Steve Woods is a retired polic   t.
Annes, Lancashire with his wife

Also by Steve Woods

When Evil Visits
The Last of the Lancashire Witches

More information about the author and titles can be found on the
blog horrorboundbooks.wordpress.com

Acknowledgements.

I need to thank family and friends for their support throughout the incarnation of this story.

In particular I am grateful to my youngest sister Irene for her tireless and uncompromising proofreads; my youngest brother Paul for the book title and bloodthirsty offerings; our friend Bridie Kent for her medical advice as a professor of nursing; my sister-in-law Ollie for her final read through of the manuscript, resulting in many excellent suggestions and identifying storyline inconsistencies, brother-in-law Tim for his IT wizardry and cover design idea and finally to my gorgeous wife Bev, who never once said "You are not on that bloody computer again are you?" when she would have been perfectly justified.

It was a collaborated effort and I am very grateful.

Cover design by Dave Armistead at www.latcreative.co.uk

This story is a work of fiction.

It is set amidst certain historical events that took place in the latter part of the nineteenth century and particular notable and named individuals; either central or peripheral to these events may be recognisable. Bearing in mind that the most recent part of the storyline occurred over one hundred years ago it was never my intention to distort their historical role or misrepresent their character.

PRIEST TOWN

Steve Woods

A Horror Bound novel
© Copyright 2014
ISBN 978-1-5118-9644-3

How It Began.

Lieutenant-General Cromwell's New Model Army of nine thousand had crossed the Pennines from Wetherby, Yorkshire into Lancashire using the Gisburn Road, then followed the north bank of the Ribble, arriving at the outskirts of Preston on Saturday the 16th August 1648.

He halted his Parliamentarian force on its push to Ribbleton Moor, where beyond this marshland, Sir Marmaduke Langdale and two thousand Royalists were guarding the northern and eastern routes into the town, while the Duke of Hamilton and eighteen thousand troops waited at Walton Bridge, protecting the south.

Sir Marmaduke had sent an advance guard of nearly a thousand foot soldiers north in search of Cromwell's army.

Come nightfall they bivouacked in open fields and driving rain, their meagre campfires visible to the Roundheads.

The intelligence Cromwell received was good news.

"Sir, our scouts report that it is a small detachment of Langdale's force. They are on the far side of the lake. There is woodland to the west of the camp and open marsh to the east. It is an invitation too good to miss."

Oliver Cromwell was an imposing figure at six foot two. Up to a few years ago he had been a farmer and Member of Parliament before he decided to act against the King.

"What are their numbers Captain?"

"Infantry sir, a few musketeers, but mostly pike men. Around nine hundred."

"Prepare the cavalry. We charge at sunrise."

Two and a half thousand cavalry troopers moved quietly through the woods. Each carried two pistols and a mortuary sword, an ideal weapon for hacking at close quarters.

That summer morning as the sun peeped over the Pennines chasing away the black rain clouds, four regiments of cavalry horsemen emerged from woodland and advanced at a quick trot in seven ranks towards the sleeping Royalist foot soldiers.

Before any defence could be mustered the cavalry troopers charged at full gallop firing off their pistols as they came within range.

Hundreds of Langdale's troops died where they lay next to their pikes as the thundering horses trampled over the dead and dying.

The impact of the charge carried the Roundhead dragoons through the camp with little opposition, the scything mortuary swords finishing off any defence as rank after rank swept amongst the sodden bivouacs. The musketeers had little time to prime their 'matchlock' weapons and a few infantrymen attempted to angle their sixteen-foot pikes towards the charging horses, but it was too late.

They took no prisoners. The troopers dismounted and with swords drawn waded amongst the fallen and quickly overpowered those threatening hand to hand fighting.

A bloodlust had taken over and against Cromwell's orders they mutilated the dead and the living, decapitating many pleading for their lives.

It is not known which officer ordered that every single Royalist to the last man, be thrown into the lake, dead or alive. History has never recorded that instruction, but over nine hundred men were hurled into the cold water, away from the reed beds. Those that resisted were shot in the head then despatched to the shallow margins with much celebration, as if it was a game of horse-shoe tossing at a travelling fun fair. Then the barrage of pistol shot began. Countless crude lead balls whizzed over the water like a black swarm of blood hungry insects, ripping into flesh and bone.

Their screams and shouts for mercy could not match the raucous cheering and roar of excitement coming from the wall of Parliamentarians now lining the water's edge, shrouded in gunpowder smoke.

It did not take long for so many men to lie still on the reddening water. A lot had sunk, but hundreds bobbed and bumped together like felled logs waiting to be transported.

As the sun's rays melted the smoky mist, the lake welcomed the new arrivals and the fish ate well that summer.

Chapter One

"Oh Charles. It's absolutely magnificent, beautiful," gasped Verity.

It must be said that the house was impressive, particularly from the driveway as it was designed to be.

He said nothing, just stared at the country mansion that was now his.

The driver kept the horse at a steady trot allowing the two occupants in the carriage to savour the building.

"Charles, darling what other secrets are you keeping from me?"

Charles smiled briefly at his wife, but remained silent.

Ribbleton Manor, built in the late 17th century was bought a hundred years later by Edwin Chadwick Cadley, the great grandfather of Charles and creator of the family wealth. It is a superb Elizabethan style stone built house with many glittering windows watched over by tall, elegant chimneys and parapets carved by local stonemasons.

It would take Charles and Verity a long time to get to know Ribbleton Manor and its forty-eight rooms.

As the hansom cab clattered over the setts a large brown rat ambled across the driveway ahead of them. It paid no attention to the strangers and disappeared into the undergrowth and only then did Verity realise just how overgrown the grounds were.

Dandelions sprouted throughout the granite-cobbled driveway and the once meticulously tended lawns were now an uncut meadow.

She looked at Charles puzzled,

"Darling. It is so neglected, what has happened?" She wore a light blue bonnet, matching kid gloves, complementing perfectly with her dusty pink long sleeved bodice, pale blue flounced dress and black velvet jacket.

Charles had visited his grandfather many times as a child, spending summer after summer at Ribbleton Manor before that fateful day. He had always been enthralled by its grandeur and it appeared just as grand to him now as it did when he was eight years old. Charles and his younger sister Lucy had played countless games of hide and seek in those long dark upstairs corridors and outside in the acres of woodland surrounding the lake.

Poor Lucy! He could clearly recall her face and long brown hair, even after so many years. He pushed the memory away.

"You must remember Verity the house has been empty since grandfather's death over eighteen months ago. Actually, that's not exactly true," he corrected himself. "Old Chandler I believe was staying on."

It was Charles' turn to look puzzled as the state of disrepair to the house and grounds began to sink in.

A man appeared from the side of the great hall and made his way to the front where another hansom cab and driver waited. He wore a black suit and topper and stood nonchalantly with briefcase in hand, smiling as he watched Charles and Verity Cadley approach.

"Good morning sir, good morning madam," the tall man doffed his topper.

"A pleasant journey I trust?" He was well into his sixties, but his bushy grey beard made him appear older.

"Ah Monk, punctual as always," Charles said to the man from Monk, Mink and Potter Solicitors, Notary Public and Commissioner of Oaths. Charles checked his gold pocket watch and smiled to himself, *ten thirty on the dot!*

He helped his wife from the cab as Stanley Monk approached.

"What a glorious spring morning to..."

The solicitor's comment was cut short

"What in the Devil's name has gone on here Monk?"

"Forgive me Mr. Cadley. I don't understand."

"Look around man. The grounds are in a desperate state of neglect. Chandler has some serious explaining to do. And where is the old fool?"

"Sir, Mr. Chandler died over twelve months ago. I thought you knew."

Charles was visibly shocked by the news of the butler's death. He had served his grandfather for over fifty years.

"Chandler dead?" He stared at the solicitor momentarily in disbelief then quickly regained his composure. "And no one thought to inform me?"

"Mr. Cadley. I can assure you, acting on behalf of your grandfather's estate, I personally wrote to your London office informing you of the sad loss of Mr. Chandler, explaining Ribbleton Manor was now unoccupied and to this day I am still awaiting instructions." Stanley Monk's indignation would take a lot of soothing.

But this was lost on Charles Cadley.

"Good God Monk, I've been in the Natal these past nine years, opening up a diamond mine at Kimberley amongst other things and would still be there if it wasn't for those blasted Boers causing trouble."

Charles Cadley at the age of forty-one was already vice-president of Cadley Industries, second only to his father Sir William Charles Cadley and heir to an industrial empire that consisted of three great cotton mills in Lancashire, a coal mine and iron works in Merthyr Tydfil, a shipping company at Bristol and Tilbury Docks, the Natal diamond mine and a huge wine growing estate just outside Cape Town.

It was the year the Boers would invade the Cape Colony and Natal, 1899, laying siege to Kimberley, now a large mining town with a population well over 50,000. Already the British army was on standby for mobilisation and Charles Cadley realised it was only a matter of months before the Boer Republic declared war on Britain. He did not relish the prospect of living in war conditions, especially as Natal was positioned between the Orange Free State and Transvaal, both Boer republics. He was even thinking the unthinkable, that the Boers may drive the British out of South Africa, so he left the family diamond mine in the hands of colonial managers and had returned to London with his wife only two weeks ago.

Stanley Monk responded,

"With respect sir, I had no knowledge of your whereabouts, but I found it odd that you did not respond to my correspondence. I am sure you will appreciate I could not act and engage staff for the Manor without your permission, as you are now the owner. As a result it has stood empty since Mr. Chandler fell down the main stairs and broke his neck. A tragic accident and it was some weeks before the gardener plucked up courage to investigate the foul smell coming from the hallway. That's when poor old Chandler's body was discovered, black and crawling with maggots, his head twisted to one..."

Again Charles interrupted the solicitor.

"Mr. Monk, that is enough information thank you. We do not need a post mortem report."

Verity had a handkerchief to her mouth and her eyes were closed against the welling tears. "That poor man. To die all alone in an empty house."

"Please accept my apologies Mrs. Cadley. I did not intend to upset you. It was most thoughtless of me. Perhaps you would care to look inside? I do have the keys to hand."

Charles took his wife's arm and walked towards the house without another word, determined to dispense with the services of Monk, Mink and Potter as soon as possible.

He looked up at Ribbleton Manor and decided that the building itself did not appear too bad at all. It had already stood here for more than two hundred years, so eighteen months unattended would not cause too many problems, he thought to himself.

The steps to the mansion no longer swept by the maid were littered with winter's leaves.

Stanley Monk reached the front door first, inserted an iron key and with some effort pushed the large oak door open. As the door swung inwards he gestured for Verity and Charles to enter. The cavernous hallway was bathed in light from the huge stained glass window overlooking the stairs branching left and right beneath the window.

The scream was loud and echoed around the stone and marble hallway.

Verity, still screaming, had both hands to her face and froze at the open door. Charles moved forwards quickly pushing past his wife.

"Oh my God!" He gasped.

The stone floor seemed to be pulsating as if alive. The white marble was now black and heaving with cockroaches. The Biblical plague of large black beetles scattered at the intrusion, fleeing under skirting, wood panels and doors. Many dropped from the stairs with a 'crack' as they hit the stone floor, a sound that echoed a thousand times amidst the panic to scurry away.

Charles pulled Verity backwards.

Stanley Monk had seen enough to tell him further inspection of the house would not happen that day and with surprising strength for a man of his age heaved the solid door shut with a grunt. It closed with a resounding bang, shaking that part of the house. A loud cracking noise from above made the solicitor incline his head towards the porticoed porch ceiling as he turned the key.

The enormous rusting wrought iron gas lantern, weighing at least a quarter of a ton, trembled for a second then dropped to the floor along with the four bolts that had held it in position for as long as anyone could remember. The point of the huge quadrant flattened his top hat and smashed open Stanley Monk's head.

Charles, still holding his wife, looked over her shoulder and stared with fascination at the thick blood and portions of brain collecting by their feet.

11

Chapter Two

Detective Inspector Albert Meadowbank was in a squatting position, struggling to examine the woman's body in the shadows of the brick tunnel. In fact it was not a tunnel at all, but one of the twelve arches of the Tulketh viaduct that connected the railway from Preston to Fleetwood, taking day-trippers to the popular seaside resorts of St. Annes and Blackpool.

This immense construction, with huge industrial grey brick pillars shut out the morning sun already rising above the hundreds of smoking mill chimneys belching out sulphurous fumes, obscured the towering white steeple of St. Walburges.

"D' wi know oo she is lad?" The police inspector was gently pulling away the blood soaked shawl.

"Aye,'appen ah do sir. Elsie Lupton. She's..." P.C. Barratt corrected himself, "she wer' a common 'ore, but 'ad an 'eart o' gold. 'As a room nearby at Lane Ends. God knows what'll come of 'er two kids nah."

He wore a black cape over his tunic to keep out the early morning chill and his helmet displayed the black night duty crest.

The detective had heard it all before and knew exactly what would happen to children of a murdered prostitute.

"Oo found 'er?" He rubbed his bloodshot hazel eyes and he felt weary. Not from being turned out of his bed at one o'clock that morning, but from having to deal with the slaughter of another young woman.

"One o' t' mill workers goin' in fer 'is mornin' shift. 'Enry Walmsley stood o' yonder."

The constable nodded towards a swelling crowd gathering at the mouth of the archway on Tulketh Brow accompanied by the clatter of clogs as some stamped about to keep warm.

"'Ere lad, 'and us yer lamp a minute."

The oil-lamp lit up the dead woman's face. She could not have been more than twenty. The wound to her neck gaped open. It was a clean cut that very nearly took off her head. It was only the spinal column keeping head and body together and the blood that covered her chest and shoulders confirmed the inspector's suspicions.

He was now searching for a maniac.

"Hmm! 'ave a look at this Constable."

The 'beat bobby' at thirty-one years old was the same age as Meadowbank, but any observer would put the detective a generation older. Not only from his appearance, but also from his deportment. He was confident in his ability and direct with his observations, a trait some confused with rudeness. The inspector was in charge of the newly formed Preston Borough Police Criminal Investigation Department. He had four detective constables and a sergeant to work with.

He was a big man, slightly overweight with dark brown wavy hair parted with brilliantine. His easy manner was unusual amongst senior police officers.

As the uniformed copper reluctantly leant forwards, his silver-coloured metal numbers worn on the collar, glinted in the lamplight.

He winced as Meadowbank's tobacco-stained right index finger ran along the raw gash.

"Straight through t' jugular, clean as a whistle. Th' murder weapon must 'ave bin some sort o' knife an' a bloody sharp 'n at that. 'Ey up! Don't step in th' blood an' mind those boot prints. I want 'em photographin'."

Meadowbank had an eternal bedraggled appearance about him, wearing his customary silk bowler and brown tweed suit, both picked up from a pawnbroker. His brown boots were scuffed and heel-worn, once belonging to a local innkeeper until his sudden demise a couple of years ago. That was his first murder case.

The inspector's gaze took in the ruffled dress and petticoat now hitched well above both knees, revealing two garters holding up a pair of shabby stockings. Underneath the shawl was a threadbare Eton jacket and a once white linen blouse, unbuttoned, showing off too much cleavage. He moved closer with the lamp and confirmed Elsie Lupton was not wearing any underwear. This did not surprise him as not many prostitutes did. The bruising on the thighs was already visible.

With finger and thumb he lifted the sodden dress higher and the source of the thick pool of blood, clotted between her pallid legs could clearly be seen.

"'Ere Inspector. Yer don't think t' same person 'as struck again d' yer?" asked P.C. Barratt as he tentatively moved forward.

"Aye I do Constable," he replied quietly.

In the glow of the 'Bulls-Eye lamp' the constable could see that his senior officer was looking at a large wound where the dead woman's genitals should have been.

He quickly lowered his head to one side and unashamedly spewed up.

Meadowbank let the dress drop with a squelch, stood up and walked away, leaving the constable some privacy to compose himself. After all it was only the second mutilated corpse Meadowbank had seen in his five years with the force and both of these had been in the past seven hours. His reaction to the first, a female still not identified, had been similar to the constable's, but with a damn sight more retching.

The detective inspector shuffled amongst the accumulated detritus on the pavement, guided by the lamp and hoping against hope that he would find a discarded weapon or a vital piece of evidence to wave under his chief constable's nose.

A noise from behind got his attention.

"I'm sorry abaht that sir, but all that cuttin' up took mi bi surprise." Constable Barratt's embarrassment was obvious even in the gloom of the archway.

"Is this 'er patch?" Meadowbank handed back the oil-lamp with a nod of the head.

"Oh aye. I've never known 'er work anywhere else. She stayed away from t' docks that's fer sure."

Preston Docks, one of the busiest ports in the country was only a quarter of a mile away with plenty of watering holes nearby to keep the visiting sailors and stevedores happy.

With cargo boats arriving from France, Holland, Denmark, Norway and Morocco not to mention various English ports, a prostitute could earn more money in the docklands and sailors were generous, but expected more for their hard earned cash. Certainly a bed for the night and a meal or two at the very least. This would save sleeping on the cramped and dingy bunks aboard the vessel or paying for lodgings in the town.

Some women preferred to do their whoring away from the docklands as many sailors were violent when drunk. Always fighting between themselves or looking to start trouble with the locals and they were not reluctant to throwing a few punches at any woman they were paying for sex, before, during or after copulation. It was considered by some seamen to be almost part of the deal.

Elsie Lupton would not have been able to take her customers back to her lodgings so conducted her business in the dark alleyways around the viaduct, preferring to attract local men on their way home from the taverns or after finishing an evening shift at one of the dozen or so textile mills in between Maudland Ward and Christchurch.

A train rumbled overhead sending a flock of pigeons into the air with wings clattering, making the constable instinctively drop his head.

"Did yer say a doctor's bin summoned?" Meadowbank was beginning to feel the early morning chill and knew it would be quite a while before he saw his bed again. He reached into a jacket pocket for his pipe and tobacco, then remembered he had left it on the table in his lodgings above the police station in the town centre.

"Doctor Archie Byers, police surgeon, 'e lives up yonder. Ah sent a lad t' fetch 'im some time ago an' cheeky bugger wanted a farthin' fer 'is trouble." Barratt said without humour and Meadowbank could not help but smile.

While both men waited for the doctor's arrival they stood in silence, lost in their own thoughts and Meadowbank could detect a whiff of cooling cooking lard from a nearby fish and chip shop causing his stomach to remind him he had not eaten for over twelve hours.

The rising sun was at last driving away the night shadows in the archway and Elsie Lupton's body was no longer in partial darkness.

Meadowbank could see there were boot prints in the blood and the macabre prints faded in various directions. Due to the blood loss around the body and the lack of a blood trail to the scene he decided that she had been slain where she lay. As this murder was near the docks he realised that he would have to establish who came ashore last night and from which vessel, which he also knew would be nigh impossible.

Any copper with 'alf a brain could work that out, he mused and hoped that the killer had not left the town on the early morning tide, especially as he was investigating a double murder and certain that the same person was responsible for both. With a bit of luck he could drop this onto the Port Authority Police and wash his hands of the whole bloody affair.

"Inspector Meadowbank!" a resonant voice called out.

Meadowbank turned towards the crowd and immediately recognised the journalist approaching with note pad and pencil at the ready.

His thoughtful frown became one of anger and his voice did not hide his animosity.

"Fuck off, Froggat."

"Can you confirm Inspector that this is the second victim to a savage murderer who has struck twice during the night?"

16

"This is a crime scene an' I'm tellin' yer t' stay back."

The reporter ignored the warning and came face to face with Meadowbank.

Edmund Froggat was several inches taller than the inspector's six foot and more powerfully built, a legacy from his days as a wrestler with a travelling circus, not many years ago.

"Go three rounds with Fearsome Froggatt. For only a tanner, win yourself ten bob," the Master of Ceremonies would announce. The wrestler retired from Barnum and Baileys 'Greatest Show on Earth' undefeated at the age of forty-five.

He was loud and brash and his tailored suits were just as hard to miss. Froggatt was wearing a bright blue two-piece, white shirt, yellow waistcoat and matching tie, brown suede boots and a foppish brown cap covered his shaved head. His spiffing sartorial style was always a hit with the ladies.

"The public and our readers have a right to know if there's a lunatic committing murder on the streets of Preston." His accent was pure Scouse, rough and gritty from the Huyton with Roby Borough of Liverpool.

"Th' only lunatic in Preston that I know's of is yer. Naw go away afore I order yer arrest fer obstructin' a police officer."

"I'll just make a note of that quote Inspector, for your Chief Constable, who as you know has an excellent relationship with my editor. A bit more cooperation would be appreciated." His false affability was unmissable.

Meadowbank was not intimidated by Froggat's close proximity, as most men would be, but realised he was in danger of losing his temper completely, not only in front of his men, but also members of the public and Froggat himself, who would like very much to report it.

"Yer know th' drill, Froggat, come t' police station an' yer'll get an official press release later. So now will yer just go an' let mi do mi job?" He said more conciliatory.

"Is there any truth in the rumours, Inspector, that these murders are connected to the grave-robbings at St. Mary's the other night?"

"Yer can allus rely on t' press t' mek up a story when there ain't one." Meadowbank answered with a smile, then moving closer to the reporter whose thin-waxed moustache twisted to a point, he said quietly "If one person is injured from yer scaremongerin' ah'll 'ave yer Froggatt. Circus strong man or not, ah'll rip yer fuckin' 'ead off."

The reporter held Meadowbank's gaze for a moment or two before saying, "I look forward to meeting you again Inspector, preferably when you are off-duty and on your own." He slowly winked one eye, his face a mask of loathing.

An increase in chatter and animation from the small crowd lingering a respectful distance away alerted Meadowbank. Constable Barratt recognised the doctor as he hurried towards them. He was fully dressed in his black three-piece tails, shirt and necktie and carried a black bag in one hand with a top hat in the other. He looked worryingly out of breath for a man in his early fifties.

"I'm sorry for the delay gentlemen, but I couldn't find a blasted cab anywhere," he panted.

"It's ok Doc, t' poor lass ain't goin' anywhere fer t' time bein'," Meadowbank replied, turning his back on Froggatt and looking at the body, grateful for the distraction, but Doctor Byers was already walking towards the deceased.

Meadowbank had found out long ago that it was best to let medical experts get on with their job without interruption rather than ask obvious questions, get in the way and become a source of irritation that could hinder the flow of information.

The black bag was open and spectacles in place as the doctor knelt by the body trying to avoid the blood. He examined the head, looking for contusions or wounds then tilted the head back to open the cut that went from ear to ear, dispensing with the obvious need for auscultation, the usual method of identifying signs of life by listening carefully for breathing or a heartbeat.

"The windpipe and gullet are severed, but the spinal cord is intact. I would say the throat has been cut left to right, which would suggest someone right handed. It is a clean cut caused by a very sharp instrument. I would say it was an attempt to cut off her head." His hands moved down her arms until they reached the lifeless hands he now held.

"Rigor mortis has begun in the limbs, the body is cold and the blood has coagulated. I estimate Inspector the time of death to be approximately four hours ago, five at the most."

Doctor Byers took out his pocket watch, "So that would make the actual time of death at around two o'clock this morning."

Using a scalpel he lifted the dress up as Meadowbank had done earlier.

"Good God! What sort of lunatic could do this?" He looked towards the inspector, his professional demeanour now one of disbelief.

"She's t' second t'neet t' end up like that."

"I need to get the body to the mortuary for a detailed examination. You say Inspector that this is your second such murder tonight, I take it then that the other corpse is already in the mortuary?"

"Aye it is. Perhaps yer could d' both post mortems Doc?"

"The sooner we get to the mortuary the sooner we can begin Inspector. I'll get a cab and meet you there if you and the constable could take the body in your wagon, it would save the time of having to wait for an ambulance."

Meadowbank could not argue with the doctor's logic even though he did not relish moving Elsie Lupton's body and transporting it across town to the mortuary.

He waved at the constable who was still with the police wagon and horses fifty yards away and signalled for him to approach. The hooves of the two horses echoed melodically under the archway as the gleaming black wagon came to a halt by the inspector.

Meadowbank spoke to the driver who had brought him to the murder scene not quite an hour ago.

"Cleggy, wi need summat t' wrap th' body in t' tek it t' mortuary. Any suggestions?"

Constable Clegg looked personally affronted by this suggestion. As the designated driver he was responsible for the wagon and the horses and its use was for transporting personnel and the occasional prisoner. He had never been asked to take a murder victim from A to B and wondered what his sergeant would have to say about this.

While P.C. Clegg pondered his dilemma, Meadowbank waited impatiently for a reply.

"Sir, can ah not nip t' police station up yonder on Waterloo Road an' get some sackin' fer t' job?"

"Cleggy, wi 'aven't got all bloody day, so get yer arse down 'ere an' find summat t' cover th' deceased wi' or guess oo'll bi cleanin' flamin' wagon? An' it won't bi me nor Barratt."

That was enough to spur the young constable into action. He climbed into the back of the open wagon, which was designed to take eight officers; four either side on bench seats. After a quick rummage he produced a cape which some officer had the misfortune of leaving behind.

"Will this do sir?"

"Perfect. Chuck it 'ere lad."

Meadowbank wrapped the woollen cape around the top half of Elsie Lupton's body, making certain her head was covered. He then realised it was not that simple. If they moved the body without supporting the head there was a good chance that it would snap free completely and even the inexperienced Cleggy knew that would not be particularly helpful to Doctor Byer's post mortem examination.

"Barratt, 'ere, you tek th' legs, ah'll 'ave th' arms an' Cleggy, you 'old th' 'ead. An' Cleggy, mek sure yer 'old it bloody proper. I don't want us goin' one way an' yer t'other still holdin' 'er bonce."

He looked at both constables and gave a reassuring nod as they got into position.

Cleggy's expression was nearly as dire as poor Elsie's.

"Reet lads, one, two, three, up!"

The three of them moved slowly and crab-like towards the wagon.

"Cleggy, yer gonna 'ave t' rest 'er 'ead on th' wagon floor, then climb in an' pull 'er towards yer." Meadowbank said between gritted teeth, as taking the strain was becoming an effort, "Oose flamin' idea wer' this?" he hissed.

They managed to get the corpse aboard in one piece resulting in Barratt and Meadowbank panting and young Cleggy having handled his first dead body.

"Cleggy, call at t' nick first. I need mi pipe an' bacca". The inspector said, ignoring the young 'bobby's' efforts to clean blood from his highly polished boots.

Chapter Three

Titus Moon admired himself in the broken mirror. He was bare-chested with both hands swirling the cold inky water as he washed away the last of the blood from his brawny arms.

He was a big man with thick black hair that matched perfectly with his untidy beard. A wide and worn leather belt holding up his only pair of trousers was pulled tight against his taut belly.

The eight bells in the tower of the ancient Parish Church told the world, or at least those interested, that it was seven o'clock. Titus knew he was late for work, but did not feel any inclination to hurry. What could the vicar do anyway?

"Titus. You in there?" a voice squawked from the other side of the door.

He carried on looking at his reflection, his battered hands running the filthy water through his hair, confident that the door was locked.

"Titus. Open up, I've sommat fer yer," the landlady said more quietly as she tried the handle.

"Begone woman. Tek yersel' away. I'm doin' mi ablutions."

"Well don't bi emptyin' t' chamber-pot owt o' th' window. I've already 'ad th' Alderman rownd givin' mi 'ell abaht t' piss an' shite owtside. Yer know t' use midden in th' yard." Her voice was back loud and shrill and without humour.

"Gi' a man some privacy yer ol' hag. I'm late as it is."

Margaret Beckett, or 'Mags' as everyone called her was landlady of the five-roomed, three up, two down hovel on Starch Houses, a slum area in the town centre.

"Yer've nowt I've not sin afore. Open th' door Titus. I missed yer last night, yer ne'er showed up like yer promised." Her tone was softer, even seductive, but her request went unanswered.

"I've a treat for yer. 'Alf a loaf an' it's only three day old. Open th' door sweet'eart an' yer can 'ave th' bread an' ah'll 'ave 'some cock."

It was a tempting offer which made Titus smile, something he did not do very often.

"Bugger off yer whore. Yer'll get no cock from mi t'day." He pictured himself sliding between her milky white thighs and playing with those big brown nipples. Yes it was a tempting offer, but he should have been at the church by seven and he knew he had at least two graves to dig before noon.

"Please yersel' yer fucker an' don't bi bangin' on mi door t'night. Two can play at silly buggers. Remember this Titus, I get no cock, you get no quim." She sounded more hurt than annoyed.

The floorboards creaked on the landing as she walked away and Titus reached for his shirt, still damp with sweat.
It had been a hard night, physically, even for a strong six-footer like Titus and he was glad that Ol' Joe had been with him.

His room was small, sparsely furnished and on the top floor of the three-storey house. The lime-plastered walls were black with damp and mildew and the lack of furniture made it harder for rats and other vermin to hide, not that a slight infestation of nocturnal creatures would have upset this lodger. Since leaving the orphanage he had slept with all manner of beasts.

Of the fifteen tenants that shared the four draughty rooms, only Titus had a room to himself. He had Mags to thank for this great luxury. She lodged downstairs in the back room and like Titus had a room to herself, but as the landlady she would quite often put another bed next to hers for the extra rent of a shilling a week.

As Titus fastened his grimy brown cotton shirt he looked out of the window and already the traders were setting up their stalls. He opened the sash window and threw out the black water he had been washing in for the past seven days, from the china basin that belonged to Mags, just like the single bed and wash stand.

He adjusted his red necker-chief, grabbed his woollen jacket from a wall peg and in his other hand held his battered hob-nailed boots and opened the door.

The piece of bread was on the floor. Titus picked it up, broke it in two, put half in a jacket pocket and stuffed the other half in his mouth.

He left his boots off so he could creep down the stairs without attracting Mags' attention, as he knew where confrontation with her would lead. There was a rolled up blanket and a sack of straw on the landing and whoever had been sleeping there for the past few nights, paying Mags a penny for the privilege, had already left the building.

Mags' room was silent, but the room next door was a din of sobbing hungry children and a screaming mother.

The front door was unlocked and Titus stepped into the early morning shadows of Starch Houses and his right foot sank ankle deep into a gully of raw sewerage that ran the length of the street, passing itself off as a drain that went nowhere. "Damn," he cursed.

He leapt onto the cobbles and removed his sodden sock, squeezing out the worst of the excrement before shoving it into his pocket along with the bread.

With his boots on, Titus strode past Brown's Prime Jug beer-house, one of the few public houses where he was welcome, then onto Lancaster Road, which joined Church Street and Fishergate. Here a newsboy was selling an early edition of the Preston Guardian, shouting the headlines with gusto and holding up a copy. "Murder, murder. Woman 'orribly slain."

Titus approached him, "What's all this abaht lad?"

With a childhood probably similar to his own, the eight-year old news vendor replied,

"Woman murdered. Read all abaht it."

"What's 'appened?"

"It's all in 'ere, mister. Buy a copy an' find owt." The newsboy turned his back to Titus and continued calling the headlines.

Titus was about to give the cheeky little sod a serious dig in the kidneys, when he heard his name being shouted.

He had not seen the police wagon outside the church, approximately fifty yards to his left and suddenly he was lost in a few moments of indecision. He avoided contact with the police, but if the opportunity presented itself, Titus would quite happily drive his fist into a copper's face, especially if he thought he would get away with it.

This was not one of those opportunities. His name was being called by a voice he recognised only too well and now a uniformed officer was walking towards him.

"Titus! Titus! Come here quickly", shouted the Reverend John Buck, Vicar of the parish church of St. John the Divine.

There was another uniformed officer with the vicar and one in plain clothes. He could spot 'a peeler' a mile away.

The burly constable still walking towards Titus had a bushy ginger moustache that met up with his trimmed sideburns. His boots were polished, uniform clean, his chin-strap was tight around his jaw and his helmet shadowed his eyes conveying clearly the message that this constable would stand for no nonsense, which Titus recognised and he finally discounted the notion of fleeing down a nearby alleyway.

"Are you Titus Moon?" The constable's accent was Scottish, Glaswegian to be exact.

"Oose askin'?"

"Don't get smart laddie, just answer the fucking question."

Even though Titus was twenty nine years old had battled to get this far, surviving whatever life threw at him by using his fists and feet, he could see no advantage challenging the glaring Scotsman verbally or otherwise.

"Aye, that's misen."

"Come wi' me laddie. The yonder sergeant wants a wee chat with thee." He took hold of a jacket sleeve and gave Titus a firm tug forwards.

They walked back to the church in silence.

"This is Titus, officer." The Reverend Buck said to the plain-clothes copper and continued the introductions.

"Titus, this is Police Sergeant Huggins and he wants to ask you a few questions."

The sergeant from the criminal investigation department was small and fat and not far off his fifty-fifth birthday. He wore a black serge two-piece suit, his white shirt was fairly clean and most of his balding scalp was covered by a brown tweed deerstalker.

"Reet lad, I know oo yer are an' yer know oo I am, so let's not piss t' other abaht, eh? Weer were yer last neet?" The accent was of a man born and bred in the town.

"In t' Prime Jug all neet."

"What time did yer leave?"

"Around mid-neet. What's all this abaht?"

The detective sergeant ignored the question.

"Can anyone vouch fer that?"

"Aye, mi landlady. I went t' mi lodgin's an' spent th' neet in 'er bed." Titus kept his eyes to the ground and did not see the sergeant give a knowing nod to the vicar who was looking mortified at the thought of unwedded fornication.

"Come wi' mi Titus, I want t' show thee sommat." The sergeant was about to put a friendly arm around his shoulder to suggest he had nothing to worry about, but the difference in height made this impractical.

Instead he kept close and maintained an amiable manner.

"'Ow long 'ave yer worked 'ere, Titus?"

"I'm not sure, but th' vicar will know. I think abaht four year or so."

"An' you're one o' t' gravediggers?"

"Not one o' 'em, th' only one."

D.S. Samuel Huggins looked impressed by this, but having already noticed the gravedigger's defined arms and shoulders was not surprised

They followed the path to the left that took them to the graveyard at the rear of the church.

The site of the parish church goes back at least to the days of the Domesday Book in 1085 and has always been a place of worship since an order of monks took possession of the land in the 8th century. It was one of many churches throughout the town, hence the name 'Priest Town' which was later changed to Preston.

"So what d' yer think abaht that?" Sergeant Huggins asked Titus.

In the middle of the cemetery sat two mounds of earth not far from each other, along with two splintered and lidless coffins made from rough untreated wood.

"Ah filled those 'oles in only yesterday. In th' name o' good Queen Vic what the 'ell is goin' on?" Titus spluttered and craned his neck trying to look into the coffins without getting any nearer.

"T' bodies 'ave gone Titus. Disappeared over neet. T' resurrectionist's 'ave struck again."

"Resurrectionists?"

"Grave robbers Titus. Grave robbers."

Two white cotton shrouds lay trampled in the loose earth.

"Any ideas as t' oo would d' this?"

"No… Why d' this?"

"That's a very good question an' at t' moment I don't 'ave th' answer. What d' yer know abaht Mary 'Ardwicke an' young Charlotte 'Ope?"

Titus looked at the detective puzzled.

"Mary 'Ardwicke wer in that coffin an' young Charlotte in that one." He pointed to each in turn. "Did yer not know that?"

"I dig th' 'oles an' fill 'em in. Until I put up th' 'eadstone I don't know oo I've buried."

Sergeant Huggins looked around the cemetery. The early morning mist hung eerily in parts allowing the illusion of marble angels and

27

alabaster cherubs akin to floating guardians rising above the graves.

This case was already puzzling him. Two graves had been attacked and two corpses taken the previous night as well. That was at Saint Mary's church, but the graves had been filled in so the desecration went unnoticed until yesterday afternoon.

He was familiar with the work of the resurrection-men, which was why the chief constable gave him this investigation.

Huggins had dealt with an incident of body-snatching before.

He was a uniform sergeant then. It was around ten years ago now, at the main cemetery on New Hall Lane, when a cadaver was secretly exhumed. The missing corpse of a ten-year old boy, who had died of whooping cough, turned up a week later, naked and staked out in the middle of Moor Park. The body had been mutilated, as had the disembowelled dog that lay across the young boy and both had been surrounded by candles, forming a pentangle. The Satanists had never been caught and whatever diabolical ceremony took place could only be guessed at.

It had caused horror and outrage at the time and Huggins had spent months hunting the devil worshippers only to find that the occult keeps mouths shut and lips tight.

He had studied Edinburgh police reports of the infamous William Burke and William Hare who practised grave-robbing eighty years earlier. They did it for financial gain, rather than to appease Satan, secretly disinterring cadavers from churchyards and selling them on for dissection to medical schools.

Sergeant Huggins knew that body-snatching was a dangerous business and those involved carried out careful planning to avoid detection and identify fresh corpses. He had even heard stories of medical students and doctors taking part in this loathsome business, robbing graves to obtain human bodies for their own research, due to the lack of legitimate cadavers being provided to the medical profession.

This legal supply of bodies always included the men, women and children sentenced to death by the judiciary. Regardless of protests from family and loved ones they would never see the body again, not even to lay it to rest, or what would be left after numerous dissections to remove organs and tissue.

Hanging was the principal form of execution in England and had been since the 5th century. The nearest gallows to Preston where the death sentence could be carried out was at Lancaster Castle, approximately twenty miles further north. Sergeant Huggins had witnessed many a 'long drop' execution inside the castle walls, a method designed to break the prisoner's neck, leaving the rest of the body intact and perfect for medical research.

The detective sergeant's plump fingers rubbed his stubbly chin and he was now lost in his own thoughts so he did not hear Reverend Buck approach.

"Excuse me Sergeant, but will you be detaining Titus for much longer? His services are needed and we need to get the churchyard back to normal."

Huggins caught the look that the gravedigger gave to the vicar. It was a brief stare of malice and unlike Titus to make eye contact. If the reverend recognised his employee's insolence, he did not respond.

Sergeant Huggins agreed there was not much else he could do here and was escorted back to the police wagon by the vicar, who was forlornly requesting assurances that the press would not be informed of the desecrations to his church.

The Right Reverend John Buck, vicar of the parish church of Saint John the Divine was a gaunt, sixty year old man with sparse grey hair, swept back. His large beak-like nose dominated his features, which allowed a pair of thick spectacles to perch in front of blue watery eyes. Many of his female parishioners were not at all surprised that their vicar had remained a bachelor and a few had even whispered that if there was ever a man born to giving his love to God, it was John Buck, as not many women would want it.

The Reverend Buck harboured a secret that his parishioners, male or female would find hard to believe, except Titus moon. He had discovered the secret by chance and had every intention of making the vicar pay for his silence.

Chapter Four

Albert Meadowbank leant against the white-tiled wall, biting hard on his pipe as he watched Doctor Byers saw into the top of Elsie Lupton's head.

He had already removed some of her long auburn hair with a keen edged razor, forming a wide parting neatly running the circumference of the skull and cut a line with a scalpel across her forehead, continuing along the circle of exposed flesh allowing the doctor to follow it with a bone-saw.

The doctor had his sleeves rolled up beyond his elbows and already his hands were smeared with blood well past his wrists, even though gravity had drained most of the blood to the backbone and vital organs. He did not wear rubber gloves, finding them too bulky and loose fitting and were not recommended for routine dissections as they greatly reduced dexterity and the sense of touch. The only occasion when gloves should be worn for protection was during the opening or removing of the stomach and intestines, but even then Doctor Byers M.D., F.R.C.P. preferred to work barehanded. He did wear a black apron that was always hung behind the door, the material crisp and stiff with blood from countless examinations such as this, and covered him from his necktie to his boots.

Elsie Lupton's corpse lay on the slate slab, mounted on a heavy white pot table with a channel around the edge, allowing fluids and human debris to run to the waste-pipe at the foot end and all supported by a sturdy central pillar. A number of instruments were carefully laid out on a nearby table, including an assortment of knives, saws, forceps, scissors, catheter, scales, magnifying glass and a variety of beakers and jars.

The police-surgeon had washed his hands in warm water and turpentine, finally rubbing in carbolic oil, a process repeated on completion of the dissection.

The corpse was naked and a systematic external examination had been completed, the doctor making notes on the colour of various parts of the body, occasionally pressing the flesh, searching for abrasions or extravasations of blood.

The doctor remarked that the deceased was well nourished and had muscular development consistent with the estimated age, and appeared in good health.

Doctor Byers had been fortunate to examine the deceased at the scene of the crime. This greatly assisted his investigation. He had already established time of death, the degree of post mortem rigidity and temperature of the body, all factors of considerable importance. The doctor, being meticulous by nature understandably adhered to the universal methodology of post mortem examination as prescribed by Rudolph Virchow, the German professor of anatomical pathology in his famous book *'Method of Performing Post Mortem Examinations with Special Reference to Medico-Legal Practice'*. This called for the cavities of the body to be examined first and in the order of head, thorax and abdomen.

It was now time for him to open the head.

"You can learn much from the dead, Inspector." The doctor was deftly sawing through the cranium, making certain he did not saw through the whole thickness of the skull. This was no easy task and required him to hold the head steady with his free hand.

"In my experience Doc, yer can learn a damn sight more from th' livin'."

"True, the dead don't answer back, but vital clues such as lifestyle, diet, how they lived and how they died are to be found, if one knows where to look."

An amiable alliance had developed between the two men long ago. Their paths had crossed many times, particularly as this police surgeon was the most sought after of the three available to the borough force.

Doctor Byers put down the saw, rinsed his hands in hot water, patting them dry with a towel then selected a mallet and chisel from his array of implements.

With the chisel he followed the saw-line that traversed the skull behind each ear, striking the chisel with the mallet inch by inch, until he was back to where he started. He then placed a towel over the top of the head and with both hands gave a sharp twist. There was a loud crack that made Meadowbank wince as the top of the head came off like a skull-cap, noisily detaching and tearing from underlying membrane and peeling free from the *dura mater* as a perfect lid revealing the brain all in one piece, allowing an inspection of the convolutions to the top of the cerebral cortex.

Meadowbank remained where he was by the open door, grimacing as he watched the cerebro spinal liquor ooze onto the grey slate surface, at the same time trying to breathe in as much smoke as possible, as the smell from the open cavity that ran from the neck to the pubes was close to making him gag.

The mortuary and its excellent facilities was part of the Preston Royal Infirmary, situated near the House of Correction, and this new hospital opened for business in 1870. The doctor was old enough to remember the hospital being built nearly thirty years ago and the facilities prior to this, or lack of them in the dead-house next to the Deepdale Workshop not too far from where he stood now. It was here where the medical men had to endure abattoir conditions when dissecting corpses.

The workshop, one of three in the town, housed four hundred and eighty adults, the overcrowding so bad that at least two had shared a single bed in gloomy desperate dormitories, where disease and infection were rampant and where Archie Byers honed his medical expertise.

But that was then.

With the brain visible the doctor eased a curved bistoury, a narrow surgical knife, between the brain and cranium, sliding it around the circumference and cutting through membrane including the optic nerves, then working under the brain detaching the *crista galli* near to the sinus and cutting free connective tissue, nerves and blood vessels, finally sawing through the spinal cord allowing him to extract the most delicate organ in the body. He placed it in a nearby metal dish and continued with his commentary.

"Just as I thought Inspector, have a look at this." The doctor was gently prodding the temporal lobe with the handle of his scalpel.

Albert Meadowbank was quite happy standing ten feet away from the body and certainly had no intention of moving closer to peer at Elsie Lupton's grey matter.

"I can see just fine from 'ere Doc, thanks," he said through a mouth of smoke.

"Mode of death was syncopation to the encephalon and heart failure caused by blood loss from the wound to the throat."

He glanced at Meadowbank as an afterthought and with his bushy eyebrows raised in a quizzical manner said in answer to the unasked question, "Encephalon is the medical term for the brain Inspector that's all, but perhaps you are familiar with syncope?" There was nothing at all condescending in his tone.

Meadowbank admitted he was not familiar with the condition.

"There are three modes of death, not to be confused with cause of death and they are syncope as in this case, asphyxia and coma. Basically they refer to the failure of our three main organs namely the brain, heart and lungs respectively and any interference with one affects the other."

He nonchalantly placed his hand with the scalpel on top of the brain and looking at Meadowbank over his half-moon spectacles said, "Syncope is the sudden loss of consciousness and posture due to excessive anaemia of the brain. In this instance it resulted from massive haemorrhaging from severed carotid arteries, this being the cause of death. The poor girl would have died very quickly, but God knows what she was going through in those final minutes of her life."

Elsie Lupton's head rested on a shaped wooden block that the doctor had re-positioned at the base of the skull, allowing the head to tilt back and expose fully the wound to the neck. Meadowbank found himself staring into the blackness of the gaping laceration, the overhead gaslight unable to penetrate the shadows of the rendered throat. He imagined her poor soul, taken by surprise at the unexpected assault, spilling out of her gurgling throat with all that blood rushing along those severed arteries with nowhere else to go, until her heart stopped pumping. What could her soul do, now disembodied and discharged without ceremony? Perhaps attempt to re-unite with its dying host and like a captain who goes down with his ship, stay with the vessel at all costs or disappear into the ether, lost and frightened, hoping for guidance or salvation from others with greater power.

Wherever the soul or spirit goes Meadowbank considered it had to be a better place than this shit hole.

He had taken in so much detail of the deceased's injuries that the inspector was feeling numb and particular words from the doctor spun in his head.

Incision to the throat...three inches below the jaw...ferocious attack...severed all arteries and muscle tissue as far as the vertebrae.

While Meadowbank struggled to control his breathing and fend off the cold tingling of his skin together with the unexpected tinnitus and blurring vision, he opened his eyes wide amidst a hot sweat and saw the doctor examining the reproductive organs of Elsie Lupton or at least what remained of them. Where the previous ten minutes had gone, Meadowbank could not explain. Leaning against the wall, gripping his extinguished pipe like a sacred artefact he had been oblivious to the surgeon's removal of the heart, lung, and both kidneys minus the intestine. Only the spleen and liver remained in place.

He did not have the pleasure seeing each extracted organ measured and weighed. The doctor was scrutinising the open wound between the lags of the deceased, at last fully comprehending the extent of the injuries, causing a seasoned medical practitioner like him to grimace. The cut had sliced between the vaginal opening and anus, through the rectum, around the uterus and bladder as far as the pubic bone in a grisly circle allowing the removal of the complete external genitalia and most of the associated internal organs, as if it was a cut of meat from a butcher's shop, leaving a wound the likes of which he had never seen before.

Doctor Byers, lost in thought, moved towards the stone sink and absent-mindedly washed his hands as he searched his memory for a distant recollection that eluded him.

"It makes one wonder Inspector, as to what type of fiend could do this to another human being. Whoever he was, I am confident that the offender was a male of some strength and with more than a smattering of anatomical knowledge. I am convinced he is a maniac on a blood-lust and will not stop with the murder of Elsie Lupton."

He paused and reflected on a childhood confiscated and now a motherhood terminated, fully understanding that Elsie Lupton and thousands like her never stood a chance in life. She had been a victim since the day she was born.

"Something is niggling me Inspector. I can't help feeling there's something familiar about this death but I can't put my finger on it," the doctor said thoughtfully, then added, "In the meantime I need to prepare my notes before I start examining the other body."

Meadowbank glanced at the figure under a white cotton sheet laid on a trestle table, waiting patiently to be transferred to the grey stone slab.

"Has she been identified yet?" The doctor nodded towards his next patient.

"No not yet. We're puttin' owt an appeal in t' morrow's Post, Guardian an' 'erald an' just 'ope fer some response. T' problem is Doc she wer also a prostitute like young Elsie 'ere, an' worked in t' dark alleyways off Church Street an' business wer done against t' nearest wall. I can't see any o' 'er customers wantin' t' identify themselves t' police officers. I've a few detectives checkin' two penny lodgin' 'ouses an' 'doss 'ouses' off Manchester Road. One o' t' vagabonds that live in them tumble-down 'ovels must know 'er."

Doctor Byers sat at the desk, shoved into a corner of the twenty-foot square room, displaying a large unlit oil-lamp. The floor was laid with terracotta tiles and a grid covered a small drain neatly sited below the slab waste pipe to receive human detritus that was washed away into the sewers. Lost in his own thoughts, the doctor prepared to write his examination notes. Picking up the steel nib-pen that lay on an open book, with a full bottle of ink nearby he made the first of many glances at the dissected corpse.

"You'll have to excuse me Inspector. I've quite a bit of writing to do for the coroner and it will keep me occupied for the best part of an hour. Why don't you have a break and I'll see you whenever you are ready. I won't start on the next one until you return."

"That's a promise I won't 'old yer t' Doc," he replied with a forced smile.

Meadowbank walked into the sunshine and fresh air, grateful for the gentle breeze whipping the perspiration away from his brow and hopefully ridding his clothes of the smell of Elsie Lupton's corpse he was so plainly aware of. He headed for the County Arms, a beer house less than a hundred yards away in an attempt to wash the last thirty minutes to the far reaches of his mind.

Back at the mortuary, Archie Byers, so used to compiling reports for Her Majesty's Coroner began to detail the post mortem in his finest handwriting.

Chapter Five

The five detectives were sat in the C.I.D. office waiting for their inspector to return from a meeting upstairs with the chief constable.

It was eight a.m. and they did not have long to wait.

"Reet lads, lets see what we've got." Meadowbank seemed in fairly good spirits, considering the workload mounting on his desk.

He pulled his chair forwards and squeezed in amongst his team of detectives.

"Where are yer up t' wi' t' vanishin' bodies Sam?"

"Not a reet lot t' tell yer sir at th' moment. Top an' bottom is wi still don't know oo or why. My thinkin' is they've been teken fer medical dissection. Of t' four dead, two males passed away through meningitis, one male a broken neck from a ridin' accident an' one female from syphilis, which came as a bit of a shock t' 'usband as they've not bin intimate for a few year o' two due t' 'is diseased gonads. Allegedly."

A couple of the detectives looked up from their reports laughing.

"Yer an irreverent bugger Sergeant 'Uggins, that there's no doubt. Mekin' a mockery o' t' dead." Meadowbank said smiling.

"I'm only reportin' t' facts sir."

"So that's two from St.Mary's an' two from t' Parish Church," Meadowbank continued, "Any connection there?"

"If there is I can't find one. Four separate families from different parts o' town. From t' wealthy, t' dirt-poor. The only difference is at St.Mary's t' coffins were replaced an' t' graves filled in which is why t' body-snatchin' weren't discovered until later in th' day. At t' Parish Church t' smashed coffins an' shrouds were left owt fer all t' see, which meks mi think oo'er it wer got disturbed second time an' fled with th' bodies. But they must 'ave 'ad an 'and-cart at least or a couple o' 'orses an' there must 'ave bin a few of 'em. One man could not dig up two graves an' remove two bodies on his own in one neet. All th' bodies 'ad bin stripped naked bi t' graveside so they must 'ave bin wrapped in sheetin' or summat, possibly tarpaulin to 'ide them during transport. An' up t' present no one's sin a thing."

"Sarge, 'ow does all this fit in wi' that grave-robbin' job you investigated a few year back?" asked Constable Ponkerton. At the age of fifty-eight he was the oldest officer in the force.

"Trust yer t' remember that one Ponky, but there's nowt fer us spendin' time lookin' back at that case t' connect it wi' these. That job in '89 was th' work o' devil worshippers an' I'm convinced, even though I could never prove owt, t' parents wer responsible fer diggin' up and mutilatin' their son's body. T' poor lad 'ad six fingers on each 'and an' some believers in black-magic circles saw that as a sign of t' devils chosen one. Th' family 'ave since moved t' York an' good riddance I say. It wer a one off thank God. No, these internments are not th' work of occultists. Someone, somewhere wants fresh cadavers fer some reason an' somebody is providin' 'em."

"An' what abaht t' vicars an' cemetery staff? 'Ave yer managed t' speak t' any o' 'em?" Meadowbank enquired as he rubbed a rough cut of tobacco in his hands.

"Aye I 'ave sir. Both churches are Church of England an' t' vicars are mortified. Reverend Kane at St. Mary's 'as now employed a night watch-man an' is offerin' a small reward fer t'return of 'is dead parishioners. As fer Reverend Buck, I don't think 'e knows what day it is. 'E seems t' 'ave other things on 'is mind at th' moment. As fer t' gravediggers, the're a strange breed any 'ow. Most o' yer already know Titus Moon, but 'e 'as kept 'issel' owt o' trouble fer a while. 'E's either a bloody good actor oo should bi in one o' Mr. Dickens' plays or 'e wer genuinely surprised by th' resurrectionists 'andy-work. Ah'll keep mi eye on 'im fer awhile though. That leaves Mungo Murdock, probably th' most miserable sod you'll ever meet. That's what diggin' graves fer forty years does t' yer, makes yer as 'appy as those poor buggers six feet under. 'E's older than misel' so God alone knows 'ow 'e manages t' put a spade t' good use. I wouldn't trust 'im mekin' a sandcastle at Blackpool sands so I wont bi wastin' anymore time talkin' t' Mr. Murdock."

Meadowbank had a lot to thank his sergeant for. Not only was he a renowned thief-taker who could smell a footpad, pickpocket or house-robber across a cesspit, but also his dry humour was ever present and irrepressible. Even though there was a twenty-year age difference between the two men, they had much in common.

Both were divorced with no children and both now married to the force. Since Meadowbank's promotion and becoming Huggins' boss a strong friendship formed between the two policemen, despite the sergeant being old enough to be the inspector's father.

There was a clatter of crockery as the door to the small office was opened noisily and in walked a large, plump woman in her early forties carrying a tray loaded with a heavy metal pot of tea and several cups and saucers. She wore a crisp white pinafore over her black mourning dress. In fact the only other item of her clothing that was not black was a white bonnet pinned to a tangle of grey wiry hair giving her the appearance of a waitress in a high-class tearoom.

"'Ere yer are lads, tea up." It was said with a big smile, which revealed a lot of missing teeth.

"Phoebe, yer a vision o' beauty an' that's t' truth, ain't it lads?" Meadowbank said and stood up to take the tray.

"Now Mr. Meadowbank, Ah'll 'ave none o' yer flannellin', thank yer very much."

It was too late she was already beetroot red.

"An' I've a bone t' pick wi' yer Mr. Meadowbank. Yer bed 'as not bin slept in fer two neets runnin' an' a man needs 'is sleep. That's what I used t' say t' mi Stan, God bless 'im."

The six 'jacks' nodded their heads with respect at the mention of her dead husband's name, which was something Phoebe Tanner referred to constantly.

"I can't 'elp bein' on neet duty Phoebe. Yer know what the' say, 'there's no rest fer wicked'. Oh! Look at these lads, some o' Phoebe's 'ome-made scones an all. Come 'ere yer beauty so I can give yers a kiss." Meadowbank puckered his lips forwards.

"My Stan wud bi rollin' in 'is grave if 'e could 'ear this Mr. Meadowbank, mek no mistake," she said with false chagrin. "An' yer must 'ave 'ad that collar on fer four days na' as t' other one I cleaned is still in yer room. So what d' yer say 'baht that?"

"What can bi said other than yer th' best char-lady this side o' t' Pennines Phoebe dear an' I promise t' change mi collar later on."

"Aye, an' mek sure yer do. My Stan wouldn't 'ave gone four days wi' same collar round 'is neck, not even on t' neet shift." She backed herself out of the office and before finally disappearing said, "Ah'll bi back later t' gi' this room a good dustin' so mek yersels scarce."
The door closed and she was gone.

Phoebe Tanner's scones and meat pies were the best in town, according to the officers stationed at Earl Street and even though tragic circumstances and a chief constable's decree allowed her free board and lodgings at the station in perpetuity in return for her char services, every one agreed that her arrival was the best thing that had happened at 'the nick' since the gas lamps were fitted. She kept the station spick and span and fussed over 'her boys' like a mother hen.

The widow Tanner was so proud of poor Stan and missed him terribly and for her, being with his colleagues, sweeping round his old locker and seeing his uniform hanging in her room kept his memory so alive.
Stanley Tanner was killed on duty a few years ago, trying to stop a runaway dray-wagon and two horses. It was headline news. He fell under the enormous iron-shod wheels, the full weight of the

front and rear cartwheels running across his neck, snapping the spine instantly, moments before the wagon smashed into a wall, shattering numerous barrels and drenching poor Stan with hundreds of pints of best brown ale. Horrified onlookers were unsure what to do first. Help the prostrate copper or save the beer that was quickly running into an open cess trench.

To this day some of Stan's colleagues still say, 'when your time has come, that is a bloody good way to go'.

Having eaten the scones and finished the tea, Meadowbank got back to business.

"Reet, were was we? Oh aye, Sam, 'ad yer finished?"

The sergeant gave a nod as his mouth was full of buttered scone.

"Good, ah'll fill yer's in abaht t' two murders." Meadowbank said as he produced a couple of type-written notes and a few more sheets of paper, hand written in pencil.

"Th' post mortem 'as revealed that t' first victim, 'oo still 'as not bin identified, wer' killed at around one o'clock int' mornin', two days ago on Tuesday 28th March. She wer' found bi PC 169 Cobbert oo wer' on foot patrol at top end o' Grimshaw Street when 'e 'eard loud screams from a female comin' from t' direction o' Church Street. 'E ran t' junction, but could see nowt. Th' ale-'ouses 'ad closed an' t' street wer' deserted. 'E used 'is whistle fer assistance an' began t' search t' north side o' Church Street wi' 'is lamp. As yer all know, that part o'town is a maze o' alleyways an' are put t' good use fer those wantin' t' avoid t' law, so it's t' Corbett's credit an' a stroke o' bloody good luck that 'e checked th' alleyway near t' Manchester Road. 'Alfway along an' wi' no gas lamps nearby, Corbett came across t' female's body. 'E reckons it were abaht five minutes after 'earin' t' scream, that's if it wer' this poor lass doing t' screamin', but I think it's safe t' assume it wer'. She wer' face down wi' blood everywhere, accordin' t' Corbett's statement and when 'e moved 'er t' check fer signs o' life, 'e saw 'er throat 'ad bin cut. 'Er dress wer' 'itched up t' knees an' thick blood wer' still runnin' 'tween 'er legs. 'Er private parts 'ad bin slashed wi' a very sharp knife, wi' deep cuts t' thighs.

It looks like t' killer wer' disturbed, possibly bi Corbett. This may explain why 'e went on t' attack Elsie Lupton a few hours later, an' on t' other side o' town. 'E 'ad unfinished business until 'e met poor Elsie. T' murderer must bi local t' move around t' town wi'owt bein' noticed, mekin' use o' th' alleyways an' accordin' t' Doc 'e would bi covered in blood. I know Ponky an' Geronimo spent all yesterday on enquiries, but it would seem no one saw nowt an' can't even put a name t' 'er. That's a thought lads, what about t' screams? Somebody must 'ave 'eard that racket at that time of t' mornin'."

Geronimo shook his head. "We've been down that line sir and I agree someone must have heard something, but they are not telling us. Ponky and I have knocked on every door we could find, made house-to-house enquiries and spoke with dozens of the pitiful sods that pack into those lodging houses. That particular ginnel was unlit and not often used at night for that reason and having been down it I'm not surprised. It's a grim place, even during the day, but at night, by God it's a black hole."

Geronimo, or to give him his real rank and name, Detective Constable Bertram Knagg had the misfortune of bearing an uncanny resemblance to the notorious Apache chief who was forced to surrender in 1886 at Skeleton Canyon, Arizona. A much published photograph of the Indian warrior posing on one knee and holding a breech-loading rifle had somehow found its way to Preston Police Station and was now pinned a few feet behind Meadowbanks' head. The nickname has stuck ever since, even though Bertram Knagg came from a very wealthy family and was probably one of the best-educated officers on the force.

Geronimo, with his long black hair and bird-like features continued,

"Because of that, I can only think the female had gone into the passage willingly to do business with her killer posing as a customer. He probably picked her up on Church Street or even Tithebarn Street. Those are the usual haunts and it's a bloody rabbit warren around there."

Meadowbank agreed one hundred per cent with this.

"Exactly! So someone must 'ave bloody well sin 'em. I want yer back owt there t' day an' find a witness an' I want a name fer t' lass. One thing I 'aven't mentioned that yer should know is that t' Doc thinks ooever wer' responsible 'as some sort o' medical knowledge. Possibly a butcher or slaughter-man or even a physician. T' mutilation of Elsie Lupton showed a distinct anatomical familiarity, t' use t' Doc's own words. Even though it wer' done in an 'urry, 'er sexual organs were removed completely, by th' use of a very, very sharp knife. Remember that, if yer think yer may 'ave a suspect. No 'eroics, no goin' in any ale-'ouse on yer todd t' follow a lead. Wi keep in pairs an' if wi do 'ave a suspect wi go in mob 'anded an' bloody 'ard. Understand lads?" He glanced at each detective to emphasise the importance of what he was saying.

The four 'jacks' left the office in quiet contemplation.

"Christ Sam, wi 'ave t' find this maniac an' soon."

Now that Meadowbank was alone with Huggins, he suddenly looked weary. Unshaven between his side-burns that ended at his jaw-line it added to his appearance of fatigue.

"Albert, get yersel' to bed an' 'ave a kip. Yer can't go on like this. If t' lads get a break through yer'll need t' bi wi' it, not fit fer t' knackers yard. Phoebe Tanner wer reet, yer 'aven't bin in that bed o' yers fer a couple a days. Anyway yer wont listen t' mi so I'm off t' 'ospital shortly an' 'opefully speak wi' some doctors oo may or may not know owt abaht t' lucrative business o' body-snatchin' an' t' illegal dissection o' corpses. So what d' yer think mi chances are o' sortin' this one owt?"

"Put it this way Sam mi ol' mate, I'd rather bi lookin' fer yer four missin' cadavers than this bloody lunatic that's stalkin' t' streets. I know 'e'll kill again an' again till 'e's stopped. I keep thinkin' abaht summat th' Doc said durin' t' post-mortem."

Meadowbank fell silent lost in his thoughts, gently drawing on his pipe. After a minute or so Sergeant Huggins broke the silence.

"What wer' it t' doctor said Albert?"

"There's somethin' familiar abaht all this."

"I don't understand. Is that what Archie Byers said or..." He did not finish his sentence.

"Yeah, that's what 'e said as 'e started t' mek notes as I wer leavin'. 'There's summat familiar abaht all this'. I asked what 'e meant an' 'e said there's summat nigglin' 'im abaht th' injuries an' attacks. 'E couldn't explain further."

"Well I've never come across owt like these murders afore. 'Ave you?"

"No I 'aven't an' I'm sure t' doc 'asn't or I'm sure 'e would remember. I've no idea what 'e was on abaht, but 'e seemed t' know summat 'e's not tellin' us yet."

"What did t' boss say?"

Huggins was referring to Colonel Sir Arthur Lawrenson, retired from The Loyal North Lancashire Regiment and now Chief Constable of Preston Borough Police Force.

Like all the corporation boroughs of Lancashire including the larger towns of Lancaster, Warrington, Wigan, Bolton, Liverpool, Manchester, Salford, Oldham and Ashton-under-Lyne, Preston was allowed to form and finance their own police force, leaving them exempt from the jurisdiction of the county police and the interference of the Home Office. Unlike the Borough Constabulary's, the County Police was established by a committee of Justices of the Peace. Following the County Constabulary Acts of 1839 and 1840 they administered the rank and file and advised the chief constable on their policing priorities. This committee appointed constables "for the preservation of the peace and protection of the inhabitants" on a ratio of not more than one officer per one thousand population. As a result it was a large force covering a huge area, unwieldy, insufficiently policed and under funded, despite a special police tax levied on ratepayers.

A borough or municipal corporation had more control over their force. The borough officials were elected by ratepayers and gave councillors a greater say in how the population was policed, in particular, resources on the day and night shifts.
It was this control that the borough councillors had, which was now giving the chief constable a headache.

"I'm surprised yer couldn't 'ear from down 'ere. That bastard Froggett 'as already bin in touch, complainin' I'm wi' 'oldin' information from t' press. Can yer believe that? Oo th' 'ell is policin' this town, us or T' Lancashire Daily Post? Well Sam, t' chief 'as med' it quite clear that 'e wants t' offender responsible fer these murders apprehendin' sooner rather than later. 'E wants a quick resolution before town's folk whip 'emselves inta 'n 'isteria an' vigilantes are formed. I mean Sam; do we want owt different? T' difference is 'e's sat on 'is fat arse expectin' me an' you an' t' lads t' find t' killer, as if t' mad-man is still walkin' round, carryin' a knife covered in blood. Shite only travels down 'ill Sam an' I can feel it round mi feet already."

Chapter Six

Titus Moon left the Prime Jug earlier than usual, he had something special in mind for tonight.

He positioned himself in the shadows of a doorway in the dark and narrow ginnel that separated the church from the row of terraced houses barely more than an arms length away and waited, leaning against the damp bricks. It was still daylight, but heavy cloud brought an early sunset and a dim light could be seen through a rear window of the Parish Church of St. John the Divine. From his previous observations he knew he was at the right place at the right time.

He did not have too long a wait.

A noise caught his attention and Titus pressed himself further into the darkness.

Titus could hear footsteps follow the passageway from Church Street, and getting nearer. Very soon a man appeared, a large man with a full dark beard. He carried a cane and the metal tip clicked on the stone path with each stride. It was a confident walk, the walk of a gentleman, confirmed by the smart black suit and bowler hat. It was the walk of someone who knew exactly where he was going.

Titus watched him approach the churchyard gate, opening it with a squeal of protest from the hinges. The gentleman continued along the path that led to the vestry, a small room where parochial meetings were held as well as being a robing room for the vicar. As the visitor opened the door without knocking, a pool of light bathed the gentleman as he entered the church and Titus recognised him with disbelief.

This was turning out better than he could have hoped for.

The watcher emerged from the shadows of his hiding place, moving quietly through the gate and wincing as the hinges again protested against the friction. Keeping his hob-nailed boots off the path, he furtively trod the grass towards the closed door where light still peeped from the bottom.

It was quiet even though it had only just gone six o'clock and some windows of the tenements and lodging houses around Stonygate were lit with flickering candles, making the slums almost appealing in the twilight.

He knew the local copper would probably be in the back room of some ale-house by now, before the end of his shift in a couple of hours, and Titus would put half-crown on it being the Eagle and Child Hotel, which was only a hundred yards away.

This was of no concern to him. A churchyard at six o'clock in the evening posed no threat to the local constabulary, but in a few hours time many officers would consider that to be different matter.

The door was closed.

Taking hold of the looped handle Titus turned it gently, feeling the bar lift from the latch, and pushed the door inwards slightly.

He could hear low voices and see a burning oil-lamp on a writing desk. Holding his breath he opened the door an inch at a time until he could fit his head through the gap. The vestry was empty and a walking cane lay across a cassock on the table in the middle of the room.

Titus silently stepped onto the floorboards and entered the room fully. There was a heavy purple curtain drawn across an alcove at the far end of the vestry, near to a door that lead into the sacristy. Someone was talking behind the curtain.

It seemed to take Titus forever to creep those few yards, but at last his face was inches from the curtain.

Titus realised it was actually two curtains drawn together and there was a small breach where the curtains should have met. The alcove was illuminated by another oil-lamp and Titus' unblinking eye peered into the room.

The visitor was leaning back against a table, his bowler hat now removed and his hands held the table edge allowing his lower body leverage and support.

The gentleman, whom Titus knew, was in his late fifties. His eyes were closed and his tongue licked his lips as he gently whispered breathless encouragement. His trousers and long-johns were dropped to his ankles revealing spindly white legs and the Reverend John Buck was on his knees, his head buried into the visitor's thighs, hands cupping genitals, his mouth open, slurping as he moved his head to and fro.

He was about to rip the curtains aside, but Titus carried on watching with mounting horror and disgust, until he saw the visitor give a spontaneous moan and shiver, placing both hands on the vicar's head calling out to God as the Reverend Buck sucked and swallowed.

Titus quietly retraced his steps, left the vestry and took up his position again in the shadows of the passageway.

A further ten minutes or more elapsed before the gentleman wearing the bowler-hat emerged from the vestry and left the churchyard with the air of a Sunday morning worshipper. Titus watched him disappear onto Church Street, but knew where he would be going.

He returned to the church.

The Reverend Buck was folding his cassock when Titus entered. This time he threw the door open, which swung into the wall with a bang, startling the vicar to put it lightly.

The look of panic soon turned to annoyance as he realised it was his gravedigger standing in the doorway.

"Good God Titus! What is the meaning of this?"

"Me an' thee need t' 'ave a little chat vicar." There was no hiding the menace in those words.

"Well whatever it is you want to talk about, I'm sure it can wait until tomorrow Titus and I don't like your manner and I don't like the way you barged into the vestry. You know you are not allowed in here. This is my dressing room, now leave this instance."

"Ya mean undressin' room don't yer vicar?" A sinister smile revealed a lot of discoloured teeth.

"Have you been drinking?"

"That I 'ave vicar, but not t' stuff you've bin suppin'."

A worried look appeared on the vicar's pallid face.

"I've heard enough. Get out now or tomorrow you shall be unemployed, that I promise Titus."

"I don't think so vicar. In fact I think ah'll be 'avin' a pay rise from t'morrow. Oh aye vicar, things are gonna change around 'ere." He took hold of a bottle of altar wine from a shelf, removing the protruding cork with his teeth then spat it to one side and took a large swig, never taking his eyes off the vicar.

Not only was the Reverend Buck finding Titus Moon's behaviour odd, he was also finding it unnerving. He had never felt comfortable about the incumbent gravedigger he inherited when he took over the role of vicar at St. John's, but he knew a reliable gravedigger was hard to come by and he had been assured by his predecessor that Titus was exactly that. The Reverend Buck was wishing he had dismissed the services of Moon on one of the many occasions he had found him in the churchyard drunk and incapable, attempting to work a spade.

"If you don't leave immediately Titus, not only will you be out of a job, but you will also be facing a constable and the magistrates. That is theft of holy wine and…"

Titus knocked the table aside forcing the vicar to step back, startled.

He took another swig from the bottle. "Theft of 'oly wine it may bi vicar, but it ain't sodomy."

The vicar's eyes widened, startled at the sound of that word which was only ever spoken when reading from the bible or condemning Satan's lust.

If the vicar was afraid it was well hidden or he did not realise the impact of what Titus was saying.

"Get out you drunken fool. I'll not be bullied by an imbecilic brute such as you. You're finished at this church Titus, do you hear me, finished. Now get out of my way. I am attending the police station to lodge a formal complaint."

As the vicar bravely moved towards the door and towards Titus, the wine bottle was hurled to the floor and as it smashed two hands gripped the vicar's throat.

"Perverted 'omosexuals vicar. Yer're not one o' those are yer? What I've just sin would mek any copper puke on t' spot. Yer nowt but a pervert oo should bi flogged." He was shaking with uncontrolled anger.

"Titus! For God's sake you're choking me."

The smell of recent sex wafted from the vicar's mouth and into the face of Titus.

"You priest's are all the same," Titus screamed against that familiar smell and head-butted the vicar's face hard, smashing his nose.

His idea of blackmail was now a forgotten memory as he dragged the pleading vicar into the church of St. John the Divine. It was a few years since Titus last fell into such a drunken rage. A rage that can only be treated with a heavy cosh and a straightjacket, so a gentle man of God, no matter what dark secret he wanted kept hidden had no chance of stopping Titus.

The vicar was pulled across the stone floor by the collar of his robe, his head kicked and punched continually.

After four years at the church Titus knew the layout very well. Even though he spent most of his time in the graveyard, he would quite often venture into the church and help himself to the contents of a charity box or rummage amongst the pews for dropped coins.

In front of the altar and hanging from the vaulted ceiling hung a large wooden candelabra, with at least a dozen beeswax candles standing proud on the heavy structure. A rope fed from the candelabra through a pulley fixed to the ceiling and tied around a piece of iron, angled down at waist height and bolted to a stone pillar.

Titus dropped the vicar, his head hitting the marble step with a sickening crunch. His face was already unrecognisable, swollen, bloody and misshapen. Blood and snot bubbled from his nose and mouth as he begged Titus to stop.

He unfastened the rope and lowered the dark wooden frame until it reached the floor. Pulling the Reverend Buck forwards, Titus violently brought his right knee up, the hard bone of the patella ramming into the vicar's face, shattering even more cheekbone and jaw.

"A man o' God, suckin' a mans cock! Yer don't deserve t' live." A white foam of spittle covered his snarling lips.

He pulled the slack rope through the iron loop and wound it twice around the senseless vicar's neck, as the candelabra sat next to the prostrate clergyman.

With both hands, Titus heaved on the rope. The dark wooden frame of six equal sides rose up smoothly, the slack soon becoming taut as Reverend Buck was pulled up into a sitting position by his neck.

At that moment the vicar opened his eyes and already the coarse twisted cord was biting into his neck. Gasping and panic stricken, his hands tugged forlornly at the rope, now fully realising what was happening. The candelabra rose in smooth elevation, taking the vicar with it. His dangling feet now off the floor kicked wildly. His fingernails dug into the rope as the coil crushed his windpipe. He tried to scream as he stared crazily at the crucifix on the altar, eight feet below him where he had placed it for tomorrow's service. Air was not getting in or out of his lungs, so there was little chance of the Reverend Buck's final scream escaping his throat.

Titus wound the trailing rope around the bracket, securing the loose end and like a harpist testing the tension of a string he plucked the rope that ran to the ceiling. It was rigid like a metal strut. Satisfied he nodded his approval and began to chuckle as if he had just been told an amusing story. His chortling soon developed into an eye watering belly laugh not dissimilar to the guffawing antics of a circus clown and the insane laughter was anything but jocular.

His grip on reality was slowly coming back.

He was sat on the front row of the wooden pews, his shirt sticking to him with sweat and trousers wet from his emptying bladder. His battered hands were bleeding at the knuckles but his breathing was no longer laboured and heaving.

Titus looked around the dark church, lit only by a low gas light in the nave adding an eerie glow to the large stained-glass windows. He got up and paid no attention to the Reverend Buck hanging by his neck in the rafters.

Once outside he collected his thoughts and decided against a couple of pints in the Prime Jug as an option. His hands were still shaking and he stank of piss, which was not unusual for Titus, just more evident on this occasion. He would have to make his way back to Mags' house.

The sound of footsteps on the passageway that bordered the churchyard from Stonygate stopped Titus in his tracks, as he strained to establish the direction of whoever it was approaching.

It took only moments to determine that they were coming his way, confirmed by the screech of the gate hinges.

Keeping to the grass, Titus darted around the opposite side of the church, climbed over the railings, dropping with a grunt onto St. John's Place, a narrow unlit ginnel of warehouses and a favourite spot for ladies and commercial sex.

He looked round, checking the coast was clear. The last thing he needed was being seen anywhere near St. John's Church this night.

As Titus Moon fled the churchyard, Samuel Huggins was looking for the Reverend John Buck. Having tried the vicarage and found it in darkness, he decided to call at the church.

He could see the light at the base of the vestry door and walked towards it. The door was unlocked. Sergeant Huggins entered and saw the upturned table, broken glass, a puddle of red wine and the cassock on the floor.

"Vicar, Are yer there, sir?" There was an edge to his voice.

He often found churches to be unnerving places at the best of times, even during daylight hours. He couldn't help but think of those two unfortunate cadavers whose eternal rest was so viciously disturbed only yards away, a few nights ago and his imagination ran riot, particularly surprising for the seasoned copper he was. He quietly prayed that he would not bump into those dear departed souls tonight, wandering the gloomy church, hell-bent on revenge.

He checked the alcove behind the partly drawn velvet curtains and then entered the sacristy. The door to the church was wide open, like the entrance to a cave and a gaslight pierced the far darkness.

"Reverend Buck! Are yer there?"

He picked up a large unlit candle in its holder and cursed for not bringing his oil-lamp. The gas mantle was within reach, allowing Huggins to increase the flame and light the candlewick. That part of the church suddenly changed from partial darkness to a shadowy gloom, which did nothing to reassure the police officer that it was a house of God.

With footsteps echoing on polished stone and marble, he ventured further into the church, not at all happy that he had found the building insecure along with evidence of some type of a disturbance. He wished Albert Meadowbank was with him. The night held no fears for that man.

He strained to see into the darkness, the candle flame reflecting eerily on metal and glass, when his right foot slipped on a sticky wet spot on the floor. Bringing the candle to his feet he saw an expanding and glistening pool of liquid surrounding his boot. He bent down and dipped a finger into the liquid, feeling its viscosity between finger and thumb when a droplet of something splattered his hand.

Huggins looked up into blackness and felt a splash hit his forehead.

Puzzled and wiping away the warm fluid, he stood up and held the candleholder aloft. He could not make it out at first. The shape was moving, swaying.

"Oh God Almighty! Jesus Christ." His profanity echoed around the altar and archways.

At last the light pierced the darkness and Huggins could see the Reverend Buck, suspended, opposing gravity like an ungodly angel.

Chapter Seven

The army of builders, carpenters, decorators and gardeners were doing an excellent job in bringing back Ribbleton Manor to its former glory. Charles and Verity had returned to their Mayfair townhouse the day of the solicitor's death. He arranged for flowers to be sent to the funeral, but certainly had no intention of attending to pay his respects for the dear departed. He blamed 'that old fool Monk' for the deterioration to Ribbleton Manor and even though he would never admit it to anyone, he felt Monk had paid a fair price for his incompetence. Instead Charles waited patiently with his wife to take possession of the country mansion that was once his grandfather's.

Since the tragic accident befalling Mr. Monk, the house had remained unoccupied. Instead, a complete restoration was ordered and one on a grand scale. Charles wanted the work completed in six months, which at first seemed an impossible task.

No expense was spared. Marble was shipped in from Italy, oak from the New Forest and hardwoods from the rainforests of South America.

Furniture and fabrics commissioned from Morris and Company, Oxford Street, London, were being handmade by William and May Morris.

Highland paintings by Landseer and huge oil on canvas figures of Christ by William Holman Hunt were already in storage, together with several pieces by John Constable, whose landscapes were becoming popular.

All in all, Charles was spending a vast amount of money on Ribbleton Manor. He wanted it to rival, if not better, the wealthy aristocratic estates that dominated both rural and urban Lancashire.

There were three neighbouring ancient and noble families which Charles particularly despised for their ancestral wealth and position and he hoped one day soon to rub their noses in his family's self-made fortune. These were William Grosvenor, 3rd Duke of Westminster, owner of huge tracts of land throughout the county, who resided at Eaton Hall in Cheshire; Edward George Villiers Stanley, 17th Earl of Derby and his numerous estates throughout England, including Preston, whose ancestral home was at Knowsley, one of the largest houses in the kingdom: and finally John Lawrenson Clifton whose family seat was Lytham Hall and the extensive acres of land the Squire of Clifton owned, stretching from north Lancashire to the borough of Preston.

Charles's father had been honoured with a knighthood by Queen Victoria in 1865 and his grandfather received his knighthood from King George IV in 1821, both for services to British industry and a way of recognising the countless pounds they had paid into the treasury coffers.

There was no reason to believe that Charles would not be a recipient of the title, *Knights Batchelore,* bestowed by a grateful monarch. In fact his father had already been assured by one of Victoria's courtiers that it would be sooner rather than later. Sir William kept this 'tit-bit' to himself, knowing full well that events could change suddenly at the whim of Victoria or her prime minister, Robert Gascoyne-Cecil, Marquis of Salisbury.

Neither Sir Philip nor Sir William had any desire to emulate or compete with the local nobility, some of who could thank Henry VIII for their fortune and land. They moved in different social circles and never 'the twain should meet'.

It is true that the Cadley dynasty was rich and powerful, but they were industrialists not landowners. Sir William was an engineer as was his son, Charles, apart from a brief flirtation with the medical profession. For some reason, many years ago, Charles had aspirations to be a surgeon. He left the company and a senior management position, but only lasted twelve months at medical school before his father gladly welcomed him back into the family empire.

Charles was a natural successor to his father, but differing in many ways. He was determined to take the Cadley Corporation from strength to strength at any price and already they were regarded as the wealthiest industrialists in the United Kingdom.

Sir William was popular and engaging, firm but fair with a ready smile. Charles was arrogant and dismissive and void of humour.

It was a mystery to some exactly what attracted Verity to her husband in the first place, even discounting the fifteen-year age difference. She was twenty-two. But this was not unusual, many of Verity's friends had much older husbands and one or two had agreed wedlock with men older than their own father. And it could not have been his fortune. Verity came from wealthy parents, who owned two large breweries in Bristol. Apart from that Verity Morgan was far too romantic to marry for anything other than love.

It would not have been his scintillating conversation or company.

Charles was tall and quite good-looking though. His deep blue eyes, straight black hair parted at the side and sharp aquiline nose lent a Mediterranean appearance to him. But it was his eyes she was drawn to. Blue like a tropical sea with hidden depths rising and falling, a refuge for deep secrets that could never be guessed at.

Many who met Charles found his 'icy stare' and 'piercing eyes' disturbing but Verity had looked hard and long into them and believed she saw vulnerability, like a lost boy longing to be found. From their first meeting she had wanted so much to hold him.

They had both studied at Oxford. Charles was reading mechanical engineering and Verity, English, with aspirations to become a teacher.

Some years later, Charles escorted his father on a trip to Bristol to sort out the unions at The Cadley Shipping Company, who were threatening industrial action. Within twenty-four hours the problem was solved and the union leaders were shaking Sir William's hand and thanking him for his understanding. They did have a point, considered Sir William. The working conditions were atrocious and bloody dangerous.

Charles wanted to sack the lot of them. There were plenty more unemployed to fill the vacancies. Sir William was more inclined to sack his board of directors. He did not use obscene or crude language very often, preferring his son to the make the most of his natural talent of giving voice to unforgiving profanities, but the six directors were told what he thought of them in no uncertain terms.

During their stay in Bristol, Sir William and Charles, before Charles was to return to South Africa, were invited to several dinner parties by the city's society. One such invitation was from George and Rosie Morgan, Verity's parents.

Charles was sat next to Verity and they chatted all evening, reminiscing about the old days at Oxford. Whether it was the quality wine or Verity that had warmed his cold heart it no longer matters. The very attractive Verity, who had suitors from Bristol and Gloucestershire's finest families and beyond, jockeying for her attention, fell in love with Charles William Edward Cadley.

After an overly long engagement, according to Verity's parents, at last they married in '88 at Westminster Abbey. A great occasion in every sense and a great celebration of the union of two distinguished English families.

Verity gave birth to a daughter, their only child eight years later, after several miscarriages. Elizabeth Rose Cadley, named after each of their mothers was welcomed into the world and having her mother's dark brown eyes and light brown hair she had obviously inherited Verity's beauty.

Chapter Eight

It was another seven days before the mutilated body of the female discovered by Police Constable Corbett was identified.

And to Meadowbank's disbelief it was her mother who came forward.

Mary Babbitt, who shared a ground floor room with her daughter at a lodging house on Bread Street, off New Hall Lane, attended the police station by the market to report her daughter missing.

Mary was not sure how old her daughter Beatrix or 'Our Beat' was, but thought she was more or less twenty.

Meadowbank sat her down in the C.I.D. office and Phoebe Tanner brought in a tray of tea and scones.

What she told Meadowbank was depressing. 'Our Beat' was illegitimate, the father a French sailor whose cargo vessel docked at the port for a weekend and has never been seen since.

He would certainly not know he had a daughter and would probably not give a damn in any case.

Mary had married a handsome man when she was seventeen and already carrying her child. She could not have been more than thirty-eight now. Meadowbank looked at the pretty woman, petite, with amazing blue eyes whose mind was addled through a lifetime of drinking. She wore a headscarf over her blonde hair and a hand held the knot to her throat as if it were a family heirloom. The china cup rattled on its saucer as she picked it up awkwardly. She told Meadowbank that her mother had died of a gangrenous leg infection many years ago and thought she would have been eight or nine at the time. She could remember her mother's big smile and soft hands but her father, she knew nothing about. His name was never spoken and she had no memory of him at all.

Meadowbank asked about her husband, diverting her attention from talk of paternalism and disguising his own discomfort.

About ten years ago, she recalled, a woman claiming to be her sister-in-law, came to the house. Her and Beat were living on The Shambles then, one step up from where the poorest of the poor lived. Mary had never seen this woman before and until then did not know she existed. Her husband's sister had bad news. "Dick's bin killed int' Zulu Wars, 'is grave is somewhere in darkest Africa."

The sister was listed as next-of-kin for some unknown reason and the War Office had issued a letter of condolence dated April 1879 stating Richard Babbitt had been killed in active service for his country.

A week before receiving the War Office correspondence his sister had received a letter all the way from that Dark Continent. She told Mary 'it wer like a bolt out o' t' blue I can tell yers'. Her brother had sent it a few days before he died. "It's as if 'e 'ad a premonition of 'is death." She had told Mary mysteriously.

His crude writing asked that if anything should happen to him, Mary be told that he had always loved her and Beatrice as if she was his own.

The sister-in-law said this in a matter-of-fact manner as if she were relaying a message from a neighbour. She gave the two letters to Mary, but Mary could not read or write. She gave no explanation as to why it had taken her ten years to pass on this information and Mary was too dumbfounded to ask.

"'E asked mi t' tell yer this pet. Don't know why 'e couldn't write t' yer direct like an' save all this rigmarole. It's not as if 'e didn't know where yer lived. But if yer can't read or nothin' that wouldn't 'ave bin much use I suppose."

She had a look of her brother that was true, tall and thin with distinguished features.

"There's no last will an' testament though. 'E left nowt t' nobody. Not a sausage, so don't come knockin' on mi door fer this, that an' t'other, cause I've nowt either."

Mary did not invite her inside for a brew, which was unlike her, she assured Meadowbank. She admitted she was too confused, but also had taken an instant dislike to her husband's sister who had not even given her name.

The long lost relative then left, returning to wherever she had come from.

In a moment of clarity, Mary explained that her husband, Richard Babbitt, whose name she had not said out loud for donkey's years, was killed at Iswandlwana in '79. Someone had read her a newspaper article reporting the blood bath. Meadowbank had never heard of the place and was amazed Mary could pronounce such a strange word.

"Iswandlwana is in Zululand," she explained, staring at the desk lost in thought.

Tears appeared as her mind was elsewhere, "Twelve 'undred British soldiers wer' massacred bi twelve thousand Zulus. S' many brave men an' s' far away."

Those blue eyes looked up at Meadowbank, "Fer ten year or more I thought t'worst of mi 'usband. Called 'im t' 'ell an' back I did. Will 'e ever forgive mi?"

At first he was not certain whether she had made all that up, but as if reading his mind, Mary produced two battered envelopes and placed them on the desk. He picked up the one bearing the broken War Office wax seal but the pain and sorrow in her eyes told him it was true. He did not need to read the letter inside.

"Why did it tek 'er ten yer?". Meadowbank struggled to understand this, but Mary said nothing, her head remained bowed, again lost in her own thoughts.

He wanted to put an arm around and tell her everything would be all right, but that was not true. In fact things would get decidedly worse for Mary. She was an alcoholic and her dead daughter had been a prostitute who brought in the money to pay for the rent, the food and booze.

Now she had nothing.

She sipped the tea and nibbled the scone, even though it was the first food and drink she had seen for over a day.

"Our Beat, murdered. I 'opes yer've caught t' bastard." She said distractedly.

Meadowbank said, not yet. He said her daughter's body still needs to be formally identified and would she come to the mortuary with him. He gently warned her as best he could that Beatrice had been dead over a week now, but it had to be done. Suddenly, something clicked in Meadowbank's brain.

"Mary, did you an' yer 'usband ever get divorced?"

"Divorced. I loved that man. Why get a divorce?" She looked hurt at the suggestion.

"'Ow long was yer 'usband in th' army fer?"

"Hmm! Over five year I think. 'E wer' quite abit older than mi sel' an' 'e wer' stationed in Aldershot fer most o' t' time an' came 'ome when 'e could."

"D' yer know which regiment?"

She was here to be to report her daughter missing, only to be told her daughter was lying in the mortuary. A God-awful journey for anyone, thought Meadowbank. He wanted so much to help this woman.

"5th Field Company. Enlisted as a driver 'e did, afore I met 'im, an' was s' proud t' wear 'is uniform. When 'e left that morning, s' tall an' smart." She trailed off, the smile fading again.

He knew what she was about to say next.

"But 'e never came back. I thought 'e'd chose th' army life or another woman instead of 'is wife an' family an' all that time 'e were dead on t'other side o' flamin' world."

"Listen Mary", he moved closer to her ignoring the unwashed stink, "'As no one ever mentioned anythin' t' yer abaht an army pension?"

"Me. Pension. Yer 'avin' a laff Mr. Meadowbank." She said without humour, brushing aside a few crumbs off her lap.

"Mary. I do know what I'm talkin' abaht. Yer 'usband wer' in t' army fer five year an' bin dead twenty. Killed in action. Yer should 'ave bin receivin' a widow's pension fer last twenty year." A lifeline had been thrown to her.

"Yer not jus' sayin' that are yer, t' mek mi feel better?"

"Bloody 'ell Mary I might bi a copper but I'm not that big of an 'eartless sod."

Mary gave a searching stare and Meadowbank wanted to weep. He looked away as if studying the photograph of Geronimo the 'noble savage', managing to compose himself and blink away the tears.

"Ah'll get yers yer pension, yer deserve that an' ah'll catch yer daughter's killer, she deserves that."

Mary put the cup to her mouth and looked at the police inspector, unconvinced.

Meadowbank had a meeting with the chief constable at two o'clock that afternoon. His superintendent told him not to be late. The detective inspector had been in the chief constable's office more times in the last two weeks than he had in the past two years.

He looked at his pocket watch as he left the mortuary with Mary Babbitt. He still had an hour.

The identification had not gone too bad, Meadowbank thought under the circumstances. The mortuary assistant had done a marvellous job of cleaning young Beatrice's face and the piece of white cloth wrapped around her head and neck covered perfectly the crude stitching that was keeping her face in position. She looked like a sleeping nun. A week, laid out in the cool mortuary had not stopped the body decomposing; nothing could prevent that, unless the dead could somehow be frozen. Blocks of ice were available but only to the gentry or anyone else prepared to pay for it, usually members of the clergy, hoteliers and fish and game mongers. Even so Mary clearly recognised her daughter.

64

There was no wailing or apoplectic sobbing, just a gentle touch of the face, followed by a farewell kiss to a cold cheek.

Meadowbank put Mary in a hansom and gave her two pounds. He had decided to walk back to the station.

It was a pleasant spring afternoon and Meadowbank removed his jacket, rolled up his sleeves and enjoyed the warmth of the sun.

He arrived with twenty minutes to spare so checked the paperwork on his desk. Geronimo and Ponky were having a brew and a thick beef sandwich, compliments of Phoebe Tanner.

"Alright boss, how did it go?" Geronimo looked up from the typewriter.

"Ok I think. It's amazin' what those mortuary lads can do. Young Beatrice laid there, hacked t' pieces an' yet I bet that's best she's looked fer a bloody long time."

"How was Mary?"

"I don't know Geronimo an' I don't think ah'll ever know." Meadowbank reflected on this for a moment or two.

Ponky offered his boss half his sandwich and pushed the mug of tea towards him. He nodded his thanks, accepting both.

The telephone rang and Meadowbank picked up the brass hand-piece. It was Superintendent Bell reminding him of the meeting in five minutes.

"Don't ever get promoted lads. Yer'll spend 'alf yer life in flamin' meetings."

The door to the office of the most senior policeman in Preston was closed and a brass plate displayed the words, 'Chief Constable'.

Meadowbank rapped twice.

"Enter!" The gruff well-spoken voice was unmistakable.

The office was twice as big as the one downstairs, where the six detectives worked.

Colonel Sir Arthur Lawrenson was not in uniform; instead he wore a smart brown check tweed suit, white shirt and brown necktie.

"Take a seat please Meadowbank." The voice reflected perfectly the old man sat behind the old desk. It was a voice of natural seriousness through a lifetime of giving orders.

The other two men nodded at the inspector. He sat next to Superintendent Bell on the only vacant chair and he was surprised to see Archie Byers sitting across from him. The doctor had a large bundle of papers on his lap and all three men were drinking tea, but none was offered to the inspector.

"Let's get straight down to business gentlemen. We'll deal with the death of the Reverend Buck first. Any developments Inspector?"

Meadowbank tried not to appear surprised by the question as they both knew damn well that the investigation had gone nowhere fast, since the body had been discovered over thirty-six hours ago.

"No sir. Sergeant 'Uggins is still at t' scene, mekin' enquiries."

"Well in that case, I think you will find it interesting to hear what Doctor Byers has discovered through the post mortem examination." On cue he turned to the doctor.

"Thank you sir. The cause of death was asphyxiation due to strangulation. I realise that will not come as a surprise. The deceased's head and body were severely bruised and bore numerous wounds consistent with being brutally punched and kicked. The frontal bone of the skull was fractured, as were both cheekbones and nasal bone. The upper jaw or maxilla and the mandible, which is the strongest bone of the face, were shattered resulting in numerous upper and lower teeth being dislodged. Perhaps more importantly though, I discovered that the mouth and stomach contained large traces of semen mixed with blood."

He paused to let this information sink in.

Meadowbank took this as an opportunity for a question.

"Doc, what exactly are yer sayin'?"

"Doctor Byers is saying Reverend John Buck was a practising homosexual who very soon, prior to his death, had indulged in oral fellatio on another male. What we now need to find out Inspector is who this man was. Would you agree?"

Sir Arthur peered over his reading glasses not at all believing his inspector would disagree.

"Of course sir. This is obviously a big lead that needs chasin' as soon as possible."

"And I Inspector, agree with you for once."

Meadowbank was well aware and almost certainly so were the three men sat with him, that homosexuality was a perversion not tolerated, in fact sodomy was a serious criminal offence, as was any improper intimacy between two men or more.

He never had cause to use the powers of the 1885 Amendment Act, which made virtually any sexual impropriety between two or more males, in public or private, a grave offence.

For him, this immediately brought to mind the recent and very public release from prison of Oscar Wilde, the celebrated playwright, who in 1895 was sentenced to two years hard labour for being a homosexual.

As far as the chief constable was concerned, the vicar had conducted an act of gross indecency within the sanctity of a house of God, making the crime even more heinous and the hunt for the 'surviving pervert will be extensive and thorough'. His perception of Reverend Buck's death was slowly moving from victim to shared culpability towards his own demise.

The offender must be caught and doubly punished, for their own crime and for that of the vicar's.

Meadowbank assumed that was the end of the meeting and stood to leave.

"With yer permission sir, ah'll inform Sergeant 'Uggins o' this information straight away."

"Sit down Inspector. I have not yet terminated this meeting. Doctor Byers has more information for you." Sir Arthur sat back in his leather swivel chair, linked his fingers over a spreading waistline and looked at no one in particular.

"Thank you sir. You may remember Inspector, during the post mortem examination of Elsie Lupton I remarked that there was something familiar about the two attacks?"

Meadowbank nodded his head, looking at the police surgeon intently.

"Well I made enquiries with some colleagues in London and I think you'll find my findings disturbing at the very least."

The detective furrowed his brow involuntarily and could detect a palpable tension descend on the meeting.

The doctor handed a report to Meadowbank consisting of several typed pages, held together with a metal binder. The superintendent and chief constable already had possession of a copy.

Meadowbank was holding a Metropolitan Police and H.M. Coroner's report listing the names of several women he had never heard of.

"Inspector. Are you familiar with the Whitechapel Murders?" Asked the doctor.

"Yes, of course."

"That report details the post mortem examination of three women whose death have been attributed to the same killer. The injuries listed on pages three, five and eight are identical to those of Beatrice Babbitt and Elsie Lupton. Apart from the fatal throat cuts to each victim, the details of these mutilations that took place over ten years ago have never been released to the press or put into the public domain."

The Inspector stared at the names in the report: Elizabeth Stride died 30th September 1888, Catherine Eddowes died 30th September 1888, Mary Jane Kelly died 9th November 1888.

"Are yer implyin' that they are all connected?" He did not want to believe what he was hearing.

Sir Arthur interjected, "We are not implying anything Inspector, but stating as fact that these murders are linked to the same perpetrator. After a ten-year absence, Jack the Ripper has struck again. This time in Preston."

Chapter Nine

The Stanley Arms Hotel built in the town centre in 1854 is a striking building on a grand design. It stands in the shadow of the Harris Library, Museum and Art Gallery with its vast façade of columns, one of the magnificent public buildings surrounding the Market Place.

Further down Lancaster Road is the police station and their close proximity, together with an amenable interior and welcoming landlord named William Walmsley made The Stanley Arms a favourite meeting place for officers, both on and off duty.

Albert Meadowbank propped up the bar side by side with Samuel Huggins.

"I mean, could the' bi wrong? Jack t' Ripper 'ere in Preston. It doesn't mek sense." Huggins said to his friend.

"The Doc presents a pretty convincin' case Sam. An' t' Colonel 'as swallowed it 'ook, line an' sinker. Problem is, suppose they are reet an' that bloody maniac is runnin' loose rownd town. It doesn't bare thinkin' abaht."

He took a gulp of ale then continued,

"Thing is Sam, once yer sit down an' look at everythin', yer know, t' case 'istory from Scotland Yard an' what's 'appened 'ere, I think only a fool would discount any connection."

"S' what 'appens now?"

"Some bloke from London is coming up. A retired chief inspector. 'E was involved in t' Whitechapel murders fer years, accordin' t' Colonel. Said 'is name is Frederick George Abberline."

Both men agreed they had never heard of him.

"I 'ope wi can keep th' lid on this fer awhile. If t' press get a whiff an' it ends up on t' front pages, yer can imagine what would 'appen. Lynch mobs, vigilantes. We wouldn't bi able t' bloody move fer mobs outside police station, mobs roamin' t' streets an' sightseers would flock 'ere, 'opin' fer a glimpse of Jack t' Ripper."

Huggins nodded in agreement.

"Yer don't think everythin' that's 'appened is all connected?"

"'Ow d' yer mean Sam?" This was a theory Meadowbank had not considered.

"T' body-snatchin', then two murders an' then t' vicar. They all 'appened within a few days. Seems a bit strange that, t' me."

"It would bi too bloody convenient fer us, that one person could create such 'avoc o'er a couple o' days. But what th' 'ell do I know. We're all pissin' in th' dark at t' moment."

The parlour was gloomy and thick with smoke. The gaslights spread around the walls gave a flickering diffused glare and trade was busy for early evening.

Neither of the two police officers had seen Edmund Froggatt sat at a corner table, but he had seen them.

The journalist was reading his notepad, checking his report for tomorrow's edition before he presented it to the editor.

Froggatt was the crime correspondent for the Lancashire Daily Post and he had never been so busy. His reporting was rarely off the front page.

First the grave desecrations had shocked the town, followed quickly by two prostitutes murdered. Froggatt thought things could not get any better, he was now passing details onto the nationals who were heading his way by the train load, and then suddenly, like manna from heaven, the Reverend John Buck is found hanging inside his very own church, like a common criminal at the gallows.

Even the editor said that a storyteller such as Jules Verne could not make one up like this.

For the first time, Froggatt was flavour of the week. Instead of reporting about drunken brawls and town centre pickpockets, he would soon be rubbing shoulders with the big boys from Fleet Street.

Meadowbank finished his second pint.

"Gerra us another Sam, while I go fer a slash."

He avoided using the lavatories in The Stanley Arms. The privy in the year yard consisted of a small brick building, housing a plank with a hole fixed above an ash pit, which regularly needed emptying, but invariably never was, so Meadowbank left by the front door onto Lancaster Road and nipped down George's Lane that ran by the side of the pub.

He was stood against a high gate, finishing his ablutions and did not see Edmund Froggatt until the last moment. A huge fist displaying a sovereign ring smashed into the side of Meadowbank's head, knocking him senseless. He remained standing, slumped against the gate when the other fist drove into his stomach.

The pain was unimaginable. He fell to the floor, on hands and knees, retching, the two pints of ale already a puddle around his fingers.

Froggatt watched the detective for a few seconds; "You're not such a hard man now Inspector."

There was no mistaking the venom in those words.

It was 1am and still quite warm, even in the shadows of the prison walls.

Titus Moon had been waiting for ten minutes at least and was becoming agitated, particularly as the police station on Stanley Street was only a few hundred yards away. He had with him a large two-wheeled cart and various tools hidden under tarpaulin sheeting. It was a good night, thought Titus, low cloud and no moon. If it had been raining it would have been perfect.

At last the man he had arranged to meet appeared.

"Fuckin' 'ell Joe. I thought sommat 'ad 'appened t' yers."

"Fear not laddie, have I ever let you down? And I am in need of the usual four half -crowns don't you know? Ol' Joe was Irish and eccentric. His manner, particularly after a skin-full was that of an actor performing on stage and his oratory tended to be loud.

"Keep yer voice down. Yer not t'bloody drunk t' d' this are yers?" Titus scrutinised the old man who must have been at least seventy.

"How dare you sir. I am as sober as a judge and resent the accusation." Ol'Joe was now holding the cart for support.

Titus considered abandoning the night's arrangements, but at least the old sod had turned up, so decided to press on with the mission. He would need another pair of hands later on.

"Reet Joe listen t' me. We're not goin' far t'neet, just up th' road. Keep yer wits abaht yer, yer drunken ol'fool. Ah'll not bi 'appy if wi get detained bi rozzers cause o' yer."

"Titus my good fellow. Should the local constabulary question us I shall respond in no uncertain terms. This is a free country by God! My family did not flee the potato blight and land on this part of this God-forsaken country to be harried by the law. No sir. I shall roam the Queen's highways as I please and…"

"Joe! Shut t' fuck up."

They set off along Deepdale Road, a main thoroughfare through the town, but after a short distance disappeared into the ginnels that inter-linked like a spider's web. The cart, which Titus stole from the market a few weeks ago and kept hidden in a derelict piggery off New Hall Lane, had been fitted with a strip of rubber over the metal bands that ran around the wheels.

Ol' Joe took up position next to Titus as they progressed along the unlit alleyways that separated row upon row of grimy terraced houses with the pervading stink of human waste wafting from the midden heaps behind each yard gate and wall. Titus knew very little about his companion even though they have been acquaintances for many a year. He was aware Ol' Joe came from Ireland, but his Dublin lilt had been supplemented with a northwest twang. He also knew Ol' Joe used to be a smithy and was still as strong as an ox.

Ol' Joe always wore a weathered cloth cap and a brown ex-army trench coat, still displaying brass buttons and epaulettes. His hefty clogs made him slightly taller than his five foot eight. Titus did not know where he lived or if he was married and had never thought to ask him.

Titus suddenly stopped and put a hand on Ol' Joe's shoulder.

"Schh!"

He turned round and was straining to see into the blackness behind.

"Can yer 'ear owt?"

His companion had been quietly singing the lyrics to a Celtic ballad about 'buxom maidens from County Kildare'. He looked at Titus puzzled.

A wind had picked up and it buffeted a discarded newspaper over the cobbles and walls. That was all that could be heard.

Titus gave a nod and they set off once again. Ol' Joe was already back in the hills of Kildare.

Their destination was Saint Paul's Church and they had not far to go, but Titus could not shake off the feeling that they were being watched. At every corner he stopped, listened and searched the night.

The church built in 1810 came into view. Situated in St. Paul's Square with houses overlooking three sides it was not ideal, even if the building was completely surrounded by a large graveyard. The beer-house called The Edinburgh Castle was less than fifty yards away and fortunately that too as lifeless as the churchyard.

A low wall with high metal railings and leafless deciduous trees were the only barriers between the living and the dead. Titus knew exactly where he was going.

The gate was unlocked and gave an unwelcome squeal as the cart was pushed through. They followed the path to the rear of the church and Titus pointed to recently disturbed earth, giving the appearance of giant mole activity.

They worked in silence.

Titus unwrapped the spades and lit an oil-lamp, which he partly shrouded with his jacket, satisfied that it could not be seen from a distance.

The two men set to work.

There was no head stone lamenting the loss of a dear departed soul, just a temporary white cross, painted with the name 'John Wilson 14 years'.

The loose soil was quickly removed and heaped onto one of the tarpaulin sheets. It did not take long for the casket to appear. Titus climbed into the grave and stood on top of the coffin.

Ol' Joe looked bemused. This was not how they had extracted the previous coffins.

Titus had a brace an' bit with which he bored a series of holes about a third of the way down and across the coffin lid. Every so often he would stop, poke his head from the hole and listen intently.

He threw the drill up to Ol' Joe and nodded.

As he had no idea what Titus was doing he stood by the edge and shrugged his shoulders, more than slightly annoyed he had not been told of a change in the plans.

"Th' jemmy fer fucks sake," Titus gave a snarling whisper.

He broke through the weakened casket lid with the iron bar and forced free the section where the head would be.

A slender form lay in the coffin, neatly wrapped in a spotlessly clean white shroud.

Titus changed his position and put his damp back against the cold earth and placed both feet on the edge of the casket. Bending down he wrapped his hands around the covered chin of the corpse and heaved.

The body moved easily and Titus soon had it upright, in an eerie bearhug.

"Joe, give us an 'and," he grunted.

Without ceremony or deference to the deceased, Ol' Joe gripped the head and lifted as Titus pushed.

The frail body of John Wilson was now out of its coffin and lay on the wet grass.

The two men unwrapped the shroud, stripped the Sunday best suit off the teenager and put the stiff naked body onto another sheet of tarpaulin. Ol' Joe threw the tweed suit and shroud back into the hole as Titus quickly wrapped the cadaver in the grimy oilcloth. With a nod to the old man, John Wilson was lifted onto the cart.

Titus and Ol' Joe re-filled the hole, gathered their tools and in less than an hour they were on their way out of the churchyard.

Edmund Froggatt was a man on a mission. It was late and he had been enjoying 'a lock in' with David Taylor the landlord of Halliday's Kings Arms on Stanley Street, which looked across London Road, directly at the House of Correction.

He referred to himself as 'an investigative journalist' and when not sat at his typewriter he was on the streets or visiting public houses.

Froggatt was desperate to get the big lead on the three murders and body-snatching he so avidly reported about and which was so avidly read by an incredulous population. The mounting unease and in some parts of the town a heart thumping fear felt by many, increased with the rising newspaper circulation.

He toured areas favoured by the underworld, choosing ale-houses frequented by vagabonds, beggars, thieves and prostitutes, believing the answer to recent events would be found there.

Someone, somewhere knows something, he kept telling himself.

The journalist had a pocket full of shillings and let it be known he would pay for information.

Having drawn another blank with locals at The Kings Arms, he nursed a pint while eyeing up an English rose who was making her intentions perfectly clear. David Taylor called for 'time ladies and gentlemen please' then promptly starting serving anyone who approached the bar, ignoring the midnight closing time an hour earlier.

Froggatt reflected on his attack on the copper, but was not unduly concerned. He did not believe Meadowbank would make a formal report and issue a Magistrates arrest warrant for assault on a police officer. That would be too easy. He knew Meadowbank would be too proud to get his revenge through the courts. He wanted blood not justice and he would fester and rage and wait for his opportunity, just as Froggatt had. And he also knew Meadowbank would seize any opportunity to come at him hard and deadly.

Perhaps in a boxing ring, adhering like gentlemen to the Marquis of Queensbury rules it could be an interesting duel, but neither man was a gentleman and certainly did not fight to rules. Froggatt had grudging respect for the police inspector. He was one of few men who would confront and challenge him, but he had enjoyed beating him senseless, like a bare-knuckle fighter.

It was approaching one o'clock in the morning and Froggatt bade his farewells to the landlord and a few locals still drinking at The Kings Arms. He had his arm round the shoulders of the good-looking lass young enough to be his daughter, his other hand was already fumbling underneath her hitched up skirt.
The breeze whipped across his face as he breathed in the fresh air while gawping lasciviously at her low cut bodice displaying an impressive cleavage. She was eagerly squeezing his groin feeling his hardness and attempting to undo the top of his trousers but close to being drunk and incapable made that simple one-handed manoeuvre near impossible.

Froggatt rented a room on Duke Street East, just off London Road near The Yard Works and only a ten- minute walk from The Kings Arms. That's where they were heading for.

Movement across the road caught his eye. At first he paid no attention to the big man pushing a cart, who he took to be a 'scavenger' with his 'treacle-wagon', on his rounds to dig out the middens and empty the privies. He preferred to direct his gaze to the delicious bosom that promised so much, but then something made him look away again.

The gas lamps outside the castellated prison façade illuminated the man and Froggatt recognised him.

Yes! It was the gravedigger from the Parish Church. The very same church where the Reverend Buck was strung-up. His name instantly came to mind.

Titus Moon.

Froggatt stepped back into the darkness, pulling his companion closer and watched with renewed interest.

He saw Moon meet up with another male, an old man in a long overcoat.

Ignoring the sexual promises whispered to him, Froggatt pushed the demanding female away a little too hard and the woman whose name he did not know, staggered backwards into the ale-house door with a bang and now unsupported, she slid to the floor. He ignored her protests of indignation and threw her a florin that landed neatly between her delightful breasts, something that she found amusing and she giggled ludicrously.

Without another word to her, Froggatt followed the two men along Deepdale Road, lurking in the shadows, listening to the rattling wooden cart, more interested in their intentions than that of a nubile wanton woman.

The journalist refused to believe his good fortune as he watched them enter the churchyard. He positioned himself at the unlit mouth of an alleyway, not daring to breathe, as the minutes ticked by.

Good God! They are robbing a grave.

Titus Moon is the body-snatcher!

He realised he needed proof. His word against two men being accused of such a despicable crime would not get very far.

Froggatt made a decision. He could follow them or challenge them.

He decided to maintain observations and establish where the body was being delivered.

It was probably a decision most would agree with, but it was one that Edmund Froggatt would most certainly regret.

His heart was racing with anticipation. He was imagining the headlines and the faces of those Fleet Street journalists, his editor and not to mention Detective Inspector Meadowbank.

Edmund Froggatt had solved the mystery of the grave-robbing and possibly the three murders. He would be able to name his own price and have the pick of the jobs that would certainly come his way.

In death there is always an opportunity to be had, his editor told him when selling him the dead end position and unglamorous title of crime reporter.

How true.

The cart, being pushed easily by Titus, trundled across the cobblestones with less disturbance, now that the cart was carrying extra weight.

They left St. Paul's Square onto East Street, then East View, crossed Meadow Street and finally entered Stanleyfield Street, which ran parallel with the rear of the infirmary.

Titus and Ol' Joe both knew where to go. It was their usual place for the rendezvous. A dark ginnel with the high wall of the infirmary on one side and gable ended terraced houses on the other. A perfect place for clandestine business.

Froggatt needed to get closer and skirted round Stanleyfield Street, reappearing at the far end near to St. Barnabas' Place, allowing an excellent view of the mouth of the dark passageway where the two men were now waiting.

A noise caught every-one's attention, and a shaft of light briefly flashed deep in the passageway as a door opened.

Assertive footsteps echoed along the walls and then a tall man appeared from the darkness.

He wore a long black apron over his waistcoat and matching black trousers. The sleeves of his crisp white shirt were secured by cufflinks.

He approached the cart, now resting at an angle on front legs, and put a hand on the tarpaulin.

"So what have we got here Titus?"

"A young boy sir. Passed away yesterday an' buried less than twelve hour ago."

Titus sounded pleased.

"And cause of death?" It was the cultured voice of a man who knew what he wanted.

"Vomitin' an'..." he paused for the word that eluded him,

"Shittin' sir."

"Ah! Dysentery. A resulting infection with the colonic epithelium. Hmm. I suppose I could still use the cadaver for tomorrow's dissection class."

Professor Daniel Bailey was a very experienced surgeon and a tutor in human anatomy. His dissection and anatomy demonstrations were in constant demand by medical students from wealthy families and they paid handsomely for private tution in his laboratory at the rear of the medical college.

Demand outstripped the supply of corpses legally supplied to the hospital by the authorities for medical research.

This inadequacy forced the professor, with the full knowledge and support of two of his doctors, to obtain cadavers from elsewhere.

How Professor Bailey and Titus Moon met initially is something that will be speculated about long after both men are dead. Suffice to say, both were corrupt, loathsome and incapable of comprehending the wretchedness of their horrific trade.

"I shall take the corpse at a reduced rate, mind you. A corpse putrefying with dysentery has limited use." He turned away, as if receiving a whiff of the putrefaction he had referred to.

"And you'll get half my usual fee and be grateful for a guinea." With a wave of his hand, indicating that Titus should follow, Professor Bailey turned, about to disappear into the dark passageway.

"One minute Professor, that's not enough." Titus said quietly

The surgeon stopped and turned to face Titus, displaying an offensive smile of self-importance.

"Not enough? My dear Titus I think you'll find it is more than enough."

"Nowhere near enough sir. I want ten pounds an' I think you'll bi payin' mi ten pounds an all."

Ol' Joe watched his friend closely, trying to work out what was going on. Even he knew ten pounds was an outrageous request.

"Now why would I give you ten pounds for a piece of rotting meat?" It wasn't really a question, but a prelude to a final dismissal.

"Cause Professor, I saw yer wi' t' Reverend Buck on neet 'e died. I think t' police would bi interested t' know that."

The colour drained from Professor Bailey's face.

"Lost fer words Professor? I know, lets call it fifteen quid t' pay fer mi silence."

Professor Bailey had regained some composure.

"Are you blackmailing me Titus?"

"Call it what yer want, but I see it as a business arrangement."

"I'll not be blackmailed by the likes of you. Go back to the sewer from where you have both crawled and take that corpse with you. You and I are finished Titus. Do you understand? Finished! Our arrangement is terminated forthwith. Who the hell do you think you are?"

His voice was increasing with anger and his chest slowly expanded like a peacock.

Titus decided to play his ace card.

"When I say I saw yer wi' t' Reverend Buck what I meant wer' I saw 'im suckin' yer cock, like t' perverted fuckers yer both are." He gave the professor an icy stare.

This time the professor did not respond. His mind in turmoil, he could only stare back.

"B'hind curtains in t'vestry Professor. Remember? An 'omosexual vicar an' a 'omosexual doctor, indulgin' in sodomy. Now what would t' press an' t' law 'ave t' say abaht that?"

"What do you want?" It was almost an admission of surrender.

"Fifteen pounds t' start wi', then we'll 'ave a chat abaht future payments."

Titus was enjoying this. He had intended blackmailing the vicar, but it turns out the doctor will be a better proposition altogether.

Professor Bailey looked deflated. He knew he had little choice but to do as Titus demanded. He attempted to reason the situation to himself. Fifteen pounds every now and then would not be too bad. He could certainly afford it. But if this did get out he would be disgraced, struck off the medical register at best or imprisoned for a long time at worst.

The revelation to one and all that he was the receiver of the stolen cadavers would probably not harm his career as much as being identified as the Reverend Buck's lover. Either was unthinkable to the distinguished professor.

The Royal College of Surgeons would not tolerate a homosexual professor amongst its ranks any more than the British public and Parliament.

All this was going through his mind with clinical analysis, so much so he did not contemplate that Titus going to the authorities would reveal his own villainous complicity.

The moment had come to concede defeat and recognise he had no other choice. Titus had won.

Titus grew impatient with the surgeon's deliberations and foolishly said something that would irrevocably alter the course of their confrontation.

"Professor! D' yer want m' t' mek an example of yer, like I did wi' t' vicar? Ha! It's a pity yer'd buggered off; yer would 'ave 'eard 'im whimper like a pup. By t' time I'd finished with 'im, I'd made certain 'is cock suckin' days were o'er."

Ol' Joe looked at both men with increasing disbelief.

Up until now, Professor Bailey had not considered Titus as being responsible for Reverend Buck's death. He had been too preoccupied pondering his own plight, but now it all became clear. What would have been obvious long ago to any student of criminology or even to a layperson in the street, now shone like a beacon of understanding to the professor.

Poor sweet John, my dearest John, my secret love.

Titus Moon is the murderer of my dear John!

He rushed forwards with a scream. Even though Titus was far stronger and much younger, the attack sent him crashing into the cart.

The professor produced a scalpel from his apron pocket and plunged the razor-sharp blade deep into Titus's left shoulder. Professor Bailey tried to extract the blade, hoping to continue his advantage of surprise, and slice the Adam's apple now staring at his face, but the scalpel was lodged in tight muscle.

Titus gripped the professor's head like a vice and with a violent twist, rammed his forehead against the side of the cart.

The professor had more fight in him than most would consider possible. He savagely jabbed an eye of the gravedigger and twisted and squeezed his nose with all his strength.

Titus screamed in shock and excruciating pain.

Somehow the professor got a hand on the scalpel still protruding from the bloody shoulder and began twisting the handle and even Ol' Joe could hear the blade scraping bone.

But Titus was a street fighter and drove his fist into the professor's stomach. Winding the older man was the only opportunity he needed to repeatedly punch him in the face. Clenched fists rained down as the professor tumbled to the floor gasping and bloody.

But Titus had not finished with him yet.

He ignored Ol' Joe's requests to stop and reached into the cart. His hand came out holding the jemmy, a three-foot length of heavy cast iron, tapered at each end.

Gripping it with both hands, dagger style, he thrust it down towards the mumbling professor's head.

It burst through his skull with such force that it pierced his brain completely and came out of the back of his head hitting the pavement with a shudder.

"Yep, I think you've killed him Titus." Ol' Joe said "I take it we won't be getting paid for tonight?" He was stood over the professor, looking at the jemmy with consternation.

"Come on Titus! Let's get these bodies moved. We may have trouble explaining this to a constable."

Without expression, Titus first pulled the scalpel from his shoulder, shoving his neckerchief in the wound and then, one handed, removed the iron bar, with some effort from Professor Bailey's skull. It slid out with a sickening slurp.

They lifted the doctor onto the cart, next to the unwanted John Wilson and pulled the heavy sheet over them both.

"That ol' bugger gi' mi a run fer mi money." Titus said with a forced smile.

Edmund Froggatt had seen and heard every word from his vantage point, not very far away.

For a man who usually acts with certainty, determination and occasionally on impulse, he remained motionless in the dark, unsure what to do.

He had just witnessed the murder of an eminent surgeon. He had no idea as to his name, but he was a professor, that much had been made clear to him. Some would argue that Titus killed him in self-defence, that the professor was the aggressor, stabbing Titus with the clear intention of causing serious harm.

But Edmund Froggatt would never say that. In the eyes of the law he is the only independent witness. Someone to swear under oath that what he says to the court shall be the truth, the whole truth and nothing but the truth and to provide an impartial account of what happened.

As far as he was concerned it was nothing less than cold-blooded murder.

He had evidence that would send Titus Moon and the old fucker to the gallows for two acts of murder.

The one he had just witnessed and the one he heard Titus confess to, the murder of Reverend Buck.

Hell fire, he mused; at last I've hit the big time. The scoop of a lifetime that could set his name in journalistic history.

His breathing slowed and a calmer rationale took over. He considered going to the police, but as soon as he lost sight of Titus and the old man, he knew those two bodies in the cart, would never be seen again, leaving him with no evidence to support his allegations that Titus Moon was a double murderer.

In fact, no matter where he followed them, once the bodies had been disposed of, he would be back to pointing the finger only on the basis of circumstantial evidence and no judge or jury would convict on the strength of a disturbed grave, a missing surgeon and his word alone.

If he was not careful, he might end up being discredited. A journalist making unfounded allegations that cannot be proved is a journalist that cannot be trusted. All his hard work for nothing. All his contacts and sources looking the other way as he approached, a man not to be trusted.

No! He had to act now.

His fear of failure, mixed with his desire for success at any price mired his decision-making process. He confused his bulk and strength as an unassailable asset, something with which to threaten, intimidate and dominate. Already he had forgotten the irrefutable fact that resulted in the cruel death he had just witnessed.

Humans are mortal and vulnerable.

With a confidence oozing from every pore, Froggatt stepped from the shadows.

"What have we got here?" His voice shattered the quiet night-time like a thunderclap.

Titus and Ol' Joe, just about to push the cart forwards, spun towards the voice.

Froggatt carried on walking towards them. He had no intention of giving away any ground.

The two men eyed him suspiciously, remaining silent.

The journalist stopped by the cart and rested a hand on the bulky tarpaulin, never for a second taking his eyes off the two men, Titus especially.

"And what do you intend doing with these two bodies then?"

Titus recognised the man mountain towering over them. He was that bloody reporter, always asking questions. Now he was here, asking bloody questions again.

"Why don't yer just fuck off an' mind yer own business?" There was no disguising the menace from Titus.

"It's my job to ask questions and solve mysteries. The people of Preston want to know who murdered Reverend Buck, a peace loving man of God, in such a cowardly fashion and what about the body-snatching? All these unsolved crimes just waiting for a name or two, to be passed onto the police."

Titus moved fast and swung the bloodied jemmy at Froggatt, hitting his upper arm as it instinctively rose to protect his head.

Froggatt responded with a lighting quick punch to the kidneys, followed by a savage hand chop to the throat. As far as Froggatt was concerned, Titus Moon was already on the ropes in the opening seconds of round one.

Retching from a ruptured windpipe, Titus staggered away from the reporter.

"Drop that iron bar or I'll take your fucking head off with it." Froggatt said, removing his favourite cap and throwing it to one side.

Titus held the jemmy aloft, beckoning Froggatt forwards.

The cart separated them and Froggatt had his back to Ol' Joe.

"Is that t' best yer can do?" Titus rasped.

Froggatt slowly moved towards him, arms raised and spread out, constantly gyrating like a true wrestler.

He feigned a charge and Titus dodged to one side, keeping close to the cart.

He charged again and this time it was for real. Titus had anticipated the move and leapt onto the cart, swinging the jemmy backwards, feeling it crash into the side of Froggatt's head. Glancing over his shoulder he saw thick blood running from the reporter's right ear, as he shook his head to clear his senses from a near knock out blow.

Froggatt took hold of one of the wheels and in a single movement, upturned the cart onto its side, spilling the two corpses and Titus onto the cobbles.

As Titus scrambled to his feet, avoiding stumbling over the dead bodies, Froggatt was onto him. Knuckles and forehead struck Titus, blow followed blow. Fists like spades dug into every part of him, and Titus, completely overwhelmed by the onslaught began slipping into unconsciousness.

And then the battery of blows stopped.

The pain, Titus could feel, but no longer could he feel those punishing punches and kicks. He was on the floor curled up with his hands protecting his head and there he lay and for the first time in his life he was afraid.

Ol' Joe had seen the iron mallet fall onto the cobblestones from beneath the oilcloth and he picked it up.

It felt good and he admired the craftsmanship that had fashioned such a heavy hammerhead, pounding the red-hot metal into shape.

It was many a year, Ol' Joe would say, since he had swung such a hammer, but swing it he did, with the experience and deadly accuracy of the blacksmith he once was.

The heavy lump of iron sank dead centre into the back of Froggatt's head, as far as the shaft would allow, smashing through the thickest part of the skull. Ol' Joe jerked the hammer free, as if it was a tomahawk, allowing the lifeless body of Edmund Froggatt to fall to one side like a felled oak tree.

Titus was hurt, coughing up thick globs of blood. His left eye was completely closed. He slowly embraced himself, wincing against the pain of countless cracked ribs and the deep wound to his shoulder.

Ol' Joe swept his eyes around the deserted street, tossing the hammer into the cart.

He said to Titus, "I know you're hurting lad, but we need to be away, sharpish. Can you move aside Titus while I get this barrow back on its feet?"

Titus crawled to the cart and slowly pulled himself to his feet with the help of Ol' Joe and step-by-step he moved away to the nearest wall for support, blood and snot hanging from his nose and open mouth and at the same time gasping in air.

Ol' Joe took hold of the upturned cartwheel, pulling with all the power and strength the old smithy possessed. The heavy cart immediately moved towards him, pivoting on the rubber rim of the floored wheel and seconds later he had lowered the cart to an upright position. Ol' Joe grabbed the dead journalist by both arms dragging him nearer to the front and with another display of amazing strength for any man, hauled the lifeless bulk of Froggatt to his feet, leaning the body against the edge of the cart then pushed back and with a grunt of great exertion from Ol' Joe, Edmund Froggatt slid along the worn planks. He quickly hauled the professor's and the young boy's corpse onto the barrow where they lay, side by side as if representing three generations staring lifelessly at the sky before the tarpaulin was pulled across them.

"Titus! Listen to me lad. We have to get rid of these three and I know just the place." He seemed hardly out of breath.

"Flamin' 'ell Joe, I wish you'd a clobbered 'im at bit sooner. By t' Christ 'e could throw a punch." Titus was slowly standing straight, grimacing against the pain.

"Your gratitude is overwhelming Titus Moon."

Without another word Ol' Joe pushed the cart forwards and already had the route planned.

They retraced their steps to Deepdale Road then into Deepdale Street and St. Mary Street, this time avoiding the police station on Stanley Street, darting between the alleyways that men from the underworld knew so well.

Ol' Joe was finding the cart cumbersome and tiring and becoming an effort to push over the cobblestones, but one look at Titus told him he was in no state to help.

They kept to the passages running parallel with London Road, towards the river.

The old man knew this would be his last night in the town and with a bit of luck this God-forsaken country. He had murdered a man and at the moment only two persons knew that and as far as he was concerned that was one too many. He trusted Titus more than he would trust most men, but everyone has their price. If Titus was arrested or taken in for questioning who knows what he may say to save himself, even though, the old man considered, Titus was not in any position to start making deals with the coppers. He would hang whatever he said, but Ol' Joe had no intention of going to the gallows with him.

Suddenly the prospect of breathing in the sweet air of County Kildare lifted his spirits and he began humming one of his mother's favourite songs, ignoring the cursing and swearing behind.

It did not take too long to reach the spot Ol' Joe had in mind.

The banks of the River Ribble near to the bridge that crossed to Walton-le-Dale, were dark, silent and steep.

The old man had hoped for a high tide, but the blackness offered no clues. He could hear the gentle lapping of the waters edge beyond the undergrowth, interrupted only by the screech of a barn owl.

"Are you up to this lad? I can't do it on my own." He stared at Titus, feeling the chill of open water waft over him and watched the big man nod his head as he moved towards one of the long wooden arms. The blood covered jemmy and hammer lay next to Edmund Froggatt and both murder weapons were close to hand should either decide four dead is as good as three.

If Titus was thinking of adding another to their tally it did not show, but the old man was certainly thinking this. Not that he was considering silencing Titus. He nurtured deep feelings of loyalty to anyone who ever helped him. One or two regulars at various taverns have been glad to buy him a pint or a bowl of soup and should tables, chairs and fists start flying, Ol' Joe would defend them to the last.

And he certainly owed Titus. They had supped many a pint together and on one occasion even bedded the same whore, all paid for by Titus.

He had an intrinsic sense of loyalty, he was not sure if Titus possessed the same. In fact he was damn certain he did not and should he rush him, the old man wanted to be ready.

Titus stooped under the shaft, his good shoulder taking the strain. The swollen face looked at Ol' Joe, waiting.

Ol' Joe positioned himself likewise. "On three."

On the count they pushed with a rush of adrenalin. The cushioned wheels slowly rolled up the damp grassy incline then dipped. They scrambled behind the cart, feeling it tug against their grip then let go and watched it roll and bounce forwards, gathering momentum as gravity took over.

Within moments of the makeshift hearse being swallowed by the night there was a loud splash and the macabre sound of bubbles popping.

With relief the old man looked at Titus who was heaving with his teeth clenched. Clearly the exertion had taken its toll.

He produced a shiny black leather wallet and said to Titus as he opened it,

"All in all dear Titus, an interesting evening and one I shan't forget for quite a while. And who said there is not a God on high?"

He had removed a wad of five-pound notes from the wallet then tossed the leather fold-over into the rippling water.

Titus said nothing, but held out a cotton bag of coins, taken from Froggatt's jacket and a big smile said it all.

"It has occurred to me Titus that we should have done in the good doctor weeks ago and relieved him of his money then. It would have saved us a lot of time and effort."

Titus wanted to laugh, but knew only too well the throbbing pain would become unbearable.

"Fifty three pounds in the Queen's currency."

Ol' Joe announced after splitting the notes and coins in two piles on the grass. Titus could not count, but recognised a small fortune when he saw one.

They headed back to the main highway that led into town indicated by the lights at the top of the steep rise of London Road.

"This is where we part company Titus. It is time for bed and alibis and don't take this personal, but I pray to The Almighty that I never see you again, particularly with a rope around our necks."

He offered his hand and Titus gripped it, nodding.

"I wish I'd met yer years ago. Wi could 'ave done some good business t'gether. Yer saved m' life t'night an' fer that ah'll allus bi owin' yer. An' if t' rozzers ever nick mi I promise ah'll never mention yer name, no matter what beatin' they gi' mi. That's t' least I owe yers."

Ol' Joe was genuinely moved by the sincerity. It was as if Titus had been reading the old man's mind earlier and for that he felt embarrassed.

The old man was the first to turn and walk away. He was heading for the countryside. He paused and looked back, watching Titus slowly limp up the hill towards a skyline of church spires and mill chimneys and the maelstrom of police activity they had started.

Chapter Ten

The black police four-wheeler drew to a halt outside Preston General Railway Station and Constable Clegg set the handbrake as Albert Meadowbank climbed from the carriage.

It was one o'clock and the London train was not due for half an hour, so he decided to have a coffee in the new refreshment room on the main platform.

He knew more about Frederick George Abberline than he did two days ago.

From police reports and newspaper articles supplied by the chief constable, Meadowbank established that the retired chief inspector possessed an encyclopaedic knowledge of the Ripper murders. He had also seen a copy of the retired detective chief inspector's personal record and he was impressed. Retired from the Metropolitan Police in 1892 with over eighty commendations to his credit.

Eighty! What th' 'ell d' yer 'ave t' do t' get eighty commendations? Meadowbank wondered, blowing at the steaming mug of coffee.

He recalled the words of Sir Arthur, "Abberline is here to assist the investigation, not run it or take charge. He is a civilian and has no authority whatsoever. Remember that Inspector. His is an advisory role only."

For the past twelve months Abberline had been in charge of the Pinkerton European Agency, the famous private investigation company. Meadowbank was unclear whether the ex-copper was representing Pinkerton or as a freelance investigator, charging the Constabulary a set fee

Something else to ask him, he mused.

There was activity on the nearest platform as the 'Bulldog' class LNWR passenger locomotive pulled in right on time. He looked at the photograph once again of a serious looking man shaking the hand of the then Home Secretary, Henry Matthews. It was dated 1892.

Through the hissing cloud of steam that wafted up towards the huge glass canopy spanning the eight tracks and platforms, Meadowbank moved next to an iron pillar and waited.

The carriages had been full and there was brisk movement all around as porters, family and friends gathered at the opening carriage doors.

He recognised him instantly, even amongst the throng of disembarking passengers.

Frederick George Abberline was not as tall as he had expected and was certainly a lot shorter than Meadowbank's six feet. He wore a black suit and tie, matching the silk bowler, dipped over the eyes. He was portly but walked with confidence and declined a porter's offer to assist with the suitcase in one hand and briefcase in the other.

When only a matter of yards apart Meadowbank approached,

"Mr. Abberline. I'm Detective Inspector Albert Meadowbank. Welcome t' Preston."

The smile was genuine and Abberline's handshake firm.

"Thank you Inspector. My first time this far north I'm embarrassed to say, but the journey has been most pleasant."

"Don't worry abaht it sir, I've never bin past Manchester."

A southern accent this far north was unusual, even though Abberline was from Dorset and forty years in the capital only accentuated the Dorset twang.

"That looks sore Inspector." He nodded at the black bruising to Meadowbank's right eye and the several stitches above the tip of his eyebrow.

"Aye it is. 'Ad a disagreement wi' someone's fist an' mi guts aren't much better either."

Abberline laughed.

"I do hope whoever was responsible is behind bars?" He said more seriously.

"Not yet, but I'm on 'is case, 'ave no fear abaht that."

Meadowbank was about to continue but stopped himself as a thought shot through his mind. *If I can't catch someone guilty of a serious assault on m' sel', a police officer, is 'e thinkin' what chance do I 'ave of catchin' a murderer?*

"T' bugger 'as gone int' 'idin'. Not bin sin fer a couple o' days naw, not even turned in fer work. Ah'll 'ave 'im sooner or later, but as yer know we 'ave more important matters t' discuss an' I need t' brief yer before yer meet t' chief. I suggest wi retire t' local ale-'ouse. I'll introduce yer t' mi right 'and man, Sergeant 'Uggins an' we'll 'ave a bite t' eat an' ah'll bring yer up t' date, if that meets wi' yer approval, Mr. Abberline?"

"That sounds excellent and please Inspector, call me Fred. I hold no rank now."

"In that case Fred, I'm Albert. There's transport waitin'. 'Ere! Let mi tek t' suitcase."

A few hours earlier Titus Moon had made it back to Mags' lodgings and as usual the front door was unbolted. He was glad for the reassuring silence that descended on wretched dwellings such as those surrounding him. It was that time between 1am and 4am when there seemed to be a natural peace, or at least that's how it appeared to Titus. The drunks had fallen into a stupor; the quarrelling husbands and wives had called a temporary truce allowing sleep to take-over; the ever squawking kids now silently followed their natural body rhythms, despite their hunger and even baying hounds rested their heads.

Only coppers and villains stalked Starch Houses at this time of the morning and it was still an hour before the knocker-up arrived to announce the time, unlike the more prosperous areas where a maid or butler would rouse the household at a more civilised hour.

He closed the door with a sigh and a familiar voice broke his reverie.

"You've a flamin' cheek comin' inta mi 'ouse at this time o' mornin' an' I suppose you'll bi as drunk as a dray man at Christmas."

Mags was stood at her open door.

"Mags! Not now. I'm not in t' mood." He answered wearily.

"That's t' trouble Titus, yer never int' mood these days. Once upon a time yer were int' mood every flamin' night. Look at yersel'! Yer can't even stand straight, yer drunken bastard. I want yers out an' I mean it this time Titus. D' yers 'ear?"

Titus moved through the gloom of the small hallway towards the stairs where the light from an oil-lamp behind Mags lit his face.

"Good God!" she shrieked, "What 'ave they done t' yers?"

Mags dashed forwards, resting a hand on his shoulder, gawping at his battered face.

"I just need rest Mags, that's all. An' if t' coppers come lookin' fer mi tell 'em I've done a bunk, eh?" Her hand prevented him from moving up the stairs.

"Come on luv, come wi' me. Ah'll look after yers."

"Ah'll bi better on mi own. I don't want yer involved wi' th' law on count o' me."

"It meks sense t' stay wi' mi, especially if t' coppers are on yers trail, don't it? If they comes a knockin' Ah'll show 'em yer room an' tell 'em yers done a moonlight flit owing rent. They wan't think o' lookin' in mi room fer that dirty rotten villain called Titus Moon." She gave a big smile and gently pushed him towards the open door.

He allowed himself to be guided by Mags, knowing full well that what she had said made perfect sense. Titus put a hand inside his trouser pocket and pushed the bank notes and coins deeper.

Samuel Huggins was already at a table in The Stanley Arms as pre-arranged and called out as Meadowbank entered with Abberline.

The introductions were made; they shook hands then sat down. All three agreed they were ready for something to eat.

"Fred, I can recommend t' steak puddin'. Comes wi' boiled spuds an' carrots. It's a proper plateful ah'll tell thee," enthused Sam Huggins and Meadowbank nodded his approval.

"Or try t' mutton broth. Delicious wi' a lump of 'ome med bread. It's allus pipin' 'ot. In fact I think ah'll 'ave that come t' mention it," continued Huggins.

"Forgive me for asking, but what is steak pudding? Surely a pudding is a dessert like rice pudding or Christmas pudding or bread and butter pudding. Are you honestly saying you eat steak in a pudding?"

Huggins looked at Meadowbank and neither knew what to say to this. After a moment's reflection Meadowbank said, "It's not a puddin' as such. It doesn't come wi' custard or owt like that. It's a tasty suet puddin' full o' meyt an' gravy. Every ones eats it around 'ere." He was pleased with his description and so was Huggins. So much so that he was ready to order it instead of the broth, but Abberline looked unconvinced.

"I know just t' thing fer yer Fred. Black puddin', wi' a bit o' mustard an' warm bread. Now that is delicious." Meadowbanks' description of more food was presenting Huggins with difficulties in choosing. He was now wavering towards the black pudding.

"Black pudding" Abberline said slowly, "Another pudding that's not a pudding and one you have with mustard?"

It was never explained to him that the main ingredient was pig's blood.

"Ah'll tell yer what Fred, 'ave t' steak an' kidney pie. Comes wi' mashed spuds an' mushy peas. In fact swap th' mushy peas fer boiled carrots. Just as good t'gether an' its t' best savoury pie in th' red rose county."

Abberline was about to query what a mushy pea was, but Meadowbank was now on his feet. He rubbed his hands together,

"Reet lads, that's three pints is it? Th' landlord brews 'is own ale here. Best in town."

He ordered the food at the bar and came back with three pint glasses, brimming with best bitter.

"Get yer laughin' tackle rownd that Fred an' taste a proper drink of ale."

Huggins grinned eagerly in rapturous support.

"Cheers Frederick. 'Ere's t' yer good 'ealth an' a successful conclusion to th' investigation." Meadowbank proposed.

All three men raised their glasses.

Chapter Eleven

Sir William sat at his huge oak desk, his back towards tall windows overlooking Victoria Embankment and the River Thames and not far from the site of the new Scotland Yard building. He was staring at a telegram he had read several times already and he looked quite pale.

Charles entered his father's office holding two cut glass brandy bowls, each filled with a respectable measure of finest cognac. He put his father's glass in its usual spot on the desk then sat in a red leather armchair by one of the windows.

As Charles took a sip from the glass, he registered his father's silence.

"Father, you look like the Queen has stripped you of your knighthood."

"Kruger is demanding the withdrawal of 12,000 British troops from the Transvaal frontiers within forty-eight hours or they will declare war." He looked at his son intently.

Charles thought about this for a moment.

"We knew war was going to happen, it was just a question of when. Remember father, that is why I got out?"

"You'd better read this."

Charles rose from the chair and went to his father's side, taking hold of the telegram, while Sir William took a large swig of the cognac.

'message…for sir william cadley…rhodes preparing for attack… town to be defended... goods still in company safe. stop... no longer safe to move them. stop. thomas travis. message ends'.

He understood the message perfectly, but not his father's anxiety.

"How much are we talking about?"

"About three million in uncut diamonds."

"Christ! What! I didn't realise it was that much." He looked at his father.

"Three million? That cannot be correct. The stones I left behind were worth a few hundred pounds at the most."

Sir William bit his bottom lip avoiding his son's gaze.

"What I haven't told you Charles is that a few months ago we had a major find to say the least. A volcanic pipe, over a hundred feet across was discovered in the dig and has produced fantastic stones. Travis contacted me and on my instructions sent a sample by personal courier to Cape Town. This all took time of course and three weeks ago the yield was confirmed by Travis."

"This has happened since my return?"

"Yes. The seam was discovered not long after you left."

"And you never thought to mention this to me?" His glare bored into his father.

"This is a bloody mess son, a bloody mess. I have a contact in the War Office, very close to Secretary Petty-Fitzmaurice himself in fact and he assured me that Kruger would not invade the colonies and like a fool I trusted his judgement. What I also have not told you Charles is that I had agreed a deal to sell the stones. That is why I wanted them to remain in South Africa. A diamond merchant from America is in Cape Town as we speak. Simon Frankel, you may have heard of him. Anyway he was to travel to Kimberley next week, examine the stones, make an offer, which I am confident would be around three million pounds, transfer the funds and leave with the stones for America."

"And when were you going to tell me of this?" Charles asked again quietly, still staring at his father. Suddenly he erupted. "I am the vice president of this company and a major share-holder and you have negotiated a deal worth three million pounds without even consulting with me, your son, not to mention the fucking board. We are a public company, have you gone mad?"

"And I am the president of this company, you will do well to remember that. I brought you into the family business, just like your grandfather brought me into it. They call it nepotism

Charles, not talent." He glared back at his son. "And do not dare speak to me like you speak to your staff."

"We cannot leave them there. If the Boers attack Kimberley and the town falls we'll lose the lot." He shouted.

"I do realise that son. Let me think this through for a minute."

Sir William ran his hands over his thinning grey hair and both men went quiet. Charles spread his arms across a window frame with his back to his father.

"Is it too late for your friend Frankel to recover the stones himself?"

"Simon Frankel is a very wealthy diamond dealer, not a soldier of fortune. He travels with several bodyguards for personal protection only and would certainly not venture into a war-zone even for uncut diamonds worth millions of dollars. He is a business man and will no doubt be contacting me soon to find out what is happening and then no doubt be returning to the States on the next trans-Atlantic steamer from the Cape."

"Did Travis know of your little arrangement with Frankel?" He was enjoying his father's discomfort despite the enormity of the situation.

"No. Frankel had a letter from me authorising the release of the stones."

He continued with a sigh, "Instead they are still locked in a vault in a God forsaken town preparing for an invading army of several thousand Boers. Travis is our only hope of saving the stones. At the moment it is not safe to move the diamonds out of Kimberley, but if they were to be hidden, perhaps buried, and recovered at a later date." He paused momentarily; "I need to think this through Charles. Without stating the obvious there is too much to lose…"

Charles interrupted and turned round,

"For Christ sake father, there's nothing to think about. Your diamond merchant may not choose to risk his life for a three million pound fortune that belongs to this company," he said pointedly, "but I have no qualms doing so. I'm going to Kimberley. I'll take Henry Frobisher with me. You know it makes sense. Henry knows the Cape like the back of his hand and apart from that, who would you now trust to hand over uncut diamonds worth over three million pounds for safe keeping in a country we are at war with, six thousand miles away?"

Sir William knew he was right.

Charles had to act quickly. There was a steamer leaving from Southampton in three days on the 11th October. His secretary sent a telegram booking two first class cabins only to be informed that the Cape liner had been requisitioned by the War Office and was not available to unauthorised personnel. This would keep Sir William busy on the phone for some time.

Henry Frobisher had also received a telegram from Charles Cadley and was already travelling from London to meet him at Southampton.

He was used to getting last minute requests from Charles Cadley. They first met in Cape Town when Henry was a major with the Colonial Cape Mounted Riflemen and Charles was managing the Cadley estate and vineyards at Stellenbosch, east of the city.

They were more than acquaintances, possibly even friends, but more importantly, Charles knew Henry could be relied on one hundred per cent to do a job properly and see it through and Henry knew Charles paid him handsomely.

Chapter Twelve

Three days later and Her Majesty's Government's non-compliance with The President of South Africa's ultimatum brought an immediate response. An alliance of the South African Republic and Orange Free State forces invaded the North West Provinces of Cape Colony and Natal Colony, attacking the British Garrison south west of Mafeking, thereby signalling the start of the war.

That Wednesday on the 11th October, R.M.S. Dunottar Castle left Southampton bound for Durban via Cape Town.

Dunottar Castle, a Royal Mail vessel that been requisitioned by the War Department as a troop ship in preparation for hostilities with President Kruger, now set sail from Southampton to much celebration. Crowds lined Princess Alexandra Dock quayside singing God Save the Queen and cheering and flinging hats into the air, when those two huge red and black funnels belched clouds of black smoke and its whistle shrieked long and loud. Then the large ocean liner, weighing nearly six thousand tons sailed away towards the River Test.

Charles Cadley and Henry Frobisher stood on the starboard deck, surrounded by smiling troops shouting and waving at loved ones. Taking no part in the celebrations, both men moved away from the bustle choosing instead to search for their accommodation.

They both wore khaki fatigues, in readiness for the African summer. Charles preferred breeches with long socks and hand-stitched boots to Henry's moleskin trousers and calf length boots. Their taste in headgear differed as well. Charles had a bespoke trilby style safari hat and Henry wore his favourite well-worn Cape buffalo hide hat.

One item they each chose to carry with them at all times when beyond the borders of the United Kingdom was a Bowie knife, now mass-produced in Sheffield. But these were both originals, created by the Arkansas blacksmith, James Black. Such a dagger, with a blade eight inches long served as a weapon and was an essential tool for the camp and hunting.

Sir William Cadley's contact in the War Office managed to secure accommodation for both men even at such short notice but any hope of a first class cabin was soon put to rest. They would be sharing a cabin along with a war correspondent, that much they had been told.

The cabin was below deck and they were searching for a door displaying the titles: Second Mate (Navigational Officer) & Third Mate (Safety Officer).

The small cabin was obviously only intended for two crew members. Bunk beds lined one side and a third bed, a green army folding type was pushed against the opposite wall where a desk had once been fixed. Already a large suitcase and a canvas bag occupied the bed.

The smell of cigar smoke hung in the air.

"At least our room mate has expensive taste." Henry recognised the smell of a fine Havana.

"Which bunk do you want Charles?"

Charles had already dropped his rucksack onto the bottom bunk, claiming it as his.

"Ok, I'll have the top one in that case," Henry said shaking his head. "I know you are paying for this trip Charles, but I do hope you don't intend taking too many liberties."

"As an ex-army officer Henry, I'm genuinely surprised you have not got used to the notion of rank." Charles raised an eyebrow to support this statement.

"But we are not in the army Charles. Therefore we are not subject to a rank structure. I would like to think of us working as a team."

"Even in team work there is a hierarchy. Look Henry, we have known each other a long time and know we work well together. I need you and you need me. It is going to be a perilous trip to get to Kimberley and you taking umbrage over the sleeping arrangements is not a conducive start to the journey. If you want the bottom bunk you may have it."

"That's damn decent of you old boy. I'll take you up on that offer Charles." Henry beamed an exaggerated smile.

"Just to prove a bloody point eh!" Charles was not too happy, but Henry was still smiling as he swung his heavy rucksack onto the bottom bunk.

Henry Frobisher was seven years older than Charles Cadley and being six foot, a similar height. But there the similarities ended. Henry had a crop of blonde hair, which covered his ears and fell across his forehead and brown eyes. He was naturally athletic, with a toned physique that Michelangelo would have been grateful to sculpt. An officer for fifteen years with the Colonial Cape Mounted Riflemen, a regiment based at King Williams Town, gave him an easy air of confidence, not to mention his skill as a horseman and crack-shot with a rifle.

It was these last two attributes that Charles had recognised several years ago and come to rely on during their time together in South Africa.

The cabin door opened and collided with Charles' back.

"Ah, Gentlemen. Good day. You must be my last minute travelling companions."

The voice was affable and cultured.

Both turned to face a smiling red haired man, much smaller and younger than themselves.

Charles shook the extended hand.

"Charles Cadley. I hope our intrusion has not put you out too much."

"Not at all. Winston Churchill, war correspondent for the Morning Post. Glad to have you on board."

"Henry Frobisher. My pleasure Winston."

Fresh cigar smoke once more filled the cabin.

This was the first occasion the three had met, but Charles and Henry knew quite a lot about this young man, as did many of the British population.

"Cadley! Any relation to Sir William and Cadley Industries?"

"Yes, he's my father and I'm vice-president of the company." He visibly puffed out like a booby bird.

"Good Lord Charles, in that case what the hell is one of the country's foremost industrialists doing on a troop ship bound for South Africa?" The Havana was now between clenched teeth.

"Henry and I have some business matters to finalise before the Boers do it for us."

Winston laughed as if he understood perfectly.

"What do you chaps say to quick shot of a rather decent malt I've brought along for the trip?"

"Winston, that is music to my ears," Henry said, already beginning to enjoy himself.

The journey would take seventeen days to Cape Town with a short stop at Santa Cruz, Tenerife, a few hundred miles west off the Moroccan coast, for refuelling of coal. During the first few days Henry and Winston struck up quite a friendship.

Churchill was travelling with his valet Thomas Walden and they were to share the cabin, until Walden's unceremonious move to other less salubrious accommodation near to the engine room to make space for Cadley and Frobisher.

Churchill was not too upset by this. During his campaigning in India and Egypt he was accustomed to sharing tents with fellow officers and war correspondents, but not his valet.

Winston Churchill came from an aristocratic background and was generally believed by many to be a titled nobleman, including Charles Cadley, who was convinced he was Lord Winston Spencer Churchill, like his father, Lord Randolph. He regarded Churchill's present role as a war journalist as nothing more than a boyish adventure of the rich and privileged. Thus, within less than twenty-four hours of meeting, he viewed young Winston Spencer Churchill with growing resentment.

Henry Frobisher's opinion was the opposite. Sitting on their cots they would exchange war stories over numerous glasses of wine or spirits, until the early hours, much to Charles' annoyance and exclusion. Frobisher and Churchill were both former military horsemen and laughed raucously at each other's tales of combat mishaps and roared at the decision-making by the military elite, agreed by both to be universally infested with 'buffoons and morons'.

Churchill, encouraged by Frobisher, explained that after leaving Sandhurst he joined the 4th Hussars, a cavalry regiment. Henry could relate to the long hours on horseback. Learning to mount and dismount from a moving horse, with or without a saddle; perseverance with practising drill instructions, manoeuvring a horse in formation, firing a rifle and hitting a target at full gallop and use of the sabre for close quarter fighting. The camaraderie was something Charles listened to, but would never understand.

From his top bunk he watched Churchill write numerous letters by the light of an oil-lamp as he lay face down on his cot.

Charles once asked, not disguising the sneer, "Who are you boring with your thoughts now Winston?"

"My mother Lady Randolph. Does Sir William not warrant putting pen to paper with news of his son and heir, especially as you and Frobisher are on a clandestine undertaking for your father?"

Charles grunted and unable to think of a suitable reply rolled onto his back, seething, his anger aggravated by Henry's drunken snoring.

He did not see Winston smiling to himself.

The following morning Henry was on deck, enjoying a Havana given to him by Churchill, when Charles approached.

"Morning Charles. Sleep well I trust?"

The deck was crowded with military personnel and civilian passengers, who Henry decided must be the press corp.

Two companies of infantry were taking part in rifle practice, firing on command at barrels thrown into the sea until they were blasted to pieces.

The ship rolled and pitched on the Atlantic waves, forcing Charles to grip the handrail to steady himself.

"No I did not. Do you know you sound like a rutting stag when you are asleep? And to make matters worse I have to listen to Churchill scratching letters until God knows when. I don't trust that fellow, far too haughty for his own good."

"The trouble with you Charles is that you are not drinking enough scotch at night. Works wonders for insomniacs like you and I."

"Have you told Churchill why we are going to South Africa?"

The smile disappeared as he turned to face Charles.

"What do you think Charles and why do you ask?"

"Well last night he referred to our trip as a 'clandestine undertaking', which suggests to me he knows something about the diamonds."

"I wouldn't mention that 'd' word on board ship or Churchill will be the least of your worries. Anyway he's not interested in your business, have you not worked that out yet? He wants to make a name for himself, be in the thick of the fighting, cover himself with glory and be hailed a hero."

"I hope he is not planning to travel to Kimberley with us."

"Charles, forget about Churchill. He's already told me he has arrangements in hand to travel from Cape Town to Durban by train, which is quicker than the onward journey of staying on board here. I know you have a distaste for nobility but Churchill regards himself as a commoner."

Charles looked out to sea. "Of course he does. Born in Blenheim Palace, the ancestral home of the Duke of Marlborough. Very common that is."

"You have been doing your home-work Charles."

"The vessel is crowded and people talk, especially about a celebrity on board. You know he's having breakfast with Buller this morning?"

"Sir Redvers Buller, the Commander-in-Chief of British forces? You've got to hand it to him Charles, Winston doesn't do things by half. Speaking of breakfast should we join the horde below and observe further destruction of eggs and bacon?"

"You go. I don't feel very well." He grimaced as the ship shuddered and ploughed through a swell.

Charles heaved and retched over the railings, not sure whether it was sea spray or vomit hitting his face in the strong easterly. The military uniforms that braved the deck, moved away from Charles, a few laughing as his stomach contents hit the waves far below, immediately attracting gulls, diving at the fresh food supply.

His face was pressed gratefully against the cold and wet handrail when he became aware of someone standing very close to him, a shoulder pressing against his own.

"Bring it up mate, you'll feel better."

He ignored the soldier. He wanted to be left alone.

"Listen mate, I couldn't help overhear your conversion with the other gentleman about some diamonds. Perhaps we can do a bit of business?" The voice had a smoker's rasp to it and the accent could only be from the Tyne.

Charles was now alert but did not move.

The face moved closer, "Let's not piss about now mate, eh! Let's keep it friendly like."

Charles turned towards the face, only inches from his own and said, "What are you talking about?"

"Blimey mate, your breath doesn't half stink." The face moved away, laughing, then continued, no longer hiding the menace.

"The diamonds you are collecting in Kimberley. You should have listened to your friend and kept your mouth shut. Now I know and if you don't want the rest of the ship to know what you are up to and have a procession of diamond hunters following you wherever you go, you'd better cut me in. I'll even settle for a cash dividend instead, but don't muck me about mate. A lot of unpleasant things can happen out at sea. Fortunately for you mate, Kimberley is where I'm heading as well, so if you do things sensible like, we'll both get something out of this."

He looked at the soldier as if he had gone quite mad and paid no heed to the cap badge displaying the initials 'DLI' in between a crown and horn or the two stripes on the sleeves, identifying him as a corporal with the Durham Light Infantry.

Charles knew the soldier was lying about his destination being Kimberley. The relief force was bound for Port Elizabeth and it was common knowledge that all the regiments under Buller's command, forming the 1st Army Corps were the vanguard force to stop the Boers invading the Natal and marching onto Cape Town, if they had not already done so. This was an absolute priority for the British government and defending Kimberley at the moment was not.

"What sort of pay off would you want?" asked Charles.

"Now that's more like it. I'm not a greedy man and without knowing the value of what you're collecting, which must be substantial for you and your mate to travel half way around the world. I'll settle for two grand as a one off payment." The leer beneath the thin moustache revealed nicotine stained teeth.

Charles nodded, "Very well. I'll speak with my partner and meet you here later. You do understand though that I do not have access to that amount of money at the moment and won't have until I arrive at Cape Town."

"I'm sure we can come to some arrangement. Be here at 1900 hours. Most of the ship will be messing then."

The Geordie soldier discreetly removed his sidearm and pushed the barrel of a Webley revolver forwards. Charles ignored the pain as the muzzle dug into his ribs.

110

"Don't be late eh! Or I'll come looking for you and I'll have over a week to hunt you down. There aint no hiding places out here."

Chapter Thirteen

The chief constable listened intently to Abberline and did not like what he was hearing.

"We have to accept sir that the Ripper has gone to ground, disappeared. It is more than six months since he struck and we are no nearer identifying the murderer. I have studied all the post mortem reports, photographs and police reports and can only agree with the eminent Doctor Byers. Elsie Lupton and Beatrice Babbitt were slain by the same maniac that took the lives of Elizabeth Stride, Catherine Eddowes, Mary Jane Kelly, Annie Chapman, Mary Nichols and Martha Tabram, who was probably his first victim nearly eleven years ago in London. Of this there is no doubt. The only deviation in the *modus operandi* is that the London victims were all middle aged, but here the victims were eighteen and twenty."

Colonel Sir Arthur Lawrenson remained still, hands together by his mouth as if in prayer.

"In effect Mr. Abberline, since your arrival, at much cost to the borough, you have not taken the enquiry any further."

Abberline fidgeted slightly on the uncomfortable wooden chair and responded to the jibe.

"I cannot agree with that sir. As I've just said there is now irrefutable evidence to link all these deaths and if the truth be known to even more victims, certainly in London. There is dispute about the true total of the Ripper's victims. Some detectives say four, some say nine. Without exception they were all prostitutes and all slain during the summer and autumn of '88."

"But how do these 'Whitechapel murders' help me catch the Preston Ripper?"

"With respect sir, I know these murders are referred to by the press and in other circles as the 'Whitechapel murders' but only two of them were committed in Whitechapel. Having said that, all the murders did take place within a single square mile of the East End of London, an area incidentally, very similar to the two murder sites here in Preston. Areas of destitution, crime and prostitution. God forsaken places. What we know is that all the murders in London and Preston took place between midnight and 6 a.m. So the murderer was absent from their home or lodgings during these times. This would suggest they live alone. A shift worker has been suggested, which is still a possibility, particularly with the preponderance of cotton mills nearby, but I would dispute this. Both Doctor Brown, who performed post mortems on several of the London victims and Doctor Byers, who you all know, conclude separately that the offender displayed an obvious anatomical knowledge and a degree of surgical skill. This is why I would exclude a mill worker apart from the fact there were no such mills offering employment in East London. In fact there was and still is very little employment of any type. We also know that the Ripper was right handed. The injuries tell us that much. There were no witnesses to the Preston murders and none as such to the East End murders but certain information can be gleaned from statements taken from witnesses who describe men last seen with several of the victims and there is a common thread. A white male, and eleven years ago aged between twenty and thirty, average height, but could be six foot and of a 'respectable' appearance. This would now put him in his early forties. What I find baffling is why travel to a small northern town over two hundred miles away after an absence of a decade or more? I believe that is the key to solving these murders."

"It is all very well, Mr. Abberline postulating theories. What I want is facts I can take to the mayor, the borough councillors and people of the town to reassure them that the murderer will be brought to justice. The town is in uproar. The local papers are canvassing for my dismissal. Can you believe that? And vigilante groups are still taking to the streets at night, pointing the finger of blame at whoever takes their fancy. Three innocent men have already been brutally attacked by one of these lynch mobs and I will not have any more of this. Do you hear Meadowbank? I want an end to this. I want the Ripper caught and I don't give a damn how you do it." He was on his feet, his knuckles taking his weight on the table as he leant forwards.

Sir Arthur was a big man with a big grey moustache and a ruddy complexion that hinted he drank too much scotch. Today he wore his uniform of rank, displaying an elaborate mass of silver and gold braiding on the shoulders of his black tunic.

"What about that Froggatt fellow? The one we fished out of the river weeks ago."

"What abaht 'im sir?" Albert Meadowbank could not follow his chief constable's deducing.

The meeting in Sir Arthur's office consisted of only these three men and this allowed the chief constable to speak with candour.

"Can we link him to the two murders?" His face lit up as if announcing a revelation.

Meadowbank looked equally as confused as Abberline.

"There is no evidence whatsoever t' link Edmund Froggatt t' Ripper murders. That line of enquiry 'as been discounted weeks ago sir." Meadowbank reminded the chief constable.

No one more than Meadowbank had hoped to prove that Froggatt was implicated in Beatrice Babbitt and Elsie Lupton's deaths, but ever since he had been found floating in the River Ribble, with his head stoved in, himself now a murder victim, there was nothing to suggest he was involved. In fact Froggatt's death remains a mystery and the file now sits on Meadowbank's desk as an ongoing murder investigation and a thorn in his side.

"Inspector, you mention lack of evidence as if that presents difficulties." He moved forward, resting his elbows on the desk and continued with his usual voice of authority.

"We are the police, we are the law. We investigate a crime and we gather evidence and we decide what evidence to produce to a court to prove a person's guilt. Basically gentlemen we hold all the cards. What I am about to suggest will not be the first occasion in which either of you will have adopted or considered an option to swing the burden of guilt in our favour during a frustrating investigation. When there is a suspect whose guilt is staring us in the face loud and clear, it is our duty to act and apprehend the suspect and worry about evidence and procedure later. Now, when there is a suspect whose guilt is probable and the crimes are of such a heinous nature and the suspect died during the course of the investigation, is it still not our duty to pursue the investigation to its conclusion and close the case book with a resounding and decisive judgement of guilty, all without having to go to trial at the assizes?"

He looked across his desk for support, Sir Arthur's face a mask of deadly earnest and the spasmodic twitching of his mouth was barely perceptible.

Only the ticking wall clock broke the silence.

Albert Meadowbank was the first to speak.

"Sir, I don't think yer could 'ave med it much clearer, but just so there is no mistake on my part, are yer suggestin' wi name Edmund Froggatt as Jack t' Ripper?"

"Think about it Inspector. We solve two particularly nasty murders, you reduce your workload and the townsfolk are reassured." He could sense the discomfort of Meadowbank and Abberline.

"What are your thoughts on this course of action, Mr. Abberline?"

Abberline chose his words very carefully.

"Well sir, I can see one or two major problems with claiming that Froggatt is Jack the Ripper. First, there is no evidence to link him to the two recent deaths, nor the East End murders. As far as I am aware he had never set foot in Whitechapel or Spitalfields and I am fairly sure the Commissioner of the Metropolitan Police and the Home Secretary will want to see cast iron evidence pointing to Froggatt's guilt, not to mention Fleet Street and the international press. You may be ready to close this part of the Ripper investigation but believe me sir, the Commissioner will take some convincing." Abberline was fighting to control his temper.

"I am not concerned with what happened in the East End slums a decade ago. It's not my problem. What is my problem is public safety now and as long as the Ripper is seen to be prowling the streets of Preston, no one will feel safe and will be constantly looking over their shoulders. Can you not feel the sense of panic gripping the town, damn you? This borough needs to return to normal and that will only be possible by producing Jack the Ripper in custody or in a coffin." His facial muscles drew tight around his fixed stare, which seemed to quell the twitching.

Abberline continued undaunted, "Secondly, Froggatt is also a murder victim and his murderer is still at large."

Sir Arthur interrupted bullishly, "Mr. Abberline you cannot say that with any conviction surely? Froggatt had been in the river for several weeks before his body was discovered rendering the post mortem result as questionable to say the least. During that time his cadaver was eaten by fish and all manner of fauna. As far as I am concerned the cause of death is questionable. It is quite possible that he fell into the river when drunk and banged his head, resulting in his injuries and drowning."

"I can think of a police surgeon oo may disagree wi' yer an' one oo 'as publicly stated Edmund Froggatt died of a massive blow t' back of 'is 'ead, probably caused bi an 'ammer or similar implement. Not only that sir, but what 'appens once you've announced t' world that th' Ripper is no more, then next week, next year or th' next decade 'e resumes 'is slaughter. What then?" asked Meadowbank.

"I think this buffoonery has gone on long enough. We are talking about a massive investigation, spanning more than ten years with worldwide press and judicial interest and you are attempting to coerce Inspector Meadowbank and I into perverting the course of justice, which all that implies, not least both of us looking at imprisonment for a very long time. Leaving that aside, this preposterous notion you've dreamt up to save your career involves falsely identifying a dead man as Jack the Ripper, the most notorious murderer of modern times, whose very name is a symbol of terror and horror. A case that has thwarted my best efforts and the resources of Scotland Yard all these years and you think you can just unmask Edmund Froggatt as Jack the Ripper and believe I would agree to this contrivance…" Lost for words, he paused, "this is beyond belief. You sir, are a sick man, a very sick man indeed and not fit to call yourself a police officer."

"Sit down Mr. Abberline and calm yourself before you say something else you may regret. I think you have outstayed your usefulness on this investigation and I cannot imagine how you may assist further. I am instructing you to abandon your role as an advisor to my police force and return to Pinkerton immediately. You have become a liability and are now actively obstructing Inspector Meadowbank in bringing these disturbing events to a conclusion. Be warned you are very close to seeing the inside of a gaol for a lengthy period of time. Do you understand now Mr. Abberline about the presentation of evidence? It is not important what facts are acquired but how they are put forward. So a detrimental depiction of your conduct during this investigation from myself, the chief constable, describing your methods as unprofessional and a deliberate hindrance to progress, due to your obsession with events over ten years ago, would render you unemployable throughout the world of private investigation and certainly discredit your reputation. Don't you think so Inspector Meadowbank?"

"What meks yer think ah'll go along wi' this deranged plan?" Meadowbank sounded calm, but his posture trembled with a seething fury.

"Because Inspector, you are a police officer and will do as you are told. And do not forget you are also subject to police regulations. As you know insubordination and refusing to obey an order from a senior officer are both offences that call for instant dismissal. If that happened you would leave the force with nothing. I would personally see to it. On the other hand this is an excellent promotion opportunity for you. Your lethargic, even dormant career could accelerate to an unforeseen level. How does Superintendent Meadowbank sound Inspector?"
Chief Constable Lawrenson assumed an expression of arrogance, lips pursed, similar to a grand-master completing checkmate in three opening moves.

Meadowbank had heard enough. Without saying a word he stood and moved quickly towards Sir Arthur. Abberline watched in amazement as the detective inspector swung his right fist, hard and fast into his chief constable's face, knocking him completely from his chair, blood pouring from nose and mouth quickly turning those grey whiskers to a deep fluid red.

"I've wanted t' d' that fer a very long time. If yer wait 'ere Fred ah'll go an' find t' superintendent."

Abberline was left alone, wondering what do to about the chief constable, sprawled on the floor unconscious.

Chapter Fourteen

The weather had changed for the better and R.M.S. Dunottar Castle at last sailed a smooth passage following a course a hundred miles west and due south off the African coast.

Charles had opened the porthole and actually believed he could smell the ancient forests of the Dark Continent even though it was invisible behind the horizon.

He was on his bunk reading an old newspaper found in the canteen, trying to ignore the childish banter of Frobisher and Churchill playing cards.

Charles checked his wristwatch; a new precision Swiss chronograph that confirmed it was not yet time to make his move.

The card game was cribbage with the crib board sat on Churchill's cot between the two men, both resting on their elbows, Henry looking intently at the position of the broken matchsticks being used as pegs. Churchill had an unlit cigar between his lips as he shuffled the cards for his deal.

"Come on Winston, make a game of it will you. I hope you are a better journalist than you are a card player," Henry goaded.

Churchill had lost the previous two games, being "double-skunked" twice.

"Your misspent youth concerns me Henry. You drink far too much whisky, especially mine, correction exclusively mine, play cards like a riverboat gambler and you are no doubt a scoundrel with the opposite sex. I don't think South Africa is ready for your return."

"Where do you think I acquired these useless talents Winston? It certainly wasn't at Harrow like you old-boy. It was patrolling the veld with a troop of hairy-arsed riflemen and when sat round a campfire under the stars there is little else to do but drink and play cards. As for the women, there wasn't a female baboon that slept soundly for five miles."

A laugh exploded from both of them.

"What time is it Charles?" Henry panted.

"Nearly time for the second dinner sitting at six forty five. Where are you dining tonight Winston?" Charles asked with a hint of sarcasm.

"Oh, I think I shall grace the mess room with my presence this evening."

"You mean Sir Redvers has not extended another invitation?" Henry quipped.

"Exactly" replied Churchill.

"So it'll be toad-in-the-hole and a mug of weak tea with the peasants instead of roast venison and vintage claret with the top brass?" he joked.

"God! Is that what the peasants are dining on tonight?"

"The peasants dine on that every night Winston. I'm praying for a few spoonfuls of gruel before we arrive at Cape Town."

"I'll have a word with Sir Redvers and arrange for him to add gruel to the menu, just for you Henry."

"Come on Winston, I think I heard your valet calling your name confirming that your table reservation is ready. We can resume this game later. Are you coming Charles?"

"Not at the moment thanks, Henry. I've no appetite just yet. All that talk of roast venison and claret has put me off food presently."

"Listen to that Winston. The man does have a sense of humour after all."

Charles was left alone, grateful for the solitude as he collected his thoughts. Laying on his bunk he breathed in the fresh air that breezed into the cabin and for once he did not feel nauseous, in fact he felt energised and excited, going over in his mind every detail of his plan.

It was that time, one minute before seven.

He jumped from the bunk and left the cabin then followed the deserted corridor to the steps leading to the port side. He hurried onto the deck and into shadows of shaded sunlight.

The infantry corporal was standing alone, nearer to the stern than the original spot he had decreed and he was now partially obscured by a large iron support strut from the bulwark to the deck above.

He obviously does not want anyone else watching, Charles thought.

The deck was quiet, the usual crowd of military personnel gathered at the bow and starboard decks at this time of the evening to make the most of the setting sun and enjoy an after dinner cigarette. Their laughter and smoke drifted past Charles reassuring him this would work.

The corporal remained slouching against the bulwark and neatly flicked a hand-rolled fag stub over his head as Charles approached. He followed this with a noisy spit of phlegm from the side of his mouth.

Charles made a casual look left and right as he walked up to the corporal. His right hand was behind his waist, holding the Bowie knife against the back of his thigh.

"I knew you'd see sense mate. I mean what's a couple of grand to a toff like you eh?"

He gave a smile and nod of acquiescence to the waiting soldier, now within arm's reach. Not faltering in his stride, his left hand was suddenly pressed tightly against the soldiers mouth at the same instant a blade of Damascus steel, eight inches long and three inches wide was thrust into his stomach. The two razor-sharp edges sliced through the stomach wall and intestines and a further thrust pierced the liver.

Charles held the knife firmly then twisted the grip allowing the serrated edge to do more damage, as he watched the corporal's eyes bulge like a terrified horse. His only sound was a guttural bark as his tongue flicked madly against the hand-palm over his mouth.

He pulled the knife out slowly, pushing his shoulder against the corporal, pressing him to the side of the ship and kept him upright as he was already dead. Charles wiped the blade on the khaki uniform trousers and re-sheathed the dagger.

Grasping the body with both hands under the armpits, Charles bent his knees then heaved upwards, lifting the corporal off his feet and over the four-foot high bulwark in one movement. In less than thirty seconds from start to finish, he was walking away casually as if promenading the deck and did not hear the splash in the ships wake.

Charles suddenly felt hungry and joined the mess deck queue and actually savoured the smell of bully beef and boiled potatoes.

Chapter Fifteen

The Lancashire Daily Post, Preston Guardian and Preston Herald reported with enthusiasm the details of Jack the Ripper's latest victim, though not many readers would have any sympathy for Colonel Sir Arthur Lawrenson, the former chief constable of the town. He had not endeared himself to the public during his four years in office, preferring to treat the local population and his work force with a regimental mind-set and indifference that had served him well since the Crimean War.

His resignation did come as a surprise to most, especially as several unsolved murders hung over the borough. The newspapers asked questions about the investigation and people wanted answers particularly the newly formed and vocal Preston Vigilante Watch who patrolled the streets and beer-houses as an angry mob in defiance of police instructions.

Sir Arthur was allowed to leave his post quietly, giving deteriorating health problems as the reason for his exit from office and at the age of seventy-two that was certainly believable. In fairness to him, those who knew the truth considered a broken jaw and shattered nose definitely detrimental to one's health and a valid reason for his departure, not to mention his surreptitious admission to the Royal Infirmary, where surgeons attempted to re-set his broken bones. That is ignoring the nervous breakdown he suffered in his final days as chief constable, which culminated with his madcap scheme to accuse a local journalist, albeit a dead one, of mass murder.

"I agree wi' yer Sam, but it don't change owt does it?" replied Meadowbank.

"True, but it's a bloody relief t' see that bastard get 'is marchin' orders, that's all I'm sayin'."

Sergeant Huggins was in a celebratory mood. It was early afternoon and already Meadowbank, Huggins and Abberline had nearly finished their third pint.

"Some of what Sir Arthur said was correct if I was being honest." Abberline said quietly. He was in no mood for celebrating. His train for London was leaving at 5p.m.

"That's utter rubbish Fred. An' yer know it. 'E were a complete nutter an' don't yer go feelin' sorry fer 'im. 'E'll still get 'is bloody pension." Meadowbank was suddenly feeling light-headed.

"Listen. He was right about one thing." Abberline looked intently at each of them.

"Since my arrival I have not taken the investigation any further. I have failed to identify the murderer. After months of sifting through evidence from here and Scotland Yard we are no nearer to making an arrest or even having a suspect, than we were before I became involved." He sounded dejected.

"That's not true. Yer tied t' investigations t'gether. Wi wouldn't 'ave known it were Jack t' Ripper if not fer you," encouraged Meadowbank.

"Come on Albert. It was not me that made the connection it was Doctor Byers. He deserves the credit for that. I only became involved once he contacted a London police surgeon. I arrived in Preston with such high hopes. Not daring to believe at last here was another chance to apprehend Jack the Ripper, identify him and see him hang. I don't want the lime-light or the glory of it all, not like Sir Arthur, I just wanted to put it all behind me. Do you understand?" He paused in thought for a moment then continued. "This has been eating me up inside for more than ten years. Ten years of torment, the letters he sent, taunting, mocking; the deaths that lunatic is responsible for will never be known and still he is a free man. He seems to come and go like a spectre, leaving behind mutilation, fear and grief and we are powerless to do anything about it. Where do we go from here? I

124

am going back to Pinkerton but my heart is no longer in detective work. You see he's even done that! The one thing I have always loved, the thrill of the chase and then moving in to feel a collar or two. I'm beaten. But what about you two? Where do you go from here? It's easy in some ways for me to walk away even though I'll always have the Ripper's shadow following me, but you two can't walk away. You still have a suspect at large for two murders and if you'll forgive me for saying, with very little prospect of solving them. He's gone, Jack the Ripper has gone. I feel it in my gut and we've missed an opportunity to snare him. He must feel unstoppable at the moment, a giant amongst pygmies, who'll go on killing." He forlornly swirled the remnants of ale in his glass.

"Two murders? Mek that four murders. People keep forgettin' abaht Edmund Froggatt an' Professor Daniel Bailey. Both found wi'in 'alf a mile of each other, washed up on t' mornin' tide, both wi' fatal injuries t' their 'eads." Huggins said through a mouthful of tripe and onions. This particular dish of white honeycombed chewy entrails had become a recent favourite of Huggins' when dining at The Stanley Arms, much to the displeasure of Meadowbank, who would wince not just at the stomach churning sight of the stuff, but the smell also.

Huggins enthused about tripe as if it was the secret to eternal life. He would point out with relish that he enjoyed eating most parts of a cow, listing the brain, heart, kidneys, liver, ribs, feet, all cuts of steak, the tail, blood and even testicles, so why not the stomach lining?

Meadowbank was becoming bored with this logic, so much so that he had on several occasions considered turning to a vegetarian diet just to annoy Huggins, but the truth was he enjoyed steak and kidney pudding too much.

The list of recent killings and macabre grave robbing now occupied the inspector's thoughts more than his sergeant's annoying eating habits.

"Froggatt th' fucker." Meadowbank said between gritted teeth, ignoring Abberline's torment and Huggins' tripe eulogy. "Froggatt is givin' mi more grief dead than 'e did alive an' I still owe 'im a bloody good 'idin' as well." Agitated, he necked the dregs from the glass and banged the empty pint pot on the table.

"Another pint anyone?" he asked as he stood up.

"Aye, go on then." replied Huggins, but Abberline remained silent, lost in his thoughts, which Meadowbank took to be a resounding 'yes' as he obviously needed cheering up and alcohol always did the job for him.

"It's strange though don't yer think," Huggins said when the drinks arrived and his plate was clean, "as soon as Froggatt gets done in, th' Ripper murders stop an' so does t' grave-robbin'. There must bi a connection there?"

"For Christ's sake Sam! Not you as well? We've just had one madman trying to claim that Froggatt was Jack the bloody Ripper and now you're at it. What is the matter with everyone? Listen very carefully, Froggatt is not, never has been or ever will be Jack the Ripper." Abberline was starting to slur a few words.

At least he sounded a bit more cheerful, Meadowbank thought to himself.

"Fred, I 'ave never suggested that an' I'm certainly not doin' now, but what abaht t' professor? A surgeon oo performed illegal dissection on anyone dead 'e could lay 'is 'ands on. 'E goes t' 'is maker an' t' killin' stops. Th' Ripper must 'ave 'ad medical knowledge, that's what all t' doctors tell us. Well yer can't do much better than a medical man oo teaches other doctors 'ow t' cut up 'uman beings, can yer?"

"'Ow long 'ave you bin thinkin' all this through?" asked Meadowbank.

"Fer a few days now," he replied cautiously.

"Flamin' 'ell Sam, why didn't yer say summat sooner? Yer could bi ont' summat."

Abberline and Meadowbank stared at Sam each not believing they had missed something so obvious.

Meadowbank was the first to speak.

"Reet Fred, bugger t' train, yer're back on t' case."

Chapter Sixteen

It took over thirty six hours for a private from the Durham Light Infantry to realise that the hammock above him belonging to Corporal Stokes had not been slept in for two nights running and that he had not been seen since the evening meal nearly two days ago.

All those engaged in military service were volunteers with a large proportion being unemployed or unemployable, others were from shady backgrounds, some were convicted criminals and not forgetting the homeless and destitute, all preferring the harsh discipline of army life to the slums and constant hunger back home. It was not only those with a nefarious past who ignored 'lights-out' to relieve the boredom and risk being caught by the 'night-watch' in a card game or drinking session, disappearing from their bunk night after night. Hence the delay in reporting the corporal's absence. Missing a night's sleep was one thing, but missing three meals a day was something completely different.

A senior officer instigated an immediate roll call to confirm that an N.C.O. from his regiment had gone absent without leave.

A more senior officer pointed out that rather than announce a corporal from the D.L.I. as being declared A.W.O.L. on a ship sailing the Atlantic Ocean, perhaps the situation should be upgraded to an emergency status of 'man overboard'.

The ships klaxon reverberated along the metal corridors and the captain confirmed over the tannoy system that a member of the relief force might be lost at sea.

Dozens of binoculars hopelessly scoured the surrounding ocean and a full search of the vessel had not found any clues as to Billy Stokes' whereabouts. Eventually a minister, masquerading under the rank of captain in the Royal Engineers, laid to rest the corporal's soul during a service on deck, ironically very near to the spot where he last stood. It was well attended. The minister had a fixed audience, thanks to an instruction from Sir Redvers Buller. A full turn out of the ship's complement, apart from Charles Cadley who stayed in his cabin breathing in the smell of Africa, lined the deck in silence and a bugler played the 'last post' as the sun set.

At the same time as Charles watched the setting sun, Verity and her maid, disembarked from the train that arrived at Preston from Euston Station, London.

A grand carriage, drawn by two horses and attended by a driver and footman waited with instructions to convey Mrs.Verity Cadley to Ribbleton Manor.

Verity was met by Stanley Monk's successor. He was a young ambitious solicitor with a far more pleasing and easy manner than the perfunctory Mr. Monk.

"Mrs. Cadley, allow me to introduce myself. Matthew MacDonald at your service." The bow was both gracious and confident and the Scottish accent unmistakable.

She was cradling her three year-old daughter, now fast asleep and wrapped in an ice blue shawl.

He took what little hand luggage the maid carried.

All manner of luggage and furniture had been shipped north weeks earlier, even Verity's golden retriever, Gladstone, would be waiting for her.

The ride to Ribbleton Manor would take around an hour, and that was good going thanks to the roads being well maintained for most of the journey or certainly as far as the moor.

Verity and her maid, Daisy Duff, sat on the rear seat. It was comfortable leather bound over horsehair. Very soon Daisy fell asleep as the sprung carriage gently rocked along Church Street passing the House of Correction and on to Ribbleton Lane.

Matthew MacDonald sat facing both ladies, with his back to the horses and had the good sense to keep his own council. He could see his client, or rather his company's client was tired from the long journey and idle chat was not something he was prone to at the best of times.

Apart from being an aspiring solicitor on the criminal circuit Mr. MacDonald was also a crack shot with a pistol, a legacy from shooting vermin on his father's estate near Edinburgh.
His brief was simple; escort Mrs. Cadley and daughter to their destination, safely.

Young MacDonald had two-loaded Austrian Lugers secured in their own discreet shoulder holsters under his black tailored suit jacket, with plenty of ammunition available in various pockets and his grandfather's dirk tucked inside a boot.

He had been informed that the threat to Mrs. Cadley was minimal, but she was very wealthy and together with her husband's fortune made her and her daughter's safety and well-being paramount whilst in the charge of Mink and Potter Solicitors. The last thing anyone needed was for the carriage to be brought to a stop and the occupants accosted by opportunistic footpads, brazen poachers or organised highwaymen. Verity Cadley or her daughter, Elizabeth Rose would make prize bargaining for any denizen of the underworld prepared to extort the Cadley dynasty. Verity was also very beautiful, something the villainous could never resist. Robbery was common on many quiet lanes, but rape of women around the confines of Preston Borough, whether hags, harlots, farmers' wives or society's most elegant ladies en-route from the darkest hovel or the finest mansion had become a local scandal.

The carriage displayed two oil-lamps to the front and since leaving behind the last vestige of the township also meant the termination of street gas lighting, these carriage lamps became the only illumination on the dark road that was now a wide dirt track.

Mr. MacDonald prior to boarding the carriage had checked with the footman and driver to establish what weapons if any, they carried. They were experienced liverymen and the footman produced a double-barrelled 18inch coach gun he kept close at hand and the driver possessed a service revolver tucked underneath his belt. The solicitor nodded his approval.

The main suspects for the recent crime wave were a large gang of 'land navigators' who had set up a makeshift camp on a hill named Walton Summit, two miles outside the town and overlooking the Lancaster Canal terminus. These nomadic labourers, known as navvies, were lawless ruffians and the remnants of a much larger workforce who had expanded the railway system and dug out canals throughout Britain. Skilled in the excavation of cuttings, use of dynamite, creating embankments and building tunnels, they followed the creeping rail track wherever it took them. Used to harsh conditions and working long hours, seven days a week, navvies became an insular group suspicious of outsiders and whether they where digging through populated areas, a remote fell side village or desolate moor land, they kept to their gangs which was their strength.

But now the arterial rail system was extensive and the canal waterways established so the need for large-scale mobile work forces had diminished. The crude encampments of navvies, some with a population of thousands, disappeared from the countryside. Some of the labourers took to road building and that is how the thirty or so navvies arrived at Walton Summit.

Fortunately they were not a headache for Inspector Meadowbank. The makeshift camp of tents and ramshackle huts was outside the town boundary and demanded attention from the county constabulary who were largely ineffective in policing the unruly gang.

A few local farmers and villagers had clashed with the navvies after finding orchards plundered, dairy sheds emptied and henhouses devastated, not just of eggs but of complete poultry stocks. These encounters, becoming more frequent, were bloody and violent and there was a groundswell of public resentment towards the navvies and lack of action by the authorities to bring them under the rule of law.

The coach arrived at Ribbleton Manor without incident. Even though it was night-time what Verity saw took her breath away. Once through the ornate gates and stone archway bearing the sculpted Cadley crest and motto: *audentes fortuna juvat,* fortune favours the daring, denoting the entrance to the estate of Ribbleton Manor and past the unoccupied gatehouse that had still to be modernised, the uneven stone sets had been replaced with a Macadamised road surface and the long sweeping drive now had its own street lighting. Tall cast iron gas lamps were positioned every thirty yards on the east side and each one glowing all the way to the house.

At last the 17th century mansion came into view and at least twelve members of staff lined the bottom step that led to the huge front door, bathed in light from the many lanterns watching over the front of the house.

Whatever trepidation Verity brought with her, vanished, and her face shone with joy at their new family home.

As the carriage halted, a footman efficiently opened the door and Verity, still clutching her daughter, stepped down and smiled a greeting at the myriad of watching faces.

A small, balding man with a severe slash of a mouth came forwards and introduced himself as Dobson, the head-butler, and welcomed her on behalf of the staff at Ribbleton Manor.

She could not help but think of Charles and was wishing so much that he was here with his wife and daughter at this moment, when Gladstone suddenly ran from the house barking and jumping up at Verity with tail wagging in excitement.

"Ma'am. Excuse me. I am returning to town now, but can be contacted at our office. I shall contact you in a day or two..."

"Not now, Mr. MacDonald. Thank you," she interrupted graciously.

"Not at all ma'am. I bid you good night and I am confident you and your family will have many years of happiness here." He held her proffered gloved hand and gave a gentle bow.

As the solicitor departed, Verity spoke to her new head butler,

"Dobson, please don't think me rude, but I would rather leave the introductions until the morning. Beth requires feeding and we are both exhausted after the journey," her smile and flash of white teeth even thawed Dobson's frosty demeanour.

"Of course ma'am. Whatever you wish. I'll show you to your suite."

As Verity climbed the steps she tried to push away the memory of poor Stanley Monk and was glad to find her instructions had been followed and the iron lantern was nowhere to be seen. The hallway, once a living carpet of black beetles was now welcoming with subdued lighting from flickering gas wall brackets and the blazing fire, which stood between the two staircases. New parquet flooring, recently varnished, replaced the cold marble tiles and reflected the most opulent chandelier she had ever seen. It was a surprise from Charles as her choice had been decidedly more modest, but she instantly adored it and everything about their house, enthusing that the transformation in such a short time was nothing short of miraculous.

The next day started as a pleasant late autumnal morning, which Verity looked out upon when drawing her bedroom curtains. This was something she had always chosen to do herself rather than have a maid fussing round her and Beth first thing.

The sun had risen over the nearby Longridge fells forming part of the Pennines, a range of hills and high fells that extended from the Peak District in Derbyshire to the Cheviot Hills in Scotland.

The estate stretched across the countryside as far as she could see and may even include the farmland at the foot of the fells, she considered with excitement. Then she spotted the battlemented tower of Saint Michael's Church in the village of Grimsargh less than a mile away to the east.

As Verity reflected on the view, something caught her eye, glistening beyond a large conifer woodland. It was water. She stood on her tiptoes and could make out the corner of a pond or lake. That would need investigating with Gladstone she decided. Ever since her days as a child sailing on the Severn with her father and holidays on the Cornish coast, Verity had a fascination with water, whether land-locked or not.

She enjoyed breakfast in the morning room and Beth made a mess with scrambled eggs. Verity looked out of the tall windows onto a magnificent manicured lawn bordered by symmetrically placed ancient yew trees, trimmed to conical perfection that led the eye to a central white stone fountain with jets of water cascading onto the ornamental stonework, agitating the surface of the large circular pond.

After breakfast Verity introduced herself and Beth to the household staff in her own time and without formality and by the end of the day she knew most by name. She toured the ground floor, visiting the kitchen first, gawping at the enormous range, a new model built into the old chimney breast that even had a separate boiler and tap providing instant hot water.

The stone floor was covered in cream linoleum, a new product gaining popularity for its extra warmth underfoot and easy mopping. A wooden table with two sturdy pine chairs at each end and two long benches provided enough seating for twelve and took up the centre of the kitchen. The cook, Mrs. Ramsbottom, a homely looking red-faced woman in her early fifties was busy rolling pastry and the kitchen maid was nearby, dutifully holding a large bowl of stewed apples and rhubarb.

Verity left them busy with her menu and made an inspection of the rooms leading from the kitchen starting with the pantry, then the serving room and then the butler's pantry which was solely

Dobson's domain. She knew he had taken a carriage into town, so using her own key had a good look around the workroom set-aside for the most senior servant. It was clearly where Dobson cleaned and stored the silverware, other than that she could not see what the room was used for and was surprised at the hushed tones adopted whenever the butler's pantry was mentioned.

She felt disappointed, expecting the butler's sanctuary to be a welcoming and comfortable room, picturing two armchairs by a blazing fire. Instead it was cold and austere, just like Dobson.

She noticed the robust wooden door, painted cream, next to a Welsh dresser and knew after familiarising herself with the architect's plan earlier that morning, that it led to the wine cellar.

The door was locked, according to the previous owners' house rules and still rigorously enforced by Dobson. Fortunately Verity had brought her own set of house keys and unlocked the well-oiled and sturdy mechanism. Steps led down to another level, too dark and indiscernible for the casual visitor to explore beyond the threshold, and into the chilled air wafting out like a gentle breath. For some reason gas mantles had not been fitted along the corridor to the wine store. An oil-lamp was placed on a shelf beyond the door and within reach but she had no inclination to start striking matches and investigate an unlit subterranean part of the house whilst holding Beth's hand.

Verity locked the door and resumed her wanderings back through the kitchen. She had a quick look into the serving room, where dishes are kept warm until ready to be served at the table, retraced her steps and found herself at another cellar, far more accessible and inviting. The door was wedged open and the white-painted stone steps led to a large, cool but well lit scullery where pots and pans were washed, vegetables prepared and some cooked meats stored when the upstairs pantry was full of provisions. The scullery-maid stopped her humming and curtsied as Verity wandered past and she smiled at the young servant, chatting to her for several minutes as she plucked a large pheasant, provided by the gamekeeper.

It was lunchtime and she was keen to search and ramble outside. She decided that once Beth had finished eating and was ready for a nap, her maid, Daisy, would look after the child while she and Gladstone stretched their legs.

An hour later Verity left the house via the nearest of two kitchen doors. One led to the courtyard where deliveries and tradesmen arrived opposite the dairy and laundry blocks. Verity used the other and entered the walled garden overlooked by the drawing room and library. The brick wall, at least twelve feet high surrounded large raised vegetable and herb beds, an apple and pear orchard, fruit bushes and an extensive greenhouse against the south wall.

Two gardeners, cutting the last blooms off the hardy perennial chrysanthemum for table arrangements nodded politely at the attractive young woman they assumed was their new mistress. She gave them a friendly wave and kept to the wide path leading to the door in the wall by the greenhouse, hoping this would take her to the lake.

The door opened to a large swathe of cut grass ending at a low dry-stone wall and in the meadow beyond, the estate's herd of Friesian cattle grazed.

Gladstone followed a worn path across the lawn with nose to the ground as if he knew the way.

Verity felt exhilarated to be on her own and outdoors for the first time since she strolled the Cape vineyards. She reached the conifers that were visible from her bedroom and the path skirted around the woodland with its dense interior turning daylight to dusk. Occasionally she stopped to listen to bird songs and was pleased to identify the call of a blackbird, pheasant and a robin.

Gladstone eagerly searched the undergrowth, trying to do what the gun dog was bred to do, when suddenly the retriever dropped to the ground and froze, its demeanour no longer excited at the prospect of finding game. Instead he snarled with a show of teeth and growled at the expanse of water now visible.

"What is it boy?" Verity dropped to one knee to soothe the dog, but he was not for being comforted.

She followed the dogs stare and then saw the lake, or part of it.

Puzzled at Gladstone's behaviour she looked around, expecting to see a deer or boar or some other large forest mammal watching them before fleeing beyond the tree line. With no obvious reason for Gladstone's agitation, Verity slowly walked forwards for a better view of the lake, leaving the retriever where he remained squatting and teeth bared.

Its full shape and size was now clear and Verity was approaching an area of reed bed.

The lake appeared to be a natural feature, rather than man made and was far bigger than she had expected. To the opposite shore at the widest point it was more than half a mile and the length of its oval shape was at least double that distance.

The surface was mirror flat, but something puzzled her. As she scanned the length and breadth of the shoreline and beyond the wooden jetty where a rowing boat was tethered, she realised what was wrong.

There were no tell tale circles, rippling undulations or small air bubbles from fish activity; none of their splashing as insects were gulped from the surface. Frowning she wondered if the lake needed stocking with freshwater fish, then she realised what else was missing. Waterfowl. There was not a single swimming, diving or flying mallard, swan, goose or water hen to be seen.

It was early autumn, the trees already losing their leaves and any lake should now be active with wild fowl making most of the autumn harvest in preparation for the winter months ahead, she mused. Verity was disappointed at the absence of wild life and would speak to the gamekeeper to see what could be done to encourage wild birds back to the lake.

She walked nearer to the reed bed, the long fluffy bull-rush were ram-rod straight and as if on cue to Verity's thoughts, a coot, disturbed by her presence, rose from the reeds with a noisy clatter of wings startling her. It flew erratically over the lake and as Verity watched she could see it had an injured wing and very soon flight was no longer an option for the stocky bird and it tumbled to the water with an ungraceful splash. It instantly surfaced, paddling frantically towards the opposite bank, head turning side to side as if in panic. The coot was less than halfway across when it suddenly disappeared, pulled from below. Verity had seen something grab the bird but it had happened so fast. She stared at the fading ripples, convincing herself it must have been a pike.

Only a pike could take down waterfowl the size of an adult coot, she told herself.

But it did not look like the voracious predator Verity had observed numerous times. It had looked like a hand, a milky white hand.

Chapter Seventeen

That eventful day, when Ol' Joe parted company with Titus Moon during the early hours of the morning, did not seem so long ago.

Ol' Joe followed the course of the Ribble from Walton Bridge as far as Avenham Park then crossed the river using the Tram Bridge, which took him south. He stuck to the path that cut across fields and through farmyards, heading towards Cuerdon, intending to put as much distance between himself and Preston as was possible in the few remaining hours of darkness.

His ageing bones and muscles felt weary from the walking and he was tired from lack of sleep.

He could smell burning wood before seeing the source and only when passing round a copse did he see the bonfire, burning like a beacon on top of the hill not too far away.

Ol' Joe headed towards the rise and the several silhouettes visible near the flames. He knew this was the camp of the 'navigators'.

He had never met any of the navvies before and knew very little about them, apart from snippets he'd heard over a pint. They were building the great road from London to Glasgow, he'd been told and were hostile towards outsiders. Ol' Joe had also been told a lot of the navvies were Irish travellers from both north and south of the island. As he trudged up the hill towards the camp he did not perceive the navvies as a threat or danger and held no fear venturing into their encampment.

Even so, as a precaution he switched his small horde of cash to an inside pocket of his trench coat.

Two barking dogs announced his arrival and the motley hounds ran towards him with wagging tails. Ol' Joe noticed about a dozen men milling around even though it was not yet sunrise. Several navvies were in a group shouting encouragement at two men, bare knuckle fighting and thrashing the life out of each other.

"What do you want old man?" The accent was Irish, possibly from the border region and coming from a man sat by the bonfire.

"Hospitality sir, nothing more. Just to share the warmth from your fire and rest my knackered bones will be enough."

"Hospitality doesn't come free. We are working men who get nothing given us and we give nothing to others, so keep walking old man you'll find no hospitality here." He had thick dark curly hair and was no more than forty years. He wore several earrings and had a third eye tattooed in the middle of his forehead that gave him a menacing Cyclops appearance.

"Surely as a fellow traveller from the mother country you wouldn't turn away a son of Limerick, baptised in the waters of the Shannon?" Ol' Joe said with a big grin.

"Limerick you say? What are you doing out here anyway old man, coming into the lion's den? Haven't you heard we are all cut-throats and vagabonds?" He returned the smile.

"No sir, I'd heard you are all law abiding and respectable pillars of society, just like me"

The tattooed man gave a roar of laughter and shouted to no one in particular,

"This man is our fecking guest."

Ol' Joe gratefully sat on a wooden box by the fire and took the earthenware flagon offered him. Whatever the liquor was it tasted vile, but the warmth felt good as it trickled to his stomach and it had a kick that made him cough.

There was a suckling pig, stolen from a nearby piggery, skewered on a metal stake and resting on a frame near the flames, crackling and spitting with large chunks of flesh already cut away. Without ceremony the tattooed man handed Ol' Joe a warm shank of pork, which he attacked like a true carnivore.

The food and alcohol took hold of the visitor and as daylight broke Ol' Joe lay down by the fire and closed his eyes.

How long he had been asleep for he had no idea, but on sitting up and stretching, he saw the whole camp was now awake and numerous men were sat around him.

Ol' Joe then realised with horror that he was no longer wearing his trench coat. He quickly got to his feet and attempting to hide the panic in his voice said to the tattooed man, who was still sat on the same spot, "I'm feelin' the mornin' chill a pinch. Where did I put my coat last night?"

"It's found a new owner. One of the lads took a shine to it. You don't mind do you?" The voice was still amenable, but his face was not. It dared Ol' Joe to challenge him.

"Now come on lads, you wouldn't steal the coat from an old man's back now, surely?"

"We haven't stolen the coat. It's been traded for the hospitality we gave you. We call that a fair trade, don't you?"

Ol' Joe was thinking fast and trying to keep one step ahead of the tattooed navvy.

"Of course that's a fair trade. I'm glad it's gone to a good home. There are one or two personal possessions I'd like to recover from it before I leave. A copy of the Lord's Book and a couple of bob," he hesitated "you know? Bits of rubbish really, but keepsakes to me, sentimental, that sort of thing, so if I could just have a look and then I'll be on my way." He was aware he was rambling, so he shut his mouth.

"I went through all the pockets and found no keepsakes, so there's no point you looking." The tattooed navvy was noisily sucking a pork rib.

His uncertainty and a palpable sense of animosity towards him should have warned Ol' Joe to leave, but he could not leave without his money. The windfall of his life had only been in his possession for a matter of hours and he wanted it back.

"Well, perhaps if I could have a quick look, I know what I'm looking for and then I'll be on my way." He was beginning to sweat and his mouth was dry.

"I did find this though." He held out the wad of notes and cotton bag of coins.

His heart sank. It was time to stop playing games.

"That money is mine. My life savings."

"Correction old man, it was yours but it's now ours. You can leave old man and you can even take your precious coat as well. This little fortune you were hiding from us will keep us in food and drink for quite a while." There was a rousing cheer as eyes wide with greed and wonder stared at the bundle of banknotes.

"That money is mine and I'll kill any man that says different and I'll fight any man for it." He tensed and leant forwards as if about to charge the tattooed man.

A large labourer standing behind Ol' Joe, who wore a vest revealing unnaturally muscled arms and shoulders, saw the nod from the tattooed navvy and understood perfectly.

He produced a well-used leather cosh filled with a lump of lead and a second later swung it hard at Ol' Joe's head. It made a sickening crunch, fracturing his skull instantly as he blissfully lost consciousness and fell to the floor.

"Bury him," said the tattooed man looking away, attempting to count the banknotes with his greasy fingers.

The muscled navvy grabbed an ankle and effortlessly dragged Ol' Joe to the edge of the camp followed by a small gang carrying shovels and exchanging jokes on how they will spend the money, some suggestions being met with guffaws of laughter.

"Here will do." The muscled Irishman said to the others.

It did not take long for a neat oblong hole to appear. This is one thing navvys are good at, digging holes, and this grave is one that Titus would have been proud of, even if it was only four foot deep.

Ol' Joe was thrown into the hole, groaning as his cracked head hit the earth, splitting the fracture ever wider, allowing more blood to ooze from his scalp.

The loose earth was replaced, the labourers chatting and joking as if filling in a construction trench and as the dirt hit Ol' Joe's face, he spluttered and choked to the amusement of the men burying him.

As the earth rose above ground level silencing the old man's screams, heavy shovels smacked and compressed the dirt into a neat mound, one of many in a tidy row on the side of the hill.

Chapter Eighteen

R.M.S. Dunattar Castle left Santa Cruz, the capital of Tenerife and the largest of the Canary Islands, re-stocked with coal and fresh produce. The local merchants in their boats bobbing alongside the large liner had done a roaring trade with the soldiers, selling tobacco, bananas, tomatoes, wine, cooked meats and fish, jewellery and trinkets from the island artisans.

Charles and Henry stood on the aft deck as the ship steamed south away from the deepwater bay of Santa Cruz. During the last few years the island had become a tourist destination with all year round sunshine and the sailing ships both large and small anchored in the blue waters were a testament to its increasing popularity. Charles looked with fascination at the towering dormant volcano of Mount Teide, with its snow covered peak, dominating the island skyline.

"Every time I see this place Henry I say to myself 'one day I'll return here' and one day I will with Verity and Beth. I think I could get used to the tropical island way of life."

"It's hardly tropical Charles, we are still several hundred miles north of the equator, but I know what you mean. I went ashore once, a few years ago and spent an interesting few days getting to know one or two Spanish maidens." He gave a knowing wink to his companion.

"That's my only reservation about the place, the Spanish."

"The Spanish are fine, especially here. There is an indigenous population of islanders called Guanches, a strange looking lot and quite a few still survive, but the majority were enslaved in the 15th century. The population is quite cosmopolitan now. You'd like it Charles, a bit of sophistication and culture. Plenty of German, Portuguese and Italian fillies. In fact most countries apart from the British."

"How did our expanding empire slip past this oasis in the Atlantic?"

"We tried to take it from the Spanish a hundred years ago. How did you think Nelson lost his arm?"

Charles looked puzzled.

"Nelson lost his arm at Trafalgar."

"I do wonder about your Eton education sometimes Charles. Good old Horatio lost his arm attacking this very port, Santa Cruz. Hit by a musket ball so his entire arm was amputated to prevent gangrene, but don't ask me which arm," he quipped.

"We were defeated good and proper and have left the islands alone since, apart from these sorties. Replenishing the British war machine. Ironic really."

Henry was unshaven, preferring to ignore the military regime that operated on board, unlike Charles who was immaculately groomed as usual. Henry wandered the vessel as he pleased and on more than one occasion had been instructed by the captain to leave the bridge as 'unauthorised personnel'.

He even managed to talk his way into the officers' mess one afternoon, and enjoy a cup of tea with Sir Redvers Buller, much to the delight of Winston Churchill who was half way through a cream scone when Henry plonked himself opposite.

He listened with interest as Winston, Sir Redvers and his staff discussed the war strategy. The Commander-in-Chief was quite certain the war would be over within a matter of weeks. "The Boers have no stomach for a protracted war. They are just farmers on horseback," he announced.

Henry was not surprised to hear Churchill agree and remark that 'the Boers' insolence must be curbed'. He had heard Winston quote the same several times already in their few days together and soon came to realise that Winston was a staunch imperialist.

"With respect Sir Redvers, if you are expecting the Boers to be a push over I'm afraid you are in for a nasty shock," Henry interjected.

The conversation went quiet as all eyes turned towards Henry.

"And who are you sir?" enquired Sir Redvers.

"Henry Frobisher at your service Sir Redvers," he beamed in reply, slurping a mouthful of tea.

"What regiment are you with Mr. Frobisher? Not military intelligence I hope." Sir Redvers, in full uniform was sitting back casually, his hands on his lap and legs crossed looking with disdain at this unshaven visitor with long hair.

"None sir. I am travelling as a private citizen."

"You mean a blasted mercenary. What the devil is a private citizen doing as a passenger on a British war ship?" Sir Redvers blustered and now sat upright he glared at Henry before looking at his Staff Officers for an explanation.

"If I might intervene Sir Redvers, Mr. Frobisher is my travelling companion," interrupted Churchill.

Henry continued without acknowledging Churchill. "My being on board has been authorised by the War Department, Sir Redvers. I am travelling with my employer, Charles Cadley and our passage to the Cape has been sanctioned at the highest level by the War Office. Charles can produce official documentation to substantiate this, if required."

The Commander-in-Chief resumed his composure and asked,

"Very well Mr. Frobisher, but why do you believe the Boers will endure the hardships of a drawn out conflict?"

"Simple sir, they hate the British. They are fiercely independent and did not make the 'Great Trek' over fifty years ago to fall submissively under British rule now."

"Kruger has ordered his forces into Natal. It is a clear act of aggression by a neighbouring country and we must protect our interests overseas. They must accept the consequences and that could very well result in the annexation of the South African Republic and the Orange Free State, and they may soon find themselves under British rule. I am not a politician Mr. Frobisher, just a soldier following orders but I will bring the full might of British forces against the Boers, who I think will find they have bitten off more than they can chew."

This was met with murmurs of approval from around the table.

"I have fought against the Boers, whom you call 'farmers on horseback'. I was with the Cape Mounted regiment for fifteen years and believe me Sir Redvers they are a very capable force. Admittedly the majority will be volunteers, but they are all committed to protecting their freedom. Their riding skills are second to none as is their marksmanship. They are probably the greatest fighters on horseback since the hordes of Kubla Khan. Your forces will be fighting in a hostile terrain, a terrain with huge mountain ranges, great rivers and vast deserts and plains that the Boers know like the back of their hands. Look what happened at Laing's Nek in '81 and at Pretoria the year before. They decimated British forces then and they are more organised now. Their 40,000 or so army of volunteers will consist of commando units of around 500 men and they will have no problems getting supplies."

"I've heard mention before of these commandos. What are they? A bunch of Calvinists with shotguns?" Sir Redvers joked and laughed with his Staff Officers.

Henry could not believe their arrogance and stupidity.

"Sir, what you should understand about the Boer army is that military leaders are elected by the rank and file. They have no brigades, regiments or companies, just a commando unit whether ten or ten thousand men. There is very little rank structure and any military proposal is discussed and voted on by the burghers. They have no uniform and wear the same clothes whether fighting the British, herding cattle or shearing sheep. There is no drill, roll call or saluting a senior officer and they come and go from their commando unit as they please. All men within the unit are equal and woe-betide any general who oversteps the mark. A Boer cannot be ordered to do anything he does not want to, for any reason, but they all want to fight the British."

Further sarcastic guffaws and snorts of derision ensued following Henry's attempt to rationalise what impels the Boers to fight.

"No rank structure? A most ridiculous notion and one that can only result in an undisciplined rabble. The more I hear about this South African adversary the more I am concluding that they are an army of untrained amateurs. Presumably they are disorganised and mutinous and from what you say Mr. Frobisher, as volunteers, they are unlikely to choose to take on and face a professional army; the world's most efficient, disciplined and trained body of armed men under any military command. The military might that will soon descend on the Boers is without doubt a fighting force with no equal. You would be better explaining that to these blasted farmers rather than expounding propaganda that they are an army to be reckoned with. These Dutch cattle herders and shepherds are in for a short sharp shock Mr. Frobisher, mark my words."

"Have you ever encountered guerrilla warfare tactics Sir Redvers?" Henry asked undaunted and ignoring the icy stare.

"Mr. Frobisher, I have never encountered anything during battle that could withstand an infantry battalion, a cavalry charge or artillery bombardment."

"A commando unit is extremely mobile. They are armed with Mauser magazine rifles not shotguns and the Mauser is a superior rifle to the Lee Metford. They can cover huge distances on horseback, attack garrisons, relief columns and any occupied position they choose then disappear into the land. Frankly Sir Redvers, no infantry, cavalry or artillery will pose a worthwhile threat to the Boers. You have to play them at their own game."

"You mean like your regiment Mr. Frobisher?"

"The Colonial Cape Mounted Riflemen did adopt tactics from the Boers. We had to and we were very successful. It is no use marching columns of troops across the savannah, flying the regimental colours to the sound of drums, accompanied by

Hussars and their garish tunics, hoping for a frontal assault with the Boers. They'll be watching from the hills, hidden, their snipers having a good day at the funfair. The secret in defeating the Boers is mounted infantry."

"I think you over-estimate the capabilities of these Dutch farmers and under-estimate the British Army. I believe this war will redefine the map and create a union of a British South Africa." He took a sip of his favourite Earl Grey before saying, "Enough of all this military speculation. Why haven't you enlisted in Her Majesty's Forces Mr. Frobisher? I'm sure someone with your local knowledge and obvious expertise would be an asset to our campaign."

"Your army does not pay enough for one thing and for another I don't agree with the war. This is more about gold and diamonds than anything else and as you've already made plain, an opportunity for the 'Uitlanders' to stake a claim to what rightly belongs to the Boers. This is nothing more than imperialism at its worst."

"That sir is sedition, where I come from."

Henry ignored the postulating major, instead looking directly at Sir Redvers and said, "And where I come from sir, that is called democracy and freedom of speech."

The Commander-in-Chief pursed his lips in thought for a few moments then said,

"Would you please excuse us Mr. Frobisher, I need to speak to my staff on military matters which are not for the ears of gold and diamond smugglers."

If Henry was affronted he did not let it show.

"Of course sir and thank you for an enlightening discussion."

Later that evening Henry and Winston had an almighty argument in their cabin and Charles was an eager spectator from his bunk.

"Henry, you made a complete fool of yourself in front of Buller and proved to everyone you don't understand the situation."

"I understand 'the situation' as you call it a damn sight clearer than you and your chief of staff and government put together. If we were not talking about the lives of thousands of British and Boer troops this would be bloody hilarious. Instead it's a national disgrace and I hope your reporting of the war reflects that."

"I am not here to play into the hands of the enemy and give them propaganda. I shall report on what I witness. Unless I am mistaken, my employment has got nothing to do with you whatsoever. I don't comment on your intended skulduggery in Kimberley so I would be grateful if you left the reporting of the conflict to the war correspondents. Henry, I am disappointed with your outburst and to be accused of sedition by a senior British officer is damn near an accusation of treason. I am amazed you are not in the hold now awaiting instant deportation at Cape Town and it would serve you bloody well right." His face had gone quite red.

"Listen to yourself Winston, no wonder you lost the Oldham by-election. You are not in touch with reality let alone the public. You must be spending too much time at Blenheim Palace."

Charles cringed with genuine embarrassment on hearing Henry spit that out.

Churchill snatched the door open and left, banging it shut without saying another word.

The snow-capped summit of Teide was just visible on the horizon and Henry and Charles were still on the aft deck, near to the blue ensign flapping noisily above the churning propeller.

"I see that you and Churchill have kissed and made up." Charles had to raise his voice above the fluttering flag and southerly wind that was whipping up.

"You know me Charles. Anyway we are at war and who knows what may happen to any one of us. It is better to sail into the unknown as friends not enemies, there will be plenty of them waiting for us once we leave Cape Town. And it's surprising, no, I should say refreshing to be able reconcile one's differences over

150

a bottle of Scotland's finest, especially one of rare antiquity. I don't know how Winston's valet manages to acquire such wines and spirits out at sea. It's as if he has brought along the entire stock of a St James Street wine merchant."

"I take it then that you are back on Buller's dinner invitation list, as we all sail together into the unknown," Charles mocked.

"No, I can honestly say that Sir Redvers and I have now officially parted company. Socially that is. We had an interesting acquaintance lasting a full fifteen minutes until the bastard accused me of being a smuggler."

"He's no fool. Having us two on board his ship as private citizens with the authority of Whitehall makes us either spies or individuals who need to retrieve valuable items from a war-zone, risking life and limb. In other words, smugglers and smugglers with powerful connections. He's put two and two together and come up with five. I just hope he doesn't get in the way of our business or leak to the Boer hierarchy of his suspicions." Charles said with a frown.

"Why would he do that? He may be an arrogant buffoon, but to contact the enemy and arrange the capture of two British subjects just because he thinks I'm an insolent privateer? No, not possible. Whatever we are after, I do believe he would like to get his hands on as well but he would not want the Boers getting to us first, but it would not surprise me if he decided to monitor our movements for his own interests, perhaps with the hope of enhancing his pension. He has the whole colonial force at his disposal, tens of thousands of eyes and ears could be watching out for us, allowing the Commander-in-Chief the luxury of detaining us on our return. Fortunately no one knows the reason for our trip to South Africa. If the true nature of our mission became public knowledge, we would have a queue of eager extortionists following us. Just to mention the word 'diamond' seems to send some men crazy and they would slit their mother's throat to get their hands on the smallest of stones, not to mention a horde worth a king's ransom."

Charles had no intention of telling Frobisher that one such extortionist had already been despatched to the brine. He would only worry, he thought, and there is plenty of time yet for worrying.

"It seems to be common knowledge on board ship that we are destined for Kimberley. I have not breathed a word, have you mentioned it to anyone Henry?"

"The only person I've mentioned it to is Churchill."

"So you tell a journalist that we are heading for the world's biggest diamond mine, presently under siege by an occupying army? Good God! I think even he could work out what our mission might be and that would certainly explain his 'skulduggery' remark earlier."

Henry tensed slightly, realising perhaps he had made a gaffe by informing Churchill of their destination during one of their card and drinking sessions.

"I told him nothing of our intentions. Damn it! I trusted the man."

"Well I never did from the first moment I met him, when he barged into the cabin, waving his big fat cigar around as if he owned the bloody place."

"Come off it Charles. The reason you don't like him is not for what he's done, but for who he is. Admit it."

"What the hell does that mean?"

"Do I need to spell it out? His late father is Lord Randolph, cabinet minister, his mother Lady Randolph, his grandfather the Duke of Marlborough, his family home is Blenheim Palace. Should I continue?"

"I seem to recall you throwing the Blenheim Palace jibe at him."

"And for that I've apologised, which has been accepted."

"Well bully for you. I would not have apologised to that jumped up bloody reporter. That's all he is you know. An employee of a bloody newspaper who is sailing through life because of his family name, family fortune and family connections, who can't keep his bloody mouth shut."

"Not like you, eh! Charles? Grandson of one of the country's first cotton magnates, now at the helm of his legacy."

"And that legacy is paying you handsomely. You would do well to remember that Henry. Anyway why are you sticking up for Churchill? He has compromised this operation."

"Churchill is a man of his word. The more I think about it, the more I cannot believe he has breached my trust. Anyway, a chap is innocent until proved guilty. I shall speak with him and decide from there."

"Well someone has got a loose mouth and my money is on it being your man."

Chapter Nineteen

The two detectives and Abberline were in the central administration office between the two gothic towered wings of the Preston Royal Infirmary, studying the file of Professor Daniel Bailey and being closely watched by the office manageress.

"Daniel Bailey, born 3rd March 1838. Status: Batchelor. Religion: C of E. Professor of the Anatomy & Pathology Department at Preston Royal Infirmary, appointed 30th June 1896. So 'e'd bin 'ere three years." Meadowbank looked up from the file he was reading out aloud.

"That's all very well, but what else does it say?" Abberline replied impatiently.

"Let's see. Reet, 'ome address, 16, Bushell Place, Preston. Where's that address Sam?"

"Bushell Place, it's just off Winkley Square, leads down t' Park. Very posh as well." Sam replied.

"How far is it from any of the murder scenes?" Abberline asked.

"T' first one, on Church Street, not far at all. A few minutes walk, but fer t'other near Tulketh Brow probably abaht two mile. A good 'alf 'ours walk, that's all." Sam offered.

The room was heavy with pipe smoke and the middle-aged manageress coughed pointedly, waving a hand in front of her face. Meadowbank ignored her, if he had registered her actions at all; instead he continued to smoke his pipe.

"What does this say? Left Addenbrookes Teachin' 'ospital, Cambridge in 1863 wi' t' followin' qualifications: MB BCHir. What does that stand fer luv?" Meadowbank turned to the manageress and spelt out "MB BCHir."

"Bachelor of Medicine and Surgery. The professor was a very eminent doctor," she answered haughtily.

"Well 'e's a very eminently dead doctor now an' strongly suspected of t' illegal traffickin' o' 'uman body parts, so I wouldn't erect a statue to 'im just yet luv." Meadowbank looked back at the file.

"That can't stand fer Bachelor of Medicine and Surgery. Those letters are nowt like that." Huggins remarked loudly.

This gave the manageress the opportunity to regain her standing,

"It's Latin of course and is an abbreviation of *Medicinae Baccalaureus et Baccalaureus Chirurgiae.*"

She spoke with the flair of a Latin scholar.

"Thanks luv. I thought it must bi sommat like that." Meadowbank muttered, glared at Huggins and continued,

"Where were we? Reet, 'e left that one in 1863 an' t' same year moved t' Kings College 'ospital in London. Stayed there until '80. So did seventeen year there afore going t' Royal College o' Surgeons in London an' was awarded a FRCS."

The manageress interrupted eagerly, "Those letters stand for 'Fellow of the Royal College of Surgeons'. It is a very prestigious honour only awarded to a select few."

On this occasion Meadowbank just smiled at her.

"'E was there until '91 then spent five year lecturin' in America. Does that fit in wi' yer investigation Fred?"

"Of course it does. He was in London from '80 to '91. All the murders we investigated took place in '88. I think we could be onto something here lads." Abberline could hardly contain his excitement."

"So what 'appens now?" Huggins asked.

"Wi need t' search 'is 'ome address. Speak wi' friends an' colleagues an' establish what family, if any 'e 'as an' try an' confirm 'is whereabouts on t' night in question. What abaht you Fred?"

"I have to get back to London and speak with the Commissioner. The Ripper case needs to be re-opened and I'll follow up the leads from that end. I'll also look into cases of body-snatching in the capital. I think I'll need to go back about twenty years to be on the safe side, bearing in mind Bailey had been practising medicine in London from 1863 to '91. Good Lord! That's twenty-eight years. This will be a mammoth undertaking. I must return to the station Albert and ring the agency. I had better let them know what I'm doing as they are still paying me."

Chapter Twenty

The new vicar of Saint John the Divine had never met his predecessor, the Reverend John Buck and did not attend his funeral. Not many parishioners did turn out to pay their last respects, once the news of the events surrounding his death became public knowledge at the inquest, which was held before the funeral, as was normal procedure.

The Bishop of Blackburn faced a dilemma now that one of his vicars had been posthumously and publicly identified as a practising homosexual. Apart from going against the laws of the land, homosexuality also went against the laws of the Church and as far as the Bishop was concerned, the laws of God as well.

In fact he was quite certain that sodomy or impropriety between men went against the Ten Commandments and only being able to recall nine of the imperatives compounded his belief. The Bishop had to refer to The Old Testament Book of Exodus chapter 20:2-17 to reassure himself and calm himself down.

Even though the other offending party or 'lover' as certain members of the press referred to the absentee visitor had not yet been identified, the mystery caller remained a prime suspect for Reverend Buck's death and the police were still very keen to trace him.

The Bishop of Blackburn was forced to take up temporary residence at St. John's to reassure the parishioners that it was still a house of God and not an ecclesiastical male brothel as some were suggesting. He realised events were in danger of spiralling out of control and often, when knelt in silent prayer he would curse that 'perverted bastard Buck' who may yet, single handedly convert overnight, most of St. John's congregation to Catholicism.

The Bishop was sat in the vestry enjoying a sherry at the very table Titus Moon had cast aside in his murderous rage. It was mid afternoon and a good time, the Bishop had found, to reflect, deliberate, worry, judge or even scheme about anything that engages one's attention, like a toothache or indigestion. At the moment the Bishop was worrying over his forthcoming sermon.

He had installed as a replacement to the Reverend Buck the Reverend Plumb, Jacob Plumb to be exact. A young minister and son of a local retired clergyman, both with impeccable antecedents.

The new vicar had a wife, the Bishop made sure of that, and she was a buxom lass with a cheerful disposition. Her name was Minnie and like her husband, no more than twenty-five. They were the perfect choice. Heterosexual and radiating love for one another, considered the Bishop at the time. They could not possibly offend anyone or have any skeletons in any cupboards at their age and the parishioners would embrace their innocence and enthusiasm, the Bishop enthused to the parish council.

Jacob Plumb was a bundle of nerves at the best of times and being elevated to the vicar of the principal parish church in Preston had aggravated his stutter to quite annoying proportions. This seems to have been overlooked by the Bishop in his haste to remove the cloud left by the Reverend Buck.

The Bishop's next sermon was the following Sunday when he would officially welcome Jacob and Minnie Plumb to the parish, hoping and praying he could get away with not mentioning the Reverend Buck's burial arrangements.

He recalled with a shudder his last appearance at Sunday morning mass when the church was electric with emotion. It was the first Sunday after the local papers had eviscerated Reverend John Buck's reputation with their front-page headlines.

The church was packed with angry and confused worshippers, all eyes on the Bishop for words of solace and guidance, and given the circumstances everything was going well until he climbed the steps to the pulpit. The very same pulpit that as a young priest and even as Bishop, he had delivered some spectacular sermons, rousing and emotive and still remembered by elder statesmen and women of the parish.

Those days seemed so long ago.

He had been heckled and badgered from the word go, not even having time to read his selected passage from the scriptures. The first voice of dissent wanted to know if he and his wife were still married in the eyes of the Church and God.

The Bishop made the mistake of asking why shouldn't they be and the reply contained the phrase 'our sacred marriage vows violated by that sodomite.'

It got worse. "What about our Jack's christening? Our baby was held by his corrupt hands, baptised by a man whose hands have fornicated with another man."

Someone had to mention communion. "Did he wash his hands and how often? His fingers have touched my lips not to mention the communion host." As if to reinforce her feelings the lady ran retching from the church.

"That deviant gi' mi father t' last rites. It's a mockery o' th' church I tell thee. 'Ow can 'e go round forgivin' sins o' t' dyin' when all 'e's thinkin' abawt is 'avin' it off wi' other blokes?"

The Bishop tried to quell the uprising. Holding his hands aloft he gestured for calm, "Please we are in a house of God after all."

"It's a pity Reverend Buck didn't remember that." A voice shouted from the back.

"I understand feelings are running high, but show some compassion, after all John Buck was brutally murdered in this very church. He strayed off the path of righteousness and paid for it terribly with his life. Whatever he is accused of don't forget he was only human, vulnerable and the vicar at this church for a good few years. You know as well as I do, John Buck was not a wicked man, but a hard working minister who lived for the Church, for God and for his parish. Surely you can find it in your hearts to forgive him and let him rest in peace. I ask you to remember the words of Christ, 'He who is without sin among you, let him be the first to cast a stone at him'."

The Bishop paused for effect, the congregation deadly quiet. He believed he had won them over and sighed with relief.

Then a voice from the other side of the church, called out, "I might be a sinner Bishop, but I ain't no arse bandit."

The Bishop gave up, ignored the reading and said "Amen."

It is now up to Jacob Plumb to sort this out, not my problem, he thought as he walked back to the altar.

There was still the dilemma of Reverend Buck's grave at the rear of the church. The head stone had been vandalised and desecrated, in particular the in-scripted 'B' of the surname, chiselled to crude 'F'. A committee of parishioners attended the vicarage demanding that John Buck should not be buried on hallowed ground and insisted his body be disinterred.

"To exhume a vicar of the Church of England from the sanctuary of a churchyard, have you all gone mad?" he shouted at them.

The reply was either you move him or we'll move him. It was obvious to the Bishop that this was no idle threat.

When Detective Sergeant Huggins returned, as part of his continuing enquiries into Reverend Buck's murder, the Bishop decided against telling him about the lynch mob that had confronted him.

The Bishop on reflection considered they were the exact opposite of a lynch mob, if such a group could exist. They weren't proposing to hang by the neck a living man but dig one up who had died by hanging. He considered what the collective noun would be for a group of parishioners hell-bent on exhuming a dead vicar and after quite some time went back to his lynch mob description.

Sergeant Huggins was requesting to go through, once again, John Buck's personal possessions. He explained to the Bishop once again, that he was looking for diaries, letters or photographs or any clue that could point to a suspect.

The Bishop explained to Jacob Plumb, that as the Reverend Buck had no next of kin, all his worldly belongings now stored in a spare room in the vicarage would eventually be donated to the poor. He suggested that he not mention to whom the clothes had once belonged. He feared that even the destitute had standards and would raise the roof in protest.

The Bishop offered Huggins a coffee, which was efficiently served by the housemaid. It occurred to the sergeant that he did not know the Bishop's name and had always referred to him as 'Sir' and on a couple of occasions 'Your Honour', though it was evident the Bishop was not a judge of the Queen's Bench Division.

Huggins suspected the Bishop to be in his sixties. He was of medium height and medium build. His hair had all but disappeared apart from remnants around his ears.

The sergeant quite liked him. He was a gentleman, decisive with a serene calmness that gave reassurance.

He wore the Anglican style tab collar shirt under his tailored black cassock with silk buttons down the centre of the front, fastened from the neck to his stout shiny black shoes. An ornate leather cincture around his protruding waist completed the garb.

The Bishop asked the sergeant if he was any nearer to tracking down the Reverend Buck's killer, even though he knew full well what the answer was.

"Wi are followin' one or two leads, that's why I need t' go through t' Reverend Buck's personal items. I know a uniform constable 'as already done so but I would like t' check fer m'sel'. Mek sure nothin' 'as bin missed like."

"Well help yourself Sergeant. You should know your way around the vicarage by now. You'll find what you're looking for upstairs in the room to the right of the bathroom. If you need anything, the housekeeper will respond to your requests."

Huggins was enjoying their chat, sipping coffee from a bone china cup in between crunching through a large piece of homemade shortcake. He asked how the new vicar was coping with the situation.

'Situation', the Bishop mulled the word over to himself, more like a living nightmare and smiled at Huggins wanly.
It was all getting too much for the Bishop, he needed to be on his own, preferably with a prayer book and a large Irish whiskey.

"If you'll excuse me Sergeant, duties of the diocese call."

"Of course sir. Just one question, does Titus Moon still d' th' grave-diggin' 'ere?"

"We have not seen or heard of Mr. Moon since the tragic death of John Buck. Why do you ask?"

"No particular reason really. I wanted t' ask 'im a few questions but I've not sin 'im m'sel' fer a while."

Left alone he finished the pot of coffee and the remaining shortcake and ten minutes later climbed the stairs.

The Reverend Buck's possessions were piled into two tea chests. One was full with books and papers, the other only part full, mostly with religious paraphernalia. One non-clerical grey suit and three ecclesiastical black suits hung from the picture rail together with several white shirts.

Huggins went through the jacket and trouser pockets first then moved onto the less full chest, gently removing educational certificates of merit, a few religious reproduction paintings of Christ, a small wooden crucifix and a bundle of letters. A quick flick through revealed them to be from grieving or grateful parishioners. Next he removed a leather bound address book. It was quite battered and well thumbed and contained a fairly comprehensive list of names in alphabetical order.

As he turned the pages at random something odd struck him. The majority of the names belonged to men. He had to search hard for a female name and some of the names had an asterisk next to them. No address was recorded under these highlighted names, just times and dates; some were crossed out with a more recent date added. It appeared to be some sort of log or record rather than an index.

Puzzled he checked under 'B' and found the name Daniel Bailey printed in scrawling capitals, highlighted with an asterisk. There were numerous dates under the name, going back over twelve months and the last entry, 9p.m. 01/08, Huggins instantly recognised was the night of Reverend Buck's murder.

Chapter Twenty-One

Starch House Square was a maelstrom of noise and it was only ten o'clock in the morning.

Two hot-potato vendors argued over their claims to a profitable pitch outside The Prime Jug, a pack of dogs ran wild in their search for food and a horde of children of all ages chased a battered football, blindly mimicking their heroes at North End, the first national league champions in '88.

Titus Moon was dozing in the parlour, as Mags called her only room with a filthy slop-stone in one corner near to the stove, which when lit was the only heat in the building. He was sat on a wooden rocking chair and cradling a crock of cider he had taken to drinking now the water from the hand pump by the slop-stone ran out stinking and brown, polluted with sewerage.

They had been together a couple of months now, since Mags found him in the hallway, bruised and battered. She had let out his old room and looked after Titus now that he wasn't working at the church any more.

Mags was happy with her lot. She had a few bob in her purse, a full house of tenants charging them a penny a night each for water, when it was available, bread and a roof over their head. A bed was usually extra. And she had a man to fuss over. It saved her going to one of the ale-houses on a Saturday night eyeing up who to invite back to her place, the more drunk the better she had found, then they would not remember how much money she had fleeced from them.

She wanted Titus to get a job. Not just to bring some cash into the house and pay his keep, but also get him out of the way during the day. He never left the house in daylight hours and only ventured as far as The Prime Jug at night.

Whatever happened that night, Mags had often thought, had changed him, but the peelers had never come round looking, so what ever did happen could not have been that bad.

The bruising and swelling around his face had almost gone and Mags' neat stitches and poultice to the scalp wound were very effective against infection and only his ribs gave him any real discomfort. Though he did not let it be known to Mags, he was grateful to her for taking him in, and looking back, did not believe he would have survived those first weeks on his own. As for the money, that was hidden in a box under a heavy paving flag in the yard. He had never told Mags about the cash and had no intention of doing so. For the time being he was quite content to live off her support and keep his head low.

He wondered what was going on at the church and had heard from gossip in the ale-house about a new vicar arriving with his wife.

A vicar and a wife! That makes a change, he said to himself.

Titus thought about Ol' Joe and whether he had made it back to Ireland after all these months and seeing as the coppers had not been round asking questions, it looked like he had.

He decided it was time to circulate round town again, stretch his legs, see what's happening and perhaps visit the new vicar and get his job back digging graves. If any one asked where had he been hiding these few months he'd say he fell down the stairs at his lodgings after a skinful. That would keep them happy and had nearly been true on more than one occasion.

In fact he would go round to the church this minute and sort it out.

Mags had already left on one of her countless errands. He never knew where she went during the day but had a good idea she was with some old hags across the square enjoying a mug of stout.

Titus stood at the front door, smiling at the din and commotion surrounding him. Street cleaners had removed most of the sewerage from the footpath for the time being, giving the area an almost respectable feel. The cobbled square, riddled with pot-holes was surrounded by two and three storey dilapidated lodging houses with leaking roofs and leaning chimney stacks, a few on this late autumn morning already pouring out black smoke. Shops traded on one side, including Sergeant's Horse Slaughterer and Livesy, Potato Merchant.

Titus had lost a lot of weight recently and Mags had trimmed his hair so it just covered his ears and his beard was clipped neatly to his face. His wardrobe had doubled in size. Thanks to Mags he now owned two shirts and two pairs of trousers, and insisted she washed whatever he was wearing once a fortnight. He rinsed his hands and face every few days and made use of the tin bath, which hung on a nail in the back yard, perhaps once a month.

Titus Moon looked a different man.

He no longer walked with his usual swagger, but instead hugged the building line and walked slowly for the benefit of his aching ribs and deep cut to the shoulder.

At this time of the day the town was busy with traders and shoppers. The horse drawn trams with both decks crowded were pulled noisily along the tracks that ran through the town on two routes, with termini at the Cemetery, Broadgate, Tulketh Road and Fulwood Barracks.

It was Friday and market day, one of the three days a week when stalls were erected and barrels set up on Earl Street and under the Covered Market.

Seeing it was a Friday and the day Catholics by rigorous tradition did not eat meat, the Lytham and Southport shrimpers and fishwives, in their distinctive clothing and hats were doing a brisk trade in shellfish and flounder, both local specialities. Stalls selling second hand clothes and shoes, local cheese, fruit and vegetables were laid out in neat rows like a military encampment, allowing the milling crowds to inspect the wares.

Titus took his usual route along the cobbled Back Lane that led to the newly constructed Market Street and onto Market Place and then he saw the crowds lining Fishergate.

Union Jacks were everywhere, waving from the crowd, hanging from shops and windows. Children sat on shoulders cheering, men clung to lamp posts and some stood on the roof of hackneys. There was a buzz of excitement amongst the spectators and as Titus approached, passing the Town Hall he could hear the sound of a marching band coming from Church Street. The crowd at this point was its most dense and the Mayor, John E. Dunn was standing on a balcony of his office in the Town Hall with his wife and officials, overlooking Fishergate.

All heads were looking left and Titus was looking for a gap in the crowd. Then the shouting and cheering tumbled along the mass of people lining both sides of the road as the Band and Drums of the 1st Volunteer Battalion Loyal North Lancashire's came into view followed by two hundred and fifty men of The South Lancashire Regiment (Prince of Wales Volunteers). The band played "The Soldiers of the Queen" and "God Save the Queen" and the crowd crammed tighter as the column, four abreast marched past.

"God bless yer lads!" "God speed an' do us proud!" "Be brave, never fear." "Three cheers for the fighting Lancastrians."

The shouting increased as men and women cheered and wept.

The second detachment from Fulwood Barracks followed. Seven hundred men dressed in full marching order, wearing khaki drab issue with the tropical pith helmet and carrying the bolt action Lee-Metford.

The crowd sang "Auld Lang Syne" in a tumultuous chorus and pressed forwards, the ones at the back hoping to get a glimpse of 'the boys'.

Titus pushed his way through the crowd to the great annoyance of the spectators he shoved aside, and barged past but in doing so quickly crossed the road, dashing between detachments. He had no interest that this army was bound for Cape Town to join Buller's forces and break the siege at Ladysmith.

He shouldered his way through the second crowd now facing him, cursing at men and women alike. He was jostled, pushed and sworn at and his broken ribs were painfully nudged by the occasional elbow in response to his aggressive rudeness. This was remarked upon several times but no one dared to challenge this thuggish brute. Titus emerged from the crowd very near the entrance to St. John's church and followed the path to the rear.

The vestry door was open, but Titus, on this occasion, knocked and waited.

Jacob Plumb appeared within seconds, his mop of blonde hair bouncing whenever he moved.

"Hallo. C-C-Can I h-h-help you?"

"I'm looking fer t' vicar."

"That is I. R-R-R-Reverend P-P-lumb."

He looked at the friendly face and enquiring raised eyebrows and took an instant dislike to the Reverend Plumb.

"I'm Titus Moon. T' gravedigger."

"Ah! Mr. M-M-Moon. Quite a lot of p-p-p-p-eople have b-b-been l-looking for you, including the p-p-olice. We thought y-you h-h-had disappeared."

"I've bin ill. Struck down w' summat. Any'ow, I've come back fer mi job."

"I'm afraid y-y-ou are t-too late."

"Yer mean you've given mi job t' someone else?" He said menacingly.

"The c-c-council has decided t-that all b-b-urials must n-n-ow t-take place at the m-main cemetery, so burials at ch-churchyards are n-no l-l-longer all-llowed. To stop all the gr-gr-grave-r-robbing I suppose. Unfortunately your p-p-position here no longer exists."

"No longer exists! What t' fuck are yer on abaht?" His voice was rising with anger.

"St-steady on Mr. M-M-Moon and pl-please r-restrain with your pr-pr-profanities, this is n-not m-m-my doing. The ch-ch-church cannot employ you as a gr-gravedigger if there are no more gr-gr-graves to dig, c-can it?"

"Fuck yersel' wi' yer fuckin' profanities." What little patience he possessed had vanished fighting his way across Church Street.

"I wouldn't dig no more 'oles for yer namby-pamby fuckers if yer paid mi in gold."

"As y-you will not be exca-v-vating further gr-graves and the ch-ch-church will n-not be p-p-p-paying you in g-g-gold, all c-concerned sh-should be happy. Don't y-y-you agree Mr. M-M-Moon?"

"Eh! Agree? I agree that yer a stutterin' fool wi' a big gob."

"Good. S-so n-now that the situation is f-fully cl-clear, I bid y-y-ou good day Mr. M-M-Moon." The vicar smiled and started to push the door to.

"Whoa! Not s' fast. I'm owed some wages."

"I d-don't think so."

"I'm tellin' yer I'm owed a couple o' bob. T' Reverend Buck ne'er paid mi."

"As John B-Buck is d-d-dead he's not likely to is he? G-goodbye Mr. M-M-Moon."

The door closed firmly, inches from Titus's snarling face. He thumped the door hard again and again, shoving with his shoulder as he turned handle, but a heavy bolt kept the door closed.

"I want mi money yer fucker." He shouted through the keyhole. After a minute or so of stomping about, deciding his next move, Titus walked away, going over in his mind the many ways of inflicting hideous pain on the Reverend Plumb.

As he reached the corner of the church the vestry door opened and Jacob Plumb called out cheerfully,

"Oh, Mr. M-M-Moon."

Titus stopped and slowly looked back with a smile of triumph.

"Mr. M-M-Moon. Pl-please do me and the g-g-good Lord a f-favour and f-f-fuck off back to the z-z-zoo. Y-you uncivilised b-b-baboon." He gave Titus a big grin then promptly shut the door and once again secured the heavy bolt.

Chapter Twenty-Two

Her maid entered the morning room with the day's post. Verity, sitting by her desk, stared at the heavy rain outside and the dark clouds hanging over the fells. She had an open magazine on her lap and did not hear Daisy approach.

"Excuse me ma'am, you have some correspondence."

"Oh! Sorry Daisy I was lost in my own thoughts. Thank you. I'll take those."

Verity wore a simple charcoal bespoke woollen dress with a cream lace collar and her shoulder length black hair was pulled back and fastened with a band.

She did not maintain the tradition of wearing several different outfits of clothes for different times of the day or events, choosing instead practical but elegant outfits from her dressmaker, who came to the house for the fittings.

Beth, sitting on the large rug doodling with crayons and a colouring book, shouted 'hallo' and giggled at Daisy.

She handed her maid the day's menu, choosing her usual soup at lunchtime and a two-course dinner for the evening to be taken in the drawing room rather than the formal dining room. Since moving into Ribbleton Manor two weeks ago, Verity had not used the large mahogany table in the dining room. It seemed silly to her, for one place to be set on a table for eighteen diners and having two servants standing by in silence, watched over by the grim-faced Dobson. She had already decided some days ago that the butler had to go and as soon as Charles returned it would be her priority to instigate his dismissal. Verity found his austerity to be bordering on rudeness and his indifference to Beth was too much. He needed to be reminded who paid his wages, she considered with a smile.

Once alone, Verity went through the mail. Nothing from Charles, but he had warned her that for the two weeks at sea there would be no communication from him. Then her face lit up. She immediately recognised her father's distinctive calligraphy and eagerly slid the opener through the envelope.

Her parents were travelling up from Bristol to Manchester on business and then intended visiting her and Beth for a few days. They would be arriving at Preston railway station the following Friday at 1 o'clock and could a carriage be there to collect them? She was overjoyed. Her parents had not yet seen Ribbleton Manor. Verity realised she had much to do as they would be arriving in three days.

The Royal Merchant Ship Donattar Castle had passed the equator and was now only two days from Table Bay.

The weather had been kind since leaving the Canary Isles and the southern hemisphere sunshine, tempered by a brisk and refreshing southeasterly trade wind, was a pleasure to soak up.

The daily routine on board was now well practised. Reveille was sounded at 5.30 a.m., hammocks and blankets cleared by 6 a.m. and breakfast at 7 a.m.

Non-military personnel were exempt from the disciplined process, which involved the ship being cleaned daily prior to the Commanding Officer's parade on deck at 10 a.m., regardless of weather conditions.

Henry had once again settled his differences with Churchill.

He had given his word, as a gentleman and former subaltern of the 4th Hussars, that he had not breached any one's confidence in his entire life, let alone a former fellow officer at arms. This was more than acceptable to Henry and he in turn apologised for even considering such a slur on his character.

Charles was not convinced and gave Churchill the cold shoulder at every opportunity. His one-man attempt at sending Churchill to Coventry caused mild amusement to Henry and Winston, who took great delight in engaging Charles in conversation as if they were old acquaintances. Charles rather predictably would always respond with, "Churchill! How many more times must I repeat? I have nothing to say to you!"

Winston was a resourceful man and conducted his own enquiries to establish who if any one had revealed Charles and Henry's objective in South Africa. He made discreet enquiries amongst the accommodation deck and mess room. He had high regard for Henry and wanted to prove to him conclusively that his honour was intact.

As a war correspondent the men were eager to speak to Churchill. Within a couple of days of detective work he had found that none of the men knew who Charles and Henry were let alone what their business was. Some speculated that they were mercenaries, a breed of fighters despised by professional soldiers.

He had occasion to speak to a private with the Durham Light Infantry who had the hammock above Charlie Stokes, the missing corporal, whose personal record was now officially endorsed, 'lost at sea'.

The day before Charlie Stokes went missing he had told the private that he was soon to come into money. They had been sharing a bottle of Newcastle Brown and Charlie planned to jump ship at Cape Town as he had some urgent business on shore that would make him a rich man and set him up for life.

Winston pressed him for more information but the infantry private clearly knew nothing more and certainly nothing of any trip to Kimberley.

Winston reported what he had found to Henry.

They discussed the events surrounding Corporal Stokes' disappearance.

"Why hasn't the private gone to his commanding officer with this information?" asked Henry.

"He did not think it important."

"Good God Winston! Not important? You don't have to be Sherlock Holmes to work out that Corporal Stokes has more than likely been murdered for something he possessed of value."

"You must remember Henry, the private is only nineteen years old and this is his first combat mission. He is not paid to make decisions, but to take orders. And you are making a rather bold accusation regarding the corporal's disappearance are you not? Murder?"

"What do you think?"

"I agree this new information does make the corporal's disappearance suspicious. The question that needs to be asked is what could make him a rich man since leaving Southampton? Something with enough value to plant the crazy idea of deserting his regiment on reaching Cape Town. To start a new life in an unstable country at war, 6,000 miles from home with the constant threat of capture and execution by firing squad hanging over his head. That is the action of a man blinded by greed and no amount of money is worth that."

"That's easy for you to say."

"What do you mean by that?" He looked directly at Henry.

"I think you should be the last person to criticise anyone's reaction to wealth. Come on Winston, you've only ever known a comfortable and wealthy lifestyle. You have no idea what destitution and poverty does to people. You've never seen the slums and the homeless of London, let alone Newcastle."

"And you have of course?"

"Yes, as a matter of fact I have. I don't suppose you have ever heard of Shoreditch have you? Near to the infamous Whitechapel. You'll have heard of that area no doubt, thanks to Jack the Ripper. The East End of London was then, and still is a stinking hole for the poor to live in. My parents and family still live there and every day is a struggle to survive. That is why I left at my first chance and I've never been back. One day I hope to return but at the moment I couldn't face them, especially my mother, who I cannot remember ever being happy. I don't think she knows what that word means. Oh yes, I know about poverty Winston believe me."

He looked at Henry thoughtfully, choosing his words carefully.

"As you reminded me a few days ago Henry, earlier this year I unsuccessfully stood for election in Oldham as a Member of Parliament for the Conservative Party. Oldham is a Lancashire mill town and I have witnessed first hand the human degradation of poverty. Perhaps not to the extent you have, but I still hoped in some small way to do something about it. So please do not judge before you have all the facts."

Henry decided to change the subject or he could envisage pistols at dawn.

They were sat on a bench on the junior officers' deck with the sun on their face and each with a glass of Burgundy.

On the deck below a sergeant major could be heard screaming orders during the never-ending rifle drill.

"You said Stokes must have come across something of great value during the voyage. Access to the ship's vault would be out of the question and I don't believe there are other great sums of money on board. I suppose it is a question of how much wealth constitutes being 'a rich man'."

"I do not believe it was money or gold or precious stones that he had obtained. I believe it was information."

"Information?" Henry looked puzzled.

"I suspect he had obtained information and he thought someone would pay a lot of money for his silence."

"Blackmail! Come on Winston, you have now shot your theory into the realms of fantasy. What information could an infantry corporal possibly have access to, that he could blackmail someone with?"

"If we knew that Henry we would know the identity of his murderer, that is of course, if there has been foul play. But if I was a betting man I would wager he had stumbled across something he should not have and what better way of maintaining an individual's silence and dealing with a blackmailer. Push him overboard into the open Atlantic with little chance of his body ever being discovered."

They both gazed out at the blue cloudless sky then Henry spoke.

"Are you going to report your suspicions to the captain or Sir Redvers? There needs to be some sort of investigation."

"It is purely conjecture on my part. Apart from that, I have searched my mind for the identity of a person or persons on board who would want certain information kept quiet and I can only think of two."

"Even more reason to officially report your suspicions Winston."

"It's you and Charles, Henry. No one knows for real what you are up to and no one really cares, but you must admit it is very cloak and dagger. And look at the rumpus caused when you both thought I had spilled the beans to Buller about your destination. Cadley is paranoid about the whole affair and you make wild accusations regarding my integrity."

"You honestly believe Charles or I or both of us have dispatched Stokes to the deep?" He glared at Churchill.

"If this were a police murder investigation and I was the officer in charge, you would both be my number one suspects, but it isn't and I'm not, so it is of no matter what I think."

"Well it bloody well matters to me. If you think I have committed murder then someone else could think that. This has to stop, now. I want you to report the matter Winston. I want everything out in the open and a proper investigation conducted before we weigh anchor in a few days."

"You may not have killed Corporal Stokes, but what about Cadley? Can you vouch for him, Henry?"

The two men looked at each other.

"Charles! Come off it Winston. What are the key ingredients for a crime, motive, means and opportunity? The last two we could all be guilty of, but motive? Why the hell would Charles want to get rid of Stokes? As far as I'm aware they have never met each other. No, this does not make sense."

"Only you and Cadley know what your business is in South Africa, but to be frank I am sure I could make an educated guess. Ask yourself Henry, if someone else knew of your intentions and was attempting to involve themselves, would it be worth committing murder to un-involve them?"

Henry said nothing, but knew what the answer would be.

Chapter Twenty-Three

The successor to Sir Arthur Lawrenson sat at the chief constable's desk reading Detective Inspector Meadowbank's report.

Major Francis Little, promoted from the rank of deputy chief constable was well aware of the investigation, but the sudden demise of Sir Arthur had come as a surprise to all who knew him and diverted attention, albeit briefly from the Ripper investigation. His behaviour had always been bullish and eccentric, but to end up in the County Lunatic Asylum at Whittingham was something that could never have been predicted.

The chief constable had regular contact with the asylum superintendent, Mr. Perceval, hoping for good news, but the diagnosis was that Sir Arthur was psychotic and completely mad.

The superintendent did not think visiting Sir Arthur would be conducive to his rehabilitation at the moment as he was threatening to murder any police officer he could lay his hands on.

The Major reverted his attention to the report. It was thorough and listed the facts and events chronologically, just as he liked, starting off with the first grave desecration at St. Mary's Church and culminating with the recent discovery of Professor Bailey's antecedents.

The newly promoted chief constable had inherited an establishment of one superintendent, one detective inspector, four inspectors, twelve sergeants and ninety-five constables to police a population exceeding 100,000.

His detective inspector now sat facing him.

"Excellent Meadowbank. You are to be congratulated. A damn fine report, if I say so myself. The Bailey lead looks promising don't you think?"

Even though the major had been a career army man, his retirement had taken him into the police service at deputy chief constable level. With his immediate commander being Sir Arthur, this had given the major a good insight into how not to lead a disciplined body of men, if he needed such practical knowledge. He had encountered many senior and junior officers in the military, who were aloof, remote, arrogant and possessing infinite knowledge, but not many had worn these attributes with such pride as Sir Arthur.

The truth was, Sir Arthur's demise was no loss to the constabulary or the town, and as far as Major Little was concerned it was a blessed relief that had not come too soon. There would have been quiet celebration from the mayor to the newest recruit now that the Guardian had printed the story detailing the former chief constable's mental breakdown as their front-page news.

Major Little was particularly grateful to Meadowbank. He would never admit this to him of course. It would have been very unprofessional, but once he had been told of the incident that occurred in this very office a few days ago, the major realised that it had been the final nail in Sir Arthur's coffin as far as his career went. The major could never condone violence towards an officer whatever their rank, but he wished to hell he had been a fly on the wall when Meadowbank landed his knockout punch.

He did not think Sir Arthur had a lot to complain about. The man had enjoyed a full and varied life, rising to the rank of colonel, receiving the honour of a knighthood from the Queen and finally achieving the position as chief constable in his seventies, an age when most men would put their feet up, but not Sir Arthur. Now he could look forward to receiving two hefty pensions paid into a bank account while he dribbles and stares at the white walls of the sanatorium.

Meadowbank did not answer his chief constable. He thought it was far too early for congratulations. There were still five unsolved murders hanging over the town.

Apart from anything else, Meadowbank could not help but feel partly or perhaps even wholly responsible for Sir Arthur's breakdown. He had a temper that could suddenly flare into a raging fury, he was well aware of that and fortunately it had only reared up on a couple of occasions and involved the arrest of offenders. Meadowbank did not worry about that, it was considered quite acceptable to strike a wrongdoer if the need arose. It was at the officer's discretion as to how much force he used to effect an arrest, to protect himself or a member of the public and Meadowbank had never abused that right, but if someone needed 'a bloody good 'iding' he would gladly oblige. He could not justify the presumption of self-defence with Sir Arthur Lawrenson. The man was elderly, seventy-three years old and had not offered or threatened violence to Meadowbank or Abberline. He had simply abused his authority and it was now clear to everyone that he was ill and not of sound mind.

He could not reconcile his actions. Meadowbank regretted striking Sir Arthur and angrily brushed aside humorous comments from other officers. Even Huggins referred to him as a hero, which was something he knew he was not and corrected his sergeant in no uncertain terms.

It was only a robust intervention by Abberline in defence of Meadowbank's action that prevented the inspector's immediate suspension. He had told Major Little that Sir Arthur had goaded, provoked and threatened Meadowbank to levels that no reasonable person would tolerate. His final remark to Major Little had been the masterstroke in defending Meadowbank. He said that if Meadowbank had not struck Sir Arthur, he most certainly would have.

The pressure was beginning to show on the detective inspector and he prayed that Abberline would come up with something conclusive. He wanted to nail Jack the Ripper and he needed to do it fast.

"Did anything turn up from the search of Bailey's home, Inspector?"

Meadowbank blinked away his wandering thoughts. At last he had some good news to pass on.

"Sergeant 'Uggins an' Constables Knagg an' Ponkerton did a grand job. They 'ave found some letters addressed t' professor from John Buck an' proves wi'out doubt they were 'avin' an 'omosexual relationship. I've asked Sergeant 'Uggins t' bring 'em 'ere once 'e 'as booked 'em ont' t' evidence record. A couple o' 'em are quite sexually explicit an' mek fer unpleasant readin'. They are all signed bi John Buck. Wi've obtained samples of 'is 'andwritin' an' signature from 'is 'ousekeeper. Th' most recent one is arrangin' their meetin' on t' night t' reverend wer killed. Sergeant 'Uggins 'as questioned neighbours oo saw t' professor leave 'is 'ome sometime after eight thirty, which fits in wi' their nine o'clock rendezvous, as mentioned in th' letter. 'Is 'ouse off Winkley Square is only a short walk t' church. So wi now know oo wer wi' John Buck t' night 'e died, but did t' professor beat 'im t' death an' string 'im up in t'church? Some'ow I don't think so. Fer a start t' professor wer not physically capable. It would 'ave teken great strength t' 'oist up an eleven stone man like that. A feat not possible fer t' professor."

"Unless there was more than one person present. An accomplice perhaps?" Major Little added.

"Wi 'ave considered that theory sir an' discounted it. Wi know both men wer lovers an' 'ad arranged t' meet at t' church. T' letter an' th' reverend's records confirm that, so it's safe t' assume it wer t' professor's semen in th' reverend's mouth which indicates that they performed a sexual act together. Why would they want someone else there?"

"Who knows what goes on in their perverted minds, Inspector? Suppose though, they did not know someone else was present.

Someone from the parish had called round for instance and witnessed the two men engaged in unspeakable acts and decided to take the law into their own hands. Your report states that Huggins found the vestry door unlocked and later the key was found on the Reverend Buck's person, so any one could have entered the vestry."

Meadowbank thought about this for a few seconds.

"An interestin' theory sir, but if someone else was present an' so disposed, why only murder th' reverend that night, why not t' professor as well?"

"We know that nothing was stolen from the church. The charity collection was still there as were the religious artefacts on the altar. The only sign of anything untoward, apart from a dead vicar of course", he allowed himself a brief smile, "was the upturned table in the vestry and the smashed bottle of wine. Your report states it was 'clear evidence of a disturbance'. So John Buck was involved in a disturbance with someone that cost him his life. You've already said Bailey could not have been responsible for hanging the vicar and twenty-four hours later Bailey disappears from his laboratory in the middle of the night. Leaves it unsecured and gaslights burning. There is a large amount of blood nearby on the street. A pathologist has confirmed some of the blood is the same blood group as the professor's and some belonging to Edmund Froggatt, the journalist, and a week later both bodies turn up in the river. Cause of death to Bailey was a fatal blow to the head. His skull and brain had been pulverised. Another feat of exceptional strength and Froggatt also had similar massive head injuries."

Meadowbank was enjoying this exchange of ideas. Sir Arthur had never once asked for Meadowbank's thoughts or opinions on an investigation, he only ever expressed his own theories and conclusions.

"So Inspector, our two homosexual lovers are murdered within twenty-four hours of each other. That cannot be coincidence."

The chief constable's office appeared much the same as it did on Meadowbank's last visit a few days ago. A portrait of the Queen hung next to one of her royal consort, the Prince Regent. Sir Arthur's certificates, diplomas and awards had been removed and a large aspidistra now sat on top of a bookcase, containing rows of heavy, dark, bound legal volumes. The desk was the same, but it was cluttered; gone was the leather diary that was always squarely positioned with ink-well and pen close to hand.

Meadowbank noticed that the papers strewn across the desk were notes and transcripts of the reports piled on his own desk, and the inspector was enjoying a mug of tea with his chief constable, which was another first for him.

The office looked the same but felt very different.

"I agree sir, it cannot bi coincidence. Possibly a blackmail attempt that went wrong. Wi also know that apart from t' professor's nocturnal 'abits, 'e was buyin' t' cadavers stolen from t' graves. What wi don't know yet is oo was supplyin' t' bodies. I think t' body o' John Wilson wer being delivered t' professor as t' others 'ad been. Summat went wrong with t' deal fer whatever reason an' t' professor wer murdered. Some'ow Froggatt got involved, whether 'e wer followin' one o' 'is own leads or wer even involved in t' crime still remains a mystery, but 'e wer also murdered around t' same time an' location as t' professor, t' blood proves that. And there's Froggatt's brown cloth cap that wer found at t' scene b'hind th' infirmary. It's unmistakably 'is. There can't bi two folk in Preston daft enough t' wear summat like that. An' ah'll tell yer summat else fer nowt sir, any one t' get t' better o' Froggatt would 'ave t' bi an 'andful 'imsel'. Froggatt wer as strong as a bloody ox. 'E used t' bi a circus strong man an' bare knuckle fighter." He winced, remembering his own experience of Froggatt's violence.

"Remind me of how the three bodies ended up in the river?"

"Wi found an 'and cart near t' Walton Bridge."

"That's the lowest part of the river isn't it?"

"No sir. The lowest crossin' point is the ford at Penwortham Bridge, ont' t' other side o' town. Any 'ow, t' cart wer stuck in t' mud an' part o' it wer 'igher than th' 'igh tide mark so it wer fairly untouched bi th' watter. Wi found quite a lot o' dried blood which t' surgeon 'ad a look at an' did whatever they do an' confirmed t' blood matches t' professor's an' Froggatt's, or at least are t' same blood types. That's t' say human an' not animal. Wi also found a large 'ammer that would appear t' bi th' weapon used t' murder Froggatt. It 'ad bin below t' tide level so wer unfortunately clean as a whistle. We've nowt t' link little John Wilson's body wi' being dumped along wi' t' other two, but it meks sense that it wer."

"To sum up Inspector, is it fair to say that whoever murdered John Buck is also responsible for the deaths of Professor Bailey and Edmund Froggatt and is more than likely responsible for the grave-robbing incidents?"

"In a nutshell sir."

"So our suspect must be either big or strong or both and I agree with your report Inspector that these deaths have no connection to those of Elsie Lupton and Beatrice Babbitt. Have we heard anything from Scotland Yard? We should have heard something by now."

"I wer 'opin' that yer would bi able t' confirm that sir."

"Hmm! I'll speak to the commissioner myself. I've known Colonel Sir Edward Bradford for some time now. Damn fine fellow I'll have you know."

The sound of a military band and cheering drifted in through the open window.

"Are you joining me at the Town Hall in the celebrations and giving the 'Fighting 40th' a jolly good send off?"

Meadowbank had no idea that was the old nickname for the South Lancashire Regiment that carried more battle honours than any other.

"No sir. I've enough battles o' mi own t' fight at t' moment."

Chapter Twenty-Four

The wizened gamekeeper known as Preston Pete stood impassively before Verity. His alert blue eyes against his weathered leathery face were the only clue that he might be younger than he appeared. He wore a green belted tweed jacket and matching breeches, knee high socks, sturdy brown boots. A mass of wiry grey hair pushed against a tattered cloth cap. And he stank of wood-smoke and sweat.

Uncertain how to address the estate gamekeeper, because of his peculiar name and to avoid any over familiarity with her staff, she remained seated by the writing desk and said,

"Mr. Preston. My husband has left me instructions that you, as the incumbent keeper, are to oversee the re-stocking of game and fish. We are trying to establish a shooting and fishing estate to rival the best in the country and it seems to me the lake is woefully down on fish stocks." She discreetly put a hand to her nose.

"Wi' respect ma'am 'ow could ya possibly know that?" His voice had a smokers rasp to it.

"Because I visited the lake yesterday and it appeared lifeless. There was no evidence of any fish whatsoever."

"In t' early spring last year, afore t' master passed on, I 'elped introduce o'er 2,000 rainbow trout in that there lake. It wer' a trial run t' see 'ow they'd fair f' next season an' there ain't no fishin' tekin' place at present, so should bi at least that many fish still int' watter."

She listened intently in an effort to understand his dialect.

"Well that's strange, as trout feed off the surface taking flies and insects, I am puzzled as to why there was no activity on the surface. Could pike be taking them?"

"Pike ma'am? There ain't no pike in yonder lake"

"Well Mr. Preston, I think you'll find there is one present in the lake. I saw one take down a coot yesterday."

"It wer'n't a pike ma'am."

"What else could it have been?"

"It wer'n't a pike I know that."

"How can you be so certain?"

"Cause I've worked th' land rownd these parts fer donkeys year an' know th' lake better than anyone. There 'as never bin a pike in Ribbleton Lake."

"Could there be some other predatory fish in the lake?"

"Such as?"

"I don't know Mr. Preston. That is why I am asking you. You are supposed to be the expert." She was finding his obtuseness annoying.

"It could 'ave bin a zander I suppose."

"A zander Mr. Preston? I've never heard of that before. What is it?"

"A fish ma'am."

"Yes, I realise you meant it was a fish, but what kind of fish? Does it have teeth? Is it big, small?"

"Similar t' pike an' often called a pike-perch. It prefers watter wi' poor visibility. I've never sin it m'sel' but 'ave 'eard stories o' one int' lake. It could tek a bird I suppose."

"Is the visibility in the lake poor? I've never heard of that being a factor to the presence of a particular fish."

"Aye, 'appen it's a bit murky I suppose."

Verity gave a sigh of relief.

"So there is a fish similar to a pike in the lake?"

"Might bi."

"Is this zander an aggressive fish?"

"I don't know ma'am. I've never 'ad owt t' do wi' it."

"I mean as a species, Mr. Preston, a species. What does the zander prey on?"

"I would imagine other fish ma'am."

"And what effect will a pike-perch have on the new fish stocks?"

"That remains t' bi sin, if it at all exists."

"Does my husband know there is this pike thing swimming around our lake?"

"I only said ma'am, there might bi a zander. Until one's caught or netted we'll ne'er know."

"Did you not think to mention it to Mr. Cadley's grandfather, before he paid for these two thousand trout to be introduced to the lake?"

He shrugged his shoulders,

"No. It's only a rumour ma'am an' may not bi true. I'm not convinced."

"Well, my father arrives in two days and he is keen on fly-fishing and will no doubt be catching whatever is still in there. And for future reference Mr. Preston, please do not bring firearms into the house." She nodded at the twin barrelled 12-bore shotgun he was cradling under one arm.

"I tek m' gun everywhere I go ma'am. Wouldn't feel reet not 'avin' it wi' mi like."

"Well it's your choice, but if you want to remain in employment here I do not want to see that weapon in this house again. Do you understand that? You will have to leave it unloaded and by the back door in future. Now thank you Mr. Preston and good day."

She gave him a forced smile and watched him slowly amble from her morning room.

Chapter Twenty-Five

The briefing was taking place in the magistrate's court, next to the police station, as it was the only room that could accommodate the twenty officers assembled.

Meadowbank was seated in the clerk of the court's chair facing the stony-faced policemen. He was the senior officer in charge of the raid that was taking place that evening.

Detective Constable 'Ponky' Ponkerton was sat near to him as he was giving the briefing. 'Ponky' let the lads settle down along the benches and light up their pipes and cigarettes before standing up and announcing,

"Right lads, I know you are eager to learn what this is all about so I'll put you out of your misery. I've received information that several dogfights will take place tonight, in an empty mill on Birley Bank, which is a side street running parallel with New Hall Lane. This will be a big event and has been organised by the Stock brothers, Charlie and Eddie. They are the main targets tonight. If you don't know what they look like stick with someone who does, as a lot of you will know these two charming fellows. They are behind most of the dogfights in Lancashire. They'll have a lookout on the street that Sergeant Huggins and myself will take care of so the rest of you can get in quickly. I want a couple of you to go round the back to cover the rear exit. Any volunteers?" He nodded at two raised hands. "Thanks lads and be on your toes round there, it'll be very dark. The rest of you, we go in hard with staffs drawn and let them have it. If they want to see a blood sport we'll give them one to remember."

Before the assembled officers dispersed, Detective Ponkerton called out, "One more thing gentlemen, keep your eyes open for Titus Moon. He's another villain you should all be familiar with and I believe he'll be having a wager or two with the Stock brothers tonight. Inspector Meadowbank here wants a word with him, so he can be detained on sight".

Dog fighting was flourishing in the northern mill towns and was a lucrative business for trainers and breeders of fighting dogs, usually the Staffordshire bull terrier. The Stock brothers were the middlemen who organised the venue, providing the pit and stolen dogs as bait and as a warm up for the fighting dogs. They were also breeders and had a reputation for raising first-class killing dogs.

Meadowbank found the sport of dog-fighting horrific but the main reason he had volunteered to join the raiding party was to follow up Ponky's tip off. He was eager for the opportunity to nab the Stock brothers red-handed and anyone else who was sick enough to regard it as a sport but it would be a bonus to catch up with Titus Moon.

Tonight would also be a distraction from his ever-demanding meetings with the chief constable, the mayor, the local press and the police committee.

Sergeant Huggins was armed with a service revolver holstered to his hip. Experience had proved that any surviving dogs would need to be destroyed, as the injuries, even to the stronger dogs, were always hideous and a bullet to the head was considered the most humane method of dispatching these pathetic trembling and shivering animals. It was nearly impossible and dangerous to attempt to rehabilitate a dog bred and trained purely to kill.

"Think on lads, yer 'ave my permission t' kick t' livin' daylight owt o' these sadistic bastards," Meadowbank said grimly.

Thirty minutes later, four polished black carriages, each drawn by two mares, trundled out of the police yard on Earl Street. Meadowbank took the lead and sat up front with the driver. The twenty officers were divided amongst the first three carriages and the fourth was a secure prison wagon.

Around the same time as the police convoy made its way through the town, Titus Moon entered the Old Dog Inn on Church Street, a popular ale-house amongst prostitutes and villains.

As soon as he saw the dark brown trench coat he instantly recognised it, but it certainly was not Ol' Joe wearing it.

"Oye you! Where did yer get yer coat from?" Titus was now stood at the bar next to the dark curly-haired man.

"And what the fuck has that got to do with you?" With one elbow on the bar he turned to face Titus, revealing fully the tattooed eye in the middle of his forehead, and placed his pint pot down.

"That coat belongs t' a good friend o' mine."

"Well put it this way, the old fucker won't be needing a coat where we left him." He chuckled and stared at Titus challengingly.

Titus knew he was a navvy and what that meant. The Irish man was not alone. Six more navvies were at the bar with him, all now watching Titus.

The inn was fairly busy and the palpable atmosphere of confrontation quickly spread to the other customers. Those near the bar moved away and those sat at tables looked on eagerly, and even the piano player, Major Harry Carruthers, a man with a dubious army career and tolerated only for his amusement value increased the tempo with his own rousing rendition of Glorious Beer.

The landlord, Thomas Cumming, understood the situation perfectly and reached for a pickaxe handle he kept behind the bar.

Titus could have walked away, left it until another time when the odds were in his favour, but that was not his nature. There was more than honour at stake; there was revenge for Ol' Joe.

He gave a smile of conciliation and at the same time swiped the pint pot off the bar and smashed it into the leering face, dragging

190

the jagged remnant of the handle along his cheek and neck, slicing through the main artery.

Their confrontation was over in seconds and Titus had made his response seem effortless.

The navvy, his eyes staring like a mad-man, made clucking sounds and pressed his hands forlornly against the blood gushing out in pulsating spurts as his knees began to buckle.

No one moved for a few seconds then Titus, with a look of satisfaction, turned round, about to leave. Numerous rough hands grabbed him, some by his arms and one pulled his hair, then the fists rained in. He put his arms to his face and kept his head down.

The landlord, like an experienced lumberjack swung the axe shaft at the nearest navvy, making a sickening crunch as it connected with bone. Two of the navvies produced knives and turned their attentions to the landlord. That was when tables were upturned and drinks spilt in the rush forwards. Old men, young men and one or two women jumped on the navvies. The whole pub erupted. Stools were flung, fists and clog-shorn feet spiralled and flurried in the bustle. It was impossible to tell whether the screams and shouts were of pain or excited enthusiasm and the ensuing pandemonium, already a violent brawl, was accompanied to music from the very drunk Major Carruthers, now rattling off My Old Man (Said Follow the Van).

Titus took the opportunity to abandon the chaos he had started, leaving behind at least one dead Irishman.

The police convoy was slowly wheeling along Church Street, when a bar stool smashed through the window of The Old Dog Inn and landed in the road, a few feet from the first carriage.

"Hell fire! What's 'appenin' 'ere?" Meadowbank said to the driver.

The disturbance coming from the ale-house reached a crescendo of noise.

The convoy stopped at Meadowbank's command and he jumped down.

'Ponky' approached him.

"Whatever is happening here sir, we could do without the distraction. We need to get into position, sharpish." He sounded concerned.

"Aye, I know that lad. You carry on. Ah'll sort this lot owt an' catch up wi' yer later."

He entered the pub failing to see Titus Moon watching from a doorway across the road as the convoy continued its mission.

Meadowbank tried to shout for order and calm without success. There were bodies all around. A fat woman with a broken and bloody nose screamed hysterically by the door. The only navvy still standing was held by four men shouting obscenities as a fifth threw punch after punch, many missing the navvy and striking the four holding him. The landlord recognised the police inspector and immediately dropped the pickaxe handle and joined in his calls for order.

Meadowbank spotted the navvy on the floor lying in a pool of blood and pushed his way towards him. On a closer look it was obvious the man was dead.

With more resolution he climbed onto the bar and shouted as loud as possible.

One by one, heads looked up. Many of the faces knew the detective inspector and he knew them.

He held out his warrant card and shouted,

"Police officer. What th' 'ell is goin' on 'ere? There is a dead man on t' floorboards an' I want everyone's name and address afore ya even think o' leavin'."

The landlord spoke up first,

"Fair do's Inspector! These flamin' navvies attacked us. We were defendin' us selves."

Meadowbank jumped off the bar with a thud shaking the sawdust-strewn floorboards.

"What abaht that poor sod Tommy? Oo sliced 'is throat then?" Meadowbank knew most of the town's licensees by name.

"It were Titus Moon Mr. Meadowbank, but 'e were provoked like. Told Titus that t' brown coat 'e bi wearin' came off 'is dead mate. Even I know it belonged t' Ol' Joe. 'E was gloatin' an' 'ad it comin', mark mi words," said the landlord.

"Titus Moon! Are yer sure Tommy?"

"I should b'. I've barred 'im enough times inspector".

"Reet. Listen up you lot! I want these navvies put somewhere secure fer t' night. We'll pick 'em up int' mornin'."

"I can lock em int' cellar. There's a room away from th' ale that'll 'old 'em," offered the landlord.

"That's grand Tommy. Ah'll bi summonsin' a doctor t' examine t' deceased. Anyone oo 'as injuries they want lookin' at can stay behind."

He realised that he could not leave a possible murder scene to arrest dog fighters, no matter what contempt and loathing he felt for them. Titus Moon was now a murder suspect and the inspector was confident he would soon be in custody, so accepted the landlord's offer of a pint while he wrote the names and addresses of everyone in the room in his note-book.

Chapter Twenty-Six

George and Rosie Morgan of Morgan's Breweries, Bristol had finished their tour of the manor with Verity and retired to the drawing room for afternoon tea.

"You and Charles have done yourselves proud Verity. It is the most magnificent home I have ever set foot in," her mother beamed.

"And you say there is a lake full of rainbow trout?" George Morgan asked.

"Well that's debatable father. Our gamekeeper assures me that two thousand rainbow trout were introduced to the lake in spring last year. I've visited the lake and it doesn't feel right. Everything is too quiet, too still."

"Just how I like it," her father joked.

"I find it a bit a creepy," Verity confessed.

"Creepy! What does that mean?"

"It is hard to describe father. I saw a waterfowl paddling across the lake and it was afraid of something. Look, I know what you are thinking, 'how can I spot a frightened duck or whatever?' Well this poor thing was terrified and you did not need to be a zoologist to recognise that. And then suddenly it was gone. Something grabbed it from below. I have been telling myself that a pike was responsible but..." she did not finish the sentence.

"Of course it was a pike. What else could it have been? In a freshwater lake set in a mature lowland meadow, undisturbed for years, ideal conditions for a pike to grow and grow and one could no doubt take a bird like that, no problem."

"The gamekeeper, Mr. Preston has suggested there may be zander roaming the deep."

"Now there's a challenge. I've only ever seen one zander landed and it was a monster. Over three feet in length and weighing near fifteen pounds. Good Lord Verity, why did you not tell me this

194

sooner? I would have been here weeks ago at the prospect of catching one of those beauties."

"George! We are here to see our daughter and granddaughter, not on a fishing trip." She winked at Verity, "Men. I dare say Charles does not talk incessantly about fishing does he dear?"

"Hold on a minute Rosie. This is not some ordinary fish. A zander is very rare and has only been recently introduced from Europe to a few select lakes. If this lake does have a zander it will enhance the estate's reputation for freshwater fishing no end. Anglers would pay a small fortune for the chance of landing one. I wonder who introduced it to the lake?"

"See what I mean Verity. Your father can only talk about brewing beer or catching defenceless fish."

"You wouldn't say defenceless if you came face to face with one. A natural predator, a born killer."

"George! For God's sake, please no more talk of this zander thing." There was no mistaking the edge to her voice.

George and Rosie Morgan were a handsome couple. Both in their mid-fifties, slim, not too tall and wore the finest clothes. His woollen suits came from a bespoke tailor on Saville Row, his shirts and shoes hand-stitched by Jermyn Street craftsmen and Rosie was no stranger to the fashion shops of Bond Street and Mayfair.

George had started work at twelve years of age as a cellar-boy to a local tavern and within ten years he was brewing his own beer for the tavern owner. Within another ten years he was the biggest brewer in the south of England and was now looking to expand to the north, unknown territory to the lad from Bristol.
He had already begun talks with Sir William Cadley about renting a disused mill in Manchester, in an area with the unusual name of Strangeways. The mill was owned by Cadley Industries and now that he had seen the premises for himself, knew it would make an ideal brewery.

"I don't suppose you would care to accompany your wife, daughter and granddaughter on a shopping trip to town tomorrow. Hmm!"

"If it's all the same with you dear, I'll stay at the house, catch up with some paperwork and familiarise myself with the estate," he said with a coy smile that did not fool anyone.

"In other words Verity, your father will be fishing tomorrow. He'd rather spend time chasing something that might not even be there than spend time with his family."

George knew his wife was annoyed, but he was not prepared to miss such a rare opportunity in the angling world.

"Come on Rosie, that's unfair. You are talking about one day out of five. I don't think that is unreasonable, do you Verity?"

Verity did not want to get involved in her parents squabbles and normally would not have bothered in the least with whatever her father chose to do, but the thought of him or anyone for that matter, fishing in that lake sent a shiver down her spine.

"Father, it would be nice if you did come with us. I could show you round the town and give you a tour of the huge Cadley cotton mill."

"That's right! Gang up against your poor old father. Well I'm sorry ladies but tomorrow will be spent fishing in the lake and that is final."

He waved them off at around eleven o'clock and watched the carriage disappear along the driveway. Rosie was still not speaking to him and Verity had pleaded one more time for him to accompany them, but his thoughts were already elsewhere.

The weather was nearly perfect, warm and not too bright. With a bit of rain it would be ideal conditions. It goes without saying that George had brought his fishing tackle; he took it everywhere just in case the opportunity of 'casting off' presented itself.

His obsession with fishing, and that is how his wife regarded it, was in contrast to his image. Very wealthy, extremely ambitious,

196

a self-made businessman who could not keep still for five minutes when at home, but put a fishing rod in his hands and he could remain stationary for hours on end.

George followed the same route Verity had taken a few days ago. His step was jaunty and as he looked around, the country gentleman way of life suddenly appealed to him. He had always lived in the city and up until now had never considered moving into the countryside.

A large wicker basket with a leather strap was slung over his shoulder. It contained everything needed for a day's fishing, including a packed lunch and a bottle of Morgan's Best Bitter.

He unpacked the basket on the jetty and placed certain items into the boat. The rowing boat appeared to be in excellent order and had obviously been stored undercover and in 'dry-dock' for the winter. The outside looked freshly painted and inside was clean and more importantly, dry.

George decided to head for the middle of the lake, as that is where the deepest water would be. To his left was the large reed-bed; the opposite shore was fringed by dense woodland and the widest part of the lake to his right, where the land gently sloped to the water line.

The dark water rippled as the oars effortlessly moved across the surface and within a few minutes George had found an ideal spot. He tossed the small anchor over the side and was surprised to see how much rope followed. It must be thirty feet deep at this spot, he estimated, and considered that this certainly improved the fishing.

Live bait would have been preferable. Any small fish around eight inches long would usually catch a pike, but as live or dead bait were not available to George he was using a home-made artificial lure, a supply of which was always stored in the basket.

He wore waist-high rubberised waders looped over a wool sweater and he always wore his 'lucky fishing hat', one of waxed canvas.

At last he cast the lure and sat back, the bamboo rod cradling in the rowlock.

Time was not important, patience was. George had no idea how long he had been dozing when he felt a tug on the line. Instantly alert, he watched and waited staring at the red float that was flipping side to side.

He felt it again, this time the reel spun wildly as he tried to grasp the handle. Whatever had taken the bait was big and swimming away.

He began to work the line, gaining control, the rod arcing with the strain, pulling back whatever was on the other end. George deftly wound the reel backwards, trying to guess what he was about to land, not daring to believe it was the zander.

No! I could not be that lucky, he told himself.

Slowly the line was wound onto the reel and George strained to see into the black water where the catgut vanished and then he saw something pale a few inches below the surface.

Excitement gripped him. Was it the silver belly of a large fish? As he lifted the rod ever higher, acutely aware of the strain, the rod recoiled backwards and the line went slack, a shredded end suddenly hanging limp above the water.

George cursed. He had been so close to landing a big one. As he stood looking over the side, searching the rippling lake for his lost catch, he felt something heavy bump the bottom of the boat. Puzzled, he leaned further over the water and in the murky depths he could see movement. Something was there and it was very pale, almost white.

A second knock to the boat was more powerful and louder, lifting one side high out of the water. George was caught by surprise and fell forwards, headfirst into the lake.

He quickly surfaced and calmly grabbed hold of the edge of the boat. He was a strong swimmer and had no fear of water, no matter how deep. As he attempted to haul himself into the boat, his right leg would not move. Something had caught his wader.

With his free foot he kicked against his right leg and his heel hit something rigid. He kicked out again, harder and whatever had snared him let go. With both legs free he heaved himself up, then stopped abruptly. Both ankles were now held firmly. Whatever was holding him had a grip of iron. Countless causes ran through his mind in an effort to stay calm. He quickly discounted debris, pondweed or discarded fishing line as the culprit, so with all his strength pulled against the boat in an effort to heave himself aboard. To his horror he felt the hold on his ankles move, as if something was readjusting its grip.

Christ! Whatever has hold of me is alive! His mind screamed.

"Help! Help!" Panic was taking over as he shouted across the lake.

It felt as if lead weights were strapped to both feet. He could not move them an inch in any direction.

Then it started.

Slowly and inextricably he was being pulled into the lake. He felt movement around his body as more of him became submerged. The top of his waders were tugged violently adding to the great force drawing him down, feet first.

"Help! Please. Help meeee!"

His white-knuckle grip was weakening and the boat was very nearly overturning with his effort to hold on, spilling the contents of the boat on top of him.

The water was now up to his neck and he became more and more aware of being grabbed and held. A hand with no nails and white as a pickled embryo broke the surface of the water and gripped his shoulder, brushing his face.

George screamed and screamed as the arm appeared and then a head, devoid of hair, revealing a huge split to the skull, caused by a cutlass long ago. A face poked through the surface of the lake, now lapping George's chin. It was so close to his own he could clearly hear it giggle with amusement. The whitewashed face of the man was shrivelled and draped with strands of pondweed, the

199

grinning mouth revealing a toothless black hole, but it was those eyes that sent George insane, moments before he vanished under water. They were empty craters emanating hatred and the mid-morning daylight glinted on the abnormally white face which continued to grin as facial muscles twitched and flexed leaving no doubt that this creature was very much alive.

Two soft wrinkled hands gripped George's head and the black mouth with bloodless lips pressed against an eye socket, sucking noisily as they stayed locked together. George flailed his arms madly as they sank ever deeper, other hands still pulling eagerly at his feet.

Chapter Twenty-Seven

On the night of October 31st, R.M.S. Dunottar Castle weighed anchor in Table Bay with the spectacular Table Mountain rising as a massive silhouette 3,556 feet above the city of Cape Town.

There was much excitement on board as news of the war was eagerly awaited.

Some senior officers expected hostilities to be over during the seventeen days at sea, anticipating capitulation by the Boers. The bundles of Western Cape newspapers dragged on board from the teeming barges bobbing around the ocean liner soon revealed the true picture.

The invasion of Natal had started. General Penn Symons had been killed at Talana Hill, forcing his four thousands troops to retreat to Ladysmith. Twelve hundred British infantry had surrendered at Nicholson's Neck and Ladysmith, Mafeking and Kimberley were surrounded by the Boers and under siege.

This was not the news that Sir Redvers Buller wanted to hear. He still had to assemble his army at Port Elizabeth, six hundred miles away and that would take another four weeks.

The British forces were to stop any advance into the Cape Colony until reinforcements arrived from England and India, then the army were to march to Pretoria for a major offensive against the Boer capital. This plan was now in disarray.

Charles and Henry did not openly react to the news that several thousand Boers surrounded Kimberley, intent on starving the town into submission. They gave each other a knowing look, both realising that their mission had become even more dangerous if not impossible.

Churchill and Frobisher made their farewells on the dockside at Cape Town. Shaking hands they vowed to get together, once the war was over, which certainly would not be before Christmas, as often claimed by some senior staff. Churchill was heading for

Ladysmith and would take the train as far as Durban. This was a quicker route than staying on board the Dunattar and sailing around the Cape of Good Hope and along the Indian Ocean to Port Elizabeth.

Charles avoided Churchill and the two men never spoke to each other again.

Henry had not told Charles of Churchill's suspicions. He would pick his own time and place and on board the Cape liner was neither. Be it true or false he knew Charles would have reacted with blind fury, taking into consideration his unreasonable loathing of the man. Ever since the notion had been put to him, Henry had spent many hours contemplating the possibility that Charles was responsible for the corporal's disappearance and could not escape from the same conclusion as Winston's.

He would not sit in judgement of Charles. They had killed several men between them for various reasons. He knew Charles was a gritty fighter and quite deadly with a knife, which was at odds with his upbringing, being the heir to a second-generation family empire and fortune. Henry had seen Charles fatally slice a man's throat with one swipe of his Bowie knife. It had happened during an attempted robbery on them both by four Dutch sailors on the Cape Town waterfront years ago.

After enjoying a couple of bottles of Pinotage in The Mount Nelson Hotel and strolling along the waterfront looking for a cab, Charles and Henry were confronted by the four sailors, who had obviously drunk more than their intended victims that evening and drunkenly ordered them to hand over their wallets, each brandishing a knife to reinforce their demands.

In a flash Charles whipped out his Bowie knife from the sheath inside his jacket and lunged at the nearest matelow cutting through his neck in the blink of an eye. The three remaining sailors gawped at their comrade as he fell to the ground clutching his throat, his legs twitching bizarrely. Immediately Charles struck again and plunged the knife into the chest of the nearest unfortunate sailor and then chased the other two as they fled for their lives. Only when Henry had caught up with Charles, as he feverishly searched the dockside alleyways, did he snap out of his crazed blood lust. A sight he would never forget.

He knew very well that Charles was not only capable of murder, but he seemed to savour it.

They spent the night at the Tudor Hotel, Greenmarket Square in the city centre, the oldest hotel in Cape Town and enjoyed their first hot bath since leaving Southampton. An evening in the hotel restaurant and bar was their immediate plan and the following day they would set off for Kimberley, but first Charles would have to contact Verity and his father to confirm their safe arrival.

Verity and her mother had arrived home a good few hours before Charles landed in Cape Town.

It was only four o'clock and already mother and daughter were looking forward to dressing for dinner in their new outfits.

Dobson was by the steps to greet them.

"Dobson, where's my father? Not still fishing surely?" She enquired helping her mother from the carriage.

"I assume so ma'am. Mr. Morgan has not been back to the house since he left just before lunch."

Verity looked at her mother, attempting to appear unconcerned.

"Is this father's normal behaviour as a house guest, mother? Putting aside good manners for a day's fishing?" She chided with a false smile.

"No, it is not. I'm worried Verity."

Those words were the only corroboration to her own fears that she needed.

"Dobson! Get help quickly and make to the lake. My father's life is in danger."

Verity grabbed Beth and with all pretence of caution now gone said urgently, "Mother, follow me."

They ran round the side of the house, through the walled garden and onto the track that led to the lake. It only took them a few minutes, even wearing a petticoat, flounced dress and heeled boots.

The rowing boat was still anchored in the middle of the lake, exactly where George had left it. Items lay on the surface, not even moving or causing a ripple. A wooden bait box, pages of a newspaper, an apple and a waxed cotton hat, kept the boat company.

Rosie froze and howled her husband's name like a snared wolf. Verity ran along the jetty, already sobbing against her daughter's head. Her mother was still by the reed-bed, hands to her face, her weeping soon becoming violent convulsions.

Dobson and Preston Pete arrived minutes later, both hopelessly out of breath, but the gamekeeper continued for another hundred yards past the jetty. He waded into long grass and shallow water, tugging on a rope until a coracle type boat made of oil cloth stretched onto a wicker frame floated into view. He climbed in with surprising agility and with the one oar paddled purposefully across the lake. The loaded shotgun rested on the seat next to him.

The small oval boat bumped gently against the larger one and the gamekeeper was not surprised to find it empty.

"Mr. Preston! Mr. Preston! Pleaseeeeeee!" Verity wailed.

He stood up and slowly shook his head.

"Noo! Nooo! Father! Noooo!"

"Oh my God! George! George! George!"

Dobson could not decide whom to offer solace to first, so walked away instead as if searching the shoreline, leaving the two women to flounder with grief.

Preston Pete collected the personal flotsam of the late George Morgan and put them back in the rowing boat. He wedged the anchor inside his boat and slowly headed for the jetty, with the solemnity and dignity of a funeral procession.

Charles was sat in the manager's office of the Tudor Hotel, reading the telegraph that had been delivered to him. There was a knock on the door as the manager entered.

"Excuse me Mr. Cadley. I've left my keys."

He gave the manager a look of disbelief.

"No, no, that's fine. I've finished thank you." He stood up slowly, lost in thought.

The manager moved to one side as Charles passed and said,

"Good evening Mr. Cadley. Enjoy your stay at The Tudor Hotel"

"What? Oh yes!"

He met Henry at the bar. He was half way through a bottle of a chilled local Chenin blanc and enjoying every mouthful.

"Try this Charles. It's nearly as good as the stuff you produce at Stellenbosh. Have you had a reply to your telegraph by the way?"

"Verity's father is dead." He handed Henry the telegram.

He read it, then read it again and looked at Charles not knowing what to say. He had never seen him so shaken.

"Drowned in the lake in a fishing accident a few hours ago. The police are dragging the lake tomorrow for his body." Charles said shaking his head. He picked up the full glass of white wine and drank it in a few gulps.

"I need something stronger Henry." He said gasping.

Henry ordered two brandies and told the barman to leave the bottle.

"What am I going to do Henry? I should be with Verity, not six thousand bloody miles away. Poor George. Poor Rosie. Oh God! Verity! Verity!" He took a few deep breaths to compose himself, He could see Charles was close to tears.

"Henry, I am going to have to get the first steamer back to England."

"I understand Charles. That is a matter for you and your father."
He did not remind him that the return journey would take at least another seventeen days and three million pounds in diamonds were locked in a safe a few hundred miles away. He would let him work that out for himself.

Chapter Twenty-Eight

Geronimo answered the phone then handed it to Meadowbank.

"Boss! It's for you. Mr. Abberline."

Meadowbank nearly threw the report he was reading into the air in his rush to reach for the hand piece.

"Fred! Am I glad t' 'ear from yer? What's t' news down there?"

"Not good I'm afraid Albert. We can find nothing whatsoever to link Professor Bailey with the Ripper murders in '88. All the evidence has been gone through again, which is why it has taken so long. If anything we have proved that he is not Jack the Ripper."

"'Ow's that Fred?" His tone reflected his plummeting excitement.

"On the night of Sunday the 30th of September when Elizabeth Stride and Catherine Eddowes were murdered, Bailey was in Edinburgh for a medical conference and he gave a talk that evening. We have verified this of course so that crosses him off the list of suspects, I fear. Anything to report your end Albert?"

"List o' suspects! 'E was our list o' suspects."

"I was afraid you might say that. No leads at all then? Not even any letters?"

"A few crank letters 'ave been delivered 'ere an' t' local news agencies, but they are obviously from fantasists or flamin' nutters. We've compared 'em wi' t' photographs o' th' ones you received durin' th' original investigation, but there's nowt vaguely similar. Ah'll bi honest Fred, yer news 'as come as a bit of a blow. Wi 'ad 'igh 'opes on t' Bailey lead."

"So did I Albert, deep down, but one thing investigating Jack the Ripper has taught me is never build your hopes up on a lead or piece of evidence. I've made that mistake and the case fell to bits and it was back to square one."

Meadowbank went on to explain the connection between Professor Bailey and the Reverend Buck and how it is now believed that at least one suspect was responsible for these deaths and that of Edmund Froggatt. He also informed Abberline about another unlawful killing he had come across the previous night and how Titus Moon, the gravedigger, was now wanted for questioning regarding that death.

Abberline could recall the gravedigger's name and thought it strange that so many deaths appeared connected in one way or another, as if there was a common thread to them all.

Meadowbank corrected him. Not all of them. The two Ripper murders stand apart as far as the other murders are concerned. Abberline joked about the new chief constable and asked how Meadowbank was getting on with him? Only Abberline could get away with joking about an issue still very raw to Meadowbank and he described Major Little as a 'breath of fresh air'.

As their conversation was drawing to an end, Abberline informed Meadowbank that he would be returning to Preston in the next few days and would bring with him the original Ripper letters to definitely confirm or refute the authenticity of any of the letters now held at the incident room at Preston, as being written by the same hand.

The raid on the dogfights had gone according to plan; at least that was some good news thought Meadowbank. As he read the report he could picture Huggins and Ponky staggering along the road, singing, holding beer bottles aloft as they approached the lookout, who they described 'as a vagrant earning a few bob'. That would not have stopped Ponky whacking him over the head with his truncheon, as soon as he was within striking distance. The poor sod was out cold for three hours and when he regained consciousness he could not remember what had happened or how both arms came to be handcuffed around a lamp-post.

Huggins had put another two 'bobbies' on the rear door increasing the number there to four. Apart from their police issue truncheons they also possessed unauthorised cudgels and pick-axe handles with the intention of clobbering anyone who approached and ask questions later, which was often a common-sense policy to adopt.

Huggins had reported that their entrance was quick and efficient and caught everyone around the fighting pit by surprise. Confrontation was imminent and a number of the cowardly dog fighters adopted a pugilistic stance, warning the coppers not to come any closer and describing in great detail what they would do to them if they did.

Meadowbank smiled to himself reading this. The first rule of engagement with twenty-two police officers with fire in their bellies, armed to the teeth and ready to take on the whole criminal world, was not to stand there and challenge them to a fight. There was no referee to stop this one. The uniformed line charged forward, yelling, what will later be described as an ungodly war cry, and waded in amongst the ruffians and thugs who were so used to ruling their underworld with fear. These villains did not have the mental awareness to recognise the time to surrender or retreat and made a serious misjudgement. It was one thing to treat the local constabulary with contempt and insolence but it was another to forget or fail to understand that most of the coppers came from backgrounds similar to theirs, by grafting a living any way possible.

The Stocks brothers and ten of their cronies made a retreat to the rear door, leaving behind their half-dead pitiful dogs. Fortunately, the four officers waiting and listening for such a move were all hard buggers. Two of them were ex-Cold Stream Guards who enjoyed nothing better than a good scrap to clear the sinuses. They had wedged the door open and could hear the commotion indoors and the sound of footsteps running towards them.

Charlie Stock, the older brother, was the first to emerge like a startled rabbit and if he did not see it, he would certainly have felt the lead-tipped truncheon smash into his mouth and the leather cudgel slap the side of his head, hard. It became a free-for-all. Hand to hand fighting in the great tradition of every man for himself. These four officers took the brunt of the violence that evening. Their unflinching defence of that door reminded Meadowbank of the battle at Rorke's Drift, twenty years earlier, where 105 British soldiers held back 4,500 Zulus. It brought a lump to his throat thinking about it, no-matter how extreme his analogy.

These 'bobbies' had taken a pastin', that much was clear from the report but they had obviously given better than they got as all twelve of the 'defendants' as the report describes them, were taken into custody unconscious and beaten to a pulp. Their injuries were not considered by the charge room sergeant to be life threatening and he authorised that they be detained, charged and presented before the magistrates in the morning.

It was Sam Huggins that Meadowbank felt for. He had the unpleasant task of destroying twelve dogs with a well-aimed bullet to the head. He described some as appearing fit and healthy, others quite mad, as if rabid, but most were in a pitiful state. A few officers had to look away, eyes brimming with tears at the blood and torn pieces of flesh hanging from trembling terriers. Two Staffordshire Bull-Terriers, one white the other a brindle lay in the pit on their sides, soaked in their own and each other's blood, too exhausted and injured to move or raise a head. With lolling tongues and chests heaving, they looked at Huggins as he approached with his smoking revolver. As if understanding completely, they both closed their watering brown eyes and barely breathing, lay there like hounds in front of the master's fire. Huggins would later say even with their grotesque injuries, it was a look of contentment from both dogs as if they knew at last that peace was only seconds away.

It was the first time Meadowbank had heard of his sergeant shedding a tear, but Huggins was not just thinking about the barbaric cruelty of dog fighting, regarded by so many as sport. He could not help but compare this evenings horrific cruelty to that inflicted on Elsie Lupton, Beatrice Babbitt, Reverend Buck and countless more victims whose names he could not even remember.

The report concluded with details of the thirty-six men and women arrested that evening and outlined the charges, ranging from aiding and abetting cruelty to animals, aiding and abetting in the staging of illegal dog fights, obstructing police, assault on police and wounding with intent to resist arrest.

There should have been more arrests made, but Meadowbank understood that logistically that was not possible, due to a transport and manpower shortage. The spectators who appeared to have got away scot-free would be dealt with by way of a summons, personally delivered by a uniformed constable and ordering the person named to appear before a magistrate on a certain time and date.

Meadowbank was satisfied with this, even though there was no sign of Titus Moon.

Chapter Twenty-Nine

Titus Moon had run back to Starch Houses as fast as he could. It had gone midnight and thankfully Mags was in bed noisily sleeping off a skinful of something or other. The dying embers in the grate gave off little glow and the oil-lamp on the table had long burnt itself dry.

He opened the back door slowly, watching Mags, before slipping out into the yard and pulling the door shut after him. The yard was laid with granite flags, each measuring three-feet square. One end of the small yard was for the midden heap and ash pit, both piled high and rarely removed by the council. The flag Titus wanted was a particularly loose one by the wall. Sliding his fingers into the space between the adjoining flags and ignoring the foul liquid seeping around him, he lifted one edge up with a grunt and rested it against the dividing yard wall. In the exposed earth was a hole containing a cigar box and inside that was a wad of money wrapped in an oilcloth. Titus retrieved the box and unwrapped the money. His intention was to leave town quickly and head for Manchester or Liverpool. Even though he had never set foot out of the borough of Preston in his life, he had a good idea that he had to cross Ribbleton Moor.

The door behind him opened noisily and Titus, still squatting, spun round to face Mags. She was gawping at the cash he was holding.

"Where's that come from?" She eyed him suspiciously.

"None o' yer business." He stood up and put the money in his jacket pocket.

"If it's bin 'idden on mi property it's varra much mi business. What th' 'ell is goin' on Titus. Where've yer robbed it from?"

"Mags! Leave it will yer? I'm goin' t' ground fer a bit. T' law will bi 'ere varra soon. Tell 'em what yer like, but 'ave no doubt that t' man I killed t'neet deserved it an' I'm not spendin' time fer

212

a thievin' scum that 'ad it comin'. I'm off Mags, I need t' leave town t'neet."

"Wait a minute Titus," she shouted, "You're tellin' mi, after all I've dun fer yer, nursed yer back from t' dead, fed yer, clothed yer, given a few bob for suppin', that you've 'ad a bloody fortune 'idden in mi own back yard? Now yer walk away wi'out s' much as a goodbye. I thought wi 'ad summat Titus. Summat goin' fer us." She moved closer and took his arm, whispering, "I love yer Titus, don't that mean summat?"

"It don't mean owt if I'm 'angin' from t' gibbert. It's too late Mags, there's nowt fer mi 'ere anymore. I need this money. It's mi livli'ood. I didn't want yer t' find owt that I'd gone 'til mornin'. I'm grateful fer what yer dun fer me Mags. I am that, but it's time fer mi t' move on."

"Grateful mi backside! Yer were goin' t' scurry away like a rat, leavin' mi wi' nowt, not even peace o' mind, lettin' mi fret mi sel' sick. Is 'e dead, is 'e alive, 'ave coppers got 'im? Is that all I've meant t' yer Titus, nothin'?"

"Mags! I 'aven't time fer all this. Ah'll let yers know where Ah'll bi, once dust 'as settled like. I promise."

She knew he was lying.

"Titus 'ow abaht an 'ug fer owd times sake? Yer can't deny mi that, surely?"

He walked into her open arms and embraced her warmly, reassuring Mags that they would soon be back together.

As they pulled apart, she put to good use her pickpocket skills and slipped a hand inside his jacket, deftly removing the cash and dropping it into her apron pocket.

She moved away towards the house, allowing Titus to leave through the yard gate.

"God bless yer Titus. Ah'll miss yers." Her tears were real.

She had reached the back door when there was an almighty roar.

"Yer thievin' bitch!" He charged after her.

Mags was in the house, slamming and bolting the door behind her, then racing for the front door. She heard the crash and knew he had got into the house and was closing on her.

Mags panicking, fumbled with the key, trying to lock the front door and feeling the floorboards pound as Titus stampeded towards her. She had the only key, which suddenly clicked the bolt into position as the handle twisted violently and the door shuddered under his hammering blows.

Mags knew she had to get away from the house and hide. The door would not hold for long. Before she had got to the end of Starch House the front door gave way with a loud crack of splitting wood, which she could hear only too clearly. She rushed along the dark street trying to think, but her heart was near to exploding with fear. The streets were deserted and for once Mags prayed for a copper to walk round a corner. She had no idea where she was going, but sobbing, ran along Back Lane for her life. Suddenly she slipped on horse dung and fell forward violently, landing on her knees and outstretched hands, the sharp cobbles gouging out chunks of flesh.

Mags lay sprawled on the road, wincing at the pain screaming from her knees and palms.

Ger up lass! She told herself, *Ger up.*

As quick as she was able, Mags was on her feet and could hear the thumping echo of hob-nailed boots not far behind. She staggered towards Clayton's Gate, a ginnel that led to Friargate and disappeared into the darkness as Titus raced into view.

On reaching Trinity Square, where Mags had fallen, he stopped and listened, having no idea which of the many lanes to take. Then he heard a loud crash come from Clayton's Gate and he ran towards it.

Mags had fallen into a pile of wooden crates in the near pitch black, but carried on towards the gaslights of Friargate not twenty yards away. She knew this was her only chance of escape.

Titus could see Mags hobbling along the passage, silhouetted against the light at the far end. With renewed determination he chased after her, his powerful arms and legs swinging and striding nearer. She sobbed at the deafening rhythmic pound of each boot closing in on her and with relief reached the main thoroughfare to the town centre.

A strong hand grabbed a handful of hair and yanked her backwards, lifting her feet off the ground as she disappeared back into the darkness of the ginnel. Before she could plead for her life his hands were around her throat, squeezing hard. He pushed her against the wall, her head slamming into the brickwork, his huge hands locked around her throat. His face was only inches from hers and even though she could hardly make out his features in the blackness, she could feel his breath and hear him panting like a large hound. He never said a word as he crushed her windpipe, starving her lungs of oxygen.

Her eyes were being squeezed from their very sockets, her mouth wide open in a scream that never left her throat. Her face turned blue as carbon dioxide poisoned her blood and her body started to twitch with convulsions.

He paid no heed to her hands flapping frantically against his arms as he strangled the woman who had saved his life. The choking rasps stopped and Mags went limp, her chin dropping forwards onto his hands. Still squeezing with all his strength he lowered Mags to the ground and only then let go. He quickly found his money and walked away without giving the body of Mags a second glance.

Chapter Thirty

The chief constable of the county constabulary, Henry Martin Moorson, had moved with unusual efficiency and already four large boats had been brought by wagon from Preston docks. The boats were identical, painted black, ten feet long and displaying the Preston borough coat of arms of the lamb of Saint Wilfrid supporting a flying pennant. The vessels were now moored off the east shore of Ribbleton Lake, ready for launching. The jetty, where several police officers stood, was located on the south side.

Access to the lake for the large wagons, each pulled by a four-horse team, was along a farm track with several gates from the driveway. It was now late afternoon, but a decision had been made that an initial sweep of the lake should be conducted in the remaining hours of daylight.

The officer in charge of the search operation for George Morgan was Chief Inspector Eddie Gilbert. He was in uniform, wearing brown leather gloves and a peaked cap that had replaced the silk hats which senior officers once wore. He was talking to a sergeant and pointing across the lake with his pace-stick from the edge of the jetty. Each boat had three police officers on board, one to row and two to use the grappling hooks. Several volunteers, including Preston Pete, all kitted out in waders and carrying a long pole, stood in the shallow margins.

Chief Inspector Gilbert waved his pace-stick and the signal was understood by the officers waiting to push the boats from the shore.

The boats formed a line, thirty feet from each other and every similar distance, the oarsman would steady the boat as the grappling irons were flung into the lake, systematically following the points on a compass as a guide to the area searched, each sweep dragging the grappling iron along the lake-bed.

The four-pronged hooks would often snag and a hard yank usually allowed them to continue dredging the muddy lakebed.

Suddenly there was a shout from a constable struggling with a taut rope indicating something had been hooked.

Verity and Rosie Morgan stood on the banking watching intently. Sir William Cadley was with them, having arrived a few hours earlier on a train from London. He had an arm around Verity's shoulder and even though he was wearing a cashmere overcoat, felt cold and gave an involuntary shudder as the activity centred on the nearest boat.

Two officers strained to pull the rope and then on the count of three gave a concerted tug. The prong moved towards them below the surface and they could feel something heavy moving with it. Grunting with effort they fed the wet rope behind them through their hands and the oarsman went to the side, ready to haul in the catch. An object burst through the surface and was quickly taken hold of by the constable. It was heavy, but he pulled it aboard and looked with horror at the slime-covered breastplate and entanglement of white bones and pondweed that dropped into the boat.

The haul of assorted skeletons and pieces of ancient armour were taken ashore while the remaining boats continued searching.

Officers lifted the tangled, stinking mass on to the jetty, poking through the aquatic detritus that clung to everything. There was a breastplate, a long-bladed rusting rapier, scraps of a leather jerkin and bones, human bones, which were remarkably white.

There was a further shout from the lake as a constable held aloft a complete skull he had fished from the depths.

"Good God!" Sir William cried out, turning Verity's gaze away.

Chief Inspector Gilbert looked on in disbelief, saying to the sergeant,

"What's that bloody lunatic playing at? This is not a fairground treasure hunt for Christ's sake. Sergeant! Order that Constable to maintain some discipline."

The chief inspector turned round hoping that the incident had gone un-noticed by the family, but one look at Sir William, Rosie Morgan and Verity told him otherwise.

Sir William looked on in horror, not daring to believe that the remains of his dear Lucy had been found after all these years. His feelings moved like a wave from heart-crushing sadness to unimaginable relief as he stared at the white skull gingerly held aloft by fingers gripping an eye socket.

Rosie was quickly reassuring Verity, who was very close to fainting on the spot, that it could not possibly be her father's head, entirely devoid of flesh and featureless in just over twenty-four hours. It just wasn't possible, she confirmed, even if there was a shoal of flesh-eating zander in the lake, she added in response to Verity's hysterical conclusion.

The uniformed sergeant, holding the cylindrical, cone-shaped voice amplifier shouted, "Officers on search duty will not display any findings until returning to shore."

"I don't like the look of this at all Sergeant. There must be a whole graveyard down there." Chief Inspector Gilbert said quietly, stroking his grey-flecked untidy beard.

The three boats had reached the deep part of the lake, the spot indicated by Preston Pete where Mr. Morgan's boat had last been anchored. The iron hooks splashed into the lake and continued to recover more human evidence as the search progressed.

Dark clouds gathered ominously around the Pennines threatening heavy rain for the evening. The chief inspector had instructed that this would be the end of the days search and ordered the sergeant to hail the boats to the jetty, once marker buoys had been positioned for the resumption of the search the next day.

The hooks were pulled on board the last boat, apart from one that refused to move. As if engaged in a tug-of-war, three officers pulled on the rope and slowly more of it emerged from the lake.

Everyone was now watching the action on board the remaining boat, the other two having joined the third, docking by the jetty.

A buzz of excitement flirted between the officers as they took the strain and heaved. They knew this was no fish and as if to confirm what they were thinking, the body of George Morgan broke the surface with two prongs of the hook protruding through his stomach. He was naked and whiter than milk. His eyes were missing, revealing dark empty sockets and his mouth was agape, as if locked in mid-vomiting and already a home to leeches and pond-snails.

The officers had the presence of mind to lash George to the side of the boat rather than manhandle him aboard. Satisfied that their catch was secure they set off for the jetty. After only a few strokes of the oars the bow hit something solid and the boat came to a sudden stop, sending two officers staggering forwards.

"Tek a look Bill. Wi must 'ave 'it a log or summat." Asked Smithy, the rower.

Bill, being the nearest, tentatively stepped forwards in true land-lubber style and dropped to his knees, peering over the bow into the murky water.

"Aye! I can see summat like, but it's not a branch or owt. Ah'll reach in an' try an' shift it." Said Bill.

He rolled his sleeve up and stuck his hand in the cold water inching past his elbow trying to reach a pale coloured object floating a few feet below the surface. Straining with effort his fingers tickled whatever it was but he could not quite get hold. He plunged his arm further down ignoring the cold water lapping round his shoulder, soaking his tunic and the soft fleshy feel of the object he was now touching, did not register immediately.

Then the thing turned over and the black eyes and mouth fixed in a maniacal grin, looked up at the officer through the gentle

219

ripples. Before he could bring his arm back or scream in terror, two hands, lightening quick, grabbed the submerged wrist and sunk like a lump of pig iron, pulling Bill over the side in one movement, headfirst into the lake.

He disappeared in less than a second.

There was pandemonium on board as his two colleagues rushed forwards calling his name.

Chief Inspector Gilbert witnessed the careless officer fall overboard and swore under his breath, expecting him to resurface at any time. It soon became clear to him that the situation had become serious, as the chief inspector would later describe it in his report, even though to the likes of Preston Pete and the young constables present, the situation was way past serious.

The remaining boats were manned once again on the command of the chief inspector and headed for the deep water.

One of the constables was still leaning over the body of George Morgan, hysterically shouting Bill's name. The other constable on board took off his helmet and tunic and without waiting for any instructions, dived into the lake, swimming deeper and deeper. The water was cloudy, freezing and swirling with pond-life minutiae. He was about fifteen feet below the surface when he stopped to look for any sign of Bill. The keel of their boat was visible and the underside of the other rowboats came into view. He was at the limit of holding his breath and having decided his search was futile at these depths, started to rise to the surface effortlessly, when movement caught his eye. Through the gloom of endless particles, floating and swirling, something was swimming towards him, fast. It was impossible to identify, but it certainly was not Bill. The thing was moving at great speed like a hunting shark, coming straight at him. Then he realised there were more of them, a shoal of creatures with black eyes and white skin, moving in unison towards him through the dismal depths.

With a kick of his feet he propelled himself higher and broke the surface a few yards from his boat.

A look of relief swept across the face of the only officer still on board as he saw his mate gasping, but alive.

"Bloody 'ell! You 'ad mi worried then Smithy." He called out to the man treading water.

"'Elp! 'Elp mi quick! There's summat..." He did not finish the sentence and disappeared as quick as Bill had.

Chapter Thirty-One

It was only 7 a.m. and already nudging seventy degrees as Charles and Henry left the hotel. They intended walking to the railway station to catch the 11a.m. train north, but first needed to arrange supplies to be sent from the waterfront traders and loaded onto the train.

The evening before, they discussed at length the options and feasibility of continuing onto Kimberley, and Charles felt that he had no choice. He was not prepared to give up a fortune in diamonds without attempting to recover them. But he needed Henry's help and doubled his payment to £20,000. Even before his pay rise Henry was certain they could get into the besieged town. ·

The railway would normally run the 880 miles from Cape Town to Mafeking, stopping at the Kimberley station, but the Boers had blown up the bridge across the Modder River. Now the train only went as far as the Orange River, some seventy miles from Kimberley and heavily defended by the Loyal North Lancashire's.

Charles and Henry had been refused permission to travel from Orange River to Kimberley as part of Lieutenant General Lord Methuen's relief force, but had been sold two cavalry horses as a gesture of goodwill by the general.

Henry had a contact with a firearms dealer from his days with the Cape Riflemen, a German gunsmith located not far from the livery warehouse.

They chose the Mauser model 98 hunting rifle, bolt action and used by the German Army, but more importantly for Henry it was an improvement on the model 95 already proven to be so effective by the Boers against the British. For a revolver there was only one choice, advised Henry, and selected the official

British Army sidearm manufactured by The Webley and Scott Revolver and Arms Company Ltd of Birmingham.

The boxes of ammunition were also despatched to the railway station and Charles and Henry jumped onto the wagon, escorting the munitions under their watchful gaze.

The British expeditionary force was divided into 14,000 troops under the command of Lord Methuen, whose objective was now to relieve Kimberley and Mafeking, at the same time as Sir Redvers Buller, commanding 21,000 troops, would break the siege at Ladysmith on his advance to Pretoria. It was the Boers' plan to wipe out or contain British forces in these strongholds and prevent contact with reinforcements.

Henry's plan was to reach Kimberley before the British Army, and Charles had agreed that they would be far quicker and more likely to slip through the Boers' offensive, scattered around a wide perimeter, than following in the shadow of Methuen's advance.

They discovered that most of the train had already been requisitioned by the army, sending support and supplies to the defences at Orange River, but they managed to find two seats together in the last carriage, after supervising the loading of their equipment and horses into the livery carriage. Both men were buoyant as their journey so far had gone without mishap and even Henry appeared to have put aside his suspicions surrounding the missing service man from the Dunottar. He had been more concerned with Charles's reaction on hearing of his father-in-law's death. Fortunately the conversation with his father seemed to have injected a dose of reality into Charles and postponed his desire to return home. Sir William had volunteered to attend Ribbleton Manor immediately to comfort Verity and monitor the police operation. He had pointed out to his son the complete impracticality and even ludicrous notion of leaving South Africa at this stage and jeopardising the recovery of the diamonds, which Charles reluctantly agreed was not an option.

Orange River station was approximately 600 miles northeast from Cape Town, leaving 70 miles to be covered by horse. Henry considered their chances of success with optimism. It had been a bonus finding the railway still running as far north as it did and he was surprised that the Boers had not taken advantage of sabotaging the track. He understood that the Boers expected to drive the British from South Africa for good and did not want to destroy the extensive rail network that ran north and east to the Indian Ocean, only to have to set about re-building the rail infrastructure after victory. Consequently extensive destruction of the railway system was not part of their campaign.

Only the bridge over the Modder River had been destroyed and fortified by the Boers, part of a deliberate plan to seriously interrupt any British advance.

Fortunately, Henry knew the Cape terrain, stretching from German South-West Africa to Bechuanaland and beyond as well as any native and was confident they could get into the besieged Kimberley.

He felt energised being back in Africa and realised he had been in Britain too long. A man could have nothing but still live like a king out here. He vowed to himself never to leave Africa and the final resting place of his dear Kathryne, ever again.

Diamonds were discovered in South Africa in 1867 and at that time Henry was living with his parents, brother and sister and grandparents in a two up, two down terraced house on Brick Lane, Shoreditch. His father was a slaughter-man at Spitalfields market, which meant they always ate well, compared to most, even if the meat he smuggled home were off-cuts destined as dog-food. Henry, at thirteen, had been working for several years on the construction of the East London Railway; a steam operated underground system that ran from Shoreditch under the Thames to Newcross, stopping at Whitechapel and Surrey Docks. Henry's job was looking after the some of the hundreds of horses that dragged load after load of excavated earth and rubble from the tunnel. He was a stable boy and this began his lifelong love of horses.

By the time he was twenty, Henry had saved enough money to pay for a single passage to South Africa and he could not wait to leave his childhood neighbourhood, which had degenerated into a slum area and had long been referred to as 'the deprived East End'. Prostitutes, vagrants, villains and immigrants had flooded the area when Henry left to search for diamonds. His mother, brother and sister waved him on his journey from the railway platform. His father was too occupied slitting the throats of cows, pigs and sheep to see his eldest son, probably for the last time, embark on a sail-ship into the unknown.

The diamond rush continued from Hopetown onto New Rush, soon to be renamed Kimberley, where diamonds were found in 1871. Henry spent the best part of five years digging in the open-pit mine known as the Big Hole and like many others did not find his fortune. A chance meeting in a saloon bar with an officer from the Cape Colonial Mounted Riflemen resulted in Henry enlisting the following week, the same week he met Kathryne De Groot.

Orange River station could not have come soon enough for Charles and Henry. The journey had taken longer than usual even though the only stop was at De Aar, a huge remote army depot that was heavily defended, given its location in the vast northern Cape veldt. The train had come under sporadic sniper fire smashing a few of the blacked out carriage windows, but as everyone was on the floor at the first sound of gunshot, a well rehearsed procedure, no one was injured.

Charles and Henry did not waste any time when saddling their horses and sorting out their equipment and within a matter of hours of arriving at the Orange River they headed north across the bushveld.

They followed a trail known to Henry rather than keeping to the rail-track and thus hopefully avoid Boer-raiding parties. They were on the edge of the Great Karoo, a huge semi-desert savannah that stretches north east from Cape Town, once a vast inland sea and now a drought stricken dusty plain that had claimed the lives of many travellers unprepared for the heat and desolation.

Henry was aware that Boer guerrilla units and rebels from the colonies used the Karoo as base camps, so he chose an old Hottentots bush-mans camp, one he'd used before as a Rifleman. It was still hidden by a small rise and shrubbery and an ideal stop for the night. Even though the temperature dropped dramatically once the sun had disappeared they dare not risk lighting a fire, so curled up under their blankets, the horses unsaddled and tethered.

Henry was awake, staring up at the clear night sky and myriad of stars when he heard a noise above the rise. He jumped up and crawled to the top of the sand dune. A large herd of Cape Mountain Zebra were grazing nearby and Henry smiled to himself, when their heads went up, alert. Something had disturbed them. He saw movement to his right and took out his binoculars immediately spotting at least six Boer commandos moving on foot, slowly towards their position, skirting round the zebras and downwind.

"Damn! How the hell have they spotted us?" He said under his breath.

Henry sprinted towards Charles, still asleep and shook him hard, holding a hand towards his mouth. Charles woke and the look on Henry's face told him enough.

"Boers, hundred yards away. They know we're here. You saddle the horses. I'll hold them off," he whispered.

Charles moved quickly and Henry grabbed his bandoleer of ammunition and saddlebag, throwing himself at the top of the rise. His rifle was already aimed and his first shot was a thunderclap in the night's silence. The nearest Boer less than fifty yards away dropped instantly with a bullet through his chest. The zebra herd stampeded revealing double the number of commandos he had initially seen.

The Boers had gone to ground but were returning fire. Henry knew they would soon circle round them. They had no choice but to make a run for it. He pulled two sticks of dynamite from his saddlebag, lit them with a match, had a quick peep then lobbed the explosives. He dashed towards the horses. Charles was already on his mount, holding the reins of Henry's, saddled and ready.

There was a boom and flash as the dynamite exploded. Henry jumped onto his horse as it reared, startled by the explosions, but with a quick flip of the reins they were away, galloping into the night.

After a mile or so of hard riding, Henry slowed his horse and spoke to Charles.

"It won't get much closer than that."

He was smiling. Charles was not.

"How did they get onto us so quickly?"

"Either followed our tracks or more likely they spotted us earlier in the day, waiting until dark for the ambush."

"Do you think they'll come after us Henry?"

Henry gave a short laugh, "Most definitely. I bagged one of them so they will be out for blood. We should head north east towards the Riet River, get onto harder terrain and make it more difficult for tracking."

"I must say Henry, I did not expect our mission to be compromised within a matter of hours and we are still a good day's ride from Kimberley."

"Not to mention the several thousand Boers entrenched around the town and now we are being pursued by an execution squad," he joked.

"I'm glad you find this amusing. I am relying on you getting me into the town rather than being taken prisoner and shot before we get there." Charles said, as he turned round, peering into the moonlit desert.

"We had better get moving then." His heels jabbed the horse for more speed with Charles right behind him.

Chapter Thirty-Two

The search of the lake had so far failed to recover the bodies of the two officers. Everyone involved in the search now wore a cumbersome life jacket on Henry Moorson's instructions. Twelve boats formed a line across the lake and extra officers, supplied by Major Little, assisted the search operation. Apart from each boat being manned with four constables, the entrance to the estate needed policing to keep out the press and public. One or two photographers had walked cross-country and managed to get shots of activity on and around the lake, which ended up in the papers and eventually forced the county chief constable to hold a press conference. Tents had been erected near to the jetty; the larger one dominating the clearing beyond the jetty was on loan from the commanding officer of Fulwood Barracks. It was intended for search personnel to rest and take refreshments and to provide Chief Inspector Gilbert with somewhere to sleep at night. After the three days since his arrival to search for George Morgan, the chief inspector had not left the scene, washed, shaved or changed his clothes and was looking close to the point of collapse.

Chief Constable Moorson and Sir William observed proceedings from the jetty.

"Damn strange Sir William, damn strange!"

William Cadley did not answer; instead he removed his spectacles, wiping away the soft drizzle that had started an hour earlier. He did not mention that his own daughter had drowned in the lake over thirty years ago.

Undaunted, the chief constable continued, "How are the ladies this morning, Sir William?"

"Hard to say Henry. Verity is in shock and bed-ridden and poor Rosie! Well, as you can imagine she is in deep mourning to put it mildly. And who can blame the poor woman? To find that her husband has drowned in a fishing accident was bad enough, but then to witness the tragic drowning of those two officers who had recovered his body, I'm afraid it is all too much for her. They are both under sedation by the doctor."

"Quite. I don't suppose this continued police presence is helping any."

"I'm not sure about that. I have an inkling that the activity here is somehow giving them some sort of reassurance, comfort even. Once your two constables have been found, Verity is talking about filling the lake in, but I think Charles may have something to say about that idea."

"Where did you say your son was Sir William?"

"Africa. Nearly three weeks sailing distance away. Trouble is he's in a remote part of the continent with no means of communication. This business trip could not have come at a worse time Henry. I just hope he is able to conclude affairs in the coming days and return home."

Both fell silent as they watched another bundle of armoured breastplates, bones and weapons hauled from the lake.

"Has any of this material been identified yet Henry?"

Henry Moorson pointed to two tall men stood by the opening of a tent. They appeared to be deep in conversation together.

"The two men in white gowns are from the Harris Museum. One is a professor of history the other a professor of palaeontology. The armaments have been dated to the English Civil War. There was a battle fought somewhere around here, between the King's forces and Cromwell's, so the professor is following that line. It would appear from the human remains recovered, that some sort of massacre took place and whoever, presumably Roundheads, disposed of the dead by throwing them into the lake. There is nothing recorded anywhere and of course Ribbleton Manor was not built until fifty years later."

Sir William did not confess that he had already introduced himself to the professor of palaeontology and established through desperate questioning masquerading as enquiries of general interest that all the bones so far recovered were of adult males.

He silently prayed to his wife asking for strength to get through this nightmare.

"Yes, my father bought the estate from Lord and Lady Fisher, whose family built the house around the late 1600s. This is the first I've heard about the lake being a repository for the remains of 17th century soldiers and I'm certain my father knew nothing of this." He paused in thought before continuing, "Now that I think about it, I was never allowed to go near the lake, my father was very strict about that. Perhaps he was uncomfortable about the lake. I did not spend much time here as a child, just the occasional summer or Christmas holiday. My parents tended to stay at their London home most of the time. It was only about ten years ago that they decided to live in the hall permanently."

The chief constable feigned interest in Sir William's family and fortune.

"But your father left the mansion to his grandson rather than you, his son. An unusual benevolent gesture, if I might be so bold as to say, Sir William."

"One can never accuse police officers of being reticent or indirect with questions Henry," he said tapping a cigarette on a solid silver cigarette case. He flicked the case open as an afterthought, offering the senior police officer a smoke.

"Not whilst in uniform and in sight of my subordinates, Sir William. Standards must be maintained."

"Verity believes there is a supernatural presence at work here." Sir William blew cigarette smoke, as if it was a relief saying this.

Henry Moorson looked at Sir William with incredulity. "Are you saying you believe this lake is haunted?"

"That is what my daughter-in-law believes."

"With due respect Sir William, your daughter-in-law has been through a harrowing ordeal to say the least and one should not place too much credence on what Mrs. Cadley says in her present state of mind. I would not like this sort of talk to become common knowledge Sir William. It could undermine the whole operation."

"So you think there could be something in what she says?"

"Of course not. To be perfectly frank it sounds to me to be the ramblings of someone hysterical. The lake haunted! I've never heard anything more preposterous. Take a look around Sir William; this is Mother Nature at her glorious best. An autumnal display of colour. What has happened here is nothing more than a tragic but freak accident and certainly not the work of the supernatural."

He shook his head in bewilderment and checked his pocket watch.

"Unless you want a horde of psychics, table-rappers or other charlatans descending here, I suggest Sir William, you keep such thoughts between you and your daughter-in-law. We have enough problems as it is with ghoul seekers wandering the streets of Preston, searching for Jack the Ripper. The thought of these lunatics hearing rumours of a haunted lake that has claimed three lives, well it would cause major problems for all of us, Sir William. I hope you understand the point I'm making. It would make the Greek mythology of Pandora's box seem as innocent as opening a biscuit tin. Now if you will excuse me, I have a meeting with the coroner shortly, to discuss the here and now of George Morgan and not his here after. Good day Sir William."

He turned without waiting for a reply and came face to face with Rosie Morgan.

She wore a long black woollen overcoat with the high collar turned up and gloved hands gripping the lapel, protecting her neatly pinned-back greying hair. Her watery brown eyes stared at the chief constable from dark hollows.

"A haunted lake, ghoul seekers, psychics and charlatans! What on earth have any of these got to do with my husband's death, Mr. Moorson?"

It was not often that the county constabulary chief constable was stuck for what to say.

Sir William smiled to himself, enjoying the senior police officer's discomfort.

"Er, Mrs. Morgan, ma'am. I was er, referring to comments that Sir William had expressed and erm, suggesting that we must be prepared for any eventuality. We would not want the wrong story on the front pages."

"Wrong story! Are you suggesting my husband's death was not an accident? William, what is going on here?"

"Henry was not suggesting anything of the sort, Rosie dear. In fairness he was responding to something I mentioned."

"Which was?" Her expression of determination was unmistakable and Sir William was well aware of her strength of character.

"Well you would no doubt hear it from Verity sooner or later, but she has got it into her head that there is a malevolent entity at work here." As he repeated it to Rosie he realised how ludicrous he sounded.

"Good God William! Say what you mean and explain yourself."

"Verity believes there is an evil presence in the lake, something supernatural. Perhaps having something to do with all the human remains we are still finding."

"And of course you believe the incoherent uttering of my grief-stricken daughter mourning her father's death. William, are you seriously suggesting George and the missing constable's deaths are connected to an underwater spectre?" She struggled to compose herself. "In two days time I am returning to Bristol with my husband's body, until then William I would be grateful if you would stay out of my way and have no more communication with Verity. In fact your immediate return to London would be most welcome."

Chapter Thirty-Three

The two chestnut cavalry mares drank their fill from the river while Charles replenished their canteens and Henry searched the countryside with his binoculars.

"Any sign?" Charles asked, emptying a canteen over his head.

"They are about five miles away and riding steady. That puts them no more than thirty minutes away so there's no time to delay Charles, we must keep going." The dust from the advancing column was worryingly close for Henry.

"What's the plan?"

"Quite simple Charles. Get to Kimberley before they get to us."

The Riet River, a tributary of the Vaal was too high to ford at this point, but Henry knew a place down river where a crossing could be made. Here the bank sloped either side, allowing them to wade part way then swim, holding onto to the bridle across the deepest stretch.

As they struggled up the muddy banking gunfire could be heard loud and clear and the surrounding shoreline 'whacked' as bullets struck the wet ground.

"Christ Henry! We're coming under fire." Charles shouted, scrambling harder, tugging the reins.

"Mausers. Bolt action. Means only one thing, Boer commandos. Damn!" Henry exclaimed.

They dashed towards shrub-land when Charles' horse made a terrifying shriek and dropped to the ground, eyes wide with fear, hind legs kicking uselessly and blood oozing from its neck. Charles sprawled next to the horse as bullets thudded into the saddle and the animals back.

Charles pressed the Webley below the mane and fired a single shot into the forehead, then used the body as cover as he reached for his rifle. Henry had made it to a small ridge, forced his horse to the ground and assessed what the hell was happening. Through his binoculars he could see a detachment of Boers regrouping on the opposite bank, ready to cross the river. He counted eight riders. Moving his field glasses east he saw that the column of Boer horsemen who had followed them throughout the night were only a mile or so away.

He knew their situation was desperate. One horse between them and hopelessly outnumbered, he had to get Charles up the ridge to hope for any chance of escape. Henry took up a sniper position on his belly and fired quickly and mechanically at the horsemen more than five hundred yards away. Two fell from their mounts instantly and in confusion the rest steered the horses inland as Henry maintained his rifle-fire until they dismounted and disappeared.

"Charles! Move now and bring what equipment you can," he hollered.

Grabbing his rifle and shotgun, the two heavy saddlebags and canteens, Charles sprinted towards Henry. Immediately shots rang out from across the river and bullets whizzed past Charles. He flung himself next to Henry, gasping for air and sweat streaking his face. Henry trained his binoculars on the far bank and as soon as he saw movement, aimed his Mauser and fired.

"How long have we got Henry?"

"Once the other detachment arrives they'll cross further down river and move in behind us. This group will wait till nightfall then cross the river as well. There are at least twenty riders so we'll have little or no chance of shooting it out. We have to make our move now, both of us on one horse and put in as much distance between us and them as possible."

Charles nodded, it made sense and was probably their only chance, apart from waving a white flag, but he suspected these particular Boers were not in the mood for taking prisoners of war.

Within a few minutes they were once again heading towards Kimberley.

It was not even noon and it was already a crazy 110 degrees and no shade from the burning sun. Henry had ridden the horse hard for over an hour and they both knew she could not keep up the pace much longer, when suddenly a decision was made for them. More shots rang out behind them. Charles turned awkwardly and saw a line of horsemen, not half a mile away, gaining fast.

"Henry, we'll never outrun them. They are nearly upon us. Make for some cover." He shouted into Henry's ear.

There was a kopje of rock, cacti and desert grass to their right.

"Come on girl!" Henry whispered, "not far now. They'll look after you lass."

They were off the mount and throwing their kit to the ground. Henry unfastened the saddle and removed the bit and bridle, giving the horse a slap on its rear, quietly telling her thanks and farewell as the mare cantered away.

On their bellies they waited and watched the Boers dismount out of range, then spreading out in a crescent formation, their senior officer raising an arm, signalling to move forwards. Stooped in a crouch the commandos approached their position. Henry spotted more activity and realised the remaining Boers had crossed the river and were now swinging west in a wide semicircle, to cut off any escape.

"Doesn't look too good eh, Henry?"

"I must admit I've been in better situations." He took out the last of the cigars that Winston Churchill had given him and remarkably, the thin metal case had kept it dry, which could not be said for his matches. Undeterred he rummaged in his saddlebag and with a huge grin produced a spare box of matches.

"Who said there's no such thing as God?" And he closed his eyes, savouring the best Havana that money could buy.

"There is something I want to tell you Henry." Charles looked at his companion in deadly earnest.

"This sounds rather ominous Charles old boy. Not a dying declaration I hope, a few words from a condemned man?" he joked, examining the glowing ember.

"I suppose in a way it is. I need to share this with you before I meet my maker or rot in hell."

"No use looking to me for forgiveness Charles, I'm an atheist."

"For what I am about to tell you Henry, the pope himself would not offer me salvation."

Henry replied with equal seriousness, "Look Charles, whatever you want to tell me, I don't want to hear. I'm not having you unburden your soul to me, while I'm staring down the barrel of a gun so you can wipe the slate clean with the Almighty. It doesn't work like that Charles. We are all responsible for our actions whatever the final cost. We've all done things we've regretted. That's life. Why should you be any different?"

The large cactus towering above them shuddered and squelched as bullet after bullet zipped through the fleshy plant showering them with pulp and chunks off the succulent.

"Save your confession Charles and add a few more souls to your redemption list." He pressed his cheek against the stock, closed his left eye, found a target and fired.

The barrage of Mauser rounds that returned fire was unrelenting, pinning Henry and Charles face down in the dust as the Boer commandos crawled closer.

Then it went worryingly quiet and a few seconds later a distant rumble could be heard, a sound that Henry instantly recognised. He turned on his side and looked back expecting to see Boer horsemen charging forwards, but instead saw a regiment of Cape Colonial Riflemen advancing at full gallop.

Three hundred fighters of the only Commonwealth force feared by the Boers raced together in formation then split left and right around the kopjes of granite rocks, leaving Charles and Henry spluttering in a dust storm.

Henry whooped, punching the air and squeezing his eyes shut against the dust cloud kicked up by the horses. Charles had no idea what was happening, having never seen a Rifleman before. They heard a few shots fired over the din of hammering hooves, but the vastly out-numbered Boers offered no resistance.

Henry stood and watched the Riflemen disarm the commandos and instruct them in Afrikaan to form two lines, a language Henry could speak fluently. He heard a lieutenant tell them they are now prisoners of war, they would not be harmed and would take no further part in the conflict.

A troop of riders approached Henry's position and the company commander, a major cradling his rifle, dismounted.

"Major Frobisher! If I had known it was you under attack, I would have held back and watched the fun."

The big man, a good ten years younger than Henry, flashed his white teeth, surrounded by a neat red goatee beard.
Henry did not hide his pleasure and relief in seeing his old sergeant.

"Sergeant Hallam, or should I say Major Hallam?" acknowledging the crown on his shoulders, "am I glad to see you."

They shook hands warmly and there was no mistaking the respect these men had for each other.

"Charles, this is Major Alex Hallam, my old company Sergeant. Major Hallam, this is Charles Cadley, a friend and business acquaintance."

"And what business brings you into the Boer infested Karoo?" he asked, shaking Charles' hand. His accent was pure Cape Colony.

"We need to get inside Kimberley." Henry replied.

If he was surprised to hear this Major Hallam did not show it.

"Do you know Major, there are over six thousand Boers under the command of General Cronje between the Modder and Kimberley?"

"Alex, it's been more than five years so let's drop the major should we? I am now a 'civvy' in the employment of Cadley Industries." He was enjoying the Havana even more now.

"You know what they say Major? Once a Cape Mounted, always a Cape Mounted. We can take you as far as the river avoiding Jacobsdal, another Boer stronghold only a few miles west of here. Our friends over there were a reconnaissance unit returning to Jacobsdal. They must have picked up your trail. I take it you've come from the Orange River Station?"

"Yes, they were onto us within hours." Henry said.

"That is one of their tactics. Hide in the kopjes between the Orange and the Riet and intercept anything that moves. A tactic that has proved very successful. We are halfway through a three-week sortie to disrupt these reconnaissance and raiding parties and basically make life bloody hard work for the Boers. Anyway, on to more important matters. I see you are in need of horses and could probably do with a drop of the hard stuff. I do not think civvy life will have changed you that much Major."

The major shouted to his sergeant for two sturdy cobs to be brought from the reserve. He produced a bottle of whisky from his saddlebag and handed it to Henry, who took a grateful gulp, as did Charles, resulting in a minor coughing fit. The watching troops found this hilarious.

"I think Mr. Cadley prefers a more refined scotch, rather than this fire-water we drink, eh Major?" Joked Major Hallam.

"Charles is a gentleman, but I'm doing my best to educate him in the ways of the Cape Mounted".

The Cape Mounted regiment wore a khaki uniform tunic, breeches and calf-high boots. Their slouch hat displayed the regimental badge on the upturned brim. They were well armed with ammunition bandoleers across each shoulder and on their belts carried a Webley service revolver and a 12" sword bayonet.

Major Hallam made an announcement to his troops.

"Lads! Listen in. Some of you will remember Major Frobisher and for those who don't, we are fortunate to be able to offer assistance to a former regiment commander and to Mr. Cadley, who have decided to do some sight-seeing in Kimberley. They have been told it is very nice at this time of the year," he paused until the laughter faded. "We are to escort Major Frobisher and Mr. Cadley as far as the Modder, or as close to it as Cronje will allow. Lieutenant Downing's company will escort the prisoners back to the Orange River and the rest of you lucky lads will follow me, attempting not to upset several thousand Boers. Stretch your legs men, we move in thirty minutes."

Chapter Thirty-Four

His decision to leave town had not got him very far.

Titus Moon had followed the old Roman road called Watling Street, which once joined Manchester and Ribchester, when he came across the infamous Preston Workhouse for the first time. He had heard many grim tales of the poor and destitute who sought sanctuary in this huge depressing building with its central clock tower rising above the long low dormitories that extended left and right, reminding him of a giant raptor, feeding with outstretched wings. In exchange for many hours of manual labour the homeless, stripped of all possessions, would receive food and shelter for the evening, some having the pleasure of sleeping on blood and urine soaked mattresses or the opportunity of bathing in water that had the colour and consistency of cold soup.

Titus peered through the railings at the countless dark windows that stared back and found it hard to believe that 1,500 homeless and starving wretches, the majority being old, disabled and children, could be so quiet.

He did not know where he was going. The idea of heading for Manchester or Liverpool lasted until he had finished his third pint of bitter in The General Havelock Hotel and he wandered the streets with little purpose and a lot of uncertainty.

Titus in all his twenty-nine years had never left the confines of the borough and even though he was wanted for murder, he had no intention of leaving town now.

The road split in two on reaching Fulwood Barracks home of 1st Battalion The South Lancashire regiment. Titus took the right fork passing two ale-houses, The Royal Garrison Hotel and The Prince Albert Inn, both opposite the barrack's short avenue leading to a massive sculptured gateway of Longridge stone.

This is where street lighting finished and beyond was Ribbleton Moor.

Both inns were in darkness as it was well into the early hours so Titus looked for somewhere to get his head down and eventually found Moor House Farm along a deserted track opposite Moor Park. He crept into the barn and gratefully fell asleep in the hayloft.

He woke with a start. It was still dark and Titus was sweating profusely. The dreams were more frequent now; images of the priest's face closing in on him, reeking of whisky and leering with anticipation.

If it was possible he hated that man even more.

Titus had never known his parents, not even their names, whether they were still alive or why he was placed into Dr. Barnardo's Home at the age of ten months. The charity workers at the orphanage had been good to him, especially Alice, who had been more or less responsible for his upbringing until his seventh birthday, when she suddenly died of typhoid from eating rotting offal.

Then Father De la Mare arrived at the orphanage to secure the spiritual guidance of the vulnerable children. The charity founded by Thomas John Barnardo in 1866 to feed, clothe, shelter and educate children less than seventeen years of age, regardless of gender or nationality, insisted on the religious teaching of the Protestant faith. Jewish and Catholic children were passed to other institutions.

Father De la Mare was the Protestant representative who spent much of his time instructing the children in moral and religious fortitude, especially the boys and particularly young Master Moon.

Titus had been found outside the town's hospital one evening, abandoned and wrapped in a blanket, pinned with a note that simply read, 'This is baby Titus'. The nurse who found him remarked how well fed and clean the infant was who stared bright eyed and smiling from the swaddling cloth, and as the moon was big and bright that evening it seemed a suitable name.

The Poor Law Amendment Act of 1834 classified Titus as *abandoned and destitute* and he fell into the category of the 'impotent poor' with no one to care for him. As a result he became a ward of the community.

After the death of Alice, which greatly affected Titus, Father De la Mare started taking the withdrawn boy for bible readings. The orphanage administrator was pleased that the Anglican priest was showing such a close interest in the boy's welfare. His grief seemed to be making him more withdrawn, moody and disobedient, but Father De la Mare was confident he could nurture Titus back to the gleeful soul he was before Alice's death. He just needed time and God's will.

The priest however had other things on his mind that had little to do with religious sustenance or bereavement counselling and his intentions were subtle and unobtrusive at first.

Gentle conversation, sarsaparilla and cakes in the vicarage, walks in the church grounds, bible readings with reassuring touches for a scripture passage read with accomplishment. Titus was seven and had no reason to be suspicious of the priest who was kind to him even though he did not like being so close as he often was. His clothes smelt of pipe tobacco and his breath had an unpleasant sour odour Titus had never encountered before. Over a period of a few weeks the priest's hands moved from brisk hair ruffling, pats to the shoulder and arms to lingering touches of his legs and 'accidental' stroking of his thighs and groin.

Titus was becoming uncomfortable with Father De la Mare's beguiling, tactile manner and his fawning attention. They were spending more time together sat on the leather Chesterfield in the vicarage parlour than the pews of Saint Andrew's.

Then Titus made the mistake of challenging the priest, asking him not to sit so close and to stop touching him. The boy was confused. The attention from the priest, his leg stroking and his whispering of the sins of the flesh were arousing feelings in him he had never experienced before. Deep down Titus knew Father De la Mare was not behaving correctly and that the wakening sensations he was feeling were wrong.

He moved away from the priest's touch and placed the heavy bible between them, keeping his head inclined to the carpet and shoving his hands in his lap. Titus was close to tears but determined not to let the priest see him cry.

In that instant Father De la Mare transformed from tutor to predator, from priest to devil. He grabbed Titus with one hand and with the other unbuttoned his clerical trousers. He shook the pleading boy violently, threatened him with damnation, an eternity in hell, while rubbing and caressing the boys' hidden erection, his demands for secrecy leaping from satanic retribution to painful corporal punishment and public humiliation.

Titus now belonged to the priest who explored the young body with his fingers and halitosis-breathing mouth. His red jowls, rough with prickly stubble, rubbed uncomfortably as those wet lips enveloped those ever so young ones.

The pretence of ecclesiastical edification now dispensed with, Father De la Mare became bolder and more predacious with his advances and Titus became further withdrawn, hating the priest, hating the staff at the orphanage but hating himself more. Like a sapling in a violent storm, Titus snapped one afternoon, in the drawing room of the vicarage as the naked corpulent priest knelt before him, eyes wide with anticipation. He took hold of a heavy ornate pewter crucifix from the fireplace. It had a solid metal base representing Calvary and the young Titus brought it down with both hands and with remarkable strength for a seven year old onto the bald head and salivating mouth moving towards him. He watched the skin fracture like eggshell and blood ooze out as if the yolk had burst. The priest fell to the floor unconscious. The brain damage was instant and permanent and would render him life-long to a bathchair, his memory and mobility deteriorating faster than his advancing years and bestowing an inability to recall past events or even Titus as the assailant or how he came by his injuries. Having to fund the care for the priest in a comatosed state was a dilemma the bishop could do nothing about and the cause of the injury remained a mystery that flummoxed the constabulary.

Titus had absconded from the orphanage that very day, two weeks before his eighth birthday, not that Titus knew what date he was born, he had more important things to consider for his survival.

Samuel Huggins had ordered Lancashire Hot-Pot, informing Frederick Abberline that 'scrag end of mutton wer' reet tasty when cooked proper'. As usual, when it came to matters of food, Meadowbank agreed with his sergeant whom he regarded as a gourmet of good fare, even if Huggins was slightly obsessive on this subject.

Abberline had not yet acquired the northern palate and was reluctant to further any culinary experiments, after tasting a few disasters recommended by Huggins and Meadowbank, such as cold pig's trotters in aspic jelly, ox heart stuffed with minced liver and oats and a cow heel and rabbit tart. He could not believe these dishes were traditional favourites and asked if the kitchen could do him eel pie and mash. The cook's reaction could be heard on the street and it clearly bordered on disgust and personal offence to her cooking skills. In the end he settled for toad-in-the-hole putting his trust completely in Huggins and his assurances that Lancastrians do not actually eat such amphibians.

Meadowbank asked for a butter pie, even though it was not Friday, as reminded by the landlord, William Walmsley taking his order. He was referring to the Catholic day of abstinence and when asked if he fancied a side portion of 'Lancashire Caviar' he agreed immediately and asked for 'a spot o'red cabbage wi' it.'

He then explained to a curious Abberline that a butter pie was basically a meat and potato pie without the meat and 'Lancashire Caviar' was in fact mushy-peas, not to be confused with parched peas. Abberline was already regretting asking. He was told that parched peas are brown and hard and eaten either hot or cold with vinegar and the best cup o' peas in town are from a street vendor on Fishergate near Cheapside, whereas mushy-peas were green and mushy.

Huggins felt that description did not do 'Lancashire Caviar' justice but couldn't think of a better one at the moment.

Their conversation moved on from food to the hunt for Jack the Ripper and Titus Moon. Abberline had read the report regarding the death of Margaret Beckett, but was glad to hear the evidence directly from the investigating officer, purely from a professional investigator's point of view.

"Wi 'ave an excellent witness. Woman next door 'eard t' disturbance, 'eard Mags scream, 'eard t' back door get kicked in, saw Mags run from th' 'ouse, 'eard front door smash an' saw Titus Moon chase after 'er. Knowin' 'is reputation and fearin' t' worse, she went lookin' fer a constable, meanwhile Mags's body is discovered by P.C. 'Smudger' Woolly oo raised t' alarm. Wi've searched 'er 'ouse an' it's now clear Titus wer livin' wi' Mags in 'er back room. One o' 'er tenants 'ave said that 'e 'ad'n't bin well, 'ad nasty cuts an' what 'ave yer t' face, said it looked like 'e'd bin bare-knuckle fightin' or summat similar. It would seem summat 'ad bin 'idden under a pavin' slab int' rear yard, so presumably whatever it were is now wi' Titus. Probably stolen property o' some kind or possibly cash." Huggins stopped to take a drink of ale.

Abberline asked, "and you have no idea where he is?"

"Not a clue. My bet is though 'e'll still bi in town. 'E's a bit of a simple soul is our Titus an' won't 'ave th' nounce t' disappear fer

246

good. 'E daren't show 'is face in t' town centre pubs an' as 'e's partial t' a drink o' two, will try some o' th' inns on th' outskirts o' town, I'm certain o' that. Some o' t' lads are visitin' 'em as we speak, so don't expect t' see them fer a couple o' days." Huggins joked, then continued, "we've 'ad a report that someone's bin kippin' in a barn near t' barracks fer past two neets. It's Moor 'Ouse Farm, run bi th' Widow Pimlet an' 'er two daughters. The're a bit skittish t' challenge t' trespasser themselves so 'Smudger' 'as volunteered t' 'ave a look first thing in t' mornin'."

A thin ravaged dog nervously wandered into the pub, sniffing the air. Huggins threw it a piece of mutton before the landlord chased it out.

Chapter Thirty-Five

The sun was unrelenting in the Great Karoo and the Cape Colonial Mounted Riflemen paid no heed to the heat as they waited for further orders from their commanding officer.

Major Hallam sat on the desert sand with Charles and Henry. A large map was splayed out in front of them.

"Kekewich has turned Kimberley into a fortress," Hallam explained, referring of course to the Commander of the Kimberley Garrison, Lieutenant-Colonel Robert George Kekewich.

"The defended perimeter is approximately fourteen miles around the town, made of barbed-wire defences, mine-fields and sandbagged redoubts, some with mounted search-lights which are in constant use at night."

"What's a redoubt?" asked Charles.

Before Henry could intercede, Major Hallam continued, "A fortified enclosure, Mr. Cadley and each one is supported by a small garrison."

"What is the strength of the Kimberley garrison?" Henry enquired.

"Around 1,600 and a population of 50,000, most of them employed by De Beers Mining," replied Major Hallam.

"50,000. That must include the women and children?" said Charles.

"Yes it does. Approximately 12,000 women and 10,000 children. Christ knows why they weren't evacuated, and now the Boers have cut the water supply to the town and it's not known what the conditions will be like. As I cannot talk you out of this madcap plan, your best route to approach the town will be from the north, between the rail-track and Kenilworth village. That is the least fortified position, as most of Cronje's 6,000 force are entrenched east to west. The main danger with this approach will be from snipers on both sides." The major's finger tapped the map.

"There are numerous debris heaps, inside and outside the perimeter. These are mounds of earth and rock excavated from the mines and they will afford excellent cover. Kekewich has fortified some as machine-gun posts. It will be to your advantage to move at night for obvious reasons and certainly not on horseback. Your only chance will be a stealth approach on foot. I would suggest you make your move approaching sunrise on Sunday morning. For religious reasons, the Boers do not initiate hostilities on the Sabbath and there now appears to be an unwritten agreement that attacks will not be conducted by either side on Sundays."

Henry was smiling and said, "You are joking of course?"

"Major Frobisher, you know me better than that. That is not to say you would not be shot by the Boers or the British if seen attempting to get through the cordon. There is nothing more certain than that you would be."

A black-chested snake eagle circled overhead, searching the bushveld for the slightest movement and a flock of ostrich moved inquisitively closer to the horses and riders, pecking fervently through fresh dung.

"Time to move gentlemen. All being well we should be at the Modder River in a few hours." Major Hallam said folding his map.

There was a sudden flash of silver as Charles moved his hand at lightning speed, slicing his Bowie knife through the head of a Cape cobra that was inches from Henry's hand.

"Impressive reactions, Mr. Cadley. Very impressive." The major watched Charles wipe the blade clean on the reptile's body. He then called out, "Sergeant! Let's move it."

"How did you know that was a deadly Cape cobra?" Henry asked shakily.

"I didn't, but there wasn't time to have a discussion on whether the species was poisonous or not. Remember Henry, I need you to get me in and probably out of Kimberley and I would rather see you die attempting that venture than from a snake bite."

The troop headed north, staying within the borders of the Orange Free State and after three hours of steady riding, just as the sun was disappearing behind distant mountains, Major Hallam called a halt to the regiment.

He explained to his guests the reason for the stop. They were to await the return of his scouts, as the Modder was less than a mile away.

It was an opportunity for a mouthful of water from a warm canteen.

"You and Mr. Cadley may be interested to hear Major, of a man-eater stalking between the Orange and the Vaal," the troop commander said nonchalantly.

"A man-eater. You mean a lion?" Asked Henry.

"Of course. What else?"

"This far west?"

"Stranger things have happened."

"Well it's the first I've heard of lions around here for a long time. The Transvaal and Cape lions were trophy hunted to extinction decades ago. It's not war propaganda is it? It's the sort of idea British High Command would come up with to put the wind up the Boers. A pride of man-eaters roaming behind enemy lines."

"Not a pride, but a rogue female. We've heard it from Boer captives. They claim that in the last seven days two farmers have been attacked. What was left of them could only point to a lion kill and the Calvinists are not known for their imagination or exaggeration to make something like this up, especially one about a bad tempered bitch with a headache."

Charles smiled slightly at the quip but Henry was frowning. "I'm not convinced Alex. I haven't been away that long for the lion population to suddenly migrate this far south and west."

"It would be unusual I admit but the whole of South Africa is presently plagued with tens of thousands of troops on the move from both armies and some prides may have been displaced and driven south searching for game. It's a big country after all. Remember Major, it was only last year we had the Tsavo Man eaters in Kenya and that story was dismissed at first. It took nine months to track and shoot the two lions; by that time the pair had killed 135 workers. Food for thought Major Frobisher, don't you agree? If you pardon the pun."

Henry did not answer, either not hearing the play upon words or choosing to ignore it, instead looking away towards the sound of approaching riders.

The two scouts came to an abrupt stop near to their major. There was no salute, just a perceptible nod that was returned by Alex Hallam.

"Sir, the Boers are entrenched across the river. It would be best to circle west of Paardeberg then head inland towards Kimberley."

Major Hallam turned towards Henry, "Did you hear that Major? You'll need to cross the river about three miles east of here, then turn west towards Kimberley. At some point you'll have to let loose the horses and hide or bury the saddles and harnesses, or whatever you decide to leave behind. If the Boer scouts find British equipment this close to their lines, it would start a bloody big search party. This is as far as we can go. Good luck Major Frobisher and to you Mr. Cadley."

They shook hands. "Thanks Alex. We would not have got this far without your help. We appreciate what you and the Cape Mounted have done for us." Henry gave a wry smile and continued, "I owe you a serious drink Major Hallam." He saluted his old sergeant.

"One final word of advice Major, if I may. Should you be captured the Boers will treat you as spies and prisoners of war, not as civilian non-combatants and you would be executed." Major Hallam said sombrely.

"That's what I've always liked about you Alex. You are such a cheerful bastard."

Chapter Thirty-Six

Charles had not spoken to Verity for some time, so he had no idea that his wife was planning to return to Bristol with her mother, for her father's funeral.

Her distress and sadness at Charles being so far away and not volunteering to return home or make contact was now turning to anger and resentment, no matter how irrational. She had requested to speak with Sir William, so she could tell him exactly what she thought of the Cadley family business that kept her husband away in a time of crisis.

When her maid informed Verity that her father-in-law had returned home a few hours earlier, she was dumbfounded. She could not believe that Sir William would suddenly leave for London without any explanation and thought it strange that he did not at the very least see his granddaughter before leaving.

Even though she was still under the doctor's orders and being administered daily sedatives by a nurse, now resident at the manor until their departure for Bristol, she expressed surprise to her mother that Sir William should do as he had done.

Rosie Morgan wanted to protect her daughter and granddaughter, so did not mention to Verity that she had insisted on Sir William's departure for repeating her daughter's fanciful theories. Verity wanted two things at the moment; rest and her husband and the family needed privacy to grieve. Rosie Morgan could offer Verity the rest she craved and give the comfort and care as only a mother can do.

She decided if Charles could not be bothered to return home to his wife at such testing times, then Verity could manage without him. Verity's irrational conclusions appeared to be contagious.

After three days of searching the lake, the bodies of the two missing constables had not been found. A horde of weaponry, bones and skulls had been recovered and lay spread out in the large tent, until a decision was made as to what to do with the human remains. A local Catholic priest had suggested that they be given a Christian burial in a mass grave at the cemetery, which seemed to be the favourite course of action between the different clergy present, the police and the Corporation.

The weaponry and artefacts had already been pledged to the Harris Museum.

There were over five hundred skulls laid out in macabre rows on canvas sheets and the officers and volunteers involved in the search had moved tables and chairs outside the tent rather than take their refreshments while being watched by so many bleached skulls still having an unpleasant whiff of pond-slime.

Chief Constable Moorson was facing a dilemma. The wives of the missing officers came to the lake each morning together with a Catholic priest, praying that their husbands would bob to the surface and swim ashore, giving a reasonable explanation for their absence. Grief can be a great comfort to the bereaved but it can also be blinding to the truth.

Henry Moorson wanted to call off the search after seventy-two hours of intense activity dragging the lakebed. The forty or so officers and volunteers involved knew as well as he did that enough was enough and the lake would release the bodies when it was ready. Henry Moorson was more concerned at the cost of the operation and the reaction of the borough treasurer once the invoices started appearing on his desk. But the dilemma presently on his mind was informing the two widows of his decision to call off the search (already he had become accustomed to referring to them as the Widows Smith and Butterworth), his announcement to the Widow Morgan and finally to the press, who bombarded him with questions at every opportunity. He could imagine the headlines already, 'Bodies Languish in Lake', 'Police Left in Watery Grave', 'The Missing Become the Abandoned'.

While he considered his approach to the Widows Smith and Butterworth, favouring a direct assault combined with sensitivity and compassion but allowing no room for plea-bargaining, Rosie Morgan approached him accompanied by Chief Inspector Gilbert.

Good God! He thought to himself on seeing his chief inspector, *Gilbert looks worse than terrible. It's as if he has recently been fished from the lake then spent a week in Newgate Prison to dry off.*

"Good day Ma'am. How is your daughter this morning?" He ignored the chief inspector.

"A slight improvement thank you Mr. Moorson. I want you to know that Verity and her daughter will be returning with me to Bristol later today. You have full access to the estate and house, subject to the approval of Dobson of course, the head butler. He will be running the estate until Charles or Verity decides otherwise.

I would also like to offer my gratitude to you and your men in the commitment you have all shown throughout this gruesome endeavour." She paused to watch the line of boats perform another sweep of the lake. "I feel terrible that those two poor men have lost their lives in recovering my husband's body. It does not make sense Mr. Moorson. Poor George was already dead and beyond help, so why has the Almighty seen fit to sacrifice two lives just so I can bury my husband?" Tears appeared around her eyes but she blinked them away. Then she noticed the Widows Smith and Butterworth stood by the shoreline and lowered her head to avoid their gaze.

"Between you and me, Mrs. Morgan, I have decided to cancel the search operation and shall make the announcement shortly. I cannot see any benefit in prolonging the hope that the bodies of Constables Smith and Butterworth will be found. Somehow they have vanished, possibly in a deep recess or hole, who knows? I hope you and your family will somehow find solace away from here."

"Thank you."

"Will Sir William be returning with you?"

She looked surprised. "Sir William! He left for London two days ago. Good-bye Mr. Moorson."

"A lovely lady. Tragedy, what has happened," offered Chief Inspector Gilbert once Rosie Morgan was out of earshot.

His joy on hearing that Sir William Cadley would no longer interfere with police procedures with talk of the supernatural, was countered by the reminder that Eddie Gilbert was still standing next to him.

"Strewth Gilbert! Have a look at yourself man. You are a disgrace to the uniform and your rank. Your tunic is shabby to put it mildly and you are unshaven, but worst of all, you stink to high heaven."

"With due respect sir, there are occasions, when circumstances are more important than appearance."

He was surprised by the Chief Constable's outburst.

"That is exactly where you are wrong Chief Inspector. Obviously you have not spent time in Her Majesty's forces or you would not come out with claptrap such as that. Maintaining one's appearance is everything, particularly on manoeuvres or engaging the enemy. One must set an example to the troops Gilbert. If they see a senior officer looking like he has been dragged through a hedge backwards, what will they think? Well I'll tell you. They'll think if the officers cannot be bothered shaving or cleaning their uniform and boots, why should we? That is what they will think Gilbert and when that happens it is too bloody late. The rot has set in, leading to a mutiny or rebellion all because you had not the foresight to maintain one's personal hygiene and grooming. Now listen to me. You are to go home or to where ever you keep your spare uniform, have a shave and introduce soap and water to your hands and face. If the press get a picture of you Chief Inspector it would certainly end up on the front page as one of our missing colleagues having returned from the dead for a breath of fresh air. I do not want any further discussion. Leave."

Chief Inspector Gilbert trudged back along the jetty, his mud-encrusted boots leaving footprints on the bleached wood.

Henry Moorson twirled one end of his superb moustache, watching thoughtfully as the Widows Smith and Butterworth gently sipped tea and consoled each other. With a sigh he too walked along the jetty to the shore.

Chapter Thirty-Seven

It was 6 a.m. and still dark when Constable 'Smudger' Woolly left the police station. His route to Fulwood took him along St. Paul's Road onto Moor Park, following Serpentine Road to Deepdale Road and opposite the track that led to Holme Slack and Moor House Farm.

It had taken him less than an hour to walk the four miles.

There was a candle burning inside the farmhouse and wood smoke was rising from the chimney. 'Smudger' knocked gently on the front door, which was immediately opened by Mrs. Pimlet.

"Ah saw yers come along t' path constable. I think 'e's still in yonder barn tha'knows luv." In her younger days Mrs. Pimlet would have been a very attractive woman. She had several suitors who still regarded her as pretty and well worth pursuing for a spot of courtship and wooing. She was on the wrong side of fifty, slim with ample breasts that pushed her ever-present pinafore to stretching point. Life as a farmer's lass had been remarkably kind to her and only now, being a widow for seven years was the daily routine of dairy farming with its early mornings and late nights starting to take its toll on her fresh face.

"Which barn is it missus?" whispered 'Smudger'.

"Well, there's only th' one luv int' there? An' it's reet in front o'thee." Mrs. Pimlet pointed across the farmyard.

"Oh aye!" He put a finger to his lips and winked before gingerly moving towards the barn.

"Ah'll put kettle on luv an' do yers a bit o' toast." she whispered back.

'Smudger' gave her the thumbs up.

Titus was laid on his back in the hayloft with his hands behind his head. He was awake and thinking about nothing in particular when a noise stopped his breathing.

He knew the farm was run by an older woman and her two daughters and he had decided in moments of fancy, should they proposition him with lustful demands he would not say no to any of them and give a virtuoso performance in unrestrained sex. Three women held no fear for Titus and expecting to see one of the buxom wenches enter the barn, as they often did, he rolled onto his stomach and peeped over the edge of the loft floor with anticipation.

It was still dark, but the oil-lamp lit up the police officer as he crept into the barn.

'Smudger' checked out the four stalls first, shining his light at the startled horses causing them to move noisily, banging into the wood partitions. The smell of hay and manure took him back to his days as a lad when he went fishing near to Ashton Park and he always took a short cut through a stable-yard and passed the steaming muck-midden.

He shone his lamp into every corner until the only place remaining to be searched was the hayloft.

Titus watched his every move.

A set of ladders reached to the hayloft deep in shadow with the inviting appeal of the mouth of an undiscovered cave. 'Smudger', with a life-long fear of heights, removed his helmet and with a racing heart cautiously took hold of a rung and started to climb up, his bulls-eye lantern looped over his right thumb as he used both hands to steady himself.

His head slowly appeared over the edge of the hayloft and numerous bundles of hay and straw towered above him. He took hold of the lamp proper and swung the beam right to left.

Two baleful eyes stared malevolently from the darkness and before his face was illuminated, Titus, now sitting up kicked the top of the ladder as hard as he could.

'Smudger' gave a choked yell as the ladder toppled backwards, his brain not having sufficient time to deduce what had happened. Even though he only fell twelve feet, landing on his

259

back it stunned and knocked the wind from 'Smudger'. The lamp was thrown from his grasp, leaking burning oil.

Titus leapt from the hayloft like a huge ape, both feet hitting the floor with a solid thump. He quickly looked around for anyone else entering the barn, but the copper was alone. Titus reached for a rusting scythe balancing on a nail above a workbench then stood astride 'Smudger', looking down at the semi-conscious face. Without further delay he raised the scythe above his head and swung it at the prostrate copper like a public executioner pleasing the crowd. The oxidised and pitted curved blade that had not even cut through meadow grass for many years, split 'Smudger's' forehead wide open and the blunt corroded point embedded into his brain as if it was a surgical instrument. And there it remained, projecting from 'Smudger's' skull.

The flames had taken hold of the loose hay that littered the floor and one side of the barn was soon ablaze. Titus burst through the barn door into the early morning twilight as Mrs. Pimlet and her daughters were running across the yard in response to the black smoke and embers billowing against the farmhouse windows.

"Ah'll 'ave yer fer this, yer swine," shouted Mrs. Pimlet at Titus, as he doubled back around the burning barn.

The three farmers entered the barn and already the smoke was thick.

Polly and Dolly Pimlet rushed towards the stalls and released the four terrified horses while Mrs. Pimlet looked for the constable.

"Oh my God!" she screamed. 'Smudger's' trousers were on fire and the blue flames were dancing higher. She had not realised he was already dead and threw a sack over his legs, patting the flames to oblivion. Then she took hold of one of his ankles and dragged 'Smudger' into the yard. It was her daughters shrieking that finally forced Mrs. Pimlet's attention to her husband's scythe protruding like a perverted antler from 'Smudger's' head.

Chapter Thirty-Eight

They crossed the Modder River without incident and soon Boer campfires were visible not far away.

Henry knew a track that ran west of Paardeberg and they had over thirty hours to make the twenty miles to Kimberley. They had travelled over six thousand miles by sea, two hundred miles or more by train and horse, but these remaining few miles would be the most dangerous.

Eventually the searchlights of Kimberley could be seen in the distance even though they where still at least five miles away. Dawn was breaking and they both agreed it was time to release the horses. They found a large kopje that would give good cover for the day and set about removing the harnesses and saddles. At first the two dappled cobs were reluctant to leave their human companions, but after encouragement from Henry they wandered off towards Kimberley.

"What will happen to them Henry? They won't die of thirst will they?"

Henry looked at Charles, feigning surprise. "Did I hear you correctly? Charles Cadley, one of the nation's foremost industrial magnates concerned about two horses. It must be the African sun either affecting my hearing or your heart."

Charles reddened slightly. "I am only concerned that they will give away our whereabouts."

"Of course you are Charles, but to answer your question our four-legged friends will be fine. The Boers will pick them up sooner or later and they will became part of their war effort and the Boers look after their horses properly, not like the British."

They hid the bulky saddles and other equipment they had decided to leave behind amidst an outcrop of rock and covered everything with shrubs and more rocks.

There was an explosion in the distance and smoke rose from a Boer position to the south of the town and a cloud of dust erupted in the empty savannah.

Henry had dropped to the sand and with elbows resting on a rock he scanned the veldt with his binoculars.

"A German Krupp 75mm field gun and they still have no bloody idea how to use artillery," he said to Charles without taking his eyes away from the lenses. "What is the point of firing a single round out of range? They should organise their guns in batteries, get in range and unleash a bombardment. Having said that, it's just as well they do not organise their artillery in any fashion, because with a bit of luck and within twenty-four hours, we shall be in Kimberley and on the receiving end of those 13lb shells."

He looked at Charles, but he was already asleep covered with his bivouac, in the shade of a thorny acacia tree. Henry kept watch and cleaned his rifle, going over in his head their plan for nightfall. He had to be honest to himself and admit it was not much of a plan. Their position was parallel with Kenilworth Village and even though Alex Hallam had advised their access into the town should be from the north, between the rail track and the village, Henry decided, after two hours of observation that an approach would fare better from the east.

He realised most of the Boers' southern assault was targeted at particular strategic defences, such as the township of Beaconsfield and three diamond mines, namely; Bultfontein, Wesselton and Premier, all well outside the town's fortified cordon.

The point of entry he was now considering, keeping south of one of the five powerful searchlights Kekewich had installed around the defensive perimeter, necessitated crossing open savannah and using the buildings of the De Beers workshops as a landmark to aim for.

The sound of approaching horses made Henry lay in the elephant grass, with his Mauser at the ready.

A large troop of Boer horsemen cantered past the kopje by no more than thirty feet. They numbered around fifty and were escorting a gun carriage pulled by two horses.

Henry immediately recognised the 120mm Howitzer on its way towards Kimberley. It fired a 35lb shell over 6,000 yards and was more powerful and with a greater range than anything the British had.

That cannon will be pounding Kimberley within a few hours contemplated Henry. *Just our bloody luck!*

Chapter Thirty-Nine

"Titus Moon 'as become a serious fuckin' problem." Meadowbank said, giving his team of detectives a fierce stare. "From t' day 'e is our number one priority. Forget abaht Jack the bloody Ripper, Titus Moon 'as murdered a police officer an' must bi caught. Where are wi up to Sam?"

"Molly Pimlet, th' owner of Moor 'Ouse Farm, 'as positively identified Moon as t' man she saw fleein' 'er blazin' barn. She knew 'im bi name. 'E did some fence repairs int' one o' their fields fer 'er 'usband a few year back an' she's also sin 'im at Th' Parish Church, attending a funeral back end o' last year."

"Wi know all this Sam, is th' search party up an' runnin'?" asked Meadowbank impatiently.

"Yes sir, it is." He gave his inspector a look of annoyance. He did not like being the target for his boss's anger and frustration.

"T' uniform lads are owt there naw visitin' all t' farms in a five mile radius from Moor 'Ouse Farm." He pointed to a map spread out on the desk. "As yer can see fer yersel' there are a 'ell of a lot o' farms t' visit. Not t' mention Ribbleton Moor. It's bleak countryside. Apart from these farms on th' edge o' th' moor, there's little else owt there, but there is this place," his podgy finger moved across the map.

"Ribbleton Moor comes under t' county police, it's well owt of our area. 'Ave we contacted Moorson yet an' get some 'elp from 'im?"

"Major Little 'as spoken wi' 'im. Funnily enough they are conductin' a massive search already in th' grounds o' Ribbleton Manor. In a lake there t' bi exact, lookin' fer t' two missin' 'bobbies'. Some of our lads are helpin' owt an all. T' search is bein' wound up today."

"That's great news Sam, it couldn't bi better. They can continue searchin' th' moor from there. How many officers are involved?"

"It's not that simple sir."

"Sam, I'm not in t' mood fer bad news."

"Well in that case Inspector you'd better put yer 'ands over yer ears. T' county lads 'ave raided t' navvy encampment on Walton Summit an' found 'alf a dozen shallow graves. Most of t' navvies 'ave bin rounded up, but a few are on th' run, so there's a search party needed that end o' town an' manpower is needed t' dig up t' graves. Moorson is askin' if 'e can keep 'old of our troops t' assist at Walton Summit."

"I 'ope th' Major towd 'im ter fuck off. Wi need every bugger wi can get 'ere an' now. We're lookin' fer a police killer fer Christ's sake, not a bunch o' navvies."

"Ironically Inspector, if Titus 'adn't glassed that tattooed navvy last week in th' Old Dog, an' you not arrested his tosspot mates, information abaht exactly what 'ad bin goin' on up there would never 'ave come owt. In fairness sir, it'll be a bloody good job once it's sorted owt. They 'ave at least six unidentified murder victims, some with 'orrific injuries."

Meadowbank interrupted. "Sam. I couldn't gi' a flyin' fuck at t' moment abaht Walton Summit. I'm only interested in findin' Moon. He's owt there somewhere an' responsible fer three deaths. 'E'll know 'e faces t' gallows so 'e'll 'ave nothin' t' lose in mekin 'is body count four, five, ten or even twenty and 'e is clearly capable of doin' that. Reet lads, get yer boots on an' yer coats, t' Criminal Investigation Department will show t' uniform boys a thing o' two abaht catchin' police murderers."

Preston Pete watched the last of the wagons carrying a rowing boat trundle from the field. Everyone had gone and the only evidence of the intense activity for nearly four days was a churned-up field, the wheel rutted shoreline and the large khaki canvas tent on loan from Fulwood barracks that remained erected near the jetty.

The macabre collection of skulls and bones had not yet been given a new home. A debate had started over who will pay for the excavation of the large grave needed to bury so many human remains and which church representative will conduct the burial service and who will bear the cost of transporting the remains and who will fund the memorial stone? The borough treasurer had already vetoed the suggestion that it should all come from public funding.

The history professor from The Harris Museum had no such problem in recovering the weaponry and finding a suitable depository. His main concern was labelling so many artefacts and he intended recruiting the help of students for that task.

Preston Pete stood at the edge of the jetty and looked out across the lake, nearly believing that the place was a setting of natural beauty. The horse chestnuts and beech trees on the opposite bank were a deep russet and the proud bull-rushes too, were surrendering to the autumnal equinox. The pull of winter was not far away and Mother Nature had decided it was again that time to prepare for sleep or death, but the gamekeeper enjoyed all the seasons and did not have a particular favourite as he could use his shotgun all year round.

The water to his left stirred with movement and large bubbles 'popped' as they reached the surface and as he watched, the body of a naked man appeared from the deep and floated face up, with arms by his side, eye sockets empty and black, and the mouth frozen in an unfinished scream.

Preston Pete struck a match and lit a cigarette as he watched the body bob and gently rock in the breeze blowing from the hills. He did not know the identity of the milk white corpse. He had never been introduced to Police Constable Butterworth.

As he exhaled lungfuls of smoke a dozen or so hands broke the surface, taking hold of limbs and flesh, gently pulling the corpse under water until it submerged from view.

Chapter Forty

It was dark and Henry and Charles knelt side by side, studying the lights of Kimberley, listening for the slightest sound.

Henry nudged his companion. "Come on Charles, time to go."

They stepped from the kopje into the night.

Campfires flickered in the distance like giant fireflies and the haunting notes from a harmonica seemed to carry on wood-smoke. They did not speak, instead communicated by touch and hand movement. Both men carried a rucksack, canteen and all the ammunition and dynamite they could comfortably bear and held their loaded rifles ready for use. They had rolled their sleeves down and wore a khaki neckerchief across their faces, tied behind their heads revealing only their eyes beneath their hats.

They kept low and moved quickly, trying to stay close to the terrain and shrubs. Henry was in his element, instinctively darting round rocks and dodging cacti that suddenly appeared in the darkness. It was so quiet, as if the lizards and other creatures of the night were watching their progress and placing bets on how far they would get.

Henry grabbed Charles' wrist and stopped, his eyes wide and head cocked to one side, listening. Charles did the same. After a few seconds that seemed like hours they both heard the noise of boots crunching on rock and sand. Henry jerked a thumb to his right and waited for Charles to acknowledge that he understood, then they crept slowly to a sand-hill and disappeared over the top.

Henry knew they had left footprints and also knew that a Boer night reconnaissance foot patrol was heading towards them. He removed his hat and gradually peeked through the clumps of pepper and ostrich grass. They were very close, talking aloud, unconcerned, the clipped tones of Dutch Afrikaan clearly audible to Henry and Charles.

In a column of two loose ranks they headed south, some carrying their rifles, some with their weapons slung over their shoulders and rather than march in regimented silence like the colonial troops, the Boers joked and chatted as they ambled across the countryside towards the Modder River, leaving behind the sweet aroma of Dutch tobacco hanging in the air.

The three-quarter moon was hidden by cloud cover and the Boer commandos trampled carelessly over the recent footprints in the sand.

It was easy to underestimate the Boers, just as the British High Command had done, treating them with indifference and even contempt. It was a mistake that would cost the colonial forces in the weeks to come, particularly as the Boers had mobilised over 48,000 volunteers and towards the end of 1899 the British troops numbered 27,000.

Commanders such as Buller and Methuen saw the enemy as bible-wielding Dutch farmers and Field Marshal Lord Roberts of Kandahar went on to describe the Boer forces as 'a few marauding bands'. They did not consider at any stage during the preparations for war that the Boer commandos would be supported by the farmsteads and villages, offering refuge, supplies and creating an extensive intelligence network, allowing the commandos to mount an attack or engage in guerrilla operations then disappear into communities. They had no warfare training and were without military discipline, but their strong sense of community and hatred for the British was their binding strength.

The British response to the underground support was systematic farm burning and livestock confiscation that only hardened the resolve of the Boers.

They wore their everyday work clothes and only the modern Mauser magazine rifle identified the Afrikaan as a Boer fighter, and these farmers and burghers introduced the British troops to the strategies of mounted commandos opening fire then moving position and also to the use of defensive deep trenches, which rendered the Boers invisible. These were unknown concepts in British tactics, who faced the enemy in formation, firing volleys at close quarters and this strategy had not changed since the Napoleonic Wars, presenting British infantry and cavalry the impossible task of advancing against entrenched or mobile Boers.

Henry was with The Cape Mounted during the Transvaal War in '81 and it was obvious to him that the British had learnt very little from those six months of conflict, after the Boers declared Transvaal independent from Great Britain.

At least the British forces no longer wore the bright scarlet uniforms, he thought to himself, which was a decision only recently made, but still they relied on regimented formation to counter the Boers stealth and mobility.

Unlike the British, Henry had acquired many skills from the Boers and even the Zulus during the Anglo-Zulu War and he was now putting them to good use.

They waited a few minutes once the Boer commandos had passed and with a nod of the head to Charles, they emerged from behind the sand dune and then Henry froze, slowly turning round, the hairs on his neck tingling.

He saw the lioness before Charles. It was no more than twenty feet away, crouching with yellow teeth bared and those keen eyes watching them both intently.

"Careful Charles. No sudden moves."

He was already reaching for his revolver.

"Don't even think about that unless you want every Boer commando within five miles descending on us," Henry said quietly, not taking his eyes off the lioness, a hand slowly feeling for his Bowie knife.

The lion was large for a female weighing at least 250lbs but emaciated, ribs visible where muscle should be and it was panting as if too hot. Even in the spartan moonlight Henry could see the animal was starving and desperate.

This was the man-eater Alex Hallam had warned them about.

The ears went back and the lioness began snarling, its body perfectly still, the yellow coat scarred with large patches of bare skin, inflamed and crusting. With two sudden leaps it attacked Charles with deadly teeth going for his throat.

The lioness had pounced in seconds and it was on top of Charles pinning him to the ground before Henry reacted.

The neckerchief still covering his mouth muffled Charles cry of surprise. Instinctively using his arms and elbows he managed to block the lion's head from reaching his and then the jaw gripped his left shoulder. The pain was instant and Charles could not move, the lioness was completely on top of him and he could smell its rancid hot breath and feel the excruciating pain as talons clawed his stomach.

Henry launched himself at the lion. His left arm went across her eyes and his right hand rammed the Bowie knife below the shoulder. The lioness released its grip and roared in pain, turning its head, deadly jaws snapping at Henry. He managed to move his left arm around the huge neck of the lion and sit astride its back like a demented rodeo rider from Buffalo Bill's Wild West Show. The lion rolled off Charles and thrashed about furiously in an effort to dislodge Henry who now had both arms around the powerful neck and held on to his knife despite the lioness's frenzied efforts to dislodge him. A cloud of dust erupted as the wounded cat growled and roared, savagely lashing out with razor sharp claws. The lioness was far too strong and ferocious and after only a few seconds threw Henry backwards into the air. He landed with a body slam that completely knocked the wind from him. The big cat was on its feet and facing him, eyes emanating nothing but death and hate, her right flank and fore leg sodden with blood.

The lioness slowly limped nearer, saliva drooling from the red tongue that flicked between savage yellow teeth as she moved in for the kill.

Henry was attempting to get to his feet when she struck. He saw the cat leap and once again fell backwards from the onslaught and still holding the knife, he grasped the handle with both hands, resting the hardwood base on his chest. He screamed in defiance as the lioness seemed to silently glide through the night air, her powerful back legs driving her forwards. She attacked Henry as she had Charles, again the throat was the target for those deadly canine teeth, but the silver steel blade pierced her neck, jaws and brain as the cat landed on Henry. The full weight of the lioness pressed down on the hunting knife and the front paws dropped lifelessly at either side of his head and the dead lioness almost head-butted Henry as it collapsed onto him.

Henry struggled to pull himself from under the big cat but once free staggered towards Charles. He was barely conscious, still laid in the dirt cradling his shoulder.

"Take it easy Charles." Henry was still catching his breath as he examined the injuries.

He ripped apart the torn and blood-soaked shirt constantly looking around for the rest of the pride to appear, or worse, a Boer patrol. Deep teeth marks forming a neat pattern surrounded Charles' shoulder blade but the wounds were clean and not ragged.

"You've been lucky Charles. You'll soon be playing cricket again."

"Henry." He opened his eyes with a look of panic. "What about the lion?"

"She's dead. Now we just need to worry about the Boers."

In silent concentration he removed the rucksack from his back taking out a small black leather bound box, first aid bag and hip-flask. He poured most of the remainder of Churchill's scotch over the wounds, then putting the silver hip-flask to Charles' mouth helped him to drink the last few mouthfuls. Henry then opened the hinged lid of the small box. Inside was cushioned with black velvet and neatly contained three hypodermic needles and syringes each filled with one dose of morphine. They were the latest design of glass and stainless steel and produced by Oppenheimer & Son of London. He made the injection into the muscle below the shoulder blade, applied the dressing and bandage, finishing the job by securing the arm in an accomplished sling. The claw cuts to the stomach were superficial. Painful yes, but nothing to worry about, Henry assured Charles, now sat up drinking from a canteen. Henry squatted on the desert sand next to Charles and it did not take long for Charles to close his eyes and drift into a deep sleep. Henry had to wait another three hours until the narcotic analgesic wore off and Charles stirred from his slumber with a euphoric smile.

They had been walking for nearly two hours and had covered four miles even with Charles wearing the sling. A searchlight to their right slowly swept the savannah in a random pattern.

As they crossed one of the many roads that linked the different mines they noticed that the township of Beaconsfield less than half a mile away was in ominous darkness and Henry assumed it was under Boer sniper occupation. Then as they approached a sandbagged redoubt apparently abandoned, Henry detected an unmistakable whiff of pipe tobacco. He suddenly threw his arm out, signalling to Charles to remain still.

Standing in the shadows of the redoubt supported by railway sleepers and sandbags mounted at least eight feet high, Henry slipped his rifle over his shoulder and drew his Bowie knife, slowly creeping around the redoubt with Charles close behind.

Leaning against the sandbags and enjoying his pipe, a Boer sentry lolled nonchalantly. His rifle rested against him, his left arm was behind his back and his right hand cradled the glowing pipe as if he did not have a care in the world. Henry moved fast and covered the two yards separating them in less than a second, thrusting the knife straight through the heart and in those fleeting moments before death took over, the guard gave out a stifled yell shattering the early morning quiet.

Henry heard raised voices all around and several Boers charged from the redoubt, ready for action. Henry did not hesitate in firing his revolver and shouted for Charles to cover him. Five Boers lay dead before Henry needed to reload. There was uproar from the Boer positions as lanterns and blazing torches bobbed ever nearer in the surrounding darkness.

Henry lit three sticks of dynamite and tossed one into the redoubt and the others at the approaching lanterns. He wanted to create confusion. The Boers had no idea how many the attack force numbered and Henry needed to take advantage of this. He told Charles to do the same and lob dynamite in all directions.

"Charles, we are going to have to make a dash for the British line," he shouted amidst the explosions. Without further explanation Henry sprinted into the night and Charles was right with him. A fusillade of gunfire came from behind when suddenly a blinding light hit them. The searchlight, mounted on a large timber platform near to the De Beers mine, remained fixed on Charles and Henry, who were forced to slow down and put their arms across their eyes.

They had one hundred yards to go to the barbed-wire perimeter.

The corporal with the seven Lancashire Signallers manning the searchlight, called for his captain urgently. Henry and Charles stumbled on towards the light as bullets hit the dirt all around them.

The signal captain climbed the ladder to the searchlight and saw the two men coming towards their position under fire. He grabbed the bar on the light and swung it higher, the beam illuminating a horde of Boer commandos racing towards Charles and Henry.

"Corporal! Sound the alarm. We are under attack. Fire at will." He bellowed.

"Open the defences corporal and allow those two men access," the captain added.

The mine sirens wailed liked tormented banshees, notifying 'battle stations'.

The flash and loud report of rifle fire blasted along the British front at the illuminated Boer targets.

Henry and Charles blinked away their temporary blindness and ran for their lives.

The Boer commandos had stopped their rush forwards and now returned fire, aiming at the searchlight.

The battle and commotion had awoken the whole garrison and within minutes, Lieutenant Colonel Robert Kekewich, Kimberley's commanding officer arrived at the searchlight post and ordered for the tripod mounted Maxim machine detachments to open fire.

Bullets whistled and whizzed inches past Charles and Henry who were uncertain as to who was firing at them and Charles became disorientated, believing they were running back towards the Boers. He called out to Henry that they were going the wrong way. Henry, without altering his pace, grabbed a handful of tunic and dragged Charles forwards.

English voices could be heard not far away.

"Come on lads, keep going, you're nearly there," someone called out.

Sand and dust erupted all around Henry and Charles as deafening explosions rocked the sandbag defences ahead of them. Shells exploded, filling the air with choking smoke, flying shrapnel and the stench of cordite. The Boers were firing a 'Pom-

Pom', a Maxim-Nordenfield piece of artillery, which discharged a continuous fire of 25 x 1lb shells, belt fed and devastating.

Both men threw themselves to the quaking ground, waiting for the salvo to stop.

British six pounders roared into life and Henry heard the order to fix bayonets.

"What the hell is going on?" Charles shouted to Henry, laid only inches away.

Henry raised his head and could see the muzzles discharging.

"Charles! If we crawl forwards we'll make it."

Henry moved first, sliding through the dirt on his belly. It was not long before hands were grabbing them and Charles winced at the pain as friendly voices urged them forwards.

The barbed-wire fence had been pulled aside allowing them to scramble into Kimberley.

"Welcome to the Diamond City, gentlemen. Now who the hell are you?" The Commander of the Kimberley garrison demanded.

Chapter Forty-One

Alexandrina Victoria, Queen of the United Kingdom of Great Britain and Ireland and Empress of India was in the sixty-first year of her reign.

The empire was expanding and the industrial revolution of the late 18th and early 19th centuries, which began with the mechanisation of the textile industry and the introduction of steam power, had left its legacy in Lancashire. Coal came to replace wood as fuel and the country had huge reserves of coal to power the thousands of steam engines in the cotton mills.

By the mid 1800s Lancashire had been transformed into the greatest textile centre in the world, despite competition from Japan and India. The largest mills in the 35 square miles of the industrial heart of Lancashire, bounded by Stalybridge, Liverpool, Colne and Preston, which made up the Lancashire cotton industry, all followed a similar design. They were several hundred feet long, up to seven storeys high, combining the production of cotton preparation, spinning and weaving and could employ 6,000 workers.

Cadley Cotton Mill was one such manufacturer and of the ninety mills in Preston was second only to Horrocks, the giant of the cotton producers.

Sir William Cadley sat in the richly panelled manager's office, situated on the third floor of the spinning mill's administration block. He had not returned to London as Rosie Morgan believed, but had booked himself into The Bull Hotel in the town centre and decided to visit Richard Oldham, in whose office he now sat. Even though Richard Oldham was not the mill owner, he was a wealthy man thanks to Sir William who generously rewarded his hard work and had personally encouraged the former weaver into management.

Sir William was alone as he read The Times, waiting for a hansom cab to take him to Ribbleton Manor. He seemed oblivious to the constant din from the adjoining single storey weaving sheds and the vibration from the huge steam engine and flywheel that powered the looms.

The front page of The Times reported news of the war in South Africa. Kimberley, Mafeking and Ladysmith were still under siege. The army of 14,000 troops under the command of Lieutenant General Lord Methuen were attempting to fight their way to Kimberley and Baden-Powell was holding out at Mafeking. Sir William prayed to God that Charles was safe.

The journey through town was not an unfamiliar one to Sir William. He had made it many times as a child, but spent most of his childhood at his parents' London mansion in Mayfair. Ribbleton Manor was used by his father Sir Philip Cadley for entertaining and as a base to increase the Cadley Empire, allowing Sir William to spend the occasional summer and Christmas there. It was only when his father retired and passed the family business on to Sir William that his father and mother moved into Ribbleton Manor permanently leaving the Mayfair house at 45 Berkeley Square, once the home of Robert Clive of India to Sir William.

He was surprised that Charles wanted Ribbleton Manor as his grandfather's bequest in view of what happened there. It was described as a tragic accident claiming a young girl's life and was similar to the tragic accident that claimed George Morgan's life thirty-one years later.

Verity knew nothing of Lucy's drowning, Sir William was certain of that, as Charles to this day had never talked about what had happened that summer's afternoon when Lucy fell from the jetty and drowned, her body never found despite days of searching by the young gamekeeper who still called himself Preston Pete.

Lady Elizabeth, Sir William's wife, had heard Charles screaming and rushed to his aid. He was in the meadow, behind the walled garden, hysterical, a paroxysm of crying making him cough and choke violently whilst shouting "the lake" repeatedly.

With overwhelming panic she shook her son asking what had happened, where was Lucy?

Lady Elizabeth shouted for Chandler and together they rushed to the lake, leaving Charles with the housekeeper.

The expanse of water reflected perfectly the summer sunshine, its surface unmarked with ripples in the absence of any breeze or disturbance.

They ran to the end of the jetty where Lucy's light blue cardigan lay. Her mother picked it up and pressed it to her face as she frantically called out her daughter's name.

Chandler saw it first and pointed at the object floating nearby.

It was Lucy's wooden hair-grip.

As the cab drew alongside the steps to the main entrance Dobson appeared and the driver deftly jumped to the ground and opened the cab door.

"Good afternoon Sir William." Greeted the head butler.

"Ah Dobson! Good to see a friendly face. Have my daughter-in-law and Mrs. Morgan left for Bristol yet?"

"Yes sir. They left yesterday afternoon. Should I prepare your suite Sir William?"

"A fine speech Dobson, a fine speech. I am tiring of the constant noise of traffic and rowdy drunks that pass below my window each night. Will you arrange for my belongings be transferred from The Bull Hotel and settle the bill in the usual manner?"

A few hours later Sir William was standing at the end of the jetty. He wore his green hunting jacket and a black woollen cap against the chill wind gathering pace.

He heard footsteps on the decking and spoke without turning to see who it was.

"I thought you would show up sooner or later." Sir William said indifferently.

His statement went unanswered as the visitor approached him.

"What the hell is going on Peter?"

The gamekeeper had no answer.

"First my daughter, then my son's father-in-law, then two police constables. If I were a religious man I would think God is trying to tell me something."

"This lake ain't reet sir, I knows that much."

He passed his cigarette case to the gamekeeper and then his lighter. Preston Pete nodded his thanks and removed two cigarettes, placing one behind an ear and lit the other, inhaling the smoke gratefully.

"Peter, you have worked for the family on this estate for over forty years. What secrets do you know about the lake?" he asked quietly.

"Secrets sir! It ain't no secret this place is evil, 'ave yer ne'r felt that sir?"

The gamekeeper did not tell his lordship of the apparition he had witnessed from this very spot, the day before.

He was perplexed. "No I haven't. My father and mother would always discourage me from coming to the lake, but that did not stop me. Now that I think about it though, I would never set foot in the water and never sailed on a boat, not even a rowing boat. I cannot explain why. Of course I feel differently about the lake now. Who wouldn't? It's become the unofficial grave for poor Lucy. Her little body is still down there somewhere Peter, of that I am convinced." He took a long draw on the cigarette, his eyes searching the lake as they had done a thousand times.

"Why do you say 'this place is evil'? Do you mean the house, the lake or both?"

"Not th' 'ouse sir, that feels as clean as a whistle. Just th' lake is evil. I would not even enter t' watter t' retrieve mi shotgun. I can feel it now. It wants us sir. Summat down there is watchin' us and waitin'. No offence meant t' yer daughters' memory but summat wants us t' join it or them down there int' watter. Th' lake is dead sir. Mother Nature moved owt a long time ago."

Sir William had not often heard the gamekeeper say so many words and thought carefully about what he said.

Suddenly the grief was overpowering and he covered his face with his hands, his shoulders hunched with sobbing.

"Please God, don't condemn the soul of a young innocent to an eternal watery hell," he spluttered.

After a few minutes Sir William composed himself and spoke to break the awkward silence.

"Verity has only been here a matter of weeks and already she is claiming there are supernatural forces at work."

"I don't know much abaht that sir, but whate'er it is that's down yonder, I 'ope it stays put. I don't want t' know what it be. I don't need t' gi' it a name. It could bi owd as time itsel' an' evil like Lucifer. I don't want t' meet it. D' you?"

Sir William, on the brink of further tears closed his eyes trying to shut out the image of Lucy helpless in the lake.

"She was only seven years old for God's sake!" he said gritting his teeth.

"I know sir. A terrible loss."

They were not alone.

Across the lake, where the roots of the sycamore and horse-chestnut broke through the soft banking like withered limbs testing the water, a figure sat in the long grass between the trees, watching with interest.

Titus Moon was hungry and he wanted see where these two men would lead him.

Chapter Forty-Two

The Right Honourable Cecil John Rhodes himself came to the billet tent first thing that morning looking for Charles. The former prime minister of Cape Colony and founder of De Beers Diamond Company and Consolidated Gold Fields pulled back the flap and strode in without consideration to Charles and Henry, both sound asleep on army camp beds.

"Young Cadley! It's true. How the blazes did you manage to get through the blockade?" asked Rhodes loudly. Charles opened his bleary eyes, "Hallo Cecil. As brash as ever I see."

"Charles, you can sleep later. Tell us news of the relief force." He then saw the sling. "And what the blazes has happened to you?"

Charles pulled the blanket aside and sat up wearily, his shoulder throbbing and noticed that Henry was still asleep, or at least pretending to be.

"A hungry lioness took a shine to me. It's nothing serious, but as far as the relief force goes, Methuen is still massing his army at the Orange River. I think it will be some time before he will be ready to advance and break through the Kimberley blockade. I'm afraid Cecil, you are going to have to hold out a while longer."

This was not what Rhodes or the besieged town wanted to hear.

"Do they understand the importance of Kimberley? We have been defending this town for nearly three weeks and cannot hold out indefinitely. Good God! How long does it take to mobilise an army by train?"

Charles did not answer. Now that he was awake it was time to visit the company office and Thomas Travis.

Rhodes accompanied him through the town, strongly criticising the tactics of Lieutenant Colonel Kekewich for not striking a blow against the enemy and still claiming the importance of the diamond mines was being underestimated. Charles did not pay too much attention to Rhodes' protests. He was only doing what he had arrived at Kimberley to do and that was to protect their interests and Rhodes had a lot more to lose than Charles.

Things had not changed much since Charles was last here a few months ago. The sprawling shanty town of corrugated iron, housing 30,000 white prospectors and 18,000 black labourers was unusually noisy for this time of the day, as most of the mine workers milled about with nothing to do.

Rhodes explained that Kekewich had put the town under martial law. Food was rationed to half-a-pound of meat per person per day, along with a tin of salmon or crayfish or brawn and the water was from a newly constructed well as the Boers had cut off the town's supply.

There was a distant explosion and dirt and dust spurted from the public gardens as a shell landed only a hundred yards away, not far from the bandstand where the Kimberley and Lancashire bands were playing. The shell had not exploded, bringing much amusement to the residents who rushed towards it, some racing others to reach the unexploded bomb first.

Charles was visibly shaken and remarked on the lack of concern shown by the town's people toward the carnage that could have occurred. There was an almost carnival atmosphere as the brass bands played God Save the Queen and Rule Britannia, encouraged on by the large audience. The garrison reserves paraded outside the town hall, marching and turning in formation to the commands of a drill-sergeant on the wide dusty street.

Rhodes ignored the commotion around the dud shell saying,

"So the rumours are true Charles. Hadley Mining has discovered a big one?"

Cecil Rhodes, English born, was a tall stocky man, forty-seven years old although he looked much older with brown wavy hair and a thin moustache. He had an undisguised air of importance and a stare that some found unsettling.

282

"As the owner of the world's largest diamond mine, I am surprised you are interested in what a small outfit like ours is doing."

"I am always interested in business Charles. I've known you and your father for some time and have nothing but respect for you as a neighbouring prospector and the way you have remained independent and, I am more than prepared to better any offer you have received."

"That is bullshit! You tried your hardest to close us down a few years ago. Our labourers were beaten and intimidated, equipment stolen, mules poisoned." He stopped walking and faced Rhodes. "I would rather give the stones to the Boers than sell them to you."

"Now steady on Charles! All that nonsense had nothing to do with me. You did ruffle one or two feathers by paying your blacks double the daily rate. There has to be a uniform pay structure to keep everyone happy. You cannot pay one Kaffir one pound when a hundred yards away the blacks are earning half that. No wonder there was unrest. If you recall, I advised Sir William and yourself how best to resolve the problem."

"The problem was we could not employ any workers because they were too scared to work for Cadley Mining. It was only by doubling the pay that we could get any labourers and you know that. And "resolving the problem," meant selling our stake to De Beers, something my father would never agree to, but you already know that and believe me Cecil our position has not changed."

"Suit yourself Charles. Your decision, but if you do change your mind, come and see me. Remember though for each day you hesitate from today, my offer drops 10,000 pounds sterling from the net value. As the town is surrounded and we will be here for several more weeks thanks to the incompetence of the British High Command, you will have plenty of time to consider my offer." His hands were pushed deep into the pockets of his beige cotton trousers. He wore a sand-coloured waistcoat, white shirt and brown tie under a summer blazer. His dimpled chin jutted forwards haughtily.

Charles moved closer and said quietly, "I wanted to slit your throat a long time ago and it was only due to my father's intervention that you are alive today. I still have a mind to permanently remove your arrogance, but I anticipate that the Boers will do it for me." He walked away unconcerned, leaving Rhodes looking round making certain no one else had heard his life being threatened.

The Cadley diamond mine was operated on a small scale compared to De Beers. Thomas Travis and his supervisor were the only white men employed by The Cadley Mining Company and they oversaw the six African Bantu labourers who worked in an ever widening and deepening pit, twenty feet down and forty feet across, revealing seams of alluvium 'blue-ground' hard rock, in later years renamed Kimberlite.

This was one of seven mines in Kimberley and the only one not under the direct control of Cecil Rhodes. The Cadley Mine was situated outside the town and the fortified cordon, halfway between the reservoir and Carter's Farm. The mine and field office were deserted, all the deposits of value now stored in a vault in the company's main office near to 'The Diggers Tavern'.

The office is where Thomas Travis had lived and slept since the siege began, behind locked doors and a loaded shotgun to hand at all times. His deputy, a rough-necked prospector called Edward Black had taken the occasional shift, but preferred to spend his time in 'The Diggers Tavern'.

De Beers Kimberley Mine was in the middle of the town. As the 'Big Hole' increased the town grew with it. Four thousand black labourers worked in the circular mine shaft which was 400 feet deep and a 1,000 feet wide. It was the biggest man-made hole in the world covering nine acres, and a further workforce of four thousand whites were at the rim of the crater, filling and emptying the swing-barrels of earth that travelled along hundreds of horse drawn aerial pulley systems, criss-crossing the chasm like a bizarre web.

This one hole produced nearly 95% of the world's diamonds.

De Beers Consolidated Mines Limited was founded in Kimberley in 1888 by three shareholders, Rhodes being one of them. The following year he had total ownership after buying out his remaining rival and shareholder, Barney Barnato, an English immigrant, for £5,338,650.00 and at the time it was the largest cheque ever written, but an amount easily afforded by Cecil Rhodes.

Charles reached the office and found it locked. He banged on the door and peered through the dust-smeared window. There was movement inside and then the door opened.

"Hallo Travis! I've come to take you for a drink." Charles was grinning at the speechless man pointing a shotgun at him.

"Mr. Cadley! I don't believe it sir. What the devil are you doing here?"

"Come on Travis, have a guess," he replied seriously.

He put the 12 bore down and clasped Charles' hand, shaking it vigorously.

"Am I glad to see you Mr. Cadley." There was no mistaking his relief as he moved aside to allow his employer access.

"I take it everything is in order?" Charles asked looking around the office, now with a camp bed behind the desk.

"Do you not trust me sir?" Travis seemed wounded.

"Good God Travis! Get a grip of yourself. My father and I trust you like a member of the family," he lied. "We do not trust the thousands of Boers massing on the veldt and trust even less Mr. Rhodes and his private army. Your telegram left me no choice but to come here. You have done more than we could have expected from you and my father is very grateful. Believe me Travis, after this display of loyalty you will not have to work again and may retire anywhere in the world you choose with the means to support your lifestyle. That is a promise from Sir William himself."

Travis's emotions were topsy-turvy. "Thank you sir, thank you. Seeing you is an answer to my prayers."

Charles could see the man was close to tears.

His attention turned to the black safe standing four feet high, hidden from view by a number of large filing cabinets.

The safe was made by Chubb of London, the best money could buy. Fire and burglar resistant, it was manufactured by riveting layers of iron plates together, forming a box, more solid than cast iron without being brittle.

"Safe keys please Travis." Charles said without further ceremony.

The large ornate key was handed over and Travis locked the front office door as Charles unlocked the safe and pulled back the heavy door one-handedly, revealing a neat row of ledgers, deeds and bank accounts. There was a compartment at the base and Charles used the smaller key to unlock it.

He slowly removed a black cotton sack, placed it on the desk and untied the leather cord. A pile of uncut rough diamonds, the hardest substance known to man, some small, some large and at least a dozen the size of quail eggs, sparkled as if glad to show off their wonder. There was an assortment of colours; most were clear crystals, a few of the largest were amber yellow, littered amongst brown and graphite stones.

Without a word Charles retied the cord, placing the large bundle inside his tunic.

He did not ask where some of these stones had come from. They certainly had not been discovered when he was last here, four months ago and did not have the diamondiferous qualities of the Cadley mine, at least he did not think they did. The less asked of Travis the better. At the moment he was not too concerned where the stones had come from, being more occupied in implementing his plan.

"Come on Travis, let me get you that drink."

The Diggers Tavern was busy with unemployed white prospectors who had nothing better to do at the moment. The Kaffirs had their own drinking dens amongst the corrugated sheds and were not welcome in any of the 'white taverns'.

Charles recognised a lot of faces and acknowledged the friendly and obscene salutations coming from all directions. He bought three pints of local brewed beer, sending one to Edward Black who was sitting on a stool, fast asleep by the bar.

Travis calmed down after a few mouthfuls of the gut-rotting ale and became more of the man Charles had known since he took him on as his manager in the early days of Cadley Mining. Charles believed Travis was wealthy in his own right and could only be trusted up to a point. After all, he had been running the mine for several years now and had the responsibility for declaring any diamonds found. He also supervised the Kaffirs, ensuring they handed all the finds to him and he in turn registered the stones. It was impossible to monitor every worker who had access to the mine and trust was begrudgingly extended to managers and supervisors such as Travis.

Theft by black and white employees was a major problem for all the diamond mines. De Beers had started searching the Kaffirs before they left the mine at the end of each shift and the volume of diamonds processed increased by 25%. The searches amounted to medical examinations and were carried out not by doctors, but by rough white prospectors who had never heard of the Hippocratic oath. They poked and pulled inside the mouth, under eyelids, inside ears, the anal passage and underneath the foreskin, all favourite places to smuggle diamonds from the mine face.

White employees were exempt from such body searches, as it would set a bad example to the natives suggesting that white men could not be trusted. This procedure of searching the Kaffirs had not yet been introduced at Cadley Mining, who had only six blacks and two whites to worry about. De Beers had 8,000 at the Kimberley Mine alone and thousands more at the Premier, Otto Kopje, Beaconsfield, Wesselton and De Beers mines, all situated in or on the outskirts of Kimberley.

Travis began extolling the virtues of Cecil Rhodes and detailing what he had done for the town since the siege began. This included forming a garrison reserve force of volunteers from his employees totalling more than 4,000, providing over 500 horses to Kekewich, enabling the commander to form a mounted regiment. Also De Beers' chief engineer had connected a supply of drinking water for the town from one of the mines and the workshops manufactured ammunition and weapons.

Charles had heard enough.

"Travis, listen to me. For personal reasons I need to get out of Kimberley tonight. I'll be leaving with Frobisher, but it is imperative we go tonight. Will you help us?"

Travis once again appeared crest-fallen. "You are leaving so soon? And what about your injury?"

"Good God Travis! This can hardly be described as a holiday destination. Yes, we are leaving Kimberely and I don't want anyone to know, especially Rhodes or Kekewich. Now, will you be able to help or not?"

"Yes. Possibly. I know a few of the Zulu Impi who go cattle foraging on the instructions of Colonel Kekewich. The Boers stole large numbers of our cattle and have them in guarded herds scattered around the veldt. The Zulus have proved very successful in recovering some of the cattle and driving them back to town. I'll speak to the Zulu commander, their camp is near to the conning tower." Travis said quietly and looked at Charles in earnest. "It will be very dangerous, even if they agree to help you, the chances of you making it through the Boer lines are slim at best. Would it not make more sense to wait here for Methuen's relief force?"

"Time is a luxury I don't have at the moment Travis. I like your suggestion that we seek help from the Zulu Impi. How many are there in Kimberley?"

"Around a dozen or so. They are here with Chief Kharma's permission. They tend the cattle and horses and bring back game every now and then. They want the Boers crushed and driven from South Africa more than we do."

Before Charles could reply, an old-time prospector burst through the tavern swing doors and called out to Charles, "Mr. Cadley sir. You'd better come quick. Your friend is behaving very strange and is going to get himself shot."

"What?" Charles asked.

"Follow me, quickly."

The old man turned around and ran off without waiting for a reply and most of the customers followed him out.

"What the hell is going on?" asked Charles looking round bewildered.

"Something is happening sir and seems to concern the gentleman you are travelling with. I think we should do as the old man asks."

They left the tavern and could feel the excitement from the crowd milling around the barbed-wire perimeter. Travis pushed his way through with Charles behind him, at the same time trying to make sense of the comments from the crowd.

"What's the darn fool doing?" "He's a goner for sure." "A Boer sniper will have him, white flag or not."

Charles got as far as the British soldiers manning the picket line and could see Henry in the distance, walking slowly across no-mans-land of open savannah.

He held his rifle high above his head and the white flag tied to the barrel flapped in the breeze. His left arm was raised and fingers splayed as he slowly walked towards the town's old cemetery.

"He's not surrendering is he?" Travis asked.

"I hope not." Charles was as confused as everyone watching.

Henry was over five hundred yards away and approaching the small iron gate leading to the resting place of Kimberley's dead.

A rifle shot rang out loudly and the desert sand not a yard in front of Henry erupted with dust. He ignored the warning shot and without faltering a step entered the graveyard. Henry knew exactly where he was going amongst the neat rows of crosses and headstones, stopping at a grave marked out by four white stone blocks and a wooden cross with the inscription, 'Kathryne Frobisher formerly De Groot. Died 22.6.1894. Adored wife of Henry.'

The desert had started to reclaim this small piece of land and the white paint was in parts sand-blasted away, but the words were still clear. Henry dropped to one knee and leant against his rifle. This is why he would never leave Africa again, his darling Kathryne was here.

Numerous Boer rifles were aimed at Henry and countless lenses glinted on both sides, his every movement watched intently, but the order to shoot was never given.

Henry scooped a handful of sand and gently trickled the grains onto the grave. He reached into a pocket and brought out a small portrait photograph of Kathryne, her delicate features smiling at the lens. Henry had been standing next to the Cape Town photographer pulling faces and making Kathryne laugh much to the annoyance of the cameraman. The photograph had been taken a few months before they married and somehow was not destroyed in the fire, which claimed her life. *I will always love you Kathryne Frobisher.* A sudden gust of wind tugged at the photo and tussled his hair.

After a few minutes he stood and once again held aloft the white flag, walking back to the gate. Once he was in open desert he turned to face the Boer lines. Apart from the cooling breeze that noisily flapped the white flag and whispered amongst the grass and shrubs sending sand into crazy spirals, it was unbelievably peaceful and hard to imagine that at least two thousand eyes and half as many gun-barrels stared directly at Henry.

He stood motionless, not really caring if a Boer sniper decided his time was up. He bowed his head for a few seconds and saluted smartly before returning to Kimberley.

"You stupid bloody moron. What the hell are you trying to prove?" shouted a sergeant with the Cape Police.

"That's enough Sergeant. Let Mr. Frobisher through," ordered Lieutenant-Colonel Kekewich.

He did not say a word, just nodded his thanks to the commanding officer, tears unashamedly streaking his dust-covered face.

Chapter Forty-Three

The four-wheeled enclosed carriage and pair swept along the manicured drive to Ribbleton Manor. Inside the carriage sat Meadowbank, Huggins and Abberline.

The detective inspector studied an Ordnance Survey map while the other two marvelled at the country mansion as it came into view.

"Apart from this place an' a few farms up yonder, there ain't much else until yer get t' Grimsargh an' Longridge. We'll 'ave a nosey round an' chat wi' what's 'is name oo lives 'ere an' if wi 'ave time 'ave a look at Sudell's Farm."

"Who does live here Albert?" asked Abberline.

"It wer Sir Philip Cadley, t' Cotton King, but 'e died last year an' t' estate were passed down. Wi don't know oo lives 'ere now or oo owns th' place. But they certainly 'ave a bob or two."

"Those two constables are still missin' in t' lake. Funny, up t' last week I'd never 'eard o' this place afore. Since then it's bin an 'ive of police activity an' 'ere wi are lookin' fer Titus Moon. Strange." Huggins said.

Meadowbank ignored his sergeant, instead he looked up from the map watching the butler descend the steps and signal to the stableboy as the carriage approached.

Abberline was first out and stood aside allowing the police officers to make the introductions.

Meadowbank had recently visited a barber's shop on Fishergate for a long overdue neck shave, haircut and trim of his whiskers. His brown tweed suit had been sponged and pressed by Phoebe Tanner, who had even polished his boots, which were more than ready for the cobblers. After a good night's sleep and hot bath it was the best he had looked for a long time.

"Good morning Gentlemen. May I enquire as to what is your business?" Dobson asked perfunctorily.

"Yes yer may fettler. Wi are 'ere t' see th' master o' th' 'ouse. I'm Detective Inspector Meadowbank, this 'ere is Sergeant 'Uggins an' mi associate 'ere is Mr. Abberline."

"Police officers! Very well gentlemen, please follow me and I shall inform Sir William you are here."

They followed the butler into the house and were shown into the study. The three men looked around the large room, recently restored and still smelling of wax, leather, wood and tobacco.

"What d' yer need a study fer?" asked Huggins, gazing at a large portrait of an ermin robed old man.

"T' keep owt o' th' way o' th' misses. This is a gentleman's domain Sam. Smell that. Breathe it in." Meadowbank expanded his chest in appreciation.

The room was on the west side adjacent to the library and an open door allowed a view into the billiard room all looking onto an Italian style courtyard. The study had a high vaulted ceiling with elaborate plasterwork reflecting the light as it streamed in through the large windows. A log fire crackled in the Robert Adams fireplace and a solid light oak desk sat in the bay window, matching the panelling that lined one wall.

Abberline was scrutinising a few of the many volumes displayed in a large bookcase dominating one wall, believing a lot could be learnt about a person from the books they read, when Sir William entered.

He wore a grey suit, black waistcoat and a crisp white shirt with the modern collar and a charcoal tie. His sparse grey hair was combed back, merging seamlessly with his bushy sideburns.

"Good morning Gentlemen and to what do I owe the pleasure of a visit from the constabulary? Do you have information of your missing colleagues?" The past few days had taken their toll on Sir William.

"Good mornin' sir. I am Detective Inspector Meadowbank, this is Detective Sergeant 'Uggins an' mi associate, Mr. Abberline.

Wi are not 'ere abaht t' drownin's, but on equally serious business. An' you are t' master of th' 'ouse are yer sir?"

"Not at all Inspector. I am William Cadley. This is my son's house, but he's away on business."

Sir William offered his hand to all three then indicated they sit down on two large maroon settees facing each other between an occasional table by the fire.

Abberline remained by the bookcase reading the titles.

"Abberline! An unusual name. Are you the former Detective Chief Inspector Abberline who led the hunt for Jack the Ripper by any chance?"

"That I am Sir William. You have an excellent memory. I am now retired of course but employed as a private investigator, presently working with Preston's Criminal Investigation Department and still actively pursuing Jack the Ripper."

Dobson entered the study and placed a tray with teapot and china on the table and proceeded to pour the beverage.

"I followed your investigation in the papers with interest Mr. Abberline. A terrible business. Were you ever near to catching the maniac?"

"To be honest Sir William we had one or two suspects which never came to anything. As far as I am concerned and bearing in mind what has happened in Preston recently, there is no doubt that Jack the Ripper is still at large."

"So what is this all about gentlemen?" He asked and turned to Meadowbank.

"There is another 'omicidal maniac on th' loose. Not yet as prolific as Jack t' Ripper but equally dangerous an' though wi don't want t' bi alarmists Sir William, wi suspect 'e is 'idin' owt on Ribbleton Moor. 'E could bi usin' some o' th' owt buildings as shelter. 'E is a desperate man an' will kill again. Wi'd like t''ave a look around t' estate Sir William, wi' yer permission."

"Of course Inspector. There is a full-time gamekeeper who patrols the grounds and he has a cottage on the estate. Who is this person you are looking for? I'll pass the details on."

"Titus Moon 'e's called. A big bugger, six foot, 'eavy build, longish black 'air an' a beard. A reet evil bastard 'e is, if yer pardon mi profanity sir, but there's no t'other way t' describe 'im. Wanted fer three murders, one of 'em a police officer, committed only a few miles from 'ere. We are visitin' residents on th' moor askin' 'em t' bi careful an' report anyone or anythin' suspicious."

"Are you a medical man Sir William?" Abberline asked casually, leafing through 'Clinical Lectures in the Practice of Medicine' by Robert Graves.

"Not at all. Those are my son's books, most of them are first editions and very valuable. Charles spent twelve months at King's College Hospital training to be a surgeon under the great Joseph Lister and Sir David Ferrier, but the medical profession was not for him. Can't say I was too upset mind you. I had always wanted Charles as my only heir, to take over Cadley Industries and hope one day he'll have a son to take over from him. To continue the dynasty so to speak."

Abberline was now flicking through an 1829 copy of 'The Anatomy and Physiology of the Human Body' by John and Charles Bell. Inside the cover was handwritten, 'Charles William Edward Cadley, King's College Hospital 1882'.
His mind had automatically clicked into investigative mode and he looked at Sir William thoughtfully.

"Has Charles always resided in London?"

"Why do you ask that Mr. Abberline?" He questioned.

"No particular reason Sir William, his name seems familiar."

"Of course it is. The family own large chunks of land in the capital, including parts of the east end, your old hunting ground. The name Cadley is on billboards and letting signs all around London. Anyway gentlemen, is there anything else I need to know about this Titus Moon?"

"Just out of interest Sir William, when did Charles last visit Ribbleton Manor?" Abberline made the question seem innocent, but Meadowbank and Huggins had picked up the subtle line of questions and so had Sir William.

"Good Lord Abberline! Am I missing something here? You seem more concerned with my son's antecedents than the capture of this murderer."

Meadowbank interceded. "It would bi 'elpful Sir William if yer could provide t' dates Charles 'as stayed 'ere in th' last six months."

"This has gone on long enough. I do not keep daily logs of my son's activities and if I did have the information I would not be disclosing it to the police. Not until someone has the decency to tell me what all this is about. Until then gentlemen, I bid you good day." Sir William stood up, making it clear their discussion was over.

"Sir William, wi 'ave irrefutable proof that in March this year two women became Jack t' Ripper's latest victims. If yer son wer in town that weekend, 'e may 'ave information which could assist our investigation. It's a routine enquiry."

"I must be hearing things Inspector. Are you suggesting that my son would not have come forward with information regarding the murder of those two young women? This is preposterous and I have heard enough. Dobson will you show these Gentlemen the way out." Sir William did not dally in leaving the room.

The three law enforcers stood by the carriage outside Ribbleton Manor talking amongst themselves as Constable Clegg patiently sat on the driver's seat, trying to hear what they were talking about.

"D' yer think it's worth gettin' a magistrates warrant t' search th' 'ouse?" Asked Huggins.

"Not yet. Wi don't 'ave any evidence. A few books on surgery an' what 'ave yer, 'ardly identifies someone as a mass murderer." Replied Meadowbank.

"But it is a starting point Albert. Charles Cadley is probably not Jack the Ripper, but it would be negligent of us not to follow up this connection. Let's face it, this is the only lead we have at the moment." Abberline said.

"Bloody 'ell Fred. Wi came 'ere lookin' fer Moon an' now on th' strength of a couple o'books you've re-opened t' Ripper file."

"Albert. The Ripper case has never been closed and could not be more open. You know that as well as any of us. I think the Titus Moon enquiry is blinkering your thoughts. Look what we have. Charles Cadley lived in London at the time of the murders. He has trained as a surgeon over twenty years ago, albeit for twelve months, but in that time he would have picked up a certain amount of knowledge and skill and there were more than a couple of medical books in there, more like a couple of shelves full. The family have land and probably own property in east London, giving him a safe house and finally, Charles Cadley recently took possession of this place and since then two women are murdered in town by the Ripper. Circumstantial and assumptive it is, I admit that, but if Sir William won't tell us what we want to know it will not be difficult to build up a picture of Charles Cadley's movements and whereabouts on certain dates. We need to eliminate him from the Ripper enquiry. Don't you two agree?"

Huggins gave his reflective agreement and Meadowbank reached for his pipe, gazing across fields to woodland that hid the lake.

"Wi 'ad similar suspicions abaht Professor Bailey, remember Fred?" Meadowbank turned to look at him directly.

"Exactly Albert. It's called leaving no stone unturned and you both know as well as I do that the flimsiest lead can provide the strongest evidence. We had to follow the Bailey connection if only to eliminate him as a suspect just as we have to do with Charles Cadley. Albert, Sam, you must agree with that."

"Ok Fred. I agree t' Cadley lead is one wi 'ave t' follow up, but at th' moment mi priority is findin' Titus Moon. Charles Cadley is owt o' t' country, so 'e is not in our jurisdiction. Wi need t' mek background enquiries an' tek it from there. It'll obviously mean further enquiries in London."

"I'll catch the first train in the morning." Abberline said without hesitation.

Chapter Forty-Four

Impi is Zulu for a group of armed warriors and can number from three or four to several thousand. The impi under the command of Lieutenant-Colonel Kekewich numbered twelve and their kraal of three beehive-shaped grass huts was sited in the shadow of the main watchtower, built on the De Beers' mine winching gear, rising 155 feet above the town.

Charles, Henry and Thomas Travis sat in the largest hut in the kraal listening to the senior warrior speak. He was with his eleven tribesmen, aged between 19 and 40 years, all sat cross-legged on colourful blankets and goatskins, staring intently at the three visitors. Four women, as was the custom sat on the left and the men on the right. Three of the women were Mandla's wives, their heads and bodies covered with antelope hide to signify their unavailability, unlike the half-naked maiden who passed wooden bowls of *amasi*, curdled milk, to their guests. Henry translated what Mandla was saying for Charles and Travis.

A fire crackled in the centre of the hut, the flames reflecting on their shiny skin as if it was painted metal. It was fairly gloomy inside; the only other light source apart from the flames was the open door, which allowed a glimpse of the late afternoon sun.

It soon became clear that Mandla was more than happy to help them leave town and slip through the Boer positions. He smiled a lot, flashing white teeth and offered Henry a clay pot containing Zulu traditional beer called *sorghum* that tasted better than the ale being sold at 'The Diggers Tavern'.

Mandla pointed to the sling supporting Charles' arm and asked Henry what had happened. He recounted the lion attack and watched with surprise as the Zulu warrior's eyes opened wide in disbelief as he listened to Henry and how he fought and killed a man eater.

The Zulu men spoke quietly amongst themselves in council, nodding their heads in agreement as they all looked at Henry with growing admiration, who in turn was feeling uncomfortable under the scrutiny and uncertain about what was happening. He glanced at Charles and his countenance confirmed that he also could sense the rising tension.

Mandla spoke first. "You are a brave warrior to kill the lioness that roamed the bush like an evil spirit. We give thanks to the one God, *Nkulunkulu,* greatest of the greats for guiding your hand and giving you strength of heart to fight the she-devil, which had already become a legend of terror to my people. Chief Kharma will sacrifice a goat in your honour and embrace you as an impi warrior once he hears the news. I shall send a runner to find the body of the she-devil and take the teeth and tail to Chief Kharma to celebrate."

Henry, embarrassed, smiled at the praise from the Zulu, but he needed their help in another way, or at least Charles did.

"Thank you Mandla, I am honoured, but my friend needs medical help from the lion attack before we leave. We do not have time to see the white man's doctor. Do you have an *inyanga* to attend his wounds?"

His demeanour changed suddenly as if he had just heard that a monsoon is approaching.

"Your heart is true Henry, like the buffalo, strong and proud, but your friend's heart is like a hyena, cunning and deceitful. The spirits are warning, do not trust this man. His greed will cost you your life."

Henry now realised that Mandla was a Shaman but did not respond to the prophecy. As much as he respected the Zulu's customs and traditions he could not accept their blind faith in spirit guidance or messages from the dead and was equally dismissive of the charlatan clairvoyants and fraudulent mediums back in England.

"Will you help him or not?"

"Only because you ask this, will we help your friend."

"Thank you Mandla. The ways of the English aren't always difficult to understand. There is a shadow over Charles I know that, and I've known it since our first meeting years ago but we have stood shoulder to shoulder through good and bad times. Ok! so I saved his life, what would you or any man have done? Run into the night and leave a friend behind to be eaten alive? I don't think so. I watch his back and he watches mine. It's that simple. Well, he actually pays me to watch his back and I won't get very much if most of him is inside a lion's stomach." His grin spread to Mandla and the other Zulus, who nodded in understanding. Charles was feeling left out, apart from being in a lot of pain.

"What was that all about?" he asked.

"I think they like you Charles."

The warrior sat to the right of Mandla was a healer or *inyanga,* a man of the trees, and after a few words from Mandla, the warrior called Lungile stood up, collected some animal skin pouches from the opposite side of the hut then placed them on the ground near Charles. Without saying a word he gently untied the sling, unbuttoned the new shirt and removed the bloodied bandages to reveal the raw looking teeth marks and bruising which covered the front and back of the shoulder.

The other warriors gathered round and looked at the wound with admiration.

Lungile used a wooden bowl to prepare a poultice made from rare mushrooms found only on ant-hills, mixed with the bark of the inshulte tree and using his hands worked it into a paste, every now and then spitting saliva into the mixture until it was the right consistency. Charles grimaced as the herbal compress was smeared onto the wounds and even though it smelt God-awful, it had an immediate cooling effect and dulled the throbbing pain. Clean dressing was reapplied, but the cotton sling was thrown aside and Lungile shook his head at Charles whose short dalliance with the medical profession was enough to leave him bewildered by what he was experiencing.

"Henry, this is some form of a miracle cure with unbelievable pain relief. It is as effective as morphine without the hallucinations. It feels incredible. Can you ask them for the ingredients?"

"No chance. Healing knowledge is passed from father to son and known only to the *inyanga*. There is nothing written down or some instructions to follow and it can take a lifetime to master. You will never know what is in the poultice, it is enough to know it will help your injuries heal more quickly."

It was already dark and the warriors would be leaving soon, so Henry and Charles returned to their tent to collect their few belongings.

Earlier that day Travis had acquired two canteens for each of them and a rucksack containing food rations, matches and dynamite.

They arrived at the mining office to go through the plan as arranged, but Travis did not show up.

"Where the hell is he?" Asked Henry.

"I don't know Henry. He may have had second thoughts about the whole venture."

"This doesn't make sense. Travis has spent weeks guarding these diamonds with his life and the moment we need his help, he doesn't turn up. There's something not right about this. You don't think he's gone to Kekewich do you?"

"No. If Kekewich knew of our intentions we would be under arrest by now. Look, Travis may yet show up, but if he doesn't we'll leave without his help."

The difficult part of their escape would be getting past the Boers, but Henry was more than confident that Mandla and his men could deliver them to safety. It would then be a question of stealing two horses from somewhere and riding like the wind to the Orange River.

Mandla had arranged to meet Henry and Charles in the deserted village of Kenilworth, one mile north of Kimberley's fortified perimeter and in 'no-man's-land' between the two forces. He explained the safest route was to follow the railway track, so avoiding the searchlight then head west until they reached the road pointing north from the village, and there they would find Mandla.

The two of them stayed in the office, to avoid contact with anyone. Henry picked up a copy of the latest *Diamond Fields' Advertiser,* the towns weekly newspaper. The headlines proclaimed that the siege would be over by the end of the week, but not many believed that. Only today an express despatch rider had galloped through the Boer lines with the news that the relief column was still at Orange River.

It was time for them to leave and there was still no sign of Travis.

It would be several hours and daylight before his body, gutted from his groin to his ribcage, would be discovered behind 'The Diggers Tavern'.

They kept to the shadows, grateful that a thunderstorm was brewing and keeping the town quiet. The wire perimeter barricades loomed in the near distance and the only soldier to be seen on sentry duty was flirting with a pretty girl who had brought him fresh fruit.

Charles and Henry ambled to the sandbagged redoubt giving the appearance of two townsfolk enjoying an evening stroll. The guard paid them no attention. His duties were simply to prevent a surprise attack by Boer commandos or saboteurs breaching the defences and entering Kimberley. He had not considered the notion that some may want to leave the safety of the town.

They climbed over the sandbagged fortifications with ease and disappeared.

It was a muggy night and lightning flashed on the far horizon, leaving Henry undecided whether that was a bonus for them or not. They reached the dusty road in good time and Henry spotted the impi warriors walking towards them. Not one of the twelve fighters was less than six foot tall. They each made the traditional and complicated Zulu handshake with Charles and Henry, most of them smiling broadly as if they were embarking on a routine hunting trip. They had bands of leather with tufts of cow tails tied around their muscled upper arms and knees. Mandla wore a lion-skin headband, the others antelope or zebra. They were all bare-chested and wearing an *ibheshu,* a knee length calfskin apron around their waists, which was more practical than the loincloth for fighting, and hunting and each had a Lee-Metford British service rifle slung over his shoulder.

The arrival of firearms to the battlefield had rendered their customary cowhide shield to be used for hunting and ceremonies, but the *iklwa,* a stabbing spear with an 18-inch blade and 30-inch shaft, was indispensable.

Mandla pointed his *iklwa* west and without further delay they set off across the veldt. The pace was between a brisk walk and a trot with Mandla at the front and two rows of barefoot warriors behind him. Charles and Henry made up the rear and a look to each other made them laugh as they both knew they would have trouble keeping up with the Zulus at this pace.

After about forty-five minutes they stopped and Mandla spoke quietly with the impi, allowing Charles and Henry to get their breath back and wipe the dripping sweat from their face and neck.

Even though Henry was an expert bushman, the low cloud covering the stars and moon and the physical exertion had disorientated him completely and on looking around he had to admit he had no idea where they were or what direction they were heading, but he assumed it was south. They both had a quick gulp of water, offering their canteens to the tribesmen, which was declined with a smile. Minutes later the nearest Zulu tapped Charles' arm to indicate they were on the move again.

Henry knew the impi could maintain this pace for twelve hours or more non-stop, and then fight a battle as they have proved on countless occasions against the British and the Boers.

After another hour or so the Zulus stopped again and Mandla told Henry they would rest for a few minutes then head south.

Head south! Henry thought to himself. For the last two hours they had been travelling east much to his bemusement as well as admiration for the Zulu orienteering skills which he considered to be without equal.

Mandla spoke to his warriors and two of them left immediately. He told Henry they were approaching the Riet River and the two warriors had gone ahead to scout.

Henry offered his canteens to the impi and he gestured for Charles to do the same, but they preferred to drink from their buffalo skin pouches. Mandla said he liked the British and Queen Victoria and KaCetshwayo, King of the Zulus prayed that her army would destroy the Boers. Henry translated for Charles, explaining that Dinuzulu KaCetshwayo, the King of Zululand since 1884 and son of the great warrior Cetswayo, was no fan of the British, this was common knowledge. Henry suddenly became suspicious of Mandla for claiming otherwise and now watched him closely.

In 1887 Dinuzulu declared war on the British and he was defeated. A year later he was put on trial for high treason and banished in exile to St. Helena and was only reinstated as King of Zululand in 1898 by the British and for that he was grateful to Her Majesty's Government, but for little else. During his ten-year absence the Zulu nation fractured into tribal chiefdoms, many had sided with the British and were now unhappy with Dinuzulu's return to power which would see the erosion of their own tribal influence. But Mandla's tribal chief was Chief

Kharma, a proven supporter of the British, which helped to allay Henry's fear that they were being led into a trap.

They were on the move for another hour at least before they reached the river. Henry was amazed. They had covered more than twenty miles on foot in less than four hours. He realised that the Zulus would have done it quicker without having to slow down and occasionally stop for his, and particularly Charles' benefit, who was finding it difficult jogging while keeping his left arm against his chest. Even so he was pleased with their efforts and that they had arrived at Riet River without incident. Mandla told Henry that they would cross the river then wait for his scouts to return. He felt obliged to agree, still uncertain of Mandla's motives. It was whilst crossing this river only two days earlier that their problems had started. At least then they had had horses.

The Zulus had made it appear so easy to bypass the Boers' offensives, making their own efforts to enter Kimberley so spectacularly clumsy.

Mandla identified a crossing point that Henry recognised. They were near to where the Riet meets the Vaal, 50 miles east from their last river crossing. The Zulus entered the river first and Henry was happy to watch proceedings from the rear. It was late November and summer was approaching, but still dark with only a hint of the dawning to the east over the Drakensberg Mountains. Henry reckoned it was approximately 3 a.m. and would be light by 5 a.m.

All was quiet and Charles fell asleep, his back against an acacia tree, while Henry watched the rising sun brighten up the eastern sky. A large group of ostrich wandered by unconcerned, tugging at clumps of feather grass, to the amusement of the impi who hunt it for food, leather and feathers, but their mission this night was different.

Some time later the dull thud of distant hooves alerted Henry. He looked round to see if the Zulus could hear the approaching horses, but they had already felt the ground vibrate and now stood together facing south. Henry shook Charles awake.

"Come on Charles! We have visitors".

The riders were not far off now and Henry estimated that four horses were galloping towards them. He and Charles cocked their rifles at the same time as the impi warriors began to silently dance together in celebration.

The two scouts came into view both grinning and riding two magnificent Arab mares and each were holding separate reins to another equally beautiful horse.

The Zulus are not horsemen, but these scouts were clearly expert riders. They had stolen the horses from an unguarded Boer livery stable some ten miles away. Henry admired and stroked the four black Arabian mares, the oldest horse breed in the world, ideally suited for desert conditions. He had never ridden such a horse before, but knew they had a reputation for being good-natured and for a willingness to please any competent rider.

Mandla was delighted and handed over the horses to Henry and Charles with pride. They had done what they had been asked to do, not expecting or asking for payment or reward.

They shook hands with the warriors for a final time and certainly Henry was humbled. They had risked their lives to help two strangers. Feeling the need to repay them in some way Henry offered Mandla his holstered Webley and ammunition belt and his prized Bowie knife. Charles grudgingly handed over his Browning pump action shotgun and cartridges. All were gratefully and respectfully accepted.

Mandla spoke English for the first time. "Go easy my friends and God bless Queen Victoria. Sawubona." Henry returned the Zulu farewell and with that the impi warriors turned away and headed for the river.

Charles was shaking his head, laughing, "Henry! This is incredible."

"Not so fast Charles. Have you ever ridden a horse bareback for seventy miles?"

"Ouch." Charles pulled a face of tortured pain.

Chapter Forty-Five

The dark clouds rolled in from the Irish Sea, effortlessly crossing the Lancashire Plain before colliding with the high fells named Belmont, Parlick, Fairsnape and Wolfs Fell. The downpour was terrific and Titus huddled in the stable block at the rear of Ribbleton Manor.

It was 5 a.m. and still a few hours until sunrise, but already gaslights burned in the kitchen and scullery of the great hall.

He crossed the cobbled yard, keeping to the shadows and the long riding coat he had found hanging in the stables, kept off most of the rain. The high elaborate wooden gate from the stable yard swung open silently and the smell of cooking food urged Titus past the laundry block and dairy buildings.

The door to the kitchen hallway was open and he crept inside enjoying the heat that blasted from the ovens.

He could hear pots and pans being used with gusto and female voices chattering together. To his right was the scullery and the kitchen to his left and he knew if any of the kitchen staff entered the hallway he would be instantly discovered. He sidled nearer to the doors and heard one of the maids ask for help in moving cases of wine from the pantry to the butler's pantry. There was a short debate about that being the butler's duty and wine should not be in the pantry in the first place. The two cooks reluctantly agreed to help the kitchen maid move the wine out of the way, but only as far as the hallway.

Titus had the sense to realise he had little time. He stuck his head around the door opening and saw the kitchen was deserted, but disgruntled voices could be heard from beyond the closed pantry door.

The kitchen was about thirty feet square, all the walls and shelves painted lime-green, proudly displaying an assortment of pots and numerous copper pans hanging from wall hooks. A large oak table in the centre of the spotlessly clean floor showed off several fresh loaves cooling on racks and a pint jug of milk was placed next to a large pot of tea and half-a-dozen cups and saucers. On the marble-topped dresser near to the range sat a cooked ham shank and a plate of smoked kippers.

He dashed to the dresser first, grabbed the still warm ham then took a loaf and the milk on his way out, spilling quite a lot in his haste. Titus headed back for the gatehouse that had become his home for the past twenty-four hours.

Mrs. Ramsbottom, the plump cook did not notice the wet footprints at first, not until she saw that the ham, which had come out of the oven only half an hour earlier, was gone. Within minutes she was banging on Dobson's bedroom door.

It was mid-morning and Sir William was sat in an armchair in the drawing room, reading the fourth detective novel by Conan Doyle, titled *Memoirs of Sherlock Holmes*. He was having difficulty concentrating on the words, his mind drifting back to what Dobson had told him over breakfast.

At first he gave little regard to the news that cooked meat and bread had been stolen from the kitchen. A hungry thief no doubt or an opportunist traveller or tradesmen. It hardly warrants informing the police, he had said to Dobson, no matter how upset Mrs. Ramsbottom was.

Sir William looked out of the window at the rain-lashed countryside recalling the police warning he received the previous day. *A dangerous fugitive is hiding out on Ribbleton Moor.*

He reached for the bell-pull and moments later Dobson entered the drawing room.

"Dobson. Inform Peter the gamekeeper to be at the front of the house at 1p.m."

"Of course sir."

"And Dobson, tell him to bring his shotgun."

At precisely one o'clock in the afternoon Sir William was stood on the steps to Ribbleton Manor. He was wearing a long rubberised Mackintosh and matching wide-brimmed hat.

"Peter. Would you do me the honour of accompanying me on a tour of the estate? I do believe we have uninvited guests staying somewhere."

Sir William carried his favourite Purdy double-barrelled shotgun that had been a present from his father many years ago. Preston Pete had a woollen cape over his tweed jacket and breeches and both wore Wellington boots.

It took them over two hours to check the buildings surrounding the house and the estate farm. The rain had eased considerably as they walked along the driveway to the gatehouse. The gatekeeper's lodge had never been occupied as long as Sir William could remember. It was single storey with a bedroom, parlour and kitchen and a separate wood store with stabling sufficient for one horse. The lodge was constructed in the same style and material as the manor house and was an elegant and impressive building.

The main door, inside a porch way facing the gates, was locked. They walked around to the rear, peering through the grimy windows, but could not identify anything through the cobweb-covered glass.

Once in the yard the gamekeeper signalled for Sir William to stand still.

"Can yer smell owt sir?"

Sir William noisily sniffed the air several times.

"Not a thing. What can you smell?" he replied curiously.

"Wood smoke."

Preston Pete walked towards the wooden door of the wood store and stable and saw that the bolt was unfastened. He slowly turned the iron ring latch and pushed the door inwards. There was movement inside and suddenly with great commotion a fat hen flew through the doorway, panicking and protesting loudly on its release. The gamekeeper deftly moved to one side as the chicken lumbered past his head, but Sir William instinctively raised his gun in a startled response.

"Sir William, that there 'en is fer layin' eggs, not fer t' dinner table an' someone 'as brought it 'ere from th' kitchen pens."

Preston Pete entered the shed and in the middle of the stone floor were the dying embers of a small fire and an empty pint jug. From a nail in the wall hung the half eaten ham shank. He moved aside and checked the small stable and saw an old bale of hay spread on the floor of the stall.

"Looks like wi've found th' rat's lair Sir William."

"Yes, but which rat? The one hunted by the unpleasant Inspector Meadowbank and his merry men or a simple vagrant or itinerant traveller? We can either inform the police, possibly starting a full scale alert, only to discover an ageing tramp taking shelter or we can be patient and establish just who is creeping around the grounds."

"D' yer want mi t' 'ave a look t' neet?"

"Not yet and certainly not on your own. I don't want the best gamekeeper in the country becoming some madman's next victim."

The gamekeeper was affronted by the remark.

"I can look owt fer mi sel' Sir William."

"I know that Peter, but this is no time for heroics. Let me think about it. I'll let you know what I decide either tonight or tomorrow. Now I want your word that you will not conduct a one-man search party. I may get some of the beaters to assist. Do I have your word?"

"Am I t' patrol t' estate as usual?"

"Not tonight Peter. Take the evening off. I don't want you challenging this Titus Moon fellow and I don't want him scared away. Do I have your word on this?"

Reluctantly he agreed and declined the offer of a large brandy back at the house, instead disappearing into the undergrowth in a huff.

Titus watched the old gamekeeper leave the cottage on the edge of the woodland now settling down for winter. Brown wet leaves carpeted the cart track that ran past the cottage and smoke rose gently from the single chimneystack. The front door was unlocked and even though he was certain the house was empty, he cautiously entered. A battered leather armchair was by the fire where a split log was gently burning. The room was warm and cosy. Titus helped himself to warm tea from the teapot on the table under the window and then sat by the fire.

He thought of Mags and how he wished he was still with her.

He couldn't remember much about that night. He remembered chasing after her, but that was as much as he was able to recall. He certainly had no recollection of killing Mags but could see her dark brown eyes wide with terror, like those of the dead rabbit now staring back at him, hanging by its feet over the sink, with congealed blood at its nostrils. He could not remember choking Mags to death, but knew he had done, because she deserved to die, just like the others.

What else could he do? She had taken advantage of him. When he needed Mags to understand, she had let him down, betrayed his trust, like his mother and all the others. Since those days at the orphanage, left in the care of God's-keepers, they had polluted his dreams, violated his expectations and abandoned him to a monster.

Titus had no idea how many men and women he had killed since absconding from the orphanage twenty-one years ago but he would argue that a few of the deaths had been accidental like the murder of Mags. Accidental or reckless would have had little effect on a jury should they have been asked to consider 'intent' or 'lack of intent'. 'Murder is murder' was always the common sense approach when contemplating a 'guilty verdict' and sending a prisoner to the gallows.

His defence counsel would have no doubt explained that occasionally Titus did not know when to stop pummelling someone's head or crushing their throat. It was as simple as that.

Titus was proud of the fact that he had never taken another's life to steal money or possessions and on several occasions when suitably intoxicated had repeated this very fact to Ol' Joe, himself no stranger to explosive violence, but even he could not follow his friend's logic.

"Robbery is as good a reason as any to do someone in." Ol' Joe would say.

Titus was an opportunistic thief and he certainly had no compunction about going through pockets or purses of his victims, which was only common sense. If he didn't someone else would. If robbery was never his motive to take another's life it was invariably the conclusion.

Only when his fragile boundaries of what was right or wrong were breached by word or deed, no matter how trivial, would his ever-present anger spiral into an uncontrollable raging fury. By then it would be too late.

It was at Barnardo's where his perverted values were forged and later enforced with sheer violence as opposed to their doctrine of turn the other cheek and love thy neighbour. He only killed those who deserved to die, he often told himself, but the simple truth was that Titus was a cold-blooded killer. He enjoyed the heart-thumping thrill when taking another's life.

But in sleep their faces came to him. Some with a look of terror, some smiling and others confused, and of the myriad of faces that whirled around him, only one could he name.

Father De la Mare haunted Titus like no other.

When he opened his eyes Titus had no idea how long he had been asleep. Looking around he was confused as to where he

314

was. His rage was overpowering and he took no notice of his wet groin and soaking trousers. He stood, taking in his surroundings like a malevolent Alice-in-Wonderland and pushed over the armchair with a roar then kicked the table across the room sending crockery and cutlery flying. He threw a chair into the fire and piled the threadbare peg rug on top and watched the flames take hold.

Fire always made him feel better.

Slowly he backed away from the rising flames and once satisfied it was unstoppable, left the cottage, feeling better already. He grabbed the long felling axe he found embedded in a short tree stump, used by the gamekeeper for splitting firewood. He did not turn to see flames licking the open doorway.

Chapter Forty-Six

They headed south and thanks to Mandla they were comfortably west of the Boer positions.

The compact Arabian horses seemed to relish galloping through the heat and desert and only now as the sun began to warm the day, did Henry suggest stopping and changing horses.

Henry poured water from his canteen into his hat and gave each of his mares a drink and Charles did the same, before taking some themselves.

"How much further?"

"We are about halfway to the river. A few more hours and we'll be home and dry Charles."

"That's a contradiction Henry. Anyway it's a pity as I'm just beginning to enjoy myself."

"You could always stay behind with me."

Charles looked at him puzzled.

"What do you mean, stay behind with you?"

"Coming back here Charles has opened a floodgate of memories and emotions for me. I've run away once before, hiding from what has happened, hoping to find answers to the eternal question that will never be answered; what the hell is life all about? I need to be here where I can feel Kathryne close to me." He looked at Charles awkwardly. "You won't understand Charles. Your family is waiting for you in England. Kathryne is waiting for me here."

Charles considered this as Henry turned his attention to the horses.

He was missing Verity and Beth; Henry had no idea how much. They were his family, not his father, whom he could barely look in the face. Charles knew his father blamed him for Lucy's death, but what could an eight year old do to help his drowning sister?

Sir William had never said anything to Charles about how he felt or pointed the finger of guilt, but Charles had seen it in his eyes.

He knows I pushed Lucy into the lake.

Charles knew his father also held him responsible for his mother's death. This abominable accusation had never been made, but Charles had seen this in his eyes as well.

How could a father think such despicable things of his son?

His parents were so desperate to fill the void left by Lucy, his mother became pregnant the following year and she died giving birth to his new but stillborn sister.

His father night after night, week after week, had staggered through the house, screaming and wailing, cursing a God that could be so cruel.

Yes father, I understand better than you.

Those many years from child to man trapped in an emotional darkness without the love of a father or mother, having to hide his heart and soul as if wrapped in a heavy blanket nurtured his passionate and insane perversions.

All he had ever wanted to do was please his father, make him proud and realise that Charles needed to be loved even more than Lucy's memory.

Only Verity had ever peeled back the blanket allowing him to feel alive and show him the secrets of a woman's desires. Now it was so hard controlling his love for her that at times it caught his breath and could even reduce him to tears. He would kill for Verity to prove his love if needed.

"When had you decided this?"

"As soon as I saw Table Mountain again. That is where I proposed to Kathryne."

"So when were you going to tell me?"

"What difference does it make to you? We shake hands, you hand over the £20,000 and we go our separate ways. You belong in England and I belong here. It doesn't get much simpler than that Charles."

"Nothing in life is simple Henry. You should know that."

A crack of rifle fire snapped through the savannah quietness and Henry dropped to the ground releasing a loud groan and a hand went to his right knee, seeping blood.

A second shot followed seconds later and the horse nearest Henry toppled over screaming as only terrified horse's do.

"Sniper! Hold onto the horse's." Henry shouted between gritted teeth.

The bullet had gone straight through his kneecap, shattering the patella. He looked over his shoulder and saw the horse was dead with a massive hole in its head. Henry painfully rolled over the dead animal for cover keeping his head down.

Charles had disappeared into the undergrowth and hidden the horses, then crawled towards Henry.

"How bad are you?"

"Bad enough. My leg is fucked. Look Charles, we need to find that sniper before he moves position and gets closer."

Another bullet whacked into the dead horse.

Henry slowly brought up his binoculars and searched the countryside and it did not take him long to find the Boer sniper.

"He's as bad a shot as he is at concealing himself. He's about 500 yards away in a kneeling position beside a thorn bush."

Resting his Mauser on the horse's side Henry took aim and fired.

"Bravo! I call that payback." Henry yelled, confirming the hit through his binoculars. "One dead assassin."

Charles with complete confidence in Henry's shooting stood up squinting to see where the fallen sniper lay and asked for the binoculars.

"Ah yes! I see him. Excellent shot Henry, excellent."

"Help me up Charles and onto my horse will you?"

Charles picked up the rifle next to Henry.

"Hand me your rucksack, you could do with a shot of the old morphine first."

"Good idea and there are still three left. See Charles you are now thinking like a Cape Rifleman."

Still sat down he awkwardly removed the backpack and passed it to Charles who took it with a smile and backed away.

"Slight change of plans Henry."

He looked up frowning.

"You must understand Henry that this is nothing personal, but it has to be this way. I was going to kill you when we arrived in Cape Town, but leaving you here to die in the desert is less messy for me and an ideal opportunity for us to part company."

"What are you talking about?"

"No one can know about the diamonds, not even you or Travis. It was always going to be this way."

"You killed Travis?"

"Of course. He had out-lasted his usefulness and only a fool would slavishly guard the diamonds for my father and be rewarded a pittance. Travis should have taken the stones and run weeks ago."

"I've never trusted you. You are just a sadistic, arrogant coward, spending daddy's cash. He should be proud of you."

"My father knows nothing of this. He believes what I tell him and when I tell him you were killed by a sniper that will be the end of that."

Henry's mind was racing, trying to stall Charles, then leap up and grab him, but he knew this was impossible. The pain in his leg was unbearable.

"So this is it Charles? You leave me here to die a slow and painful death after all we've been through together. I saved you from a man eating lion for fuck's sake?"

"Death is death. Where, when or how are irrelevant. You are still making the mistake of taking this personally Henry. It's not. Believe me if there was some way I could let you live I would. I respect you Henry, I honestly do, but no-one can know about the diamonds."

"What are you talking about? It was common knowledge in Kimberley that the Cadley Mine had found something big. Do you intend annihilating the whole town?"

·"Now you are talking like a fool, which I know you are not." His eyes narrowed as he glared at Henry. "I am hoping the Boers will do that for me. What you don't understand Henry is that these diamonds are mine. They no longer belong to my father or Cadley Mining. They belong to me. I shall prove to my father that I can survive on my own, stand on my own two feet without the help of Cadley Industries. I shall tell my father the diamonds were lost in the escape and fell into the hands of the Boers. This will teach him to go behind my back as if I am irrelevant. I already have a buyer lined up and these stones shall make me very wealthy indeed and no longer shall I have to ask for handouts, like a child requesting pocket money. Have you any idea how humiliating that is Henry?"

"This doesn't make sense. You have wealth in your own right and are heir to a fortune. You have never wanted for anything in your life, so why steal from your own family?"

"My wealth is nothing compared to some. I am living off my grandfather's inheritance and Ribbleton Manor has eaten into most of that. As for my father, it will be years before I inherit anything worthwhile from him and I cannot wait that long. These diamonds will make me millions; more than enough to start my own business empire, one that will make others give me the respect I deserve."

"So you murder just to prove a point and in your twisted mind gain respect." Henry started laughing. "I've been a fool Charles. You are nothing more than a cold-blooded murderer. You should have drowned all those years ago, not your sister, and made the world a better place."

Charles rushed forwards and brought a foot down hard onto the shattered knee. He pressed his Bowie knife against Henry's windpipe as it released a scream of pain. With their faces only inches apart, Charles shouted above Henry's cries of agony.

"If you ever mention my sweet Lucy's name again, I'll forget that you and I are friends. Do you understand that?"

Henry did not answer as he fought against the mind-numbing pain, so Charles pressed his foot down harder.

"Do you understand?"

"Aaaarrgghhhh." That single scream pierced the wilderness causing creatures both the hunters and the hunted to stop and listen.

"Yes, yes, yes. I understand," he gasped.

Charles kicked the canteen away from Henry and picked it up.

"You won't be needing this. No use prolonging the inevitable Henry old friend," he said smiling and moved towards the horses, climbing onto the back of one.

"I'll be back in a minute or two so don't go away, will you old chum?"

Charles rode to the dead sniper and a short time later returned with another horse, rifle and water bottle.

Without further conversation he approached the three Arab mares, gripped the reins, withdrew his revolver and shot each one in the head. He then smashed two rifles against a granite boulder and stamped several times on the most recent canteen he had acquired.

"I prefer a horse with a saddle Henry, far more comfortable, don't you agree?"

Henry stared back with pure hatred.

Charles mounted the Boer cob, gave Henry an informal salute then rode south, leaving Henry in the full glare of the African sun.

Chapter Forty-Seven

In less than forty-eight hours after arriving back in London, Abberline was sat in The Commissioners office at New Scotland Yard. He was not his usual self. His composure had deserted him and he fidgeted as he listened to Sir Edward Bradford.

"How sure are you Mr. Abberline?"

The Metropolitan Police Head-Quarters had moved from Great Scotland Yard in 1890 and was now on The Victoria Embankment, overlooking the Thames in the Norman Shaw building. The Commissioners office had marvellous views of the Houses of Parliament to the right and Saint Paul's Cathedral and Tower Bridge to the left, but neither man was interested in spectacular skylines on a murky winter's day, instead their attention was on a bundle of case papers on the Commissioner's desk.

"Sir, as you know the Ripper murders have pre-occupied my time both as a police officer and as a private investigator for over eleven years. What has been discovered about Charles Cadley in the past twenty-four hours leaves me in no doubt that he is Jack the Ripper."

"What worries me Mr. Abberline is that we are not dealing with some East End ruffian, but the son of one of the wealthiest and most powerful men in the country. There is no hard evidence. What you have shown me about the medical training and the fact that he was in London and later Preston at the time of the murders is circumstantial. Even if we knew his present whereabouts, there seems little to be gained by bringing him in for questioning, unless you are hoping for a quick confession to multiple murders. Any barrister worth his salt would have this kicked out of court immediately then sue for wrongful arrest."

"I agree sir, at the moment, yes. What we need is to find a murder weapon or direct evidence, such as the missing body parts."

"And how do you propose to do that Mr. Abberline?"

"A magistrate's warrant to search Cadley's address in Mayfair and his stately home in Preston."

"Hmm. I see." He stroked his beard as he considered the suggestion. "Another aspect of the case you present against Charles Cadley that troubles me is the lack of Ripper-style letters since the latest two victims. During the Whitechapel investigation, as you know, we were bombarded with correspondence from people claiming to be Jack the Ripper. I accept most were hoaxes, but a few contained details only the perpetrator could know and have been authenticated. Is this not so?"

"That is not quite correct sir, with respect. First of all Preston police have received numerous letters purporting to be from Jack the Ripper. Inspector Meadowbank and his team, including our graphologist who is now assisting up north, have painstakingly compared each one with the hundreds we received and a conclusive match could not be made. Not only that, but the letters did not contain any information that could not have been obtained from the newspapers so they have been dismissed as hoaxes. Secondly, as for the hundreds of letters we received eleven years ago only one remains a possibility of being penned by the Ripper. That is the famous 'From Hell' letter that accompanied the piece of kidney sent to Mr. George Lusk in October 1888. It has been accepted that the kidney probably came from the deceased Kate Eddowes, but there is still a split between medical experts and it cannot be proved conclusively. And the third and final point sir is that not one letter we received contained information that only the murderer could know. Some make inaccurate claims and the rest have details that were printed in newspapers. So in answer to your question sir, I do not think we can place any importance on the lack of or presence of letters claiming to be from Jack the Ripper. And certainly not until we obtain a sample of Cadley's handwriting for comparison."

Sir Edward Ridley Colborne Bradford, who succeeded James Monro as Commissioner in 1890, was a thin man with a moustache that completely covered his mouth. He picked up Abberline's report once again and read it for the second time.

"How would you explain the eleven year gap between the apparent re-emergence of the Ripper? Do you have any thoughts on this Mr. Abberline?"

"Up until a few days ago sir, I was as much in the dark as the next person as to why the killings suddenly stopped. I've read the theories as to what had happened to Jack the Ripper. He had gone to prison for another crime, moved abroad or he was dead, possibly suicide, are just some of them, but the truth is no-one has known. That is until now. In November 1888 Charles Cadley went to live in South Africa to manage his father's huge estate and vineyard near Cape Town. He was thirty years of age then. The Whitechapel murders stopped that month with the death of Mary Jane Kelly, on Friday the ninth to be exact. Two days later Cadley caught a steamer to Cape Town and by this time had already spent a year at medical training college from '82 to '83. He has lived in South Africa from '88 to '99, only returning occasionally and apart from the most recent visit, he last returned nearly four years ago to get married in London. On Sunday 26th March this year Cadley and his wife came to Preston by train and stayed at The Bull Hotel. That night the two women were murdered."

"Have enquiries been made at the hotel, what is it called? The Bull? Presumably, if Charles Cadley is responsible for these deaths, he would have returned to the hotel in the early hours of the morning in quite a state and perhaps his wife may be able to assist in discovering her husband's movements that night."

"Inspector Meadowbank has spoken to the hotel manager and has confirmed that Mr. and Mrs. Cadley did stay at the hotel for one night on Sunday 26th March on a bed, breakfast and dinner basis. They had separate single rooms due to a mix up by the receptionist. The original reservation had been made by the solicitor dealing with Sir Philip Cadley's estate. A double bedroom was requested, but an overbooking by the hotel left the Cadleys with no choice but to accept the alternative single rooms."

"Could they not have gone to a different hotel?"

"The Bull is one the finest hotels in town sir. I stop there on my visits to Preston and accepting a single room is no hardship. All the rooms are of the highest standard and I don't believe there is a serious alternative. In fact, Mr. Charles Dickens himself stayed at the hotel some years ago, whilst researching his book 'Hard Times'. Anyway sir, that leaves Charles Cadley to come and go as he wishes as far as his wife is concerned. You ask did any hotel staff witness Cadley's movements once they had retired to their rooms? In short sir, no. The hotel employs a night manager and a porter and both have been questioned. They have their own duties which take up considerable time and quite often the reception is left unattended, so it would have been possible for anyone to enter or leave the hotel undetected with the use of a guest key."

"If Charles Cadley is the homicidal maniac you believe, surely he would have carried on his slaughter in South Africa."

"My thinking exactly sir and I have contacted the police at Cape Town through an international telegram. One thing you must appreciate sir, as I do now, is that Cape Town is still a growing frontier town. The Cape has only been a British colony for a hundred years, when we took it from the Dutch and it was only in the last seventy years that the Crown has actively encouraged emigration there. It is a city in its own right, populated by European settlers and around forty thousand black slaves freed during the abolition in the 30s. Basically sir, it can be a dangerous place and not every murder is reported and probably not even investigated. So a madman like Jack the Ripper could satisfy his bloodlust with impunity in the sprawling city of Cape Town. They certainly have not recorded any suspicious deaths that could be attributable to the Ripper, but that does not discount the probability that there are some."

"All that aside Mr. Abberline it is now six months since the Preston murders and Cadley has been residing at his Mayfair home throughout this time. And yet there have been no further Ripper-style killings either here in London or elsewhere. How do you account for the sudden halt in his killing spree and Cadley maintaining the role of a model citizen?"

"I cannot answer that sir. This is one aspect of the case that I find baffling and until Cadley is apprehended and asked this question directly I do not think even the remarkable young Doctor Freud could offer the true explanation. Having said that, Charles Cadley is now vice president of Cadley Industries, which, I'm sure you know sir, is the most powerful business conglomerate in Great Britain. He is never out of the papers as one of London's most extravagant socialites. He and his wife dine at the finest restaurants, visit the capital's grandest casinos and hold parties with a guest list of which The Prince of Wales would be envious. Since returning from South Africa, Cadley has adopted a flamboyant and lavish lifestyle. Even the restoration of his country manor in Lancashire is regularly reported on due to the amount of money he is said to be pouring into it."

"His lifestyle is that of a multi-millionaire perhaps?" offered Sir Edward.

"Quite so sir."

"I have attended one of Charles Cadley's dinner parties that you mention. It was a splendid evening. The food and wine were first class and he was a perfect host. I was sat next to the Home Secretary and only spoke to Cadley briefly, but he was most charming and certainly gave no hint of a dark side to his personality. As for him being Jack the Ripper, well on face value it does appear incredible to say the least."

"I only mention his lifestyle sir, to offer a possible reason why he has not struck again since March. Cadley has immersed himself in the family empire and certainly taken to the high society in London. Perhaps his celebrity reputation has curtailed his other interests."

The Commissioner put the report down and again stroked his beard thoughtfully. The minutes ticked by as Commissioner Bradford pondered over the report in solemn silence. Abberline was finding the waiting too much and was about to break with traditional rank etiquette and stand to stretch his legs when Sir Edward said,

"Mr. Abberline I too am drawn to your conclusions. On reflection I cannot afford to ignore the facts that you have presented, which do provide sufficient evidence to treat Charles Cadley as a murder suspect. There is far too much at stake here to worry about the immediate after-shock that is bound to hit me from all directions. You shall have your search warrants, but as you are no longer a serving police officer I shall appoint a senior officer to take charge of the investigation and you shall accompany him, having full access to police and intelligence reports. In short Mr. Abberline you are once again in the employment of The Metropolitan Police and shall remain so, until Cadley is either charged with murder, released due to insufficient evidence or can provide solid alibis. Carry on Mr. Abberline while I brief the Home Secretary."

Abberline was in a state of semi-shock. After all this time could he really be close to naming and catching the Ripper? Carrying the bundle of files he rushed along corridors searching for an empty office and a telephone.

Meadowbank on receiving the news was as ecstatic as Abberline. He needed some good news. He enthusiastically agreed to sort out the search warrant for Ribbleton Manor, assuring Abberline he would not execute the warrant until he had heard from Scotland Yard.

Meadowbank was under pressure from Major Little, who was becoming increasingly impatient by the lack of progress in finding Titus Moon, even though he was not given extra resources in the search for him.

The operation on Walton Summit was still ongoing and so far seven shallow graves had released nine bodies in various stages of decomposition, making identification difficult. Henry Moorson was optimistic that within twenty fours he could release most of his officers from this investigation to assist in the manhunt for Moon.

"At last!" Meadowbank said to his detectives. "Some progress. This should 'ave 'appen days ago. Moon is at large in an area under 'is jurisdiction an' I'm getting' it in t' neck from every bugger, includin' th' Major, th' Mayor an' t' press."

"The front office has received a telephone call from Sir William Cadley. He's reporting a suspicious fire that has destroyed one of his farm buildings and he believes someone is sleeping rough in another building on the estate. What should I tell the Sergeant? He has Sir William on hold?" Ponky asked placing a hand over the mouthpiece.

"Ponky, tell 'is Lordship wi are on our way." Meadowbank rubbed his hands briskly as he often did when moving in for the kill, as he describes making an arrest.

"Reet lads, no talk o' warrants or owt in front o' Sir William. Wi are there t' find Moon. Th' warrant is a completely separate investigation regardin' 'is son an' Sir William will find that owt soon enough. Until I say different, our priority is arrestin' Titus Moon. Ok?"

The five detectives squeezed in the brougham, a fast and lightweight carriage and Meadowbank climbed on top next to Constable Clegg who was at the reins for the six-mile journey to Ribbleton Manor.

Preston Pete stood a safe distance from his smouldering home. The thatched roof and joists had disappeared and one of the gable ends had already collapsed because of the heat.

"It wer' 'im. I know it wer'."

"We don't know anything yet Peter. You did say you left the fire burning this morning. Perhaps a spark or ember started the blaze." Sir William offered, not really believing that theory himself.

"This 'as bin mi 'ome fer more than forty year." He said to no one in particular.

"The police are on their way. Let's leave things to them, should we?"

"I ain't stayin' around t' listen t' their shite. 'Ow long fer now 'ave th' bin tryin' t' snare this Titus Moon, eh? Well ah'll tell thee sir, ah'll bi snarin' this fucker mi sel' an' I won't bi 'andin' 'im over t' coppers neither. 'E'll end up in t' lake, mark mi words."

Sir William had never heard his gamekeeper utter profanities before and was uncertain how to pacify his brooding rage.

"Now look here Peter. You'll have to come and stay in the manor until we can sort out other arrangements for you. I'll speak with Dobson and he will provide you with accommodation in the servants' quarters and some clothes. How does that sound?"

"No thank ya sir, ah'll bi makin' mi own arrangements."

"What the devil does that mean? You have no family and nowhere else to go. No Peter you'll do as I say and stay in the house. My father would turn in his grave if he could hear you. As you rightly point out, this estate has been your home for most of your life. It will take months to rebuild the cottage and we cannot do anything until Charles returns."

"Whatever yer say sir, but ah'll bi stoppin' out on th'land until I've hunted down that bastard." He cradled his shotgun; grateful he still had that if nothing else.

Titus was back near to the kitchen door and this time he was not searching for food but somewhere to hide. He knew his chances of staying hidden in woodland, quickly losing its cover, was not good and the winter weather could arrive at any moment. He needed to get indoors, now that his gatehouse den had been discovered, and find somewhere they would not look for him and Ribbleton Manor seemed the ideal place.

He had tied a rope beneath the axehead and the other end along the shaft so he could sling the felling axe across his back. The kitchen was quiet and Titus was not to know that the kitchen staff were having a tea break with Dobson in the serving room, going over the week's menus and Sir William's shopping list, in the absence of the lady of the house.

There was a doorway opposite to the one he stood by; he had not noticed it last time. He crossed the kitchen quickly, found the door unlocked and entered the butler's pantry. It was about a half the size of the kitchen with polished floorboards and white walls. A large table carried solid silver platters and terrines in the process of being polished. As Titus scanned the room he saw a grey butler's jacket on a hanger near to the door. A quick feel through the pockets revealed a large bunch of keys and a packet of cigarettes, which he kept. He also picked up a pot flagon of cider from one of many stored under the table. There was another door, painted cream as opposed to matt green like the others within the kitchen area and was situated by a large sideboard and dresser. Titus turned the doorknob slowly but found it locked. Using the keys he soon selected the right one and pulled the heavy door open revealing stone steps disappearing down into darkness. On a shelf by the top step was a large oil-lamp and matches. He lit the lamp, closed the door behind him and locked it before descending the steps.

As Titus reached the bottom step he held the lamp ahead of him, lighting up row upon row of dust covered wine bottles, stacked floor to ceiling. He smiled to himself as he walked along the central aisle, thinking this was a perfect place to lay low for a while.

His footsteps on the stone floor echoed in the cavernous cellar and Titus saw another door ahead. This was unlocked and daylight lit the small office, from a skylight adjacent to the ceiling. Two well-worn armchairs were by a table with a ledger, ink-bottle and numerous wine glasses and decanter for the ceremonious tasting by the head of the house and his guests. Very few men and certainly never a woman had been invited into the wine vault and allowed to select a particular vintage for tasting and this honour, all be it unintended and unofficial, Titus intended to make the most of.

He lit a cigarette, blew out the lamp and settled into one of the armchairs looking forwards to finishing off the cider before he started on the wine.

Chapter Forty-Eight

It was Tuesday 7th November and at 4 a.m. that morning the bombardment of Kimberley commenced.

Four hours later and approximately 50 miles due south a lieutenant of the 10th Royal Hussars, through his field glasses watched the lone rider gallop across the veldt.

"Well, who ever he is sir, he'll soon have to explain himself to several thousand British servicemen," he said to his major.

The Hussars were on scout and reconnaissance patrol in advance of Lord Methuen's gathering army.

The squadron wore khaki uniforms and cork foreign service helmets, blending perfectly with the desert landscape, which is why Charles Cadley did not see the hundred or so British cavalry watching him.

"Is he a blasted Boer, Lieutenant?"

"I think not sir. Looks European and so do his clothes, but that cob is certainly a farmer's nag. Would you like him intercepting sir?"

"Due to his direction I do not think we need worry about a lone horseman, riding hell for leather into the jaws of a lion. No Lieutenant, leave him. We have bigger game to hunt."

Charles reached the Orange River less than an hour later and stopped to take in the scene before him.

Thousands of drab khaki tents spread out from the railway track in uniformed rows on the south side of the river and countless Union flags and regimental pennants flapped in the hot wind.

A silent train was in the station unloading troops, horses and artillery, adding to the breathtaking spectacle of military might on a massive scale. Line after line of 15 and 12 pounders and 5-inch Howitzers already hitched to gun carriages were ready for immediate deployment.

Carabiniers, New South Wales Lancers, Household Cavalry, Scotts Greys, several brigades of mounted infantry, Rimington's Scouts, 16th Lancers from India and horse artillery waited impatiently in their tents for the command, 'Prepare to break camp. We march at dawn.'

The relief force commander, Lieutenant-General Lord Methuen, 3rd Baronet was still in Cape Town and would not arrive at Orange River for another five days and then would not march his army of 14,000 the sixty miles to Kimberley until the 21st November. By then Charles hoped to be passing Gibraltar on R.M.S. Dunattor's return sailing.

As Charles cantered towards the station following a well-worn track, a squadron of horsemen from the Southern Rhodesian Volunteers rode towards him, forming a single line blocking his way.

Twenty rifles were aimed at Charles as the captain demanded to know who he was, his destination and purpose.

Fortunately he still possessed the letter, obtained by his father and signed by the Secretary of State for War, Henry Petty FitzMaurice, 5th Marquess of Lansdowne, allowing Charles and Henry access to military transport, subject to the approval of a commanding officer.

"This letter refers to yourself and a Henry Frobisher. Where is Mr. Frobisher?"

The captain was unfriendly, suspicious and disdainful of civilians entering war zones, especially ones who were arrogant, wealthy and well connected.

"He was killed by a Boer sniper as we left Kimberley."

"Kimberley! The town is under siege. Are you telling me you have managed to slip past General Cronje's army?"

"That is exactly what I am telling you. Now if you don't mind I would be grateful if you could introduce me to your commanding officer as I have a train to catch."

The captain handed back the letter, "Follow me Mr. Cadley."

Without further conversation Charles was surrounded by heavily armed South African horsemen and escorted into the British camp.

Charles donated his stolen horse to the war effort after enjoying several cups of tea in fine china with a colonel from The Green Howards offering the colonel his views on Boer positions at Kimberley and lying about his reasons for entering and leaving the town. Charles produced diagrams as best he could and identified on a map their route to and from the besieged town, describing in layman's terms and not military jargon what he saw, much to the frustration of the colonel who had hoped Charles would prove to be a valuable source of intelligence. He explained that Boer defences included deep trenches along the Modder River, concealing the positions of Boer marksmen, but his observations were dismissed as a preposterous strategy.

"A mobile militia would not be placed in such a static and vulnerable position as you describe Mr. Cadley. It would be a strategic disaster," expounded the army officer.

The colonel had heard quite enough of Charles's non-military perceptions and politely excused himself.

He was accompanied to the train station by two sergeants from the military foot police who remained with him in total silence, until he was allowed to board one of the carriages. He expected the long train to be empty but it was surprisingly full with military personnel returning to the capital for various reasons, the most common being sickness, in particular typhoid, which would eventually claim the lives of over 8,000 British soldiers during the three years of war.

The steam locomotive was disconnected and the carriages shunted to a siding so the locomotive could be moved and reconnected to the opposite end. This manoeuvre took some time and Charles was becoming agitated.

At long last the train lurched and heaved, a loud shrill whistle declaring the locomotive driver's intention as the train rolled from the station, through billowing steam towards Cape Town. He settled back into his seat, the rucksack and diamonds held securely on his lap.

In September 1899 the Orange Free State Government imposed The Commando Law, instructing all burghers between 16 and 60 years to be ready to fight the British to protect their country when called upon. Each must provide for himself a horse and saddle, a rifle with 30 rounds of ammunition or half a pound of gunpowder plus enough provisions to feed himself for eight days.

The company of mounted Boer militia united under The Commando Law, looked at Henry curiously, until one of them fired a single shot at the nearest hyena. It was a large male Spotted Hyena and too occupied ripping out the stomach of an Arab mare to be concerned by the onlookers. It dropped dead with a yelp and the gunshot scattered the clan reluctantly, jabbering at the intrusion to their feeding frenzy and excited interest in Henry. High above, numerous huge Lappet-faced vultures circled leisurely waiting their turn.

The burgher dismounted and approached Henry with a finger on the trigger of his Mauser rifle. He prodded Henry with his hippopotamus hide *sjambok*, but he was somewhere between delirious and unconscious, his wandering mind and trembling body not registering the jabbing of the thick whip.

The Boer turned to his commander and said in Afrikaan, "He could be British, certainly a colonial, but he is close to death."

More of the commandos dismounted to get a closer look at Henry. He was given water while his tunic and pockets were searched. A shout came from the distance when the body of the dead sniper was discovered.

The commander of the unit, Thomas Leak, a veldkornet or lieutenant, examined the dead horses. He was lanky, in his forties and had a thick beard caked with dried tobacco juice. He wore a

335

short jacket, heavy cotton trousers and waistcoat over a dirty calico shirt. His wide brimmed hat shadowed his dirt-streaked face. He struggled to make sense of all this and walked towards Henry who was now gulping water from a canteen held to his mouth.

Veldkornet Leak spoke to Henry in Afrikaan, "Who are you?"

"Henry De Groot." He gasped.

"Are you English?"

"No. Dutch Cape."

"Why are you here?"

"I'm a prospector from Kimberley and escaped the siege and was heading back to Cape Town. I was ambushed by colonial mercenaries."

The veldkornet looked at Henry with suspicion and said in English,

"You lie! You are English. So maybe a spy?"

"No, no. I tell the truth. I am a diamond miner. I had a horde stolen from me. They left me for dead." He replied in accented English.

"Who killed the burgher sniper?" The question was in Afrikan.

"I did. I had to. He was trying to kill me. He did this to my leg. Then the mercenaries came, shot my horses, stole the diamonds and left me to die without water."

One of the commandos handed the veldkornet a photograph found in Henry's pocket.

"Who is this?" He read the name scrawled on the back.

"My wife. Kathryne. She is buried in Kimberley."

Leak took hold of Henry's hands and examined both palms then nodded to the commando holding the canteen for Henry. A few minutes later two stout branches, supporting either side of his knee were being strapped to his leg.

"Can you ride?" asked the veldkornet.

Wincing with pain as he was helped to stand he replied, "We'll soon find out."

Henry nearly passed out with the pain of being manhandled into the stirrups and throwing his shattered leg over the horses back. He gave a stifled scream, sweat covered his face and his stomach desperately wanted to heave in protest at the agony.

The Boers, all farmers from around the town of Bethlehem and known as the Bethlehem Commandos set off east at a gentle walk towards Bloemfontein. Henry was now a prisoner of war.

Chapter Forty-Nine

Albert Meadowbank smiled to himself as three police wagons from the County Constabulary drew up outside the front entrance to Ribbleton Manor and watched six uniform constables climb out of each one. There was also an inspector and sergeant which Meadowbank was relieved to see as technically he had no authority over subordinates in the county force.

'Better late than never.' He said quietly.

Meadowbank had his full team with him: Detective Sergeant Huggins and Detective Constables Ponkerton, Knagg, Tomkins and Quinney. They were in the kitchen enjoying hot tea and Mrs. Ramsbottom's apple pie while going over a map of the estate provided by Sir William. Preston Pete was also present and identifying possible places where Moon could be hiding, even though he had checked them all himself during the night without success.

The uniform inspector and sergeant were invited to join them in the kitchen as they discussed a search plan and Meadowbank left it for them to brief their own officers.

Sir William remained in the study, becoming concerned at the lack of contact from Charles. He had even rung his friend in the War Office, a senior civil servant, but news was slow to come from South Africa. Sir William was assured that as soon as any word of Charles was received he would be contacted immediately. This would have to do, he knew that and thanked the Whitehall Mandarin for his efforts.

Looking out of the window he sighed at the resumption of police activity on the estate and was beginning to believe that Verity was right, maybe there are malevolent, supernatural forces at work here. He was ready to return to London and be as far away from this place as possible and only a sense of responsibility for his father's home kept him at Ribbleton Manor, at least until that outrageous inspector and his detectives had completed the search. Sir William conceded that it was in everyone's interest that this murderer called Moon be apprehended if he is taking refuge on the estate. He did not want to abandon the staff during a crisis, in particular Peter the gamekeeper.

Dobson was making enquiries with members of staff to establish if any of them had seen his set of master keys. He was convinced he had left them in his jacket pocket the day before and had conducted several searches of the house himself since then. It was a mystery and most unlike him to misplace anything, as he was annoyingly punctilious by nature. He was beginning to worry. Dobson was reluctant to involve Sir William at this stage. He had the only other set of master keys which were kept in the study safe. Dobson thought about it carefully. He only needed keys for the gun cabinet in the study and the wine cellar door, the rest were obtainable from Mrs. Ramsbottom and Miss Campion, the housekeeper and he just hoped the keys would turn up, before he was forced to report them missing.

Not very far away Titus Moon was enjoying his second day of hiding and was still in a drunken stupor. He was grateful for the cork extractor he found in the office and had nearly finished a sixth bottle of a classic 1885 Burgundy. He remained in the armchair preferring the gloom of the small office at night where he slept fitfully in between swigging wine, to the absolute blackness of the cellar. A stone sink in the office served as a toilet and already it was stinking with faeces and urine.

When he woke it was dark and he was hungry. He took a mouthful of wine before leaving the room and lighting the oil-lamp. Titus made his way to the top of the stone steps and pressed his ear against the door.

It seemed quiet enough.

He unlocked the door, pushed it open slightly and carried on listening. The butler's pantry was in darkness and then instantly illuminated as he stepped from behind the door. A quick search proved there was nothing to eat in here so he moved towards the kitchen door and repeated his ear to the door routine before deciding to unlock and pull it open. Likewise, this room was deserted and dark. As he stepped inside, the axe, once again slung across his back, hit the doorframe with a thud that froze Titus. After a few seconds of intent listening, he emerged fully into the kitchen, saw no evidence of food and continued to the pantry beyond the door in front of him. This was unlocked as was the pantry and once inside the windowless and cool storeroom Titus was spoilt for choice.

The light revealed a wooden bowl piled with fresh fruit next to a muslin cloth covering half a fruit pie. Yesterday's bread lay on a marble board below numerous shelves loaded with tinned meats, fruits, vegetables and jars of chutneys and jams.

He shoved a couple of apples in his coat pocket, selected the nearest loaf, a jar labelled 'Red Cabbage Chutney. March 99' and the plate with the pie. He fought the urge to eat there and then, so quietly retraced his steps. The house was silent apart from the gentle ticking of a large wall clock in the kitchen. He remembered to lock the correct doors and was soon back in his hiding place, stuffing his face in the meagre moonlight allowed in by the window.

The gamekeeper was passing the kitchen during the early hours of the morning, still looking for Titus Moon even if the police had called off the search, when he saw the glow of a lamp move across the window.

The windowsill was a good six-feet from the ground, too high for Preston Pete to look into. He gripped the stone sill and scrambled up and peered into the kitchen. It was completely dark. He clung there as long as possible, staring into darkness until he had to let go and drop to the floor. There was no one there, but he had seen someone's shadow he knew that. He tried the kitchen door and found that locked. Puzzled, he lit a cigarette and sat on the kitchen step watching the windows until the morning staff arrived.

Preston Pete mentioned the activity he had seen to Mrs. Ramsbottom as soon as she unlocked the back door to let out Truffles the ginger tom and resident mouser.

The trouble with Mrs. Ramsbottom was she either worried about cooking or worried about cooking in between cooking and at the moment she was fretting about breakfast so had little time or inclination to worry about anything else. Not even someone prowling about her kitchen in the early hours could distract her from kippers, two poached eggs and thick cut rashers, just how Sir William likes them.

The gamekeeper decided to speak to Dobson, who preferred to eat food rather than talk about it and ate probably more than was good for him, looking at his portly stomach, but at least he would listen to Preston Pete.

Dobson was most interested to hear about what the gamekeeper had to say and thanked him for his diligence. Only two members of the household are allowed the freedom of the house once the master has retired and they are himself obviously, and Miss Campion. To consider a member of staff had made an unauthorised visit to the kitchen during the night was outrageous. He would investigate the matter immediately after his lunch.

Chapter Fifty

They arrived at Bloemfontein later that evening and Henry was taken to the railway station. A line of cattle trucks were under heavy guard and Henry was ordered off his horse, a moment he had been dreading. He placed his left leg in the stirrup and gingerly swung his right leg over the horse's flank, lowering his foot to the floor. As soon as contact was made and he put his weight onto that leg he immediately fell backwards with a cry of pain.

The mounted militia who had captured and accompanied him this far left him on the ground unconcerned and in the charge of new custodians. Henry was told to stand up. He explained his injury made that impossible and a hard kick to the face, sending him backwards was intended to help him reconsider.

"I'm bloody well crippled. Don't you understand? This leg has taken a Boer round." He shouted in Afrikaan through a mouth full of blood and spit.

The sliding door of the nearest truck was unbolted and opened by a guard who ordered Henry to get inside. He crawled the few yards to the track and pulled himself onto his good leg oblivious to the gagging stench of sweat coming from the opening. He was about to haul himself inside when a number of hands took hold of him and an Australian voice said, "Take it easy mate. There's plenty of room for all of us. Don't worry we've got you."

Henry was carefully lifted up into the dark wagon, but his shattered knee hit the metal edge of the opening sending a mind-numbing shock wave of pain through him, knocking him unconscious.

He was aware of a gentle rocking motion as he opened his eyes to the darkness and could hear voices chattering away in English and feel bodies pressing next to him on either side. Now he could taste the smell of sweat and urine.

"What regiment are you with mate?" The accent was again Australian and close by.

Henry looked round trying to adjust to the partial darkness, blinking at shafts of light that pierced the gloom from cracks in the wood and unable to put the pain from his leg to the back of his mind.

"Oy mate! I'm talking to you. What regiment are you with?" Henry felt a gentle dig to his ribs and looked left coming face to face with a silhouette framing blue eyes and white teeth.

Henry was confused. "Are you talking to me?"

"Well who else?"

He considered that to be a strange question, as the wagon appeared to be full of people.

"Where are we being taken?"

"Pretoria." The same voice answered.

He did not know who was listening so maintained his cover story and Cape accent.

"Pretoria. Why?"

"Away from the front line and repatriation. What happened to you mate?"

"Took a bullet in the knee from a sniper."

"Strewth mate, that sounds bloody painful. You've been out cold for nearly half an hour. Who are you with anyway?"

"I'm non-military. I was a diamond prospector in Kimberley when the Boers arrived and I got fed up with horse meat, beer like piss and dodging nine inch shells so decided to make a break for it with a pocket full of diamonds. Nearly made it as well."

"Don't tell me you still have the diamonds?" His eyes lit up.

Henry laughed. "I wouldn't have told you that part of the story if I had. No, British mercenaries took them after shooting my horses."

"So you've been buggered by the British and now it's the Boers' turn. Doesn't pay to be neutral mate."

"Whose neutral? I'd like to see these Calvin preaching bastards driven from Africa for good, but this war has nothing to do with me. The problem is I think they think I'm a spy."

A hand came across to Henry. "Pleased to meet you sport. Jack Cobb, Staff Sergeant with the 4th Australian Light Horse Infantry. Most of the lads here are from my unit."

"Henry Frobisher, formerly a major with the Cape Riflemen, now a freelance diamond hunter. Good to meet you Jack." Henry shook the hand firmly.

"When did you get nabbed Henry?" He offered a cigarette and flicked a match alight as Henry nodded his thanks.

"I'm not too sure. A couple of days ago I think. To be honest if they hadn't have found me I would certainly have died that day. Crazy isn't it? I owe my life to a Boer commando unit and a few hours earlier I'd shot and killed their sniper who shot me."

"And they think you are a spy. That could be a problem Henry."

"Something I'm well aware of, but not a lot I can do about it. Just hope they believe me before they start pounding my feet to a pulp with a hammer."

Both fell silent, listening to the banter and enjoying the smoke.

After a few minutes Henry asked, "Where are you from Jack?"

"Bulla, north of Melbourne. Worked on a cattle ranch before enlisting. Seemed a bloody good idea at the time." He said laughing.

Suddenly from across the gloomy interior pierced by flickering shafts of light someone had a coughing fit followed with violent retching.

"Shit! The captain is puking blood." A panic-filled voice shouted. There was some commotion and Jack Cobb stood up and deftly stepped over and around the men sat down.

"Where are you Billy?" He asked.

"Over here sarge. Keep coming. The Captain's not moving now."

"Ok lad, keep calm."

Jack reached the stricken captain and winced at the rank stench of vomit. He pressed his fingers against the captain's neck.

"Captain MacDonald is dead." Jack announced quietly.

Henry dropped his head against the wooden sides, closed his eyes to the nightmare he was in, with a single thought dominating all others, Charles Cadley will die for this.

Chapter Fifty-One

Dobson took a deep breath and entered the drawing room where Sir William was reading The Times and enjoying afternoon tea and scones. Dobson had been left instructions to select an '85 Cabernet Sauvignon from the cellar for dinner, which now posed a problem for the butler.

"Excuse me sir, may I have a word with you?"

"Of course Dobson. What is it?"

"We have a slight problem sir."

Sir William put down his newspaper and looked at the butler over his reading glasses.

"As long as it does not involve those blithering idiots from the local constabulary Dobson."

"No sir. I'm afraid I've misplaced my set of house keys."

It took a few seconds for the implications of this to register fully.

"You mean a set of the master keys?"

"Yes sir. I last saw them Tuesday evening. I could swear I left them in my pantry and none of the staff have seen them either. I don't suppose you have sir, have you?"

"Good God Dobson, if I had I think I may have mentioned it, don't you? Tuesday evening, that's nearly two days ago. What about the safe key?"

"You have the only safe key, but at the moment I do not have access to the wine cellar."

"This is not good enough Dobson. The keys to the whole estate missing! You don't think they have been stolen do you?"

"Not at all sir. I am sure they will turn up soon, probably been picked up by a member of staff unwittingly. I am terribly sorry sir. I realise it is an inconvenience to you, but if I could borrow the wine cellar key it would be helpful."

"You had better find them before Charles gets back. He has enough on his plate without the worry of changing every lock on the estate."

Sir William produced the only remaining set of master keys from a desk drawer in the study and returned to the drawing room, handing them over without so much as a word to accompany his baleful stare.

Dobson felt suitably chastised and did not like it. He had not lost the keys on purpose and after ten years service to the family as a valet before his promotion to Chandler's former position as head butler; he expected a bit more loyalty than was shown by Sir William. He had to admit that Sir William becoming annoyed in such a manner was out of character and he wondered if recent events were getting to him.

Now armed with the keys he made straight for the wine cellar door. There was an '82 Medoc that had caught his eye on his last visit and he had decided to sample it tonight in the privacy of his room. Helping himself to several bottles of wine each week was considered a perk of the job, as far as Dobson was concerned.

It was approaching four o'clock in the afternoon and the kitchen was busy, so no one paid any attention to the aloof butler silently passing through to his pantry.

He unlocked the heavy door and saw that the oil-lamp and matches had gone from the shelf, which is where they had always been. With a curse he searched the pantry and produced another lamp, filled that with oil, lit the wick and set off down the steps, leaving the door open behind him. In his eagerness to return the keys as soon as possible, he did not stop to consider where the lamp was, why wasn't it there and who had moved it?

Once he had reached the cellar he became aware of a peculiar smell. He had trouble placing the noxious odour but it reminded him of the open cesspit next to his parents' cottage on the back road to Feniscowles.

Dobson began searching the racks of dusty bottles for Sir William's particular choice, still trying to identify the obnoxious pong that was even more pungent now, when he noticed a smashed bottle of wine on the stone floor near to the office door.

Not possessing an efficient suspicious mind that should have identified the possible cause of the clues now known to him: fugitive on the estate, missing keys, nocturnal prowler in the kitchen, missing oil-lamp and the broken bottle, Dobson calmly opened the office door as if by invitation.

Titus was fast asleep, snoring in the armchair when Dobson blustered, "Who in the blazes are you?"
Dobson came from the old school believing that authority would never be challenged.
Titus came from a different school believing that authority was there to be challenged and if necessary beaten senseless.

"Speak up! Who the devil are you sir?"

Titus was instantly alert and on his feet, the felling-axe resting against the armchair. He did not answer, just stared at the butler weighing up his options of whether to kill him now or later. He decided to see what the butler intended doing first.

Dobson looked around the room, at last seeing the empty wine bottles, food debris and the oil-lamp on the floor by the chair, but it was the stinking pile of excrement in the stone sink that seemed to shake him from his reverie.
Titus had taken hold of the axe, ready to strike.

The realisation hit him and took effect immediately. It was if a bolt of lighting had struck the ground inches away, indicating that he was in imminent danger and should flee for his life. Dobson, a fat man who drank too much pilfered wine, moved with impressive speed through the cellar. Titus was right behind him and calmly swung the axe forwards with great force, keeping hold of the shaft as the blade embedded into the butler's right collar-bone, the momentum forcing him to veer left, crashing into wooden racks of priceless wine.

Dobson was prostrate and whimpering with pain and fear, both hands pressing on broken glass and vintage claret soaking through the seat of his trousers as Titus wrenched the axehead free from the shattered clavicle. He raised the axe in true executioner's style and one look into those crazed eyes told Dobson a last-minute reprieve was unlikely.

He put his glass encrusted hands out and screamed as the heavy axehead smashed both arms aside and hit the skull bang in the centre of the forehead, shattering the frontal bone with such force that the face literally split into two bloody halves as far as the mouth and sliced deep into the frontal lobe of the brain.

Even Titus, a homicidal maniac without equal, looked down with fascination at the end result of Dobson's slaughter.

He went through the butler's pockets and found more keys, which he tossed aside, but there was nothing worth taking. Titus then checked the steps and saw the open door. He quietly climbed the steps, closing the door and locking it. He grabbed hold of the nearest bottle of wine as he trudged back to his armchair to resume his nap.

Chapter Fifty-Two

R.M.S. Dunottar was already in Cape Town harbour when Charles arrived in the city, but his first priority was to get to the telegraph office as soon as possible.

He sent two telegrams. One to Verity at Ribbleton Manor and one to his father at Belgravia Place informing both he would be leaving Cape Town within twenty four hours. He included a message to his father stating 'No longer possess the goods. Ambushed. Henry dead. Too dangerous to remain here.'

Charles was able to secure a cabin to himself and was looking forward to some peace and quiet and catching up on a week's lost sleep.

The passenger list was in stark contrast to the outward journey. The steam liner was still under War Office requisition but most of the military passengers were the walking wounded and the seriously injured, or ill and no longer able to carry on the fight.

He purchased a new shirt, cotton breeches and tunic before making a visit to The Tudor Hotel where he booked a room for the day just to have a bath and a meal in the restaurant. Before he returned to the harbour Charles emptied the bag of diamonds onto the bed and for the first time was able to appreciate them in safety.

He spread out the stones, stroked them, rubbed them, enjoying the sensation of touch. Some he held up to the light between forefinger and thumb admiring the facets, colour and clarity, appreciating their tactile quality. Smooth, hard and even angular the stones sparkled in the daylight.

Three million pounds! You must be joking father? Someone has seriously undervalued these stones. Probably that idiot Travis. Not that it matters now. My father will never know otherwise.

Charles had also purchased a leather money-belt for around his waist and under his shirt. It was a perfect size for carrying the diamonds.

On his return to the harbour he called into the telegraph office a final time, but there was nothing for him.

Walking along bustling Adderley Street he passed Groote Kerk, the oldest church in South Africa, as column after column of marching infantry foot soldiers stomped up the cobbled street away from the waterfront, followed by the clatter of countless hooves and rattling field guns.

It was as if an invasion had taken place, which in effect it had. An invasion of colonial armies from Canada, New Zealand, Australia and India poured from the many steamships, liners and sailing ships in the harbour.

Charles walked in the opposite direction, crossing the Strand next to the railway station and finally reaching the Victoria and Albert harbour with its two basins and huge warehouse facilities.

He stood on the deck of R.M.S. Dunottar watching the clouds roll off Table Mountain and brought to mind that famous quote by Sir Francis Drake when he sailed into Table Bay aboard the *Golden Hind* in 1580, "The fairest Cape we saw in the whole circumference of the earth". Looking at the breath-taking beauty of the mountain he understood what the ancient mariner meant.

It was to be the last time Charles would look upon the mountain and across the bay and he knew that, but could not say why. It was if the howling southeaster was ushering him away, back to where he belongs, back to Verity and Beth.

Frederick George Abberline stood on the pavement with Detective Inspector Robert Sagar, an experienced officer with nineteen years service, who was part of the Ripper investigation as a young detective in '88 when his commanding officer was Inspector Abberline.

They were outside Charles Cadley's London address on George Street off Hanover Square, Mayfair. Two Metropolitan Police carriages had also brought along a uniform sergeant and five constables to execute the search warrant at the three-storey town house. The property was empty of furniture, that much they knew and they had no key. The only available ones were at Ribbleton Manor or with Verity Cadley in Bristol and the Commissioner was not prepared to wait for either of those to be hand delivered. So, in accordance with the powers of entry into the premises as stated on the warrant, Inspector Sagar had already decided to break the door down.

Two constables had hold of a heavy cylindrical lump of iron with two large grips, one welded in the middle and one at the end, allowing the door ram to be swung with maximum effect. It took five strikes before the gleaming black door crashed open.

The house was empty apart from one or two lonely tea chests, even the rugs had gone to Ribbleton Manor allowing the sound of heavy boots on polished wood to echo sadly.

Inspector Sagar sent two officers to each floor and he and Abberline would search the basement. It was a large house and it went back further than appeared from the street, but within fifteen minutes every one had rendezvoused back in the dining room. There was nothing to report from the house search, which just left the rear garden. The key had been left in the back door and the small formal garden was dominated by a single storey brick building, once used as servants' quarters and stables. A heavy dark wooden door, which would not have looked out place in Newgate Prison, prevented access inside.

The two constables who had done such a fine job on the front door were instructed to open this one. It took more effort and considerably more time before the cracking of splintering wood gave way to breaking metal as the lock surrendered its hold.

Sager entered first. The room was cold and dark but the gaslights were soon lit revealing a type of laboratory, clinically clean and smelling of chemicals unknown to most of the officers.

But Inspector Sager had studied medicine for four years and instantly recognised the smell of formalin and was drawn to the large glass jars and vials on a shelf.

"What's that smell Bob? It seems familiar. Is it formaldehyde?" asked Abberline.

"Not exactly. It is formalin, a mixture of formaldehyde, water and methanol. You've probably smelled it at undertakers, they use it for embalming."

Sager stared with disbelief at the preserved tissue in the nearest sealed and unlabelled vial.

"Oh my God! It's part of a vagina and uterus." He looked at Abberline, eyes and mouth wide open.

"You mean from a woman?"

"Of course from a woman." He turned his attention to the vial, making no pretence to hide his annoyance at Abberline's obtuseness.

"I meant a woman as opposed to a primate, horse or whatever. So it definitely came from a woman?" Abberline replied, holding his breath as he stared at the preserved organs.

"Frederick, I have confirmed to you what it is and where it has come from. Why are you finding it difficult to accept?" he replied rather pompously, resenting the presence and interference from his old boss.

"Do you realise the implications of this?" He returned the wide eyed gaze to the police inspector.

It was Inspector Sager's turn to furrow his brow.

"Annie Chapman. She had these organs removed eleven years ago and they have never been found and the same happened to Elsie Lupton a few months ago. Identical *modus operandi*. And Catherine Eddowes was missing her womb and a kidney. What are in those other jars Bob?" His voice was cracking with nervous tension.

"Good God Frederick! Calm down and let me take a closer look." Beginning to share Abberline's excitement and without picking up the vials he peered into each one. "Left kidney, part of it missing. A womb, a bladder and a portion of intestines. Christ! This is a chamber of horrors. These are all human organs."

"More than that, they are the body parts removed by Jack the Ripper. This is it Bob, this it! We have found the lair of Jack the Ripper."

"Not so fast Frederick. These need to be examined by a police surgeon at the very least before any conclusions can be made."

Abberline looked awe-stricken at his former junior officer as if he had discovered the meaning of life when in fact he had discovered something more important to him.

"Charles Cadley is Jack the Ripper." Abberline said quietly.

Chapter Fifty-Three

The train stopped at Pretoria Station and the cattle trucks were emptied one at a time as the prisoners were transferred to open horse-drawn wagons. Boers, armed and unsympathetic, forcibly ushered their captives onto the wagons and any complaint was met with a rifle stock to the face or stomach.

Henry was eased from the rail truck with the help of Jack Cobb and a trooper. The platform was well guarded and any chance of escape at this point was impossible, but that did not stop two Australian troopers slipping underneath a cattle truck. As they dashed across the adjacent tracks towards a siding, a salvo of rifle-fire cut them down amidst a lot of shouting and whooping from many of the guards. Henry heaved himself slowly into the open wagon, being watched over by Jack Cobb, and a short time later a convoy of horse-drawn wagons carrying silent and thoughtful men, now prisoners of war, left the station, escorted by many mounted commandos.

The wagon carrying Henry stopped outside a large school with a high corrugated-iron fence topped with barbed wire and the outside perimeter patrolled by armed guards.

The prisoners were lined up on the road, facing towards the school, and a burgher paced the line, examining each uniform insignia then separating the officers from non- commissioned officers. Henry was pulled forwards away from Jack Cobb and ordered in English to move to one side together with the group singled out. Henry turned and winked at Jack, giving him a smile and thumbs up before limping away through an opening in the metal fence.

It was a state school being used to contain prisoners of officer rank, war correspondents and spies. Henry was to learn that the majority of prisoners of war were taken to the city racecourse and up to two thousand British and colonial servicemen were under guard there.

Henry had not eaten for over thirty-six hours and was feeling hungry despite the throbbing pain in his leg. He was eventually led to a classroom empty of desks and chairs and was left with several officers of different ranks. They began their introductions, discussing how badly the war was going, what the prospects were and how they could escape, which was considered their duty.

The following morning three burghers entered the classroom and ordered Henry to stand up. He did not know the time but it was light and having spent the night talking to his fellow prisoners about the course of the war, knew it was just after sun-up. The guards watched with indifference as Henry struggled to his feet and shouted 'No' at several prisoners who came forwards to help him.

A captain with the Cheshire Yeomanry protested loudly.

"For God's sake, the man is injured. He needs help, damn you."

It was met with insolent silence and three rifle barrels pointing directly at him.

Henry was on his feet and followed the Boer who was waving him towards the door. He nodded his thanks to the Yeoman Captain who nodded back saying loudly, "bastards".

He was taken outside and he used the wall as support in an effort to keep up with his captors who prodded him forward with rifles whenever the pain began to slow his pace. He found himself at the rear of the school in a large fenced compound and the guards moved away leaving Henry blinking at the rising sun as he adjusted to his surroundings.

He was against a high gable wall and facing eight Boer riflemen, standing in a line twenty feet away and facing him. Their weapons were carried on the right shoulder and they stood to attention.

He understood perfectly why he had been brought here.

A veldkornet approached Henry with a hood, but he refused. He wanted to see his executioners. He ignored the shrieking pain from his knee, standing straight with his legs together, hands now tied behind his back and chin raised.

The veldkornet moved aside, standing next to the commandant in charge of the firing squad who had loaded one of the rifles with a blank. Only he knew which one that was, the burghers only knew one of their squad would fire a blank. This was believed to make the execution process more efficient as each shooter could believe they fired the blank thereby not having the responsibility of the fatal shot on their conscience, which seemed to matter to some. Also it was to prevent wild shooting by the executioners in a deliberate effort to miss the target. It was a much-used military tradition throughout the Empire.

He gave the command in Afrikaan.

"Present arms."

Henry took a deep breath and with open eyes staring at the blue sky he spoke quietly.

"My darling Kathryne. This is sooner than I planned. I will be with you very soon my love. Please be there, waiting."

"Take aim."

He calmly inhaled his final breath.

"Fire."

A simultaneous blast of rifle fire echoed around the compound and seven bullets tore through his chest propelling him backwards into the wall. Henry fell lifeless to the dirt.

"At ease."

The commandant turned to the veldkornet, "Their spies die with more dignity than their soldiers."

"So he was a spy was he sir?"

"Who knows? Who cares? We have too many prisoners to interrogate but he wasn't one of us, that I do know." As the young commandant stared at the corpse he instructed the veldkornet,

"Make certain he is dead then bring out the next one."

Chapter Fifty-Four

It was early evening, the light was fading and Titus was returning to his roost. He had left the wine cellar at five that morning, just before Mrs. Ramsbottom started her day. He needed to stretch his legs after five days underground and spent the day away from the estate, reconnoitring the moor towards the east.

Sir William was sat by the drawing room desk and his shaking hand held the telegram from Charles, redirected to him from his London home. He was in shock, those few words on a piece of paper pounded in his head. *No longer possess the goods. Ambushed. Henry dead. Too dangerous to remain here.* The fact that Dobson had not been seen for over twenty-four hours no longer concerned him.

Not since the telegram arrived.

He was sat in the gloom, lost in his thoughts, listening to the burning coal crack and splutter in the grate, when movement at one of the large windows reaching from floor to ceiling caught his attention.

Titus was peering into the drawing room, testing the windows, trying to find a way in, as the kitchen was not an option at this time of the day. The room was in darkness apart from the glow off the fire and he did not see the figure sat by a writing desk at the far end of the room.

Sir William seemed to snap from his thoughtful meanderings and watched the male pull at different windows. He moved towards Sir William's position who caught sight of those eyes which seemed to blaze like the drawing room fire and were as black as coal. He knew instantly who this man was. His name was already scratched onto his memory.

Titus Moon.

Rage filled Sir William. He had lost much in life, his wife and daughter, his love for a son and now a fortune in diamonds, but he had always kept hold of his pride, no matter what. Dignity in victory and fortitude in defeat had been his dictum, but no longer. It was time for revenge and to hell with propriety and decorum.

As Titus sloped away Sir William jumped to his feet, fuelled with anger and feeling invincible, even though a knight of the realm in his late sixties. He called out in a voice cracking with emotion, *'audentas fortuna juvat'* as if it was a war-cry to rally the faithful. He went to the gun cabinet in the study and found it locked, remembering Dobson had his keys. He cursed aloud at the butler's incompetence as he took a heavy chrome-plated letter opener from the desk and wrenched the door open. He selected his Purdy shotgun, loaded the weapon and shoved a handful of cartridges into his pocket, then left the house by the front door in search of Titus Moon.

The former gravedigger was now at the back of the house patiently tugging at each window when he heard a noise. It was the rusting hinges of the wrought iron gate at the side of the house. He had heard them screech many times. Titus moved away from the house, jumping over an ornate wall that separated the formal gardens from the ha-ha beyond. Laying face down he watched the path, peeping between sandstone columns.

Sir William made no pretence of stealth or of advancing with caution. Instead he strode along the footpath, his face flushed with fury and his metal-shod brogues noisily striking the stone underfoot. He held the shotgun at waist height, brandishing it forwards as he turned the corner. The only light was from a full moon, constantly blinking as banks of cloud swept past in an unorganised procession.

Titus watched Sir William as he came into view. He stopped, searching around him and straining to look across the dark lawns, where Titus lay.

A voice from behind, shouting, pierced the night.

"Oy! You. What yer doin'?" Preston Pete called out.

Titus turned his head to see the gamekeeper standing below the ha-ha, no more than thirty feet away and looking along both barrels raised towards him.

Instinct took over and Titus leapt the low wall as shotgun blast tore chunks from the stone balustrade. He carried on running across the lawn towards the house.

Sir William had no idea what was going on or who was dashing towards him or who the hell was discharging firearms on family property.

"You there! Stop and present yourself."

Titus already had the axe in his hand and charged forward like a Huron Indian from the James Fenimore-Cooper novel, *Last of the Mohicans.* Sir William, in panic rather than a controlled endeavour, fired both barrels from the hip sending the 'shot' on an uneventful trajectory. Before Sir William had chance to react further, to compensate for his foolishness in discharging both barrels, Titus had reached him. He swung the felling-axe in a wide arc and never broke his stride as the axehead sunk into Sir William's head, cutting through his left ear, striking deep into the cranial cavity and dislodging the left eyeball, leaving it dangling by the optic nerve like an obscene Christmas tree bauble.

In a single move he yanked the axe free and continued running towards the house.

By the time the gamekeeper had made it to the top of the steep embankment and climbed over the wall, Sir William was dead and Titus was nowhere to be seen. He rushed to his employer's aid, but soon realised the next formal occasion for Sir William would be his funeral.

Preston Pete ran towards the kitchen to raise the alarm.

Titus had positioned himself in a doorway to the laundry room offering an excellent view of the kitchen door. He saw the gamekeeper dart inside, followed by a woman's shriek and wailing, then several of the kitchen staff dashed outside to find Sir William. Preston Pete chased after them, attempting to dissuade them from seeing the body. For a few seconds everything went quiet as the kitchen party disappeared from view, allowing Titus to move from cover and walk towards the kitchen.

The door was open and he slowly looked in. It was empty, the only noise coming from large copper pans steaming away on the range. Titus quickly headed for the butler's pantry, grabbing a loaf of bread from the table before unlocking the door to the wine cellar and re-locking it prior to descending the steps.

Dobson still lay where he was slain, the blood on and around the body now congealed, adding to the rotting stench of decay pervading the vault.

He sat in his favourite armchair, swigging from a bottle of Cadley Vineyards Cape Chardonnay, smirking to himself, his amusement soon developing into a full blown belly laugh, leaving him gasping for breath several minutes later.

Chapter Fifty-Five

The steam liner R.M.S. Dunottar Castle was two days into its journey to Southampton and Charles had no idea of the developments unfolding back home and fortunately for him, no one there had any idea that he was on his way back to England, apart from Verity and Sir William.

He only ventured from his cabin to use the bathroom and check the healing progress of his wounds and with each passing day since receiving the poultice, the recovery had been remarkable. He was still considering returning to Mandla's village sometime in the future and using any means of persuasion to ascertain once and for all what exactly went into Lungile's concoction. Charles knew a money-making opportunity when he saw one.

Since departing Cape Town he had not eaten for those first two days. He had no appetite in between long spells of restless sleep and a recurring dream that always involved Henry watching him sleep from somewhere above, as if he was fixed to the ceiling looking down with eyes searching the room, searching for Charles but never seeing him.

Several thousand miles away the Mayfair home of Charles and Verity Cadley was still the scene of intense police activity. The 'laboratory', having been photographed for evidential purposes, was now empty and the specimens in the care of and being examined by a professor of pathology. Surgical instruments, racks of sterile test tubes, flasks and all manner of laboratory equipment along with a stack of pornographic literature were all labelled and removed to Scotland Yard.

Two senior detectives from Scotland Yard had travelled to Bristol to interview Verity and of course they had to explain the reason for the questioning, and what had been found at their London home, without giving too much detail away. The investigation was at a sensitive stage and Verity was considered an accomplice until proven otherwise.

The detective superintendents wanted a full list of staff in their employment and details of all previous members of staff. They wanted the name of the company who transported their belongings to Ribbleton Manor, details of family and friends who were frequent visitors and those who had access to the outbuilding.

They wanted the key for the outbuilding, which Verity did not have. Only Charles possesses keys for there, she explained.

How often had she been in that building? Never, she answered.

Did she not think that strange? No, she said that Charles very rarely set foot into the place anyway. He said it was a storeroom for Cadley Industry documents. She had no reason to question him or any reason to enter the building.

She was questioned as to her movements on particular dates in October and November 1888, the year she married. At this stage her mother stopped the interview, insisting it would only resume with a family solicitor present. If they were suggesting her daughter had some involvement in the Whitechapel Murders eleven years ago, they had gone too far.

Rosie Morgan ordered them out and told them to return only if they possessed a search warrant or enough evidence to make an arrest.

Verity gave her mother a look of desperation.

"Mother, they can't honestly believe that my Charles is Jack the Ripper. Surely?"

"What do you believe Verity?"

"What do I believe? In the truth of course. I love Charles and so does Beth. He's been my husband for eleven years and this is all some sort of mistake and when Charles gets back he will explain everything."

Her mother could see Verity's bloodshot eyes brimming with tears.

"Why did you not mention to the police about the telegram Charles sent you a few days ago?"

"I need to speak with him first in private, rather than with an audience of bloodthirsty policemen accusing him of unspeakable crimes he has not committed."

As her daughter burst into tears and fled the room, Rosie moved towards the window and watched the two detectives climb into a hansom cab, not certain of anything anymore.

Albert Meadowbank came off the telephone with Abberline and clapped his hands together with a beaming smile.

"Reet lads. This is it. T' big 'n. It's lookin' like Charles Cadley is our man fer Elsie Lupton an' Beatrice Babbitt's murder. Wi need t' get our arses down t' Ribbleton Manor an' rip th' place apart an' tek no more shite from Sir William bloody Cadley. But first there is t' small question of obtainin' a search warrant from t' magistrates. Ah'll speak with th' Major first an' tek it from there. Ok!"

"Are we going up there t' night sir or what?" asked Geronimo.

"The Yard want us t' sort it as soon as possible. Trouble is though if wi don't do it t'neet an' whatever evidence there is, if any, is moved before wi get there t'morrow we'll look like a bunch o' flamin' idiots. Wi could put a couple of uniform lads on t' front door t' mek sure nothin' leaves th' 'ouse overneet I suppose. Ah'll see what t' Major sez first."

The telephone rang and Geronimo picked it up. He did not say a lot to the caller apart from "right" a few times and finishing with "someone from C.I.D. will be up there soon."

"Hang on sir, before you go. You'll find this interesting. Sir William Cadley has just been found murdered in the grounds at Ribbleton Manor. Titus Moon's name has been mentioned as well."

"Bloody 'ell! What's goin' on? 'Ave they emptied Whittingham lunatic asylum? Oo was on t' telephone then?"

"The housekeeper, Miss Campion. Do you want me to contact a doctor to examine the body at the scene and sort out an ambulance to transport the body to the mortuary? It'll save time calling for one from down there."

"Good idea an' contact Sergeant 'Uggins will yer? Yer'll find 'im at 'is usual table in Th' Stanley. You lads get down t' manor 'ouse an' start th' ball rollin' while I sort things owt this end with t' Major. 'E'll probably want t' come an 'ave a look an' stick 'is two penn'th in."

Sam Huggins, Ponky and Geronimo stood aside as Doctor Byers examined the body of Sir William Cadley.

"Hmm. Very nasty. Death would have been instantaneous. The left parietal bones of the skull are fractured resulting in massive brain damage and blood loss, caused by a blow of considerable force from a sharp instrument, probably an axe or similar. The time of death fits in with what your witness has told you, about three hours ago now. The eye spilling from the socket is interesting. Have you ever seen anything like this before?"

The three police officers grimaced simultaneously as Doctor Byers gently lifted the eyeball and moved his head close to the shattered socket, inserting a finger into the cavity. Even Huggins who once enjoyed a meal of braised sheeps eyeballs with suet dumplings and onion gravy, felt unusually nauseous at what he was seeing and already regretting having that second black-pudding an hour ago.

"Ok Gentlemen. I can confidently say the victim is dead. He has not taken his own life nor is it natural causes, therefore I suspect foul play. We need to get the corpse to the mortuary. Can I leave that with you Sergeant?"

Huggins, who had met the doctor on numerous occasions during the course of their work, could never decide whether the doctor was being sarcastic in his observations or enjoyed stating the obvious or was painfully professional at all times.

"Reet y' are sir. Leave that wi' us. Once mi colleague 'ere 'as teken a few snapshots we'll 'ave Sir William in th' back o' th' ambulance. Ah'll need t' tell Inspector Meadowbank when th' post mortem will tek place. Any idea at t' moment?"

"Tell my good friend Inspector Meadowbank, if he cares to attend the hospital at eleven in the morning I shall enlighten him further," he said with a smile.

Ponky positioned the camera and tripod and proceeded to take several shots of Sir William from various angles and in particular the gaping wound to his head.

Chapter Fifty-Six

The decision not to immediately execute the search warrant at Ribbleton Manor was made by the Chief Constable, Major Francis Little, and not for operational practicalities or to further the investigation to apprehend Jack the Ripper, but to prove a point. He would not dance to the Commissioner's tune and would implement the warrant when he decided and not on the say so of Bradford, Ridley or Abberline.

Somehow, even the High Sheriff, William Huntington and the Lord Lieutenant, the Right Honourable Earl of Sefton, had got wind of proceedings and arrived together in a carriage at the major's office just as he was about to leave with Meadowbank. They were quite clear about what they expected from the major and wanted 'the cloud of terror' lifting from the town as soon as possible. 'This murder enquiry has been going on for four months and that is three months three weeks too long' the chief police officer had been told. In reply he pointed out that the Jack the Ripper investigation had been ongoing and getting nowhere for eleven years and it was his own officers' enquiries that were now drawing events to a conclusion.

Needless to say this exchange did nothing for his wellbeing and reinforced his entrenchment in doing things his way.

Meadowbank remained silent during the bumpy ride along Watling Street Road, not even listening to his chief constable's lamentations against 'interfering bastards in high office', instead concentrating on the recent news from Abberline that a positive match had been made with Charles Cadley's handwriting and the famous 'letter from hell'.

'E's as good as 'ung, he thought to himself, *once 'e's bin caught that is.*

Their journey to the manor had been a waste of time. The body of Sir William Cadley had already been taken away and the detectives soon established that the only possible witness was the gamekeeper, Preston Pete. He was in the kitchen being questioned by Sergeant Huggins when the chief constable and detective inspector arrived.

"So what have we learnt from this witness Sergeant?" asked Major Little.

"Nowt much sir. 'E took a shot at a male 'e spotted snoopin' about t' grounds, but 'e don't thinks 'e 'it 'im."

"What is your position on the estate sir that allows you to shoot first then ask questions later? This is rural England not the Khyber Pass," the major asked, already out of his depth in the handling of potential witnesses.

"Gamekeeper."

"That does not answer my question sir."

"It do' fer me."

"What is your name sir?"

"Preston Pete."

"That's not a name, just a nickname. What is your proper name?"

The gamekeeper looked up for the first time. "I think I knows mi own name."

"I beg to differ. Preston is a town and Pete is short for the Christian name Peter. It is like Her Majesty the Queen, God bless her, calling herself Windsor Vicky. Quite preposterous. Are you saying your name is Peter Preston?"

"No. I'm sayin' mi name is Preston Pete."

Major Little turned to Meadowbank. "This man can hardly be treated as a reliable witness if he does not know his own name. You cannot go round adopting names that take your fancy. What is the point of being baptised?"

A look of horror descended on the major.

"You have been baptised haven't you sir?" his voice rising.

"Nope."

The major stopped to control his thoughts. "This explains it Inspector. The man is a heathen. How could he hold the good book in his right hand then take the oath as a non-believer? Exactly! He could not, therefore whatever evidence he offered to a magistrate or judge would be treated as a pack of lies and rightly so."

Huggins gave his inspector a conspiratorial nod.

"Sir, should wi leave t' witness interviews t' Sergeant 'Uggins while wi examine t' scene of the crime?"

Before the major answered, two more police officers entered the kitchen, one they all immediately recognised.

"Major Little! What the blazes is going on here?" demanded Henry Martin Moorson.

"Ah Henry. Good, you received my message. Allow me to bring you up to date."

"I received no message from you, but fortunately William Huntington, the High Sheriff of Lancashire, saw fit as the Sovereign's judicial representative of the county to inform me of a murder investigation that I know nothing about, taking place within my force area by a Chief Constable who has no authority or jurisdiction whatsoever. You have completely ignored protocol, not to mention the Home Secretary's regulations regarding policing force areas." The county chief constable made no attempt to hide his anger.

Both men were of similar height and build and wore their uniform of rank, including cap, gloves and pace-stick.

Major Little appeared personally affronted by his counterpart's outburst.

"Now look here Henry, the murder of Sir William Cadley may well be connected to the hunt for Titus Moon or Jack the Ripper or both and I don't think this is the time or place for nit-picking. We are here following a lead that came direct to us and you have been made fully aware of and kept up to date about our search activities on the moor, so to find my officers here can't come as any surprise. And for the record Henry, I most certainly did send a constable to your office with a memorandum from myself, not two hours ago."

Suitably placated and certainly more conciliated, Henry Moorson listened to the major's chronological summary of events, starting with the London address search warrant.

Major Little then asked Meadowbank for their own search warrant and in an act of deference and feeling somewhat relieved, handed the warrant to Henry Moorson, with the assurance that borough officers are available to assist if needed.

Even if either of the two chief constables had the desire to execute the search warrant at Ribbleton Manor there and then, they most certainly did not have the manpower or equipment to conduct such an operation in such a big house, so the Lancashire County Chief Constable made the decision to delay the search until later the following day.

It was 11a.m. and once again a posse of police officers gathered outside the front door of Ribbleton Manor. Chief Constable Moorson, together with a superintendent and twelve officers, including Meadowbank's four-man team waited impatiently for the house keeper, Miss Campion, now unofficially running the whole estate, to read through the details of the magistrate's warrant with red, puffy eyes.

"Very well. You must do as you see fit, please be mindful that there are priceless works of art on display, particularly in the drawing room, dining room and library. I don't just mean the paintings. Some pieces of china are particularly valuable as are the Egyptian artefacts. You should also know Chief Constable that for the past few days certain keys have gone missing, preventing access to the wine cellar and the safe in the study. I take it you will want to examine beyond those locked doors?"

"We'll worry about that when faced with that problem. Now if you could stand aside please madam, my officers will start the search from the ground floor and work their way up dealing with the cellar last. Thank you Miss Campion and have no fear of breakages we are all professionals you know."

Miss Campion had taken it upon herself to make a tearful contact with Verity in Bristol, before she read the news of her father-in-law's death in the papers. Verity had her own problems. There were numerous journalists camping outside her mother's home waiting to pounce on anyone who had the misfortune to leave the house. An unidentified source at Scotland Yard had leaked the news that Charles Cadley was to be questioned regarding several unexplained deaths in East London during the last decade. It did not take long for the news-desks to read between the lines and print front page headlines declaring that Charles Cadley is a police suspect for being Jack the Ripper.

Less than twenty-four hours after the Mayfair house was searched, newspapers worldwide clamoured for information, sending journalists to London and Bristol and very soon to Preston, once the family connection was made public.

By 2p.m. the search officers rendezvoused once again outside the front door. A thorough search had not revealed anything incriminating against Charles Cadley, much to the disappointment of all the police personnel present.

A locksmith had been summonsed to hopefully deal with the safe rather than the suggestion of using dynamite. That was to be the second option.

As for opening the cellar door, a quick debate had narrowed the solution down to a 20lb sledgehammer smashing against the locks, a very successful tried and tested method of opening locked doors in the past.

A burly sergeant, six feet tall and a former dray-man used to swinging 36 gallon oak beer-barrels and even larger hogshead casks, removed his helmet and tunic, rolled up his sleeves, revealing heavily tattooed arms and took hold of the sledgehammer.

"Stand back," he shouted unnecessarily, as his colleagues detailed to search the cellar had already moved away a considerable distance.

"Go on sarge! Show it oo's boss," a constable called out.

Like a heavy beam striking a Buddhist temple bell, the hammer blow resonated around the butler's pantry. The hammer was swung again and the iron door handle dropped to the stone floor to the sound of ruptured metal and splintered wood, but the door remained closed. The sergeant raised his right leg and gave the door an almighty kick with the flat of his foot and the door flew inwards on its hinges, crashing against brickwork.

There was a roar of approval and admiration, which the straight-faced superintendent decided to ignore. Even he had to admit it was an impressive display of strength. Conscious of his subordinates watching intently, the superintendent ventured towards the dark opening. Straining to see inside he moved to the top step, when the smell hit his nostrils and tastebuds, forcing him to lean against the doorway, gasping as his stomach contents became an unstoppable surge, splashing his boots and accompanied by a gargled retching.

Meadowbank stepped forwards, taking charge.

"Reet lads, wi need lamps afore wi go any further. I need six o' yer wi' strong stomachs t' come wi' mi. Any volunteers?"

"What's that pong sir? What's down there?" a voice enquired, moving away from the smell.

"Whatever it is, it's dead, that's fer sure." Meadowbank replied.

"If it's dead, summat must a killed it," the same voice offered.

"Yer reet lad an' that thing might still bi down there, waitin', or then again 'ave yer never 'eard o' natural causes or blocked drains? Fer God's sake, get 'old o' yersels. Yer supposed t' bi Lancashire's finest."

The burly sergeant standing like Thor holding his war hammer said, "Count me in sir and my five lads would love to accompany you. Isn't that right lads?"

A few voices reluctantly murmured, "Yes sarge" from behind.

Armed with oil-lamps Meadowbank led the search party down the steps and put a hanky to his nose and mouth attempting to mask the acrid stench already making his eyes water.

The smell was suffocating like an invisible gas and someone at the rear puked noisily and for the second time in as many minutes no one found it amusing.

"Christ Almighty Fred, mind mi boots!"

Meadowbank could see movement in the gloomy passageway and raised his bulls-eye lamp to cast its beam further. A colony of rats swarmed over the corpse of Dobson, hundreds of unsettling eyes glinting in the light, staring at the intruders, before they scurried under wine-racks and stacked barrels.

The procession moved closer until they reached the gnawed body and two halves of a skull stripped of flesh.

"Oo is 'e?" the sergeant asked.

"Th' 'ead butler, lookin' at 'is clothin'. Dobson's 'is name. Bin missin' nigh on four days now, poor sod an' I suspect this is th' 'andywork o' Titus Moon," said Meadowbank, sweeping the beam around the vault.

He saw the closed door ahead and reached inside his coat, producing a Webley revolver and slowly walked forwards, with numerous shafts of light from behind dancing around him in silence.

Meadowbank motioned for the sergeant to try the door and as soon as it opened he darted in with the revolver held out and finger on the trigger. The smell in the small room was if anything more nauseous and soon they found the sink layered with putrefying human waste, crawling insects feasting and breeding on the filth.

He had seen and smelt enough.

"Check b'hind t' wine-racks afore yer leave, just t' mek certain there's no one lurkin' in t' shadows. Ah'll see yers back in th' kitchen fer a brew," he said wearily.

Titus was several miles south on the outskirts of the village of Longridge by the time the butler's body was discovered. Sat in a hayloft he enjoyed a whole roast-chicken, compliments of Mrs. Ramsbottom's kitchen, while taking shelter from another wet November morning. He rolled the house keys between his fingers as he decided what to do next.

Titus was not a social beast and not one to crave another's company or seek companionship, but after ten days since fleeing Preston he was ready for a pint in The Prime Jug and he had unfinished business with the Reverend Plumb.

Money was not a problem. Titus still had the horde of cash safely kept in a jacket pocket but he was not in any hurry to start spending yet as he had managed to survive quite nicely by thieving and murder. He was surprised how easy it had been to maintain the basics for human survival: food, warmth and shelter, and the previous seven days in the wine cellar still brought a smile to his face.

Titus had developed a taste for wine, especially red, even though he was completely ignorant of the need to appreciate the sensory evaluation of fine wine.

Nonetheless his palate recognised tannins and acidity without the knowledge of assessing the wine's quality, determining the maturity, studying the colour and clarity, detecting the aromas and flavours or gauging its complexity. After all he was not a sommelier and lovers of wine did not usually swig the stuff straight from the bottle. But two strands of a new certainty came to mind for Titus. First, even after three bottles and falling asleep, he never woke up with a banging head, and second, it tasted a damn sight better than that gnat's piss the Reverend Buck had the nerve to pass off as altar wine. With this in mind, he pulled a ten-year old claret out of the sack and removed the cork using the corkscrew he had had the sense to take along, with unusual accomplishment for a gravedigger. He settled back to wash the chicken down with a decent vintage accompanied by bouts of loud belching.

He had no plan and had never heard of the concept of contingency. At the moment he was quite content to stay amongst the bales of hay with enough food and bottles of the finest wines money could buy, to last him three or four days.

Titus lived from day to day, each new dawn presenting him with opportunities or obstacles or both, and on occasions it was difficult to distinguish one from the other.

He tried not to dwell on the past as the past had memories and some memories made him very angry, very angry indeed.

Chapter Fifty-Seven

Three days later the Royal Merchant Ship Dunottar Castle docked at Southampton and Charles disembarked anonymously, eager to contact Verity.

Unknown to him, the funeral for his father was to be a very private affair and Sir William's solicitor had asked Verity, as the wife of the son and heir, if she would take on the responsibility of making the funeral arrangements for her father-in-law.

She declined. Still raw from the death of her own father the last thing she felt inclined to do was oversee the burial of Sir William. That was left to his solicitors, in the absence of any contactable family or next of kin.

Sir William Cadley was buried side by side with his wife and infant daughter in Highgate Cemetery the morning Charles arrived at Southampton. He was despatched without pomp and ceremony and with minimum mourners invited, unusual for a knight of the realm, but being identified as the father of Jack the Ripper and himself a murder victim, the family solicitors decided the less publicity the better.

The newspapers decided otherwise.

Charles headed for the nearest telephone exchange and put a call through to Ribbleton Manor. It was answered by Miss Campion, her soft border country accent a stark contrast to her austere countenance.

"Miss Campion, this is Charles Cadley. May I speak with Mrs. Cadley?"

"Oh Mr. Cadley! Thank Heaven you've rung. We have all been so desperate to contact you. How are you?"

Charles was not accustomed to exchanging welfare enquiries with a member of staff and his need to speak to Verity outweighed any inclination to start now.

"Will you just bring my wife to the telephone," he asked curtly.

"But Mr. Cadley, your wife is not here. She has returned to Bristol with her mother several weeks ago." There was a pause as this unexpected information filtered through his mind, the silence allowing Miss Campion to continue, "and Mr. Cadley there is something you need to know about. Your father..."

Charles sighed, "not now Miss Campion," he interrupted and hung up.

He put the next call through to Bristol and was connected within a few minutes.

Charles immediately recognised Verity's voice over the crackling line.

"Verity, my darling. It's Charles!"

"Oh Charles, Charles my sweet, where are you?" she sobbed.

"I've just arrived from Cape Town. It's so good to hear your voice. How's Beth?" Charles was close to tears, his voice trembling with emotion.

"Charles, they are saying such horrible things about you, horrible sick lies. The police have been here looking for you. What is going on Charles?"

His eyes opened wide and he caught his breath. "Why are the police looking for me? What are they saying I've done Verity?" he asked quietly.

With emotion and tears washing over her she said with a gasp,

"Charles. It's too unbelievable to think about. I feel I'm losing my mind. First my father, then yours and now this. Charles, I cannot cope any longer. I need you here to put a stop to what the papers and police are saying."

"Verity! What are you talking about? What has happened to my father?"

"He's dead Charles, dead," she wailed, "I'm so sorry darling to tell you. His funeral is taking place within the hour in London."

He felt dizzy, as if he had slipped into a nightmare, no longer listening to Verity's lamentations and unconsciously pressed the diamonds around his waist.

377

Charles wanted more information.

"Verity, listen to me. Calm down, take a deep breath and tell me slowly what has happened while I've been away."

After a few seconds his wife managed to compose herself in an effort to tell her husband how his father died.

"Sir William was murdered last week by some maniac on a killing spree. No-one knew how to contact you Charles. The press are outside as I speak and they swarm over me like pigeons in Trafalgar Square as soon as I step from the house. That is why I have not attended Sir William's funeral. Please come home Charles, we need you."

"My father murdered? Where? Who by? Verity, give me some answers for God's sake."

"At Ribbleton Manor. There is a madman on the loose. He killed Dobson as well and the police are still hunting for him on the estate."

Charles slumped against the cubicle wall and as realisation hit him he joined Verity's sobbing.

"Darling. I'm so sorry I wasn't with you. I should have been there. Please forgive me."

"What about you Charles? You need to put a stop to these lies. They are destroying yours and your father's reputation."

He loosened his necktie, hoping to breathe easier. "What harm can words now do to my father? Where is the funeral Verity? I may still have time."

"Charles, be careful. The police are looking for you and will almost certainly be at Highgate Cemetery."

"Why are the police looking for me? You haven't said." Butterflies were fluttering madly in his stomach.

Her cries resumed. "They are saying you are Jack the Ripper. Charles you must come here to Bristol and put a stop to these monstrous allegations."

Those two sentences contained one that he believed he would never hear.

"What are they saying exactly?" He fought to control his breathing.

"Does it matter? A lie is a lie and I know the truth. You would never harm anyone. We shall face your accusers together and prove them wrong. Do you hear Charles? Every single newspaper that has printed slander about you shall present a front page apology…"

"Verity! Tell me what you know."

"They have executed a search warrant at our London home and supposedly found human parts in your store room along with press cuttings and some letters. When are you coming back to me Charles?"

"Soon, very soon. We shall meet at the Manor. I will travel there today. You and Beth get there whenever you can, but tell no one of our plans. Do you understand Verity?"

"Yes Charles. Everything will be alright won't it?"

"Of course. I'll make certain of that. Are the servants still at the manor?"

"As far as I know, but I have not been up there since my father's death and so much has happened since then. Be careful Charles, I believe this maniac who murdered your father had been living in the wine cellar. He is some sort of axe-wielding madman."

"Living in the wine cellar? That cannot be correct."

"That's what the papers and the police are saying. That is where they found poor Dobson's body, in the cellar."

"How did my father die?" It was almost a casual question.

"Does it matter? He is dead Charles. Your family needs you now."

Even with his own mounting death toll the news of the killing spree at his own home was hard for him to believe.

"Verity, for God's sake, I need to know. I need to know how my father was murdered."

"Yes. Of course you do," she replied and with some effort composed herself. "Your father disturbed this maniac in the grounds one evening. Mr. Preston, the gamekeeper went to assist and fired his gun at the intruder, but he escaped by attacking Sir

William with an axe. He received a fatal blow to the head. I believe death would have been instant, which will be of little relief to you, I know."

He wiped his streaming eyes and took a deep breath before continuing, "Travel light Verity. Don't bring Gladstone with you. It may be an idea for us to get away for a while, until the dust has settled, so to speak."

"I would not have thought that to be a good idea, Charles. Better to face the music and get it over with I say."

"You are probably right of course darling, but we will not make any decisions until we meet at Ribbleton Manor."

"I'm certain I'll be able to catch a train travelling north sometime tomorrow. Until then, take care Charles. I feel better and more confident already. God I love you Charles Cadley"

He replaced the handset gently, already planning his next move. He needed to stay one jump ahead of the police if he hoped to leave the country, possibly go back to South Africa if the Boers are defeated, or even Tenerife. Now that he had the diamonds, money would not be a problem.

Charles paid the operator for the two calls then headed for Southampton Railway Station Left Luggage Department. He produced a tattered receipt and the clerk handed over a leather handgrip holdall. It contained clean clothes, cash, soap and towel. Both he and Henry had left similar luggage on their embarkation as a matter of routine when leaving the country and Charles was grateful for Henry's foresight.

After washing and changing in the public lavatories he transferred the Bowie knife and revolver from his rucksack, which had never left his side since leaving Kimberley, to the holdall. His route north would be Southampton to London, then a train to Manchester and finally Preston. According to the timetable he should arrive at Preston late tomorrow afternoon followed by an hour's cab ride to the house.

He purchased a copy of The Times from a seller and settled back in the waiting room next to a well kept coal-fire, reading the front page and the latest information in the hunt to find Charles Cadley, alias Jack the Ripper. The article contained a detailed description of the suspect but fortunately for Charles, he had given up shaving and grooming the first night in the Karoo and now his thick dark beard, straggly long hair and suntanned complexion gave him the appearance of someone who is not the heir to a multi-million pound industry and now the most wanted man in the country.

Then something made him smile. At the bottom of the front page, underneath the Jack the Ripper story were several paragraphs stating that Winston Churchill had been captured by the Boers outside Ladysmith and was now a prisoner of war.

My name had relegated Churchill's to a lesser headline. He will not like that at all, will our dear Winston.

Winston Churchill had been taken prisoner in South Africa that was certainly true. The British armoured train with six carriages that ran from Estcourt approximately twenty five miles south of the besieged Ladysmith set out on a reconnoitre towards Colenso.

Churchill was on board the train as a war correspondent when it came under artillery fire causing it to derail at a speed of forty miles an hour. A fierce battle ensued between Boer horsemen and a company of Durban Light Infantry and Durban Fusiliers. They had occupied two of the carriages and in heavy rain approximately 100 troopers took up a defensive position around the train until they were surrounded and overwhelmed by the Boers.

The prisoners were taken to Pretoria and Churchill was detained at the fortified school where Henry Frobisher had been held only weeks earlier.

Unlike Henry, Churchill was soon to escape from the school and make his way to Lourenco Marques, the capital of Portuguese Mozambique.

The journey on the *London & South Western Railway* to London took longer than scheduled and Charles arrived at Vauxhall station too late to travel north so he booked into The Nags Head Inn on James Street, Covent Garden. A lively tavern with unassuming accommodation by his standards, but he would be unknown amongst the noisy hustle and bustle of market traders, street entertainers, revellers, shoppers and theatre-goers.

He settled in a corner of the public lounge with a pint of stout and a copy of *The Evening Standard.* The front page was dominated by the funeral of Sir William Cadley, the London millionaire industrialist, laid to rest that morning at Highgate Cemetery. It recounted the details of his murder, even naming the suspect wanted for questioning about the death of Sir William.

Titus Moon. The second most wanted man in the country.

The named jumped out at Charles. He had never heard of Titus Moon before, but read with interest that he was believed responsible for his father's murder and several more victims in the Preston area, including a police constable.

He mulled the name over in his head. He planned on Titus Moon being Jack the Ripper's next victim.

Charles had mixed emotions over his father's death. He had had nearly a day to think about it and was already coming to terms with his loss. Emotions such as grief, sorrow, heartbreak or pain were not what he was experiencing. It was relief.

No longer would he have to strive to reach his father's unattainable heights of achievement. No longer would he have to look into those eyes, blazing with accusation and mourning, and no longer would he have to instinctively seek approval, like a faithful terrier.

I did not kill them father! For God's sake I was a young boy when mother died. I did not ask for another sister. You have to take responsibility for your own actions and consequences, don't you? That's what you told me so often and so often how I wanted to throw those pathetic, hypocritical words back into your face.

Practise what you preach dear father and don't you dare look at me like that. Do you hear me?

As for Lucy, of course I pushed her into the lake. It served her right for teasing me, how was I to know there was something in there that wanted her as much as you and mother did. I only wanted to teach her a lesson, not for her to disappear. She should not have said those nasty things about me, should she? That white thing in the lake must have agreed she needed punishing. It gave me a smile as Lucy disappeared as if saying 'this will teach her respect', but those staring black eyes and open mouth, how could I tell you about them father? Would you have believed a young boy claiming there is a monster in the lake and it wants to be my friend?

Considering the dramatic turn of events that had erupted and were still massing around him like black storm clouds, Charles was remarkably cheerful the next morning. He caught a hansom to Euston station to board the eight o'clock *London & North Western Railway* service to Manchester.

Around the same time that Charles was enjoying a bacon sandwich for breakfast at Euston station, Titus Moon was deliberating about his future, an unusual occurrence in itself. He'd had a belly full of country life and deep down yearned for Starch Houses, The Prime Jug, gaslights, cobbled streets, but most of all to have a Church Street whore.

Somehow four days and nights of solitude in a hayloft had focused his mind or perhaps it was because he had run out of food and drink or that he felt indisposed to masturbating amongst bales of hay.

Whatever was driving Titus got him to his feet and into the cold air.

A mist, waist high hung over the surrounding fields and Titus, chilled and hungry tried to keep to the soggy bridle tracks that criss-crossed the marsh when a large buzzard waiting patiently on

383

a favourite hunting perch gave off a piercing cry, as if welcoming Titus to the moor.

He headed towards Preston, feeling better in himself already, intending to make a final visit to Ribbleton Manor to see what else it had to offer.

Uncertainty hung over the staff at Ribbleton Manor. The master of the house was sought by the police with the unbelievable allegation that he is Jack the Ripper, the mistress of the house had shut herself away in Bristol and the head butler had been murdered.

Miss Campion, as housekeeper assumed authority throughout the house and estate, until someone such as Mr. or Mrs. Cadley or their solicitors said otherwise.

The police had left the estate after a fruitless search for Titus Moon and the search warrant revealed no further evidence that Charles Cadley was in fact the Whitechapel murderer, much to the disappointment of Henry Moorson.

The large safe in the study had proved challenging to the locksmith, but after two days he eventually drilled through the lock allowing the contents to be examined by the chief constable. Apart from £20,000 in assorted Bank of England notes it contained nothing of interest to the investigation.

The money was handed to Miss Campion for safekeeping and she in turn demanded a police escort into town so she could bank the cash or Lancashire County Constabulary provide the estate with a replacement Chubb safe at their cost. Needless to say her first option was agreed to.

The door to the wine cellar was beyond repair and Henry Moorson refused point blank to even consider compensation for a new door. He told the family solicitors, who were not used to dealing with criminal law to read the small print on the search warrant and had to remind them that if they had not smashed the door down the dead butler would still be laying there undiscovered.

Abberline had returned to Preston the day before and now sat in The Stanley Arms with Meadowbank and Huggins ready for a late lunch.

To say Abberline was buoyant, over the moon or full of the joys of spring would have been a gross understatement. He could not keep still or quiet and had even insisted on paying for the meal and drinks. Meadowbank always said ale tasted better if someone else was paying for it and Huggins could not agree more, already enjoying four excellent pints of the superb draught bitter with a plate of brawn and boiled potatoes.

Huggins had recommended the brawn, a new addition to the menu and explained in salivating detail that it consisted of braised pig's head, heart, tongue, trotters, lemon rind, spices and vinegar, boiled together for hours, then allowed to set. And should always be served cold and sliced, he added.

Even Abberline, still maintaining his 'Scrooge on Christmas morning' countenance was tempted to give it a try until he saw the prepared dish presented to the sergeant. It looked bloody awful, he decided. Trying to fathom out the local dialect had always been a problem for Abberline, but dealing with local food was proving to be more of a headache.

Meadowbank and Abberline both had the tater-hash served with red cabbage and pickled beetroot. The London detective considered potatoes boiled with onions in milk and butter, then mashed with corned beef was the safer option and hoped it was as nourishing and 'reet gradely' as Meadowbank claimed.

"S' ya reckon 'e's still in South Africa d' yer Fred?" Meadowbank asked through a mouthful of meat and potatoes.

"Probably. This has come from the highest level in the War Office via the Home Secretary to the Commissioner. His father, the late Sir William Cadley, arranged passage to South Africa for his son and another male named Henry Frobisher, on board a troop ship. That in itself is unusual, allowing civilians other than war correspondents to travel with an expeditionary force. Anyway Sir William pulled a few strings and they sailed on a liner called the Dunottar Castle. We've made contact through the War Office with some of the officers now in Cape Town, who were also on board and it has been confirmed that Cadley and Frobisher disembarked at Cape Town."

"D' wi know why they travelled t' South Africa in t' first place? Seems strange enterin' a war zone." Huggins asked.

"It must 'ave bin bloody important then," added Meadowbank.

"Exactly. Cadley Industries have a diamond mine at Kimberley in South Africa and there were rumours on board the ship that's where Cadley and Frobisher were heading. The problem is, as you may already know that town is under siege by the Boers and has been for nearly two months. Nothing enters or leaves the place so we don't know whether they made it or not, or if Kimberley was their destination."

"So basically Fred, wi don't know where Cadley is at th' moment."

"Not for definite. Information coming from South Africa, other than through war correspondents is sketchy to say the least. It is a huge country and both Cadley and Frobisher are no strangers to that continent."

"What d' wi know abaht this Frobisher bloke?" Meadowbank enquired.

"Not a lot. A soldier of fortune. He spent many years out there as an officer with the Cape Colonial Riflemen, a respected and feared cavalry unit and then left to work for the Cadleys on their wine growing estate outside Cape Town. If you intended travelling through enemy lines for whatever reason, Frobisher is the man to have with you."

"An' there's no sign of 'im either?"

"Not a whiff. South Africa is not a good place to be at the moment, especially for English adventurers. They could be dead or taken prisoner of war like Winston Churchill."

"I've 'eard o' that name."

"I'm not surprised Sam. He's a member of the aristocracy. His grandfather was the Duke of Marlborough of Bleinham Palace fame. That's someone else who shouldn't be out there. Funnily enough Churchill shared a cabin with Cadley and Frobisher for the two week journey to the Cape and by all accounts Churchill and Frobisher struck up quite a friendship."

"Y' don't think our two friends could 'ave bin wi' Churchill then, an' now prisoners o' war?" Meadowbank asked.

"No certainly not. We know they left the ship at Cape Town and from the newspaper reports and details from the War Office, Churchill continued his sea voyage to Durban and then travelled across land. They were in completely different parts of the country."

"So wi strongly suspect Charles Cadley is Jack t' Ripper."

"Correction Albert! Can prove he is Jack the Ripper," added Abberline.

"Ok, wi can prove 'e is Jack t' Ripper, but do not know 'is whereabouts other than possibly somewhere in t' continent o' Darkest Africa."

"Succinctly put Albert."

"Tek this a stage further, if a mass murderer wanted t' disappear, 'e could do a lot worse than choosing Africa t' disappear into."

Abberline raised his eyebrows in agreement feeling slightly deflated.

"So at last wi know th' identity o' t' Ripper, but may now never find 'im."

They both looked at Meadowbank in silence.

"And if t' Boers win th' war an' drive t' British out, any chance o' trackin' Cadley in South Africa would be impossible?"

Their silence said it all.

"What about 'is missus an' daughter?" Huggins said.

"What about 'em?" answered Meadowbank.

"Well 'e may want t' mek contact at some point. Not just abandon 'em."

"It's a good point to make Sam, but being realistic Cadley has butchered at least seven women and must know by now that his secret is out and all over the papers and therefore the police will be looking for him. I think he'll walk away from his wife and child. He has already lost the family empire. The company assets have been frozen by a high court judge and once convicted and hanged, his wife and daughter will inherit the lot. Cadley has left them a hell of a legacy."

"If 'e is arrested, found guilty an' 'ung," quipped Meadowbank.

"Arrested or remains at large, either way Cadley has lost everything. If he shows up in this country and makes claim to any of his business interests he will be apprehended immediately. If he crawls away and hides, after a number of years his wife can lay claim to his assets, business and personal. One way or the other Cadley will die a wealthy man, and until then he won't see a penny of it."

"Fer all wi know 'e may 'ave come t' some arrangement wi' 'is wife. 'E keeps 'is 'ead down in Africa, she cops th' lot, they secretly keep in touch. They already 'ave business interests in South Africa, a perfectly reasonable excuse fer 'er t' sail owt there, they meet up an' live 'appily ever after on a 'uge estate in t' middle o' nowhere."

Abberline and Meadowbank looked at Huggins with a mixture of admiration and annoyance as neither senior detective had considered this possibility.

"Flamin' 'ell Sam! You an' yer theories, but what abaht this? If 'is wife now knows all abaht th' allegations against 'er 'usband, s' why would she stand bi 'im?"

"Albert, oose t' say she 'asn't known from t' start an' might even bi an accomplice."

"Because they married at the end of '88 and until then she lived in Bristol." Abberline said.

"So what? She may bi as sick as 'im. 'E made a confession t' 'er, she forgave 'im or was fascinated by it all, oo knows? It's a thought."

"I some 'ow don't think so Sam. M' money is wi' Fred's conclusion at th' moment. I don't think we'll see 'im again."

"And what about Titus Moon?" Abberline asked.

"Don't mention that bloody name t' me Fred. Fer someone oo is described as thick as pig shite by t' general populace, 'e's doin' a bloody good job o' stayin' ahead o' t' pack. I'm convinced someone must bi shelterin' 'im somewhere. Let's change t' subject fer a while an' seein' that Fred is payin' I'm gonna get kaylied."

Chapter Fifty-Eight

Charles Cadley arrived at Preston station a few hours after Verity and Beth.

His wife and daughter were already at Ribbleton Manor and Verity was doing her best to reassure the servants that all was well and they would remain in employment come what may.

Charles left the bustling station main entrance, ignoring the newspaper and flower sellers and the pungent smell of sulphur dioxide from the smokey fog that swirled around the gas lamps as he crossed Fishergate Bridge. Dodging trams and hansoms he made his way along Fishergate, pushing through the crowded street, keeping alert for pickpockets, thieving louts and begging urchins until he came to the biggest cab owners in Preston, Hardings Carriage and Livery Company in the Old Vicarage off Tithebarn Street.

He hired a two horse closed carriage and driver for twenty-four hours and paid from his last fifty pounds, reassured in the knowledge that there was £20,000 cash in the safe at Ribbleton Manor. His plan was for them to travel to Hull overnight then hire a boat and crew to take them to Amsterdam and travel overland towards the Mediterranean until the situation in South Africa resolves itself one way or another.

Charles could not foresee any problems.

Verity put Beth to bed then wandered the house finding it difficult to believe what had happened here in a matter of weeks. She had fallen in love with Ribbleton Manor when she saw it for the first time that sunny spring morning, now an eternity ago. Even the tragic death of the poor solicitor, Mr. Monk had not jaded her excitement and enthusiasm in overseeing the restoration of the house and Charles had told her from the beginning that money was not an issue.

She had secured craftsmen from all around the country. Stonemasons, carpenters and plasterers were put in paid accommodation in town and brought to the house each morning by carriage for a minimum twelve hours work. An architect and foreman prowled the building site and any worker found drunk or asleep was dismissed without pay immediately. The huge building programme had been excellent for the town's economy. Hundreds and hundreds of pounds had poured across sale counters in one way or another and the renovations at the manor were the talk of the town as were the soon to be incumbent owners who were still a mystery to most.

But now the place made Verity feel uneasy. Perhaps it was her father's death that made her skin tingle and reluctant to return, and the prospect of visiting the lake sent a shudder through her that she could not explain. She needed to speak with Charles and tell him she can no longer stay in this house and it could no longer be their family home. They would return to London tonight or stay with her mother in Bristol, all three as a family and Charles would clear his name and this house would be put up for sale.

This thought process made her feel slightly more reassured so she visited the kitchen for a mug of tea and the company of the staff. Even the prospect of conversing with the gamekeeper had become an appealing task.

Meadowbank was summonsed to the enquiry desk by the station sergeant to speak to a visitor asking for him by name.

He grudgingly put aside the pathology reports recently received from the Metropolitan Police detailing the examinations of the various body parts recovered from Cadley's London address, and entered the public area. He came face to face with a woman whom he recognised but could not put a name to.

She obviously recognised him.

"Oooh! Mr. Meadowbank. I 'opes h'im not puttin' yers owt t' much, but I 'ads t'come an' see yers".

He knew the soft voice, wheat coloured hair and amazing blue eyes, but still struggled to identify this attractive woman.

"I's can't thank yers enough Mr. Meadowbank an' would like t' buys yer a pint sometime. In fact it would bi an 'onour. What you've done fer me Mr. Meadowbank 'as changed mi life an' mek no mistake on that."

"Mary Babbitt! I don't believe it. You look incredible," enthused Meadowbank, immediately moving forwards and giving her a hug.

"I've gotten that army pension after yer wrote t' War Department. Backdated an all, just like yer said. Some good 'as come from all this and I 'ave poor Dick's death certificate an all now."

He was still smiling taking in the transformation of Mary Babbitt.

"It wer' nowt yer don't deserve Mary. I'm as pleased as Punch those civil servants got their fingers owt fer yers."

She wore a black woollen jacket over a white blouse fastened at the neck with a cameo brooch and a matching ankle length skirt, revealing polished black boots. A black brimmed hat was pinned to her fair hair and even in mourning she looked radiant. Meadowbank could not take his eyes off her.

"I've got proper lodgins now, wi' a privy inth' yard an all. Reet swanky on Fishergate 'ill, an' it's thanks t' you Inspector. You 'ad faith in mi. Instead o' leavin' mi in t' gutter like most would, yer 'elped me an' ah'll never forget that, just like ah'll never forget what yers are doin' fer our Beatrice." She was close to tears.

"What's yer 'ouse number? Ah'll come callin' an' 'ave a brew in a day or two. I might even tek yers up on th' offer of a pint as well."

"It's a long time sin' any gentleman came a callin' on me, but if yer serious it's th' front room o' number 22."

Even with her hat Mary's head did not reach Meadowbank's shoulder and she inclined her head staring intently at his grizzled unshaved face.

"I 'ope t' 'ave some good news soon. We are close t' catchin' Beatrice's killer. Not much consolation I grant thee, but may 'elp a little."

She gave a nod and said, "I've laid our Beat t' rest up int' yonder cemetery an' put up an 'eadstone an all an' a memorial plate t' my Dick. I catch tram up there once a week t' say a few words. I couldn't 'ave done all this wi'owt th' pension money."

Mary put a gloved hand on Meadowbank's arm. "Don't forget about mi Mr. Meadowbank. I've lost m' daughter an' 'usband, I wouldn't want to lose a friend an all."

She teetered on her tiptoes and gave him a gentle kiss on his cheek, turned away and left the enquiry office.

Meadowbank watched her leave without saying a word to her. He did not know what to say. As he breathed in her mild perfume his mind was reeling, his skin tingling and heart racing. For the second time in six months Mary Babbitt had made him fight back brimming tears. He dashed for the door and stood on the steps searching for her, but she was gone.

Meadowbank slowly walked up the stairs to his office and for once he was not thinking about Charles Cadley or Titus Moon.

The dry-stone wall that marked the boundary of Ribbleton Manor estate was six feet high and ran left and right following the contours of the land as far as the eye could see, but Titus climbed it effortlessly despite the damp moss and lichen that clung to every stone, and dropped feet first into a tangle of undergrowth.

He was cold, wet and hungry but more importantly he was seething with anger. Titus had got lost on the moor several hours ago, straying from the path because of the mist and had fallen into a bog up to his waist, his sodden clothes now extremely cold and uncomfortable.

The house was still some distance away and not yet visible through the denuded woodland, but Titus knew which direction to take and hacked at the undergrowth with the axe until he came to one of the many deer and boar tracks that criss-crossed this part of the estate. His vexation drove him on and he made no effort to conceal his presence, unconcerned and unafraid of whoever may discover his whereabouts.

Secretly Titus was nurturing a desire to be discovered trespassing on the estate land, then he could unleash the axe which had already proved to be a good friend to him and one that was steadily becoming indispensable. Once his anger had been directed and sated Titus would feel calmer and less agitated, as if he was reacting to a dose of morphine (it had occasionally been administered whilst in custody to regulate his self-control) but for the time being he was in a lethal frame of mind.

The carriage arrived at Ribbleton Manor less than an hour after departing the livery yard and Charles instructed the driver to remain at the reins, as he did not intend being any length of time.

He felt no sorrow in returning to the scene of his father's murder, if indeed he had at all reflected on his father's passing, mournfully or otherwise. Instead he focused his attention on what must be done and he did not have a lot of time.

It had just gone nine o'clock and the outside of the house was illuminated until ten o'clock in the evening when the lights were doused by the hall boy, a sixteen year old lad, the youngest and lowest ranked male staff in the house.

Charles entered the hallway and met the housekeeper as she secured the fireguard for the night. Miss Campion looked as if she had seen a ghost.

"Pardon me sir, I had no idea you were returning," she spluttered.

"A flying visit Miss Campion that's all. No need to attend to me. Please carry on as normal. Has Mrs. Cadley arrived yet?"

"Yes sir. She's in the drawing room. I'll instruct the maid to prepare your room."

"Miss Campion I have just said there is no need to attend to me. We shall be gone within the hour."

"Would you like some refreshments preparing before you leave?"

"No. I shall help myself shortly," he replied as he was leaving the hallway to find his wife.

The drawing room was lit by two ornate oil-lamps and several split logs were burning in the grate, their dancing flames reflecting curiously on the gold patterned cream wallpaper.

Verity stood by a window attempting to identify the mysterious fells that she knew were out there in the darkness. The high limestone moorlands that dominated the landscape and split the country in two had fascinated her ever since she first saw the huge whale-back ridge of Fair Snape, but she no longer had the desire to venture the few miles and gentle trek to its summit. She wanted to be away from the house, the fells and the lake, especially the lake, as soon as possible.

"Darling! At last I can hold you." Charles said as he saw her for the first time in weeks.

She turned and ran towards him with relief and hope beyond comprehension, repeating his name over and over. They embraced passionately and kissed with the fervour of lovers. She stroked his long hair and nuzzled his full beard and he breathed in her beauty. As they held each other she did not feel the knife strapped to his waist beneath his jacket.

"Verity, listen to me. We must leave this house of death tonight."

"Oh Charles! I am so glad to hear you say that. We could go to my mother's house in Bristol."

"No Verity, we cannot go there. Get Beth and your belongings. Bring only what you can carry in a case. There is a carriage waiting outside, we must leave soon."

She became worried. "Charles what is the hurry? I too want no more nights here, but I need time to pack and make arrangements with my maid. I cannot leave at the drop of a hat."

"Verity, you must trust me. I need to clear my name and I cannot do it from behind the bars of a cell. We leave the country tonight."

Still holding each other she looked intently into his eyes and recognised the panic that was gathering pace inside him like a thunderstorm.

"Charles I will follow you anywhere. I've missed you so much and will never let you go away again. Ever! Have you got that Charles Cadley?"

They kissed again before Charles urged Verity on. Time was not on their side.

She left the drawing room and Charles walked briskly to the study. The door was ajar and the desk lamp lit. He edged nearer and gently pushed the door open and the voice of a woman speaking quietly could be heard.

He listened with mounting anger and crept into the dimly lit room. The tall woman was alone, by the desk with her back to the door as she cupped the telephone mouthpiece with one hand. Her voice reflected a tone of consternation, a trait not normally associated with Miss Campion's demeanour.

She replaced the handset with a sigh of relief, then suddenly aware of someone close behind her.

A hand came over her mouth squeezing like a vice as Charles whispered,

"I am disappointed with you Miss Campion, very disappointed."

The Bowie knife cut deep across her throat in one quick stroke, slicing through the trachea and oesophagus, silencing her gagged scream as blood from the severed jugular veins spurted over the green leather top of the desk. He let the lifeless body slowly drop to the polished floor, dragging her to one side and out of sight.

Charles wiped his knife clean on the housekeeper's dress before cutting through the telephone wire, then turned to the safe, already searching for the key in one of his pockets. With a look of horror he noticed the safe door was wide open. He rushed towards it and kneeling down he searched through the contents. There was nothing but innocuous legal papers and certainly not the £20,000 he was expecting to find.

His mind was whirling and he fought to control his breathing.

"What have you done, you meddling bitch?" he hissed at the body of the housekeeper.

Charles walked to the desk and poured himself a glass of brandy from the decanter to consider his options. As he stared out of the window deep in thought, a shadow moved across the formal terrace, eerily illuminated by the house lights, and Charles diverted his attention to who or what was out there.

Moments later a lone figure trudged along a path, past the house. Charles watched the man whom he did not recognise. He was a big man with a mop of dark hair and a thick beard. He wore a long riding coat and carried a felling-axe in an easy manner.

Titus stopped and stared back at the figure watching him from the house. After a few seconds Titus nodded an acknowledgement to the unknown man at the window, which Charles ignored and he continued to watch the stranger disappear from view.

He quickly assumed the man was a new member of staff, recruited in his absence and from his appearance, one of the ground staff or possibly working with the gamekeeper.

Charles dismissed the stranger from his thoughts, resuming his planning for leaving the country.

Chapter Fifty-Nine

As Meadowbank returned to the C.I.D. office the phone rang. He picked it up before Huggins reached over.

"Meadowbank," he announced abruptly. As he listened to the caller his eyes widened and his face took on a countenance of incredulity.

"'E's there now?" he asked quickly. "Now listen t' mi Miss Campion. Don't stay on yer own an' get all t' staff t' gether. We're on our way."

Huggins and Abberline looked on curiously.

"Yer won't bloody well believe this but Cadley is at Ribbleton Manor."

"Ah'll sort out a carriage." Huggins said already on his feet.

"No Sam. Wi 'aven't time fer that. Get three 'orses ready while I raise th' alarm wi' t' Major. Wi need every bugger wi can muster down there an' this time Jack t' Ripper won't escape."

Five minutes later Meadowbank entered the cobbled yard checking the ammunition in his revolver as Huggins and the stable lad were efficiently strapping the saddle onto the third horse. Without a word he took one of the reins from Abberline and deftly mounting the large horse he said, "'Ow are yer on 'orseback Fred?" He had no such concerns about his sergeant's riding skill.

"You lead the way Albert I'll be right behind you." Placing his left foot in the stirrup he swung his leg over the saddle in a manner that told Meadowbank he was an accomplished rider.

With a flick of the reins and jab of the heels Meadowbank urged his mount through the yard gates then galloped off into the night followed by Abberline and Huggins.

They thundered along Lancaster Road, onto Meadow Street then Deepdale Road, past the infirmary and onto Ribbleton Lane leaving behind the township of Preston as they rode onto the dark moorland.

Charles entered the kitchen, waiting impatiently for Verity to appear, but now feeling decidedly hungry and with a long journey ahead looked for some of Mrs. Ramsbottom's creations to take with them. Even though he was not certain who the housekeeper had been informing of his arrival at the manor, he concluded it probably had been the police and estimated he had no more than thirty minutes before they arrived.

In a few more minutes we will be gone from here.

The gamekeeper was sat on his own at the table devouring a cold meat pie and drinking 'kitchen tea', a blend especially for the servants, strong and cheap.

"Sorry t' ears abaht yer father Master Cadley. Sad business, varra sad," he said through a mouth full with meat and pastry.

"Yes it is." Charles knew his father had a soft spot for the gamekeeper, but he found him repellant and even as a child avoided him and his staring eyes and that peculiar smell. Even now with his back to him Charles could feel those eyes boring into him. As a child it was disconcerting, as if the gamekeeper was constantly watching him, but now as an adult Charles found it infuriating to say the least and the stale unwashed smell even more distasteful.

He took one of the small meat pies left to cool on a wire rack and moved to the window, away from the gamekeeper and filled a glass with water. Charles saw the tall stranger still carrying the axe; emerge from the dairy swigging from a bottle of milk.

"Peter. This new chap you've taken on. He seems too damn familiar for my liking and is taking liberties already. I want rid of him, do you hear and I want him off the estate by morning. Is that understood?"

Preston Pete stopped chomping and swallowed noisily before answering.

"No sir. I've no idea what yer on abaht."

Charles turned round to face the gamekeeper. "Peter it's quite simple. There is a man wandering the estate with impunity and appears to be under the impression that theft from his employer is acceptable. I do not care who he is or who took him on. I want him dismissed from my service immediately. Now do you understand?"

If anything the gamekeeper was even more confused.

"Wi' respect sir I still 'aven't a clue abaht any o' this."

"Good God man! How the hell you have managed to stay employed by this family for over forty years I'll never know? A large male with a beard, long coat, scruffy and carries an axe. Behaves like a cretin so he must be one of your associates. Any clearer now?"

The description sent a shiver down the gamekeeper's spine.

"Where 'ave yer sin this man?" he asked slowly, eyes wide and focused on Charles.

"Now you look here Peter. My father may have tolerated your impudence but I certainly won't…"

The gamekeeper interrupted as he rose to his feet.

"That bi Titus Moon. Th' one oo killed yer father an' burnt down t' cottage. Now where t' fuck 'ave yer sin im?" he roared across the kitchen.

Charles spun round but the yard was empty. He whipped out the Bowie knife and ran into the yard.

Titus saw the carriage waiting by the front steps and headed towards it.

Young James, the hall boy had offered to pass the cases to the driver, prior to his evening task of dousing the driveway gas-lamps, his final duty at the end of a sixteen-hour day. Verity appeared at the front door looking for Charles, her packing now complete.

She watched the large burly man approach and as he did so he threw the half full milk bottle aside and Verity flinched as it smashed noisily.

"James, who is that ruffian?"

"I dunno ma'am, but ah'll soon find owt," his bravado spurred on with the knowledge that the beautiful Mrs Cadley was watching.

Verity foolishly came down the steps as James turned to face Titus.

"You there! Explain yersel' t' lady o' th' 'ouse an' state yer business." He called out with a voice of authority far exceeding his tender age.

Titus said nothing as he strode nearer. The end of the wooden shaft was in his right hand and the axe head by his ankle. He struck with amazing speed and swept the axe, one-handedly in a blinding upward arc, decapitating young James instantly, the blade embedding into the gleaming coachwork with a loud splinter of wood.

Verity watched in horror and screamed, seconds before her legs gave way and her central nervous system shut down automatically in a vain effort to protect her sanity, she slumped to the bottom steps.

The coach driver on seeing the headless body fall against his carriage, leapt from the driver's seat with an impressive display of agility, hit the tarmac running then fled down the driveway without once looking back.

Titus towered over the unconscious Verity, then knelt, cupping and fondling her small firm breasts, thinking of the only woman who had ever loved him, Mags, with her ample figure that could keep a man happy for hours. His rough hand wandered down her tweed jacket and skirt following the contours of her thighs and groin, fingers pushing between her legs, a salivating mouth moving closer to hers. His arousal needed satisfying.

Charles heard Verity's scream and his sprint became a charge. As he cornered the house the coach driver ran past him in blind panic, then he saw Titus with his mouth pressed hard against Verity's, a hand unbuttoning her jacket eagerly, her dress already pulled past her thighs revealing the top of flesh coloured silk stockings.

"Noooo! Face me you cowardly bastard," he shouted.

Titus reared up with a perverted smile displaying his decaying teeth and took a few steps towards Charles; his left hand beckoning him closer, the axe in the other was moving to and thro menacingly.

"What 'ave wi got 'ere. A gentleman oo want's t' fight? Mek it quick squire as this bitch is waitin' fer some proper fornication."

Charles ran at Titus, holding the knife like a sword and when only five feet separated them Charles dived forwards into a roll and as the sweeping axe head missed his face by inches, Charles lashed out with the knife slashing calf muscle to the bone.

Titus winced at the burning wound and took the weight off his right leg to ease the pain at the same time spinning round looking for Charles.

Charles attacked again, hoping to maintain the advantage and leapt at Titus, driving the pointed blade forwards, but Titus grabbed his wrist, pushing the hand with the knife down in a painful wrist lock. Charles rammed his fist into the snarling face, shattering bone and cartilage and releasing a pouring of blood.

Titus ignored the punch and his broken nose and jabbed hard with the base of the axe shaft connecting with Charles' windpipe. He tried to re-grip the axe nearer to the blade for more control, but did not dare let go of the hand still gripping the Bowie knife, wavering inches from his stomach.

As Charles took a few moments gasping for air, Titus struck with a head-butt that hit the side of Charles' face with a loud smack. Titus repositioned his grip and instantly chopped down with the axe-head shattering the ball and socket joint of the still healing right shoulder, dislodging the humerus. Charles released a yell of pain as the axe was raised menacingly and this time Titus intended to dispense the fatal blow.

Locked together in a fight to the death, Charles in desperation brought a knee up with great force connecting solidly with Titus' testicles, driving the scrotum up into the prostate gland and then beyond into the bladder.

Even Titus could not ignore such an infliction, which to most men would have proved fatal. He groaned and slumped forwards against Charles, the pain rendering his floundering arms useless which released his grip on the axe and the knife. The Bowie knife, now free was thrust forward, tearing through the stomach wall and Charles with all his strength pushed the blade up and up causing massive tissue damage, rupturing every internal organ in the abdomen, ignoring the warm blood pouring over his hand.

His jaw fell onto Charles' right shoulder, his body almost lifeless, blood oozing from his open mouth like a volcano spewing magma. Charles let go of the knife and pushed Titus away, watching him topple backwards his head hitting the ground with a crack and there he lay, next to the headless body of the hall-boy.

The three detectives raced through the open gates of Ribbleton Manor, their sweating steeds steaming in the night chill.
Meadowbank was the first to spot someone running towards them and raised a hand as he slowed down.
The coach driver was still hysterical.

"You there! Stop an' give an account o' yersel' lad. Wi are police officers," barked Meadowbank.

"Oh! Thank God. Thank God. There's bin murder, unspeakable murder. 'E chopped 'is ruddy 'ead clean off," wailed the coach driver.

Without another word the three horsemen galloped away.
Minutes later they arrived at the front of the house and saw the carnage welcoming them.

Charles had heard the sound of approaching horses and moved away from Verity but not before touching her soft warm lips.

"I have to go my darling, but I'll be back for you and Beth. That I promise," he whispered as he smoothed her dress.

Holding his shattered arm close to his chest he recovered the Bowie knife from Titus's stomach. He still had the diamonds and if he could get to the estate farm he would be able to take one of the horses from the riding and equestrian school and then on to freedom.

With this new plan now his sole objective he disappeared into the night and did not see the gamekeeper watching from the undergrowth.

Meadowbank had dismounted and on examining the body of Titus Moon, felt no relief in finding him dead.

"She's alive. I think she only fainted." Abberline called out.

Fanny Ramsbottom appeared at the front door in a terrible frenzy. It was a rare sight to see her beyond the boundaries of the kitchen with or without her hands clagged with dough, but discovering Miss Campion's body had driven her to drastic action.

She howled with all the power a fifteen stone woman could muster. The cook could not begin to explain between her breathless howls and moans, what catastrophe had befallen her and continued with an unintelligible bawl as she waved her arms and stamped her feet. She had not been this hysterical since the Christmas goose became a burnt offering to the French Ambassador in '82.

Preston Pete stepped from the shadows of the copse-wood and spoke to Meadowbank.

"Master Charles thinks 'e's escaped. Follow mi an' 'e'll bi yers fer tekin'. 'E's gone towards yonder lake."

"Fred, you stay wi' lasses. Me an' Sam 'll go wi' th' gamekeeper after Cadley."

"Have you gone mad Albert? After eleven years do you honestly think I would give up the opportunity of apprehending Jack the Ripper?"

Meadowbank nodded, understanding his conviction then said to the gamekeeper,

"Reet ol' man. Tek us to 'im."

The moon was big and bright, the dark lunar 'seas' clearly visible as if the giant face was watching events with interest. There was no cloud that evening and the woodland had turned white with hoarfrost and only the eerie screech of a barn owl broke the silence.

Charles hurried along the grassy track unaware of the wet footprints following him. Then he came to the lake.

He stopped and stared at the expanse of water as a blanket of fog moved across it from the cooling countryside.

No! This is not the time to think of Lucy.

The jetty pointed north like a compass arrow, indicating to Charles which direction he should take.

The boat! Yes of course. I can still cross the lake with one good arm.

The decking was frost-covered and wet underfoot and his boots, the same ones he had escaped South Africa in, crunched the ice.

A gunshot shattered the silence.

The three detectives were by the reed bed and Meadowbank fired a warning shot into the air.

"Charles Cadley. Wi know all abaht yer. Give up now. Yer've nowhere t' go," the senior detective shouted.

Charles ran along the jetty and one-handedly, frantically untied the rope that held the rowing boat in place.

Another shot blasted the night tranquillity.

"Charles Cadley. This is yer final warnin'. Gi' yersel' up." Meadowbank continued.

Charles ignored the calls to surrender when escape was so close.

Twice before he had very nearly been caught and on one occasion, when disembowelling Mary 'Polly' Nichols in Bucks Row, Whitechapel, he fled the scene before he could finish his work thanks to that damned workman who had to walk down that gloomy passageway and find the body.

On the second occasion, a few weeks later Charles Cadley struck twice in the same evening. First he slaughtered Elizabeth Stride on Berner Street, severing her throat in his trade-mark way but saving his best handy-work for Kate Eddowes on Mitre Square an hour later.

He cut her throat good and proper and opened her up, slicing away a kidney and part of her womb, both later found in one of the specimen jars.

If the steward of the International Working Men's Club on Commercial Road had not driven his horse and cart along Berner Street to the rear gates of the club and to the very spot where Charles hunched over Elizabeth Stride, about to commence his dissection, she too would have been ripped apart and ravaged.

Charles had fled to the safety of the slum house he still owned to this day on Leadenhall Street in Whitechapel. That had been his masterstroke in evading capture, having a 'bolt-hole' no one else had access to, on the very doorstep he worked.

The house was empty and even now remained undiscovered by the authorities, but he only kept a bed, spare clothing and his hunting knife there, when he did not need it.

On occasions, Charles would dress as a hawker or vagrant, spending an evening and late night amidst the slums and squalor, visiting taverns, going over in his mind how he could rid the streets of the prostitutes that were on every corner.

He had once read that there were over 1200 prostitutes alone in the East End. There was so much work to do and sometimes it seemed overwhelming.

But for now he must escape for Verity and Beth's sake so he could find a new home for them and continue with his cleansing. They would want him to do this and surely they would understand one day what compelled his carnage? It was not God's work, a noble crusade or an evangelistic zeal; Charles would never claim to be carrying out the Lord's Will to make the world a better place and had given up speaking to The Almighty a long, long time ago. It was a waste of time.

And he had seen no evidence that even hinted at an omnipotent all forgiving divinity and many years ago abandoned the notion of celestial contact offering congratulations on his work rate. So huge was his challenge, Charles once believed Jesus Christ himself would put in an appearance and shake his hand, but deep down he had known that he was alone in his undertaking. Despite this he remained certain of what he must do and just like Almighty God in Heaven; Charles could only offer death as the best option.

He had once heard Edward Benson, the Archbishop of Canterbury say, when visiting his father at Sir William's Mayfair home, as he often did many years ago that only a mad man would compare himself to a deity with the power of death and life.

At first Charles laughed at this, but the more he considered those words the more he believed that Edward Benson, 'Primate of All England' needed to be shown that eternal salvation was as dead as the nails on the cross, it does not exist and never has and Charles could prove this with a single swipe of a knife.

As for the existence of the human soul, well he had searched hard to find one, probably harder than most, certainly with more diligence than the so-called clerics that were everywhere, whose hands only ever got wet with holy water, but Charles had seen nothing looking remotely soulful as his hands paddled and pulled amongst the beautiful blood and gore. It certainly did not shelter in the body from the neck to the groin or else he would have found at least one in existence. Perhaps he should extend his search to the adult brain?

He had only considered this recently and could not explain why he had ignored such potential of the rarely explored *cerebrum* with unfathomable secrets, considering he had handled many during his medical student years.

The truth was simple enough, Charles thrilled for the heart thumping frenzy of exposing, touching, tasting and removing female genitalia and his trophies were his reward.

Life is for living and you have to make the most of the short time you're given, his father had repeated such platitudes on numerous occasions. *No! Life is for living until I decide otherwise.*

Charles was more than content with his achievements, particularly his most recent, killing his father's murderer. That had been a matter of pride, purely personal and certainly not to avenge his father's slaying, but for daring to touch his Verity. That alone had driven him to new heights of bloodlust to kill Titus Moon and it was the same adrenalin rush allowing him a sense of invincibility as he stood on the jetty, looking back at his pursuers.

Charles leapt the three feet drop into the boat and landed with skilful balance as the small boat pitched from side to side. He untied the rope, pushing against the jetty and the boat, already facing the lake was smoothly propelled towards the gathering fog.

By the time Meadowbank reached the end of the jetty, Charles had nearly vanished into the dense mist and only his bobbing head could be distinguished. Abberline and Huggins had followed the shoreline and were now running to the opposite bank.

Meadowbank was joined by the gamekeeper and side-by-side they watched him disappear, the inspector not daring to believe that Charles Cadley may escape once again.

"D' ya think yer can tek 'im from 'ere?" Meadowbank asked, ignoring the revolver in his hand.

"'Appen. I 'ad mi chance afore, but it don't seem reet. I keep on thinkin' what Sir William would want mi t' do. I'm not sure 'e would want mi t' shoot 'is lad in cold blood even if 'e is a cock-sure bastard."

"Sir William is dead an' 'is son is Jack the Ripper. If wi don't stop 'im now it will bi on yer conscience if 'e kills again. Oh bugger it! Gi' mi that gun."

Ignoring the inspector Preston Pete looked intently across the lake, snapped his shotgun open, removed two cartridges and replaced them with two more from his jacket pocket, as if he had all the time in the world to spare.

"A lead slug is better than a blast o' pellets at that there distance."

He brought the gun to his right shoulder and aimed along the rock steady barrels.

Charles was standing in the boat, finding it easier to work one oar in this manner and still maintain some control over direction. He had reached the deepest part of the lake and a quick glance revealed that the shoreline all around was invisible through the fog as it swirled and recoiled from the slightest turbulence.

He allowed himself a grin as his escape looked promising and the farm was not very far from the north side of the lake.

The shotgun blast sounded like a thunderclap, as the gamekeeper fired one barrel of the 12 gauge.

A lead ball hit Charles in the lower back to the left of his spine, the force instantly lifting him off his feet and sending him crashing overboard. The water was cold, freezing like an Arctic sea.

Charles sank deeper and deeper, unable to gain momentum with one arm and the numbing cold could not disguise the wracking pain from his back. But soon he slowed his descent and by kicking his feet felt himself going up and he ignored the reddening bloodied water that circulated around his face.

Christ! It is so cold.

He believed he would never feel warm again.

Something caught his attention to his left. A shape twisting, turning and circling darted around him like an inquisitive sea mammal, its constant movement and distance defying identification.

He was still fifteen feet from the surface when close movement in his peripheral vision made him search the gloomy water around him and focus on a white, almost child-like object that dropped from view.

He felt a bump to his legs and even through his trousers it felt as if a large fish, with skin colder than the lake itself had swum into him.

His lungs demanded air and Charles could almost touch the surface when something sinewy grasped an ankle preventing further lift to the surface. He struggled against the hold for a few seconds and kicked down with his free foot. Close to suffocation he bent his body to see what was keeping him submerged and came face to face with his sister, grinning with genuine pleasure as she held onto his foot.

The scream started below the surface, his open mouth allowing water to enter the trachea, forcing the larynx to seal and protect the lungs, diverting water to the stomach. Charles was experiencing the initial phase of drowning.

The hand let go of his ankle and Charles rose to the surface close to a cardiac arrest and unconsciousness. As his face broke the surface the larynxospasm relaxed and his lungs gulped in air and his stomach emptied itself of pond water. Coughing and retching loudly Charles floundered on the surface in terror, splashing his good arm in an effort to stay afloat.

"Help! Help me for God's sake," he gasped.

The four men now in pair's and on opposite sides of the lake could clearly hear the commotion and cry for help, but the thickening fog kept the plight of Charles Cadley hidden from view.

"We cannot just stand here, listening to a man drown and do nothing. No matter who he is." Abberline said in earnest.

"Fred, th' only t' other choice yer 'ave is t' swim out yonder yer sel'. An' would yer risk yer own life t' save Jack t' Ripper?" Huggins replied.

Charles continued thrashing the water and then through the fog gently drifted the empty rowing boat. He splashed and kicked his way towards it, laughing and sobbing deliriously and when little more than an outstretched arm's reach away as his fingers brushed the wooden side, he was yanked below the surface.

Lucy was so pleased to see her brother again, but her empty eye-sockets as black as tar could not reflect her joy, that was left to her wide grin, revealing toothless decaying gums.

I always knew you would come back for me Charles, dear Charles.

These were not spoken words; still they reverberated through his skull.

His face was inches from hers.

Why did you do it Charles and why did you not help? Please answer me this.

A freezing hand cupped his face tenderly as the other held his injured shoulder and pushed him deeper and deeper.

His breathing reflex released the final precious air supply from his lungs; apnoea no longer an option and Charles could only stare at the monster that was now his sister.

A few remaining strands of hair straggled her ageless face; her body naked and waxy, like a church candle. Whatever clothes this pretty girl was wearing over thirty years ago had long disappeared, ripped apart by the others, her pre-pubescent skin bleached white now the need for nourishment ended with her last breath that summer's day.

Charles shook his head in disbelief as if to rid himself of the apparition like a wayward daydream, but Lucy had waited such a long time for this moment. She wished the others were here to watch, but they had vanished when their bones were sanctified and laid to rest in hallowed ground.

Now she was no longer alone, she had Charles.

His feet hit the lake-bed abruptly, the disturbance releasing a cloud of sediment around them.

My sweet big brother, how you've changed, now a man, just how I remember father. I hear him Charles, calling my name from the jetty. Did you know he was so sad?

Hold me dear Charles, hold me and tell me you won't leave me again.

Lucy embraced her brother as loving siblings do, her black eye-sockets aching to weep.

As her deathly cold cheek nuzzled his own fondly, his frozen scream of terror was not dissimilar to the many he had marvelled at.

Only his deep subconscious recognised and recoiled to her touch. The deterioration to his oxygen-starved brain was irreversible and death was only a final heartbeat away.

His return had released her.

How it ended.

The three detectives and gamekeeper had regrouped on the jetty, deciding between themselves nothing could be done until the fog lifted in the morning.

They kept their own counsel as the hours passed, each staring at the lake and each hoping and praying that Charles Cadley would be found one way or another.

Major Little and Henry Moorson arrived leaving a phalanx of officers to patrol the lake perimeter and wait for further orders while the two chief constables joined the group on the jetty.

Preston Pete ambled away to search the shoreline and prepare his oilcloth coracle, a small oval boat he made from willow branches years ago, in readiness to sail across the lake if needed. He was a loner and was grateful for the excuse to avoid further discussion on his excellent shot that had more than likely ended the reign of Jack the Ripper.

He had spoken to more people in the past two weeks than he had in the past decade and people made him uncomfortable. Some looked at him with disdain, others derision, laughing as he passed, but not Sir William. That man was a true gentleman who spoke to him as an equal, respecting his knowledge as a woodsman and lover of nature.

It was a sad day for the gamekeeper when Sir William died, but he was grateful that the old man was not around to witness what had happened to his only son and have to listen to the incredible stories of his unbelievable violence and the monster he was.

No father should have to hear such things of his son, true or not.

Preston Pete was confident Master Charles was dead. He had aimed slightly right and low, despite the surface fog and would bet anyone half-a-crown that a lead slug would be found in Master Charles' left kidney.

At last it was dawn, the time of day according to some when evil spirits and demons are obliged to disappear and the dead return to their graves. And now as November sunlight peeped from behind the Pennines pushing away the night, those cold and quiet men on the jetty began to stir.

The sun rose less than an hour later and slowly the radiation fog, a phenomenon occurring only at night during autumn and early winter when conditions are calm and the sky clear, began to dissipate.

A doctor arrived at Ribbleton Manor and after heavily sedating Mrs. Ramsbottom, checked Verity's condition before examining the bodies of Miss Campion, James the hall boy and Titus Moon, still lying where they fell. His primary role this evening as a police surgeon was to pronounce life extinct and provide the coroner with first hand medical evidence of injuries.

Attending to the living was an unexpected chore.

The bodies were now on their way to the Preston Royal Infirmary for a post mortem to establish the cause of death and to discount or conclude whether foul play is suspected, a principal aim in any murder investigation. It was not necessary to be a police surgeon to recognise a severed jugular vein, be it internal or external or decapitation as the most likely cause of death, though the internal injuries to Titus Moon would require further investigation.

Ribbleton Manor was once again the scene of intense police activity.

Dolly Crabtree, the kitchen maid had been elevated to the position of cook, now in charge of the kitchen in the absence of Fanny Ramsbottom, who was serenely asleep in an armchair placed especially for her, in the the butler's pantry.

To her credit, Dolly immediately arranged for hot tea and sandwiches to be taken to the officers by the lake and announced that refreshments would be available in the kitchen throughout the day. It soon became full with cold and grateful police constables despatched by their sergeants in shifts.

Huggins had eaten three bacon sandwiches made with thick slices of bread and dripping and could not help but think about the roast chicken that was on the lunch menu. He was ready to share his considered reflections on the pleasures of a roast bird with Meadowbank, but after a quick glance decided against it.

Meadowbank was not contemplating food but the blossoming of Mary Babbitt and the start of his wooing campaign. It was a long time since a woman showed romantic inklings towards him, excluding of course the occasional night he spent with 'Sweaty Betty' in her room behind Yate's Wine Lodge and paying her for the privilege, but even he could not fail to recognise the advances made towards him a few hours ago.

He assumed Mary was now a reformed alcoholic as she did not smell like the many drunks, male or female; he regularly had contact with and no longer had the glazed eyes or ruddy complexion she had on their first meeting, months ago.
Then something occurred to him.

If she was off the drink then Mary must be teetotal, there could be no other explanation, as Meadowbank was well aware there had to be no half measures when giving up the drink. It was all or nothing. The situation now presented him with a dilemma. If Mary had cleaned herself up and come off the booze and he was pretty certain she had, would she expect him to do the same if they began courting?
The thought of forsaking his daily jaunts to the beer-house on or off duty caught his breath. Then a more heinous thought popped into his head. Was she part of the Temperance Movement? Being a teetotaller was one thing but a God fearing, church-going teetotaller was a different matter completely.

His own father, God rest his soul and may he rot in hell, for reasons still unknown to Meadowbank was a member of the Temperance Movement. In fact he was one of the founder members in 1832 and together with his good friend and fellow Prestonian Joseph Livesy adopted and signed the pledge 'to abstain

415

from all liquors of intoxicating quality whether ale, porter, wine or spirits unless as medicine'.

Meadowbank never got to know his father who was a distant and impatient disciplinarian with his family and twenty years older than his mother. He ran off with the church organist from Saint Michael's in Ashton when he was twelve, abandoning a distraught wife and rejoicing son.

Meadowbank still held the same opinion of his father as that of his mother, he may have been of sober character but he was nothing more than *a deceitful, cruel, lecherous bastard* and she took that opinion to the grave with her.

He considered the Temperance Movement to be a monumental failure, just like his father. For a start, Preston had the highest mortality rate in the country and this was not due to the ravages of demon drink as some suggested, but poor diet that for many bordered on starvation together with wanton neglect by the borough and dire housing and working conditions.

It was not the 'carriage class', to which his father belonged and represented, who frequented the ever growing number of beer-houses amongst the never ending back-to-back terraced dwellings, but the working man and woman who had little else to look forward to other than obliterating their squalor through drink as often as they could afford. And as the beer-houses opened at 6am to accommodate the mill workers before the morning shift and after the night shift, there was plenty of opportunity to imbibe.

Then the words *Salvation Army* rang out loud and clear and stopped his thought process dead, just when he believed his conclusions surrounding Mary Babbitt's rehabilitation could not get any worse.

Meadowbank was well aware that the *Sally Army's* road to redemption was to refrain from alcohol, smoking and gambling amongst other pleasures and he pursued all three with a passion.

Drawing on his favourite briar-root pipe with a well-chewed bit he consciously savoured the sweet Virginia tobacco and was rapidly coming close to the decision that he could live without a woman's company but not that of a pint and a pipe after a good day at the betting office.

His confused reverie, now in danger of jeopardising his efforts of courtship before they had even started, was interrupted by a shout. Abberline had spotted an object floating towards the middle of the lake at its deepest point.

"Over there, to the right of the boat by a few yards. Something has just appeared on the surface."

Henry Moorson searched the spot through binoculars.

"It appears to be the body of a man floating face down. Can we organise its retrieval Mr. Meadowbank?" he said calmly, handing the field glasses to Major Little.

Meadowbank turned to address the gamekeeper and finding him gone looked further afield. Preston Pete had seen the body as soon as the fog began to clear and was already sat in his small boat working the single paddle effectively.

It did not take him long to reach the corpse that had now drifted alongside the empty rowing boat, gently rocking against the wooden hull.

Without any change to his usual staid expression Preston Pete took hold of the body and rolled it onto its back, now looking down at the face of Charles Cadley.

He shuddered involuntarily.

The features were a grotesque mask of terror as if frozen with ice.

The mouth was obscenely twisted and gaping, stretched to the limits of facial muscle, but it was the missing eyeballs that sent a chill along his spine.

Both sockets were empty apart from a large haemophagic leech, its own five pairs of eyes forlornly searching the cushion of fat that would normally protect the eyeball. The blood-sucking carnivore using its three jaws and 100 teeth noisily chewed the mucous membrane of its host in a quest to find nourishment.

417

Preston Pete looked away and fed a rope under the corpse, immersing his arms up to his elbows before lashing both ends around the seat plinth and not stopping to consider how much warmer the lake felt. He noticed the unusual leather wallet beneath the torn shirt and removed the wet pouch of diamonds. The gamekeeper did not know what sort of precious stones he was looking at, but was certain they would bring a bob or two at the pawnbrokers and he put them in a pocket of his jacket along with the sopping bundle of one and five pound notes.

As he paddled towards the shore, a skein of geese looking for a roost warmer than a dark Scandinavian winter skimmed the treetops, their honking and powerful beating wings grabbing his attention. The twenty or so geese circled the lake before descending and one by one they settled on the surface immediately drinking and washing their delicate flight feathers.

The gamekeeper could only watch the large black-necked waterfowl with fascination, suddenly distracted from his gruesome task, as the migrating birds explored their winter home.

Within minutes more birds announced their arrival and two pairs of ponderous, but magnificent Mute Swans with six-foot wingspans, landed on the lake near to the reeds eagerly calling to each other in low grunts.

The officers on the jetty noticed the winter visitors with indifference and even an ornithologist would not have considered their arrival unusual or exceptional, but to Preston Pete it was the first wildfowl he had witnessed on the lake in his forty years as gamekeeper and he nodded his head with respect to Mother Nature welcoming her back as he paddled towards the shore.

If he caught sight of the brown leech he did not respond as it slid down the lifeless face of Jack the Ripper and still hungry the parasitic annelid plopped into the lake searching for warmer blood.

Printed in Great Britain
by Amazon